THE EX

THE EX
Anne Billson

THE BROOLIGAN PRESS
LONDON
NEW YORK

This edition published 2019 by The Brooligan Press

ISBN: 978 1 9160 578 4 5

"When I took my departure that evening, it was not with the feeling that this had been one of my more successful investigations."

Sidney Gilliat & Claud Gurney,
Green For Danger

"Needless to say, the woman was not approaching straightforwardly."

Robert Aickman, *The Fetch*

THE EX

ONE

I<small>T WAS</small> hard to tell where the water ended and the sky began. If it had been me flying the plane, we would probably have ended up in the lagoon, but fortunately for everyone on board, I was as far as I could possibly be from the cockpit: right at the back, next to the lavatories.

The flight had been fully booked, yet I had somehow found myself with two whole seats to myself. It might have been the clothes that had put people off—I was wearing a hooded sweatshirt, and borrowed tracksuit bottoms so large the bunched-up fabric made it seem as though I had a permanent erection. Or maybe it was the lacerations across my face, which made it look as though I'd been in some sort of razor fight.

Or it could have been the smell; I'd taken a shower, several showers in fact, but couldn't do much about the stench seeping from the damp clothes bunched up in the plastic bag I'd stuffed beneath the seat. I began to wish I'd thrown them away.

But even without the smell and the lacerations and the sex pervert outfit, I would have been the sort of traveller's nightmare you would normally go out of your way to avoid on a two minute bus-ride, let alone a two-hour international flight. I could feel my features subsiding into a scary thousand yard stare, but I was simply too exhausted to try and arrange them into something more amenable.

All I could think was, *Oh Lord, what have I done?*

I'd only been trying to help, and all I'd done was make things worse. Much worse. Maybe if I'd stayed at home, everything would have turned out OK. Maybe if I hadn't agreed to take the job in the first place, none of this would have happened, and Alice and Nick would even now be . . .

"Tea? Coffee?" The voice jerked me out of my reverie. A

3

meticulously groomed stewardess was leaning over me with a forced grin, like a nurse greeting a patient with a terminal disease. I didn't even try to smile back, but managed to whisper, "Coffee."

Just as she was handing me the plastic cup, the plane hit a small air-pocket and some of the scalding black liquid slopped into my lap. I yelped in agony, and the stewardess backed away in a hurry, scowling as though I'd done it on purpose, just to get attention. Other passengers craned their necks, trying to see what the smelly degenerate in the clown trousers was up to now, so I stared fixedly out of the window, pretending to be a regular tourist searching for a last glimpse of St Mark's Square, or the Lido, or the Isle of the Dead. But below us the lagoon had already given way to fume-belching factories, and soon even those were obscured by thick grey cloud as the aeroplane continued its climb.

At around 30,000 feet, there was a muffled burbling that I eventually traced to the plastic bag beneath the seat. I was surprised to hear the mobile working at all, even if it did now sound like a heavy smoker coughing up phlegm. I made no effort to extricate it; you didn't need to be a genius to guess who was calling, and she was the last person I felt like talking to right now. So I let the phone burble on and ignored the dirty looks until, mercifully, it finally let out one last splutter and gave up the ghost.

I squirmed around on my two seats, trying to get comfortable, but too tense to relax; the muscles in my legs were taut as elastic bands and the flight stretched ahead of me like an unbridgeable void. I had nothing to read; my knowledge of Italian was limited to names of pizza toppings, and I'd already looked at all the pictures in the tattered copy of the *Corriere della Sera* I'd picked up in the departure lounge; the only items in the seat pocket in front of me were a sick-bag and a laminated card of emergency instructions. There was nothing, nothing at all, to distract me from stewing over my mistakes. If only I hadn't drunk so much champagne at the party. If only I hadn't been so blinded by lust. If only I'd taken the time to study *Old Egbert's Almanac of Eerie Things* more carefully . . . There was a long list of 'if onlys' and I'd duly flunked them all, one by one.

Sleep was out of the question—every time I closed my eyes I could see that horrible figure with its peculiar loping stride, arms outstretched and sleeves trailing uneven lengths of cotton like thin dark streams of vapour . . . Oh for heaven's sake, how was I supposed to have known?

So, in the circumstances, it was almost preferable to torment myself by rewinding the events of the past week and running through them again in my head, trying to decide exactly where I'd gone wrong.

Let's face it, I was pretty much spoilt for choice.

TWO

SHE WASN'T my type. Of course it didn't help that she was taller than me, which is never something I appreciate in a woman. And I didn't much care for her expression, the one that seemed to say, *Yes, I know I've trekked all the way across town just to talk to you, but don't think for one moment that I actually enjoy being stuck on this floating death-trap.*

She had a point there. The barge looked as though it might start taking in water at any second. It belonged to my friend Kevin, who'd always spent barely enough to keep it afloat and who, unlike other barge-owners, had absolutely no interest in painting it cheerful colours or festooning it with pots of geraniums. Kevin was currently raking in a fortune as an engineering consultant in the United Arab Emirates, though you'd never have guessed it from his furniture, most of which looked as though it had been rescued from a skip.

But I couldn't pin all the blame on Kevin. The books and papers and CDs and socks spilling out of plastic bags were my own, as were the leftover chop suey cartons and empty beer cans. And it was my cat and no-one else's whose tray was giving off the sort of smell that indicated a change of litter was long overdue.

Plus it can't have helped that I was lolling around in my underpants. Had I been expecting a visitor, I might have made an effort and put on a clean shirt and trousers. Hell, I might even have got round to shaving. But she turned up out of the blue, and since it was still morning and I was sprawled on the sofa with my usual hangover, there hadn't seemed much point in getting dressed.

Instead, I was idly leafing through a computer magazine with a glass of Alka-Seltzer to hand, *Man on the Silver Mountain* blaring out of the speakers, Boris the cat throbbing away on my chest and basic decorum preserved only by the blanket I was using as a buffer-zone between my pet's neurotic treadling and the more delicate parts of my anatomy.

Fortunately, boarding the barge was a precarious business; she had to negotiate three deep and rather slippery wooden steps down into the main cabin, which gave me just enough time to tip Boris on to the floor and pull on the crumpled Chinos that were still lying where I'd left them.

In fact, her feet were the first thing I saw, and I was able to get a good look at them because she wasn't wearing shoes *per se*; more like a couple of ice-picks held in place by strips of vermicelli. They hadn't been designed for clambering on and off barges, so—luckily for me—she was forced to watch her step. By the time she'd made it safely down to my level, I was buttoning up my shirt.

Too late, I noticed there were bright orange chop suey stains down the front.

It could have been worse. At least I wasn't stoned. Her mouth moved, but all I could hear was Ronnie James Dio. I lunged for the keyboard and hit pause.

For a while, she stood and stared at me, as if dazed by the sudden silence. Then she smiled, a little shyly, and in an unfeasibly posh accent said, "Croydon?"

I nodded and waited for her to make a smart comment about my name, but all she said was, "I tried calling, but there's something wrong with your phone."

"Um," I said, improvising wildly. "They said they might be able to fix it next week."

She made a small tutting sound, whether directed at me or Kevin's phone company I couldn't tell, but held out her hand. "Alice Marchmont. How do you do."

I shook the proffered hand, then took a step back and rubbed my eyes and wondered if I was dreaming.

What had I done to deserve a vision like this at ten thirty on a dismal autumn morning? She was tall and slim-hipped, and although she was wearing jeans they were a lot smarter than any of my so-called smart trousers. She was also wearing a jacket made from leather so soft-looking you wanted to bury your face in it, and a filmy blouse unbuttoned just enough to reveal a hint of cleavage. Her hair was brown with gleaming auburn high-lights, cut in one of those deceptively simple styles that undoubtedly required a hairdresser's attentions every other day, and so unnaturally neat I itched to reach out and muss it up. Her lips were big and it seemed to me as though she was having to work hard to keep them under control, and she had a tendency to talk out of the side of her mouth, which lent everything she said a droll quality that reminded me of Mae West, of all people. But she was polished and classy and extraordinarily well groomed, which automatically made her attractive to a slob like me.

Then again, it might have done, if only she'd been my type.

"The gate at the top of the path was open," she said, looking around with the wide-eyed gaze of a prize-winning heifer that had accidentally strayed into a blood-splattered abattoir.

"The catch is broken," I said.

"You should get that mended," she said. "I mean, around here . . ." She broke off to ask, "You are Croydon? John Croydon?"

"That's me. Er, take a seat."

She looked around and finally perched uncomfortably on the edge of a chair, as though preserving the option of being able to sprint for the exit at a moment's notice. The coffee had just finished percolating; I asked if she wanted some and she shook her head. She turned down the offer of a microwaved bagel as well, as though she imagined this were the Underworld and that if she allowed anything to pass her lips she'd be trapped here for the next six months, like Persephone. I rounded up a pencil and a notepad and sat back down on the sofa, trying to look suitably businesslike.

"How can I help?"

She seemed reluctant to look me in the eye. "To be frank, Mr Croydon, I'm not so sure you can."

"Why don't you let me be the judge of that," I said, flashing my most charming smile, the one Kate had always told me was irresistible, and trying not to sound too desperate. It had been six weeks since I'd last tracked down a teenage runaway, two and a half months since I'd warned the magistrate that his wife knew all about his kerb-crawling activities and that if they didn't cease forthwith she would leak details to the press, more than a year since the Barnum brothers had talked me into posing as a junkie to intercept one of their rivals' drugs deliveries (don't even ask what had happened to the drugs) and getting on for a decade since the Kitchener case (but it was best not to think about that).

In short, I needed work and I needed it badly.

Alice Marchmont took a deep breath.

"I've got a stalker."

"Oh, right." I relaxed. I was in my element here. I knew all about stalking. I'd done a fair bit of it myself, though admittedly that had been back in the days before anyone had actually begun referring to it as *stalking*. Hanging around all night outside your ex-girlfriend's flat, perhaps. Getting into a punch-up with her new boyfriend, maybe. Strangling her in a fit of jealous rage and hiding the corpse under the floorboards, absolutely. I hadn't gone that far, of course, but mutual friends had reacted as though I had. Before you could say 'Quattro Formaggio with Extra Mushrooms and Anchovies' I'd been dropped from everyone's party list.

But that was all in the past. I'd learned my lesson. I was never going to get involved with a woman again.

"Jealous boyfriend?" I asked, chewing the end of my pencil and wondering why Alice Marchmont had come to me, as opposed to a more upmarket outfit with proper offices and headed notepaper.

"Don't tell me. He hangs around all night outside your flat, gazing up at your bedroom window with a soulful look on his face."

It seemed like yesterday.

"No, nothing like that." All of a sudden she seemed fascinated by her hands; flawless French manicure, elegant fingers, engagement ring with diamond the size of a small Brussels sprout. I glanced down at my own hands, and the contrast was humbling. My fingernails were ragged and dirty and one of them was turning black where I'd shut it in a door.

"I think it's my fiancé's ex," she said in a voice so small I had to strain to hear it. "His first wife."

First wife? This was already more interesting than a jealous boyfriend. Girl-on-girl stalking? You didn't get a lot of that. Maybe it would lead to catfights. Kicking and hair-tugging. *Crêpage de chignon*, as the French called it. Hellcat mud wrestling. All-nude lesbian orgies . . . I struggled to keep a cool head, but the stream of associative imagery was difficult to resist.

You could tell I didn't get out much.

"So, er, what's this first wife up to?"

"I feel as though I'm being watched," she said. "Like today, when I got a cab over here—I could have sworn there was someone following me."

"In a car?"

She shrugged. "I never really thought about how she gets around."

"But that's all it is? A feeling?"

"No, of course not."

She made an odd little gesture with her hand, as though brushing a non-existent lock of hair out of her eye. "She's been phoning me up. Several times a day, sometimes during the night . . ."

"You tried callback."

"I'm not stupid."

"And?"

"Number unobtainable."

"And what does she say when she calls?"

"Nothing."

"*Nothing?*"

"But there are strange noises on the line . . ."

"So how do you know it's her?"

Alice Marchmont glared at me defiantly. "She's been sending emails as well."

Feelings of being followed? Crank calls? Unsolicited emails? I was a little disappointed. I got this sort of thing all the time. In fact, I'd been on both ends of it. This was low-level harassment—if you could even call it that. Hardly worth getting upset about.

"What kind of emails?"

"Photos of dead things. Corpses. Murder victims. Threats."

Threats was slightly more interesting.

"Such as?"

She started examining her fingernails again. "If I don't cancel the wedding something bad will happen."

"And you reckon it's this . . . ex-wife?"

"Georgina. She always was a one-man girl, and now she can't bear the idea of Nick marrying someone else. And I don't reckon, I *know*. I've *seen* her."

"You've seen her following you?"

She took a deep breath.

"Every night this week she's been standing on my doorstep, ringing my bell."

"And you let her in?"

"Of course not," she snapped.

"Then how do you know it was her?"

"I saw her on the video entryphone."

"Oka-a-y," I said slowly. "And what does your fiancé think about this?"

She looked uncomfortable.

"He still has feelings for her, obviously. It's only natural, they were together for years, and it wasn't his fault it ended so badly."

She stuck her chin out, as though challenging me to disagree. but I didn't see any reason to; it sounded like a classic case of some poor sod caught between his ex and his current, unable to let go of the past, feeling obligations, trying to keep both women happy and everyone ending up thoroughly miserable—the sort of thing that goes on all the time. The eternal romantic triangle.

I asked, "Is he still seeing her?"

Her mouth twitched.

"No. Oh no."

"You're sure of that?"

"It's just not possible."

She sounded almost too certain. I glanced down at my

notepad. I hadn't taken any notes, but there was an elaborate skull-and-crossbones doodle that was coming along just fine.

"And you're getting married when?"

"The thirteenth."

"Good thing you're not superstitious," I chuckled, but she didn't crack a smile. "A week tomorrow?"

She nodded.

Saturday. I jotted that down, then printed the name GEORGINA.

When I looked up again I was startled to see Alice blinking back tears. I'd always thought the idea of getting married was supposed to make women happy. I wondered if maybe she was weeping with happiness, but then decided she was simply upset about the possibility of her big day being spoiled by this other woman. Oh Lord, there was no need to cry about it, for heaven's sake. I couldn't stand seeing women cry; it made me feel like a heel, even when it wasn't my fault.

I struggled to get back on track.

"Let's see if we can sort this out. You're being harassed by your boyfriend's ex. But it's just heavy breathing phone calls and mildly threatening emails—nothing serious enough to warrant going to the police."

"I did go to the police," she said. "That was when they gave me your name. They said this sort of thing was right up your street. They seemed to find the whole thing hilarious."

She stared down at her hands again and took a deep breath, and when next she spoke there was a slight wobble in her voice.

"So, Mr Croydon, do you think you can help me?"

"Call me John," I said, stalling for time.

"*John . . .*"

She repeated my name as though it were an exotic word she was hearing for the first time. Maybe the only guys she knew were Tristrams or Ruperts.

I sighed, wondering if it was worth continuing. But then a depressing vision of my latest bank statement swam into focus in my head. The stalking of Alice Marchmont didn't sound like a very exciting case, but maybe it would lead to more lucrative work. Alice looked flush enough; she was bound to have a few equally flush friends who would require the services of someone like me.

"They had no right to laugh," I said, turning on my best sensitive male expression. "But you can't expect the police to understand. Why don't you tell me more about this ex-wife . . ." I glanced down at my pad. "This *Georgina*."

"She was very beautiful," said Alice. I turned the words over in my head.

"Was? *Was?* You mean she isn't beautiful any more?"

She shuddered. "God, no."

"What happened?" I was thinking acute eczema, or smallpox, or maybe a tragic accident with a box of matches.

"She was really beautiful when she was alive."

I tried to wrap my head around that, but I couldn't, not really. I was still wondering whether I'd misheard her, or whether she'd been playing fast and loose with her tenses, when I heard Alice Marchmont saying something else.

"She died two years ago."

"Wait," I laughed nervously. "We are talking about the same person here? The person who keeps phoning and sending you emails? Your stalker?"

"Georgina Fitch, yes. Nick's late wife."

After a while, I said, "I see."

But I didn't see at all.

THREE

I MOVE IN the sort of circles in which people, if they're lucky, live in flats. But the price of London property being the sick joke it is, the not-so-lucky ones often have to make compromises. Sometimes they're forced to share digs well past the optimal digs-sharing age. Sometimes the really desperate ones are forced to move back in with their parents—something that in my case, of course, was out of the question. And sometimes they're forced to shack up in the dilapidated barges of absent friends—barges where the roof-beams are so low there's barely room for someone of even below average height to raise an arm to scratch his scalp, let alone swing Boris the cat.

What I'm trying to say is, when you emerge from the subway into one of the swankiest parts of the London Borough of Kensington and Chelsea and find yourself gazing up at a large Victorian terrace house which is not divvied up into flats but owned in its entirety by a couple still in their thirties, you know you're dealing with folk who have at their disposal the sort of figures from which you could add or subtract a nought or two without anyone really noticing.

Of course, I was still evading the *real* questions here, such as, *'Stalked by a dead woman, eh? How is that possible?'* Or, *'Of all the private investigators in town, why did you have to come to me?'* Or, *'Why don't you just go away and leave me alone, and we'll pretend we never met?'*

But when I looked at Alice Marchmont, I found I didn't want her to go away, not just yet. She'd only just stepped into my life, but I was already searching for excuses to keep her there. Although she was not my type and never would be, just the way she talked and dressed couldn't help but remind me of Kate, and I was curious about the kind of life she led, the sort of people she hung out with. It was a world from which I'd long been banished, and I wanted to get a whiff of it again, take a stroll there and sniff the flowers, just to see for myself if it was how I remembered, or if, as I suspected was the case, time and yearning had exaggerated its fragrant charms.

Either way, Alice Marchmont was a gateway.

And, oh yes, I really needed the money.

From the outset it had been obvious that Alice was well off compared to the likes of, say, me. And while I hadn't actually set eyes on her bank statement, her immaculate yet understated grooming (that manicure, those gleaming highlights, the way her clothes didn't look as though she'd just scooped them out of the laundry basket) were a dead giveaway, as was the way she'd casually let drop that she'd spent a couple of years in Paris, working for French *Vogue*. Not even common or garden British *Vogue*, mind. Plus she hadn't so much as blinked when I'd demanded a sizeable advance for agreeing to lay to rest whatever it was that was stalking her.

A little reluctantly, but realising that if I wanted to do the job properly I would need to give my client some way of contacting me, I went straight out and bought a mobile phone, which worked out cheaper than getting Kevin's line reconnected and also had one big advantage over a regular phone—it had an 'off' switch, which meant it would be relatively easy to keep my mother at bay.

That was the theory, anyhow.

It was agreed—or rather, Alice had decided—that I should casually bump into Nick at a party that evening, which would allow me to pump him for any information I might need without tipping him off as to the exact nature of my relationship to his fiancée. "We can pretend you've met before," she said. "It's OK—he won't remember. He meets so many people, and he's got a rotten memory for faces."

"Hold on," I said to her. "Nick doesn't know about any of this? You haven't told him?"

Alice chewed her bottom lip, which seemed to have taken on a life of its own and was threatening to get out of control. "He was very depressed after Georgina's death. People were worried about him. What he needed, what everyone *said* he needed, was a lot of tender loving care from a woman who was well-balanced and stable and down to earth. Someone who didn't have *mood swings*."

I eyed her sceptically. I had yet to meet a woman who didn't have mood swings.

"And I take it that someone is you?"

She relinquished her lip and smiled weakly. "I can't have him or any of his friends thinking I'm flaky, or that I'm imagining things. I can't have them suspecting that my life is not … *normal*. That's why I came to you, Mr Croydon."

"John," I said again.

"No-one knows you, you see. We don't move in the same circles."

This was already self-evident. But it wasn't until the party that the reality of it was hammered home.

ALICE HAD already given me the lowdown on our hosts. They were Selina and Jolly, the latter apparently being short for Jolyon, a name that up until then I'd encountered only in BBC serialisations of *The Forsyte Saga*. Selina was the daughter of a well-known writer I'd never heard of. Jolly was a well-known chef who'd liberated himself from the grind of punishing slog and unsociable hours by lending his name to a brand of kitchenware and signing on as culinary consultant to a chain of organic fast-food restaurants. I'd never heard of him either.

The extent of the difference between me and the people in Alice's world began to make itself as soon as I turned up on Selina and Jolly's doorstep, clutching what I reckoned was a decent bottle of red wine. The front door was opened by a handsome middle-aged guy with salt-and-pepper hair. He was more formally dressed than I'd expected, but I consoled myself with the certitude that my weather-beaten leather jacket and faded jeans were hardy fashion perennials. I'd even remembered to comb my hair.

"Jolly, I presume," I said, thrusting the bottle into his arms.

The man didn't smile. In fact, he didn't look very jolly at all. He accepted the proffered bottle as though I'd handed him a small furry animal of indeterminate species and glanced at the label with just the tiniest suggestion of a sneer. Then he stood to one side and said, "May I take your jacket?" and I realised I'd made my first *faux pas* and mistaken the hired greeter for the host.

I hung on to the jacket.

I became aware of my second *faux pas* when The Man Who Wasn't Jolly directed me down some steps, through a conservatory at the rear of the house and—even though it was early October—out into the garden, where I saw that in place of the arrangement to which I was accustomed—a scrum of revellers helping themselves from a muddle of cans and bottles while small puddles of lager accumulated around their feet—a fleet of sleek waiters was gliding nimbly between guests, offering them a choice of champagne, fresh orange juice or mineral water pre-decanted into small plantations of slender crystal flutes. Other waiters were carrying trays laid with small squares of bread and smoked salmon, miniature vol-au-vents and dwarf vegetables on sticks.

Too late, I realised this was not a bottle party.

Nobody seemed to be touching the food, which was a shame as it had been so prettily laid out, so I stuffed some of the miniature vol-au-vents into my mouth and reached for a glass of champagne to wash them down. The instant my fingers made contact with the crystal a small explosion went off in my face. Once I'd recovered my eyesight I spotted the man who'd blinded me with his flash; he was working his way through the guests, doggedly recording each new arrival on camera and it was just my luck to have been captured for posterity with my cheeks bulging with tuck.

He wasn't the only photographer; I also spotted a woman in elbow-length black gloves weaving in and out, leaving a trail of developing Polaroids in her wake. I sipped champagne and considered my options. Up until now, I'd assumed I would be able to blend into the crowd and strike up casual conversations with whomever I pleased, but now I wasn't so sure. The jeans and leather jacket, instead of coming across like a universally acceptable fashion classic, were making me feel like an ageing hippy adrift in an ocean of overpriced couture. It wasn't particularly smart—the hired caterers easily out-formalled anybody they were catering to. In fact, there was something diligently *drab* about it, but it was the sort of drabness only money could buy. Black predominated, of course, but there were also sprinklings of grey, beige and—obviously we're talking about the more rebellious elements here—an occasional flash of red. It was as though they were all extras on a film-set, dressed so as not to distract from the exciting foreground action.

While I was trying to work out where this foreground action was, I managed to finish my first glass of champagne and get stuck into a second. As I drank, I scanned the ranks of tastefully-clad guests, trying to gauge which group might be easiest to infiltrate, but they'd somehow arranged themselves into tight little clusters as impenetrable as squares of Waterloo infantry. It was clear I would have to be tread carefully. Having scanned the day's newspapers in preparation, I'd imagined I would be on safe ground with popular culture, if not with politics and world affairs, but all the books and films being discussed here seemed to be books and films that not only hadn't yet come out, but were actually still being written or produced by the people discussing them.

I was glad I'd hung on to my jacket as it was decidedly nippy, though this didn't seem to worry any of the women swanning around in sleeveless dresses. Alice was nowhere to be seen and, since no-one was making an effort to be friendly, I arranged my face into a vaguely amused expression to suggest I was standing on my own for lofty and mysterious reasons, rather than because no-one wanted to talk to me. Years of practising in front of the mirror had helped me perfect the art of conveying that I was really a lone wolf sort of personality—a non-conformist rebel like James Dean, say, or a pre-fat Marlon Brando—and that if they didn't have the bottle to approach me it was their loss, not mine.

I drained my flute and swapped it for a full one, dimly aware this wasn't such a bright idea as champagne never failed to leave me with a splitting headache, but knowing also that requesting beer in this company would have been tantamount to asking for pork scratchings in a mosque. To my right an earnest young man with pink cheeks and wire-rimmed spectacles was holding a gaggle of impeccably groomed women in thrall with *bons mots* clearly ripped off from La Rochefoucauld. To my left a clutch of men of about my own age were gurning like village idiots at an attractive teenage girl who endearingly assumed she was impressing them with her sparkling personality.

"So who do *you* know?" whispered a soft voice at my left ear. I turned my head and found myself gazing into the deep green eyes of a foxy redhead. She was definitely one of the rebels because she had elected to dress in red despite—or perhaps because of—the colour of her hair. She was several inches shorter than me, and I liked her immediately.

Definitely my type, this one.

I liked her breasts too; they were compact but shapely beneath the tight red silk. But I forced myself to concentrate on the eyes, which probably made me appear more outgoing and confident than I felt.

"Come again?" I riposted.

"Are you one of Jolly's or Selina's? Or someone else's?"

"Someone else's," I replied with what I hoped was a mysterious smile. "*Et vous?*"

She didn't bat an eyelid at my suave schoolboy French.

"Selina and I were at school together, oh, about a hundred years ago."

"That's an awful long time to stay friends with someone."

She roared with laughter, though I'd never intended it as a quip.

"Selina *never* drops anyone. Her address book just gets fatter with each passing year. She manages to stay in touch with *everyone*. It's *amazing*."

"However does she find the time?"

I was rewarded by the redhead laughing her head off again, as though I'd come out with a Dorothy Parker-type witticism.

"You're funny," she said.

"I do my best."

I couldn't help but feel flattered. This was looking promising. The redhead seemed to have bypassed the formal early stages and was already behaving as though we were old buddies, so out of genuine curiosity I asked, "Have we met somewhere before?"

"And you were doing so well." She shook her head sadly. "But I'm afraid that line's older than the ark. You know the score: if you land on the head of a snake you slide all the way down again."

"It wasn't a line . . ."

I started to protest, but decided it would be better to change the subject before she could drop me and start afresh with a more auspicious candidate.

"Perhaps you could tell me who some of these people are."

To my surprise, she grabbed my free hand and hauled me fearlessly into the fray. The earnest young man with pink cheeks looked vexed as the well-groomed women redirected their attention to my new friend and me. "Hi Molly, hi Janie, hi Blanche," said the redhead. To my sorrow, she relinquished my hand, but I was almost consoled by the subsequent flurry of air-kissing that broke out around my head. *Mwah mwah mwah*. It was like being surrounded by a swarm of sweet-smelling butterflies.

"And this is . . .?" The redhead looked at me inquiringly.

"John," I said. And then, because we'd killed the conversation stone-dead and everyone was staring expectantly at me, and because at the last minute I'd decided it might be prudent to adapt an alias, I added, "Barnes . . ."

"Like that nice black footballer," said one of the women. Too late, I realised I'd plumped for the wrong London borough. I should have gone for John Islington, or maybe John Hampstead.

"There's more than one black footballer nowadays," I said, trying to laugh it off. "Long gone are the days when Clyde Best had to force his way through an unforgiving wall of white faces."

I'd gone too far. Everyone was looking politely baffled, apart from the redhead, who smiled sweetly, as though enjoying my discomfiture, and said, "So, John *Barnes* . . ."

"Barnes-*Wallis*," I added in a reckless attempt to leave football behind and thinking, by the by, that the double-barrelled name had a comfortable-sounding ring to it.

There was a stunned silence, and then someone finally piped up, "Any relation?"

"To what?"

An anorexic-looking brunette started to giggle nervously.

"*The Dam Busters!*"

The big blonde to our left started humming the theme tune, and I realised too late why the name Barnes-Wallis had tripped so comfortably off the tongue—it had already been worn in by the scientist who had invented the Bouncing Bomb. I felt like kicking myself, but couldn't very well back down now.

"Very distant relation," I said, gesturing in a way that suggested *comme ci, comme ça*. Unfortunately I'd forgotten there was a glass in my hand, with the result that the remaining champagne slopped all over the nearest pair of shoes. They were strappy grey suede with heels like steel knitting needles, though this wasn't enough to prevent the owner from leaping backwards like a startled fawn.

"Sorry," I said. "Sorry. But hey, I *do* know how to get that stain out."

"How?" asked the redhead, though the stick-insect had already fled our group and attached herself to another, drier one. The young man with pink cheeks, aggrieved at no longer being the centre of attention, had also realigned himself, leaving the remainder of the well-groomed women arranged in a semi-circle, looking expectantly at the redhead and me as though we'd been hired to provide the entertainment. For a giddy moment, I felt like bashing her over the head and cackling, "*That's* the way to do it!" just to see everyone's faces.

But I didn't really want to hit the redhead. Not when she was being so nice to me.

She asked, "How *do* you remove champagne stains from suede?"

"With a rubber!" I replied triumphantly.

The redhead frowned prettily. "You mean . . .?"

There was a titter from our well-groomed audience. Too late, I realised they thought I was talking about condoms.

"No!" I corrected myself hurriedly. "I mean an *eraser*."

The redhead relaxed. "And that really works? I can get marks off my suede jacket with an eraser?"

"Champagne stains," I said. "I don't know about the other

stuff. Well, actually I do know. Salt gets rid of red wine. Hot vinegar gets rid of hard water deposits."

The redhead gawped at me. The well-groomed women, cast in the role of chorus, did likewise. "How do you know these things?"

"I know lots of things," I boasted. "I used to be Brain of Britain."

They seemed impressed by this, and it was true I had once been part of a team that had shared first prize in a pub quiz of the same name. But being the focal point of so much attention was beginning to go to my head, and I made the mistake of trying to show off.

"I can tell you the names of all the American state capitals," I announced. "I can give you all five of the Mighty Handful, all six of *Les Six*, all ten of the Hollywood Ten and all seven of *The Magnificent Seven* and the actors who played them, not forgetting Brad Dexter. Plus all the names of the Japanese actors in *The Seven Samurai* as well."

This last accomplishment was my *pièce de resistance* and never failed to impress film buffs, but the redhead was staring at me as though I was babbling in classical Greek.

"But *why?*" she asked. "What's the *point?*"

I was losing my audience. The well-groomed women were drifting away, but politely, like well brought-up wraiths, leaving the memory of their perfumed smiles behind them. But my redhead remained, watching me attentively, lips slightly parted to reveal a row of impressively small and even teeth. I had an urge to press my mouth up against hers and force those lips even further apart with my tongue, but just managed to restrain myself. I suspected the urge was showing in my face, though. I was certainly starting to feel it at the level of my groin.

"I can see you're easily impressed," I said, trying desperately to keep her gaze from straying down south.

"Not really," she said. "I think you're talking a load of old bollocks. But I do think that, compared to most of these other stiffs, you're intriguing. I don't know, you're . . . *different*."

This wasn't what I wanted to hear. I was supposed to be blending in. I was supposed to be one of them.

She smiled wickedly. "So tell me, *Mr Barnes-Wallis*, what do you do for a living?"

I remembered Alice had told me she worked part-time in an art gallery. "I'm a, er, conceptual artist."

Only afterwards did it occur to me that maybe I should have prepared my alias in advance, given it a bit more thought, furnished it with some credible back-up.

"Really?" She smiled as though I wasn't fooling her for one second. "Then how come I've never heard of you?"

Blimey. How many conceptual artists did she know? "I'm not a household name," I said hurriedly. "Not yet."

She leant closer and whispered, "I think you're full of shit."

The words on their own might have been discouraging, but the way she said them was most definitely not; she might as well have been saying, *I want to fuck your brains out.* I caught my breath; it seemed aeons since a woman had come on to me like this. It was a perfect moment; two souls locked in passionate collusion. We gazed into each other's eyes and she seemed ready to take the cross-examination to another, deeper level, one that I both yearned for and dreaded. I was so dizzy with desire that when someone grabbed me from behind and spun me round, I almost fell over.

It was Alice Marchmont, pecking me on both cheeks as though we were social equals. "John!" she squealed.

"Alice!" I shrieked back. "Alice!"

My frustration at her monumentally bad timing was tempered by the thought that now the redhead could see for herself that I was indeed one of the crowd and not some lowlife gatecrasher. Nevertheless she raised one eyebrow, looking sceptically from me to Alice and back again. "You two know each other?"

"Of course," said Alice. She was wearing a shimmering grey dress and sandals with heels so high they made me feel like a garden gnome. She smiled coolly at the redhead and said, "John and I are old friends."

I might have been imagining things, but there seemed to be an undercurrent of competition between them. Surely they couldn't be fighting over me? On the other hand, why not? I wasn't so bad looking; I'd been told I looked rakish, which I thought more than made up for the lack of inches. So I relaxed, and relished the moment.

The redhead was scowling, but somehow this just made her seem foxier than ever. She slipped her arm through mine and purred, "Don't you just adore men who wear grungy old leather jackets?"

Once again I felt the urge to kiss her, but didn't get the chance to act on it because Alice immediately grabbed my other arm and peeled me away. "Come and say hello to Nick."

The redhead shrugged helplessly and waved goodbye as Alice yanked me across the garden so violently that my heels tore wet brown scuffmarks in the lawn. I cast a wistful backward glance.

"You behave now," mouthed the redhead, trying not to laugh.

"I intend to," I replied, though I doubt she heard because already there were a dozen or so people between us, most of them buffeted sideways as Alice hauled me in her wake like a piece of wheeled luggage.

As soon as she'd pulled me clear of the crush, she turned and asked, a slight edge to her voice, "What did you tell her?"

"Nothing. Absolutely nothing."

"That's good."

She turned back and continued to drag me towards where two men were deep in conversation beneath a small pergola. Alice launched herself at the shorter of the two and kissed him on the cheek.

"Nick!" I exclaimed, holding out my hand.

"This is Charlie," Alice said in a warning voice.

I rallied swiftly. "Charlie! So pleased to meet you!" I shook his hand heartily before swivelling to face the man to whom he'd been chatting. Aquiline nose, receding hairline, very tall. Well, over six foot, in fact. How could I not have guessed? Though, to my relief, he wasn't as drop-dead handsome as Alice's breathless description had painted him.

"Nick Fitch! So good to see you again." I peered up at his face; he reminded me of a younger, better-looking Prince

Charles without the sticky-out ears and tainted genes, and there really did seem to be a hint of tragedy in his face. Here was a man who had known true sorrow, who'd been touched by a grief undreamt of by most of his peers, who had looked death in the eye and lived to tell the tale, albeit with emotional scars. He looked—there was no denying it—a little haunted. Whereas Alice's eulogising had made me hate him, now I'd actually met him I began to feel a curious kinship. Maybe we weren't so different after all.

Charlie had disengaged himself from Alice's embrace and was now looking me up and down as though he really did know me from somewhere, but before I could say anything further he murmured something about having to see a man about a dog and slipped discreetly away, leaving me at the mercy of the happy couple.

"You remember John," Alice prompted.

"How could I forget?" said Nick, bluffing like mad and pumping my hand as though he thought he might get water from it. He was good, I had to give him that, but I thought I could detect just the faintest trace of panic in his fixed stare. *Who the hell is this and where did I meet them?* "How are you doing, John?"

"Not so bad, old buddy. It's been a while."

"It certainly has," said Nick, still staring fixedly. "I take it you've heard our news." He draped his arm around Alice's shoulders, but it looked awkward and he didn't leave it there long.

"Congratulations." I nudged him in the ribs, which thanks to his height was easier said than done. "You jammy bastard. You son of a gun . . ." How *did* normal men speak to each other? I took a deep breath and started to improvise, which perhaps wasn't wise. Blame it on the champagne. "I might as well confess," I confided, "that I was thinking about asking Alice to marry *me*. I've had this crush on her for years, ever since I saw her on that pony. And now it's too late! You got in there first, and I missed my chance. And now I'll never, never ever be happy again."

Nick seemed a little dazed by this speech. I wondered if I'd overdone the *nevers*. Alice was looking at me uneasily, but gamely took up the conversation. "You *must* come to the wedding," she said. "Mustn't he, Nicky?"

"Absolutely." Nick's eyes were darting back and forth. He was still trying desperately to place me. It was obviously going to be a lengthy and altogether fruitless process.

It had been so long since I'd socialised with men who were neither drug addicts nor computer nerds nor out-of-work musicians that I'd forgotten what came next. What the hell did you *say* to them? They liked sport, didn't they? All men liked sport. I decided to try a more robust approach. "You're in good shape!" I punched his arm. "Been working out?"

"Not really," he said, rubbing his arm and tilting his head slightly, as though still trying to place me in the scheme of things. "But I'm always on the lookout for squash partners. Are you up for it?"

"Why not?" I chortled in relief, elated by the realisation that this was working, it really was working. He didn't suspect a thing. "But you must promise to be gentle with me. I'm more accustomed to the lager and crisps workout." I laughed heartily and moved my hand up and down, up and down, miming the action of lifting a can of lager to my lips. I glanced at Nick, expecting to see him laughing too, but instead he seemed uncomfortable and it occurred to me he might have mis-interpreted my gesture.

Once again, Alice came galloping to my rescue. "Talking about crisps, oh God, only one week to go and half a stone to lose! I'll never get into that dress!"

We went on to discuss the dress, or rather Alice talked about it in brain-numbing detail, until I thought I saw Nick's eyes glazing over, and decided it was my duty to draw him back into the conversation.

"So where's it to be? Church or registry office? Madame Tussauds or the London Eye?"

"Nothing gimmicky, I'm afraid. We're sticking with family tradition. St Cuthbert's, Little Yawning."

I must have looked blank because he added, "Framptons," though that didn't help much.

"Hmm," I said, trying to sound knowledgeable. "That's Frampton as in Peter, as in The Herd and Humble Pie?" He laughed, making me feel deliciously witty.

"*Framptons*. Rhymes with Hamptons. Alice hasn't told you about it? Fitch family pile. Falling to pieces, of course, aren't they all. I'd flog it to the Trust if I could."

Out of the corner of my eye, I saw Alice being hauled away by a large bosomed blonde, which left me on my own with Nick. Luckily, he seemed to have taken a shine to me and I began to see what Alice had meant about his charm. He had a way of smiling that made you want to caper around like a court jester, just to please him. I responded with a fair bit of capering, meta-phorically speaking, and soon we were getting along famously. He started making disparaging remarks about the quality of the champagne we were drinking, which led to a rather one-sided conversation about wine.

"I hear you lived abroad for a bit," I said, trying to steer the conversation back to the case in hand. Alice had told me that after Georgina's death he'd spent time in France and Italy, which had immediately conjured a vision of a bronzed playboy basking on the *Côte d'Azur*, surrounded by a bevy of bikini-clad Euro-cuties all too eager to comfort the wealthy widower. But now I'd met him I adjusted this mental picture to that of a pale aesthete passing his days in a spartan hotel room, gazing mournfully at a cameo of his lost love.

"More than a bit," he groaned. "Too long, in fact. Europe's all very well where food and drink are concerned, but . . . well, it's full of *Europeans*."

"Ghastly," I agreed.

"You've read the Nigel Molesworth books?"

I nodded enthusiastically. During my adolescence, *Down With Skool* had been my bible, its contents etched into my memory more thoroughly than any of my school set-books.

"Well, it's just like that," he said. "The French *are* slack, and the Germans *are* unspeakable."

"And the Russians are rotters!" I added. "Though maybe not as much as they used to be. What exactly were you up to over there?"

"Oh, couple of business deals." He waved his hand vaguely. "But mostly trying to get away from things after . . . you know."

I decided to jump straight in.

"I was so sorry to hear about Georgina."

For one brief moment I thought I saw a flicker of uncertainty somewhere deep behind his eyes, but then it was gone. "Thank you. It was a pretty dreadful business, you know . . ." There was a pause before he added, not very convincingly, "But I guess life goes on."

"It certainly does," I said. "Even after a tragic accident like that . . ."

Alice had not been forthcoming with the details; all she'd mentioned was that Georgina had drowned. I was hoping he would fill in a few of the gaps, but all he did was look down at his feet and say, "I appreciate your saying it. There are still rumours, you know, that it wasn't an accident . . ."

"Of course it was an accident," I said. "What else could it have been?"

He looked uncomfortable. "Some people suggested it was, you know, suicide. Of course, it was nothing of the kind. Georgina would never have . . ."

He tailed off and took a fortifying swig of champagne. I noticed his hand was shaking.

"Terrible business. I thought I'd never get over it, you know... And then I met Alice."

He cast such a fond glance in his fiancée's direction I sensed that to persist in talking about his dead first wife would have been tactless.

"I envy you," I said, nodding in Alice's direction. "She's very, er, solid and down to earth. Not at all flaky."

"And thank God for that," said Nick. "She's exactly what the doctor ordered. Good looking, well-connected and independently wealthy."

I must have looked shocked because he coughed and launched into a hurried explanation. "Which means I don't have to worry she might be marrying me for my money." He gave an embarrassed laugh.

I nodded sagely. "Must be a concern."

"Oh it is," Nick said in a tone so insouciant it had to be deadly serious. "You have no idea how many greedy little gold-diggers I've had to fend off through the years." He glanced around nervously, as though half-expecting to see a mob of social-climbers closing in on us, and lowered his voice. "They're OK for the odd fling, of course. But marriage, well, it's different."

"Absolutely," I agreed.

"There are traditions to be observed. Links to the past to be maintained. Genes to be propagated. And then, of course, I have to think of the house."

"Of course," I said, wondering whether he was having me on. "One *always* has to think of the house."

A waiter made me jump by silently materialising at my elbow. Nick and I helped ourselves to fresh glasses of champagne.

Nick asked, "What are you up to these days, anyway?"

I thought I might as well stick to the same cover story I'd given the redhead. You never knew when these folk might get together and compare notes. "I'm a conceptual artist."

"Excellent!" He flashed another of those disarming smiles. "You must show me some of your work. What's your speciality?"

I did some quick thinking. "Actually I've been working on something rather exciting recently. Something cat-related. A series of litter trays."

To my amazement, Nick was still looking interested. "I'm always on the lookout for something a little different. Something to invest in," he said.

"Well, you've come to the right place."

My pulse was racing. Maybe I really could make a go of this. Maybe Boris and I could make a killing on the art market.

The temperature suddenly seemed to drop, and I sneezed violently, several times in succession, just managing to keep the champagne from slopping over the side of my glass. "Isn't it a bit chilly out here?" I ventured. "Maybe we should go inside . . ."

"Summer nights are colder now," Nick said before adding, "They've taken down the fair."

What the hell? I narrowed my eyes suspiciously, trying to work out if he was taking the piss. Ninety-nine point nine per cent of the people at this party would have had no idea what he was talking about.

But I, on the other hand . . .

"All the lights have died somehow," I said, a little cautiously. "Or were they ever there?"

I half expected him to start sniggering, but he didn't.

We looked at each other, and something clicked, and we opened our mouths and chorused as one, "No sighs or mysteries, She lay golden in the sun . . ."

There was a pause, and then we both burst out laughing. And that was it! We'd bonded!

I'd been dead wrong about Nick. He was nothing like the playboy wanker I'd been expecting. After all, it wasn't every day you ran into someone with whom you could trade lyrics from *Rainbow Eyes*, possibly the loveliest ballad ever written and one that never failed to leave me with a large lump in my throat. Nick and I grinned at each other. We were on a roll. We began to discuss Rainbow, and the Sabs, and whether Ronnie James Dio was a better vocalist than Ozzy Osbourne, which as far as I was concerned was a no-brainer, though we both reckoned Osbourne deserved respect, at the very least, because, after all, he *was* Sabbath.

"Just don't let on to anyone here that I still listen to heavy metal," Nick said in a stage whisper. "I'd never live it down."

"I don't exactly go around bragging about it in public either," I assured him.

We were obviously destined to be firm friends.

We were playing air guitar to each other, satirically of course, when Alice came up and spoilt it all. I noticed her face was a little pasty, but didn't think anything of it until she put her mouth to my ear and whispered, "*She's here.*"

After that, the evening turned a little hazy.

FOUR

THERE WAS a riff playing, repeating itself again and again without actually getting anywhere, like a truncated sound-track loop on a DVD menu. What the hell was that song? It was so familiar it was driving me nuts. But I couldn't turn it off, because it was in my brain.

The first things I saw when I opened my eyes were black dots. I waited for them to go away, but they didn't. If anything, they were multiplying.

My God, so this was the DTs: not the pink elephants from *Dumbo*, nor even the bats and mice from *The Lost Weekend*, but dots, fuzzy black dots swarming all over the curtains and the bedside lamp and up the bedspread towards my face . . .

Once the initial surge of panic had subsided, I saw that not only were the dots real and not imaginary, they were in fact an integral part of the decor. Predominant theme: fake ocelot, with a sprinkling of pink and a dash of aspidistra. I could see pink boxes piled up at the bottom of the bed, a pink carrier bag marked with the words *Agent Provocateur* in curlicue print, a couple of antique medicine chests, and long necklaces looped like a glittery bead curtain across the corner of a large mirror. On the bedside table were a fancy glass jug of water, a box of pink tissues and a couple of anthologies of 19th century poetry.

One thing was clear. I was not at home.

The rest of the scene gradually filled itself in. I was lying on my back, and I had no clothes on. To judge by the thick coating of fur on my tongue, my mouth had been open all night. And for a very good reason, I found as I attempted to close it – my sinuses seemed to be stuffed with cotton wool. I was forced to keep the mouth open in order to breathe. And my throat hurt like hell, as though I'd been gargling with sandpaper.

I experimented with sitting up. Big mistake. My stomach felt as though it was full of dirty laundry being churned around in a gastric spin cycle. I cursed and slid back down again. I was going to have to take this slowly.

Only now did I see I was not alone in the bed.

"How are you feeling?" my companion asked in an unnecessarily cheerful manner. The words had a familiar ring to them. I remembered Kate asking me the very same thing, many times. But this couldn't be Kate, unless I was dreaming. I rubbed my eyes again, just to make sure.

No, not Kate.

Kate hadn't had red hair.

I relaxed. Hey, at least I'd done *something* right. I couldn't remember what exactly, but here was living, breathing proof that I hadn't entirely lost my touch. Her breasts, now liberated from the red silk I vaguely remembered had been encasing them, were firm and ripe, like apples. Though not the same colour, obviously. I'd been obsessed with breast similes ever since reading one of Ed McBain's 87th Precinct novels in which he'd described a policewoman as having 'cupcake breasts'. Since the cupcakes I remembered from my childhood were flat and covered with orange or lemon icing, the image that had lodged in my brain was a slightly discomfiting one, and no matter what alternative food-related metaphors I tried to conjure up, I couldn't quite seem to banish it.

But the redhead. *The redhead.* I couldn't understand how I hadn't noticed her earlier, since she too was naked, and lying only a few inches away, propped up on one elbow and regarding me with an amused expression. I'd seen that expression before, but where? And when?

Ah yes. Selina and Jolly's party.

Hmm. The party. Fragments of memory creaked into action like peeling wooden figures in an antique amusement park. I remembered arriving with my bottle, and spilling champagne on somebody's shoes. And oh yes, I remembered meeting Nick Fitch, and deciding that he was a capital fellow. But after that it was a jumble of confused impressions, as though some clod-hopping couch potato with access to cable and satellite had been merrily channel-surfing with my brain.

"What happened?" I groaned. "Did we fuck?"

"You're coy," she said. "I like that in a man."

"*Did* we?"

"Sadly, no." Though she didn't look sad at all. In fact, she appeared to be having trouble keeping a straight face. "You weren't up to it."

"Sorry."

The grin finally broke out on her face. "No need to apologise. You made up for it in other ways. You were most entertaining, Mr Barnes-Wallis."

"For example . . .?"

"You talked in your sleep. Babbled, in fact. I thought you'd never shut up. It was a real laugh riot."

Uh-oh. This was bad. "I trust it wasn't too embarrassing."

She shrugged. "There was an awful lot about your mother. You're obviously very close."

"*Au contraire*. Not close at all. I hardly ever see her."

She looked almost apologetic. "There was some X-rated stuff as well."

"Not with my mother, I hope."

"Worse. You were ranting about severed heads. Bloated corpses. A bit sick, really. I do hope you're not a serial killer or anything, *Mr* Barnes-Wallis." She emphasised the 'Mr' with another sly grin.

I winced. "Must have been a movie I saw." No matter how hard you tried to keep the rotten memories buried, they kept oozing to the surface, like pus from an old infected wound.

The thought of pus set off a chain reaction in which the dirty clothes in my stomach not only started spinning again but threatened to rise up and spill out. The redhead watched in mild alarm as I clamped a hand to my mouth and rolled sideways out of bed, and wordlessly pointed me in the direction of the bathroom. I made it just in time to puke a small amount of yellowish bile into the toilet bowl.

Afterwards, I felt better, but not much. I stared at my reflection; my complexion had turned a delicate shade of *eau-de-nil*. I stuck my head under the cold tap and sprayed mousse into my armpits under the mistaken impression that the aerosol can contained deodorant, and hobbled back into the bedroom with a towel wrapped around my waist and my underarm hair nicely coiffed.

In the meantime, the redhead was pulling on baggy jeans and a white T-shirt with the words CHEDDAR GORGEOUS printed in red letters across the chest. She looked even sexier than when she'd been all dolled up in her party frock and heaven knows she'd looked sexy enough then. That much I *could* remember. My penis twitched into life beneath the towel. Maybe now I could prove to her I wasn't gay. But I wasn't operating at full-speed either, and before I could co-ordinate my limbs sufficiently to attempt an advance she was leading me into her kitchen and sitting me down at the table. She plopped a large orange tablet into a large glass of water, where it started to bubble and fizz.

"Drink that. It'll make you feel better."

I took the glass sceptically, but as I sipped, I did indeed begin to feel like a human being again.

Something brushed against my leg. I looked down and saw a Jack Russell rubbing up against my ankles and panting laboriously in that way dogs have. A little disappointed that my hostess had turned out to be a doglover instead of a cat person, I reached down and scratched its ear. But at least she liked animals—a big point in her favour, even if the mutt was busily depositing a trail of cold canine snot across my shins.

"What are you doing?"

I looked up and saw her watching me keenly from the other side of the kitchen.

"Playing with myself," I told her, and then, because she didn't seem to think I'd been joking, added, "I'm scratching your dog's ear."

She burst out laughing and said, "Of course you are," and returned to her tea-making.

The kitchen faced east, and the light streaming in through the window was making my eyes water. The window-ledge was crammed with cookbooks and jars containing witchy-looking herbs. There were a lot of different sized saucepans hanging on the wall, as well as a great many utensils to which I couldn't even give names.

"You like cooking?" I ventured by way of conversation.

Her reply was, "Doesn't everyone?"

Not me. Microwaved bagels was my limit, though in another lifetime, back when I had been half of a couple, I had been hailed for my pasta sauce.

I looked down, but the dog had wandered off, leaving me with damp ankles. The redhead handed me a mug of tea, sat down and offered me a cigarette.

I told her I didn't smoke.

"You did last night."

At least that explained the sore throat. "What else did I do?"

She chuckled. "You're kidding me. You don't remember?"

"Come on, stop tormenting me."

She propped her chin in her hands and looked at me intently. "You go first. How do you know Alice Marchmont?"

Blimey. Alice. I'd forgotten about her. But now the thought of her made me feel obscurely guilty, as though by sleeping with the redhead I'd somehow betrayed my client's trust. Which was ridiculous of course. What I got up to in my spare time was no concern of hers.

"Go on, tell me," pestered the redhead. "How do you know each other?"

"We go way back." I thought it best to keep it vague. That way, I thought, I couldn't dig myself into too deep a hole.

The redhead leant forward. "Really? So how come she never mentioned you?"

"You two are friends?" She ignored that, and I remembered the undercurrent of rivalry I'd sensed between them. And then I had what, in my hungover state, seemed like a brainwave.

"I guess she didn't want Nick to find out about us."

The redhead's gaze didn't falter, though her green eyes narrowed. "And what is there to find out?"

"Nothing."

She looked sceptical.

"And who's Kate?"

That threw me.

"How do you know about Kate?"

Had someone been talking about Kate? Might there have been someone at the party who knew her? I couldn't work out whether this made me happy or sad.

"You've got her name tattooed on your bottom," said the redhead.

"Oh, the *tattoo*."

Funnily enough, I really had forgotten about it. It just happened to *be* there, like a scar from open-heart surgery.

"Just an ex," I said.

"And you called me Kate last night as well," said the redhead. "In fact, you called me just about everything but my own name."

"I did?"

To my dismay I found I couldn't remember what her real name was. What was I to do? I couldn't very well say it had slipped my mind. I scoured my memory, but the relevant file— "Redhead, Name Of"— remained obstinately tucked away on a shelf out of reach.

She was still watching me intently.

"You also mentioned . . . *Georgina*. You knew her as well?"

Georgina.

I felt almost relieved at the change of subject, but the name *Georgina* triggered something in my head and I had a sudden debilitating flashback to a vision of skin stretched tight and so translucent you could almost see the skull beneath it, a face half-obscured by strands of dark hair and fingernails grimy with grave-dirt . . .

I gulped hot tea to hide my confusion but only succeeded in scalding my tongue.

"Wasn't she Nick's first wife? It's weird, I think I was dreaming about her."

"Nick? You mean Nicholas Fitch?"

"Of course I mean Nicholas Fitch. Alice's fiancé. He was there last night. You must know him."

"Oh, Nicholas *Fitch*." She made a peculiar face. "Not really. Not as well as you, anyway. You two looked very chummy last night. In fact, you were pretty chummy with a whole load of people. You can't blame me for having been so monstrously attracted to you. You were the life and soul of the party."

This was slightly baffling, since I couldn't recollect having been on party animal form. On the other hand, I couldn't recall anything much. "So, all in all," I said hopefully, "I didn't behave too badly?"

"You behaved," she said, "*atrociously.*"

My spirits sank. I could tell she wasn't joking.

"Give me the bad news."

So she did. And it turned out to be even worse than I could have imagined. My sins included the annihilation of several herbaceous borders, repeated yelling of *Nobody expects the Spanish Inquisition!* and getting into a fistfight with the pink-cheeked man, who had punched me on the nose, after which I'd left bloody handprints all over the living-room wall.

"Weren't we in the garden?"

"It started pelting with rain," said the redhead. "There was thunder as well. Everyone went indoors, though you took some persuading. You kept yelling and running round in circles, as though you were being chased by a wild boar or something. We were worried you were going to get struck by lightning. By the time we got you inside you were soaking wet and semi-hysterical. It was grand entertainment."

"I'm sure it was," I muttered darkly.

This was bad. What would Alice have thought? I was clinging to the knowledge that it could have been worse, like the time I'd dropped a lit cigarette down the back of someone's sofa cushions, when I noticed the redhead trying hard not to laugh.

"Ooh, I've just remembered something else." She was squirming on her seat like a small girl wanting to go to the lavatory.

"*What?*"

"You told Alice Marchmont to call off the wedding."

I turned this over in my head. The redhead was still watching me closely, and all of a sudden I knew she was lying. As little as I could remember of the evening, I was sure that—ratfaced or not—I had never said any such thing. I would never have been that stupid, even when drunk. But why would she lie about a thing like that? It didn't make sense.

But all I said was, "Oh dear."

"I wouldn't have thought she was your type," she said. Ah, that was it. She was just trying to gauge the exact nature of my relationship with Alice.

"Maybe she is my type," I said cautiously. "It all depends on how jealous that would make you."

The redhead refused to take the bait.

"I wouldn't worry. You probably made her evening. Poor Alice."

'Poor' was the last word I would have used to describe Alice Marchmont, and I said as much.

"Poor people don't go and live in Paris. Not unless they're Ernest Hemingway."

The redhead made a soft noise in her throat, like a cat flexing its jaw at the glimpse of a bird.

"She told you she lived in Paris?"

"She'd just got back from Paris when she met Nick at some dinner party. Where was it? Don't tell me. Oh yes, Dan and Eva's."

I felt unreasonably pleased with myself at having been able to dredge up a trivial little detail like that, but the redhead was shaking her head slowly, smiling to herself.

"I can't believe she would say that."

"Well if she wasn't in Paris, where was she?"

"Your guess is as good as mine," said the redhead, still smiling.

I wanted to find out more, but she clammed up, and I wasn't feeling sufficiently robust to prise anything further out of her. Maybe next time I saw her, I thought. Maybe next time we might even get round to having sex.

I finished my tea and dressed myself in crumpled clothes that reeked of stale sweat and cigarettes, trying all the while to get a glimpse of an envelope, a postcard, a bill—anything that might tell me the redhead's name. But she seemed reluctant to leave me alone for a second, as though she feared I might slip some of her witchy herbs into my pocket while she wasn't looking.

In the end, I gave up, pecked her fondly on the cheek, patted her Jack Russell and set out for home.

I ROAMED up and down identical crescents for about ten minutes before finally stumbling across a street I recognised. Portobello Road. So I'd passed the night somewhere in the region of Notting Hill, an area that held so many bad memories I'd been avoiding it for years. Well, maybe the redhead would help me replace those bad memories with some more pleasurable ones.

I headed north, to Westbourne Grove tube station and the Metropolitan line. The train had crept as far as Baker Street before it struck me that not only had her name completely slipped my mind, not only had I forgotten to ask for her telephone number, but now I couldn't even remember which of the identical crescents she lived in, which meant I would never see her again, because after my behaviour at the party Alice would certainly refuse to speak to me, let alone encourage me in my quest to track down someone I hadn't even been sober enough to shag.

FIVE

I MADE IT back to the barge without throwing up, which felt like a major achievement. After feeding Boris, I collapsed on to the sofa bed and switched on my mobile phone to see whether Alice had got round to firing me yet. There were three text messages waiting. I spent ten minutes trying to make sense of CMGCLS, FTCCRS and LCWLDFSHWDSNK before laboriously copying the letters into my notebook so I could erase them from the phone's memory.

It was still reasonably early, so I allowed myself a couple of hours chilling out to *Lock Up the Wolves*, flat on my back on the sofa with Boris squatting like a Fuseli incubus on my chest, where he stared unblinking into my eyes. I drifted in and out of a shallow doze in which, every now and again, fresh new instances of my utter stupidity would plop to the surface of my memory like fart bubbles in the bath.

Talk about blowing it. No wonder someone had punched me. Now I would never get invited to Alice and Nick's wedding. It was a crying shame. I loved weddings, and receptions, and stag parties—*especially* stag parties—anything that encouraged people to get merry and take their clothes off and give tactless speeches and so forth. Given my love of such occasions, it was a source of never-ending mystery to me why I'd never got married myself. Maybe the fact that I'd never popped the question might have had something to do with it. Maybe the fact that I'd never fallen in love . . .

There I went again, trying to pose as a cynic when I was nothing but a big old softy romantic. Because I *had* fallen in love, deeply and passionately, and then I had stupidly gone and told her the truth about myself, and it had all ended in tears. It was just too tragic, and I knew from experience that it wasn't a good idea to dwell on it. Dwelling on it only led to even more drinking than usual, and ragged black holes in my memory, and waking up in a police cell . . .

Just as I was drifting perilously close to the pit of depression that invariably opened up at my feet whenever I started thinking too hard, I was snatched back from the danger zone by what sounded like the chirruping of a budgerigar and Boris immediately switching from cuddly household pet into search-and-destroy mode. I traced the sound to my mobile and made a mental note to replace the ringtone with something less annoying. I didn't think my mother would have got hold of the new number this quickly, but answered in my best Gorbals accent, just in case, ready to deny all knowledge of my own existence. Not that it would have made much difference; she seemed to have an uncanny knack of knowing when she had me cornered.

"John? Is that you? Why are you speaking like that?"

I groaned inwardly. It wasn't my mother. It was Alice Marchmont, no doubt ringing to announce she had no further need of my services.

I dropped the accent. "Alice!"

"Enjoy yourself last night?" she asked.

This had to be a trick question. I hesitated, trying to rate the frostiness of her tone on a scale of one to ten. If I said yes, it would allow her to come back with, "Well, I'm so glad, because you fucking well ruined it for everyone else." But without the *fucking well*, obviously.

If on the other hand I replied in the negative, she would say, "Nya nya, serves you right."

Or words to that effect.

In the end, I chickened out and said, "Had a little too much to drink, I'm afraid. Champagne goes straight to my head."

I didn't go so far as to *apologise*, because there's nothing more pathetic than a drunk *apologising* for his behaviour, as though he expects everyone to forgive him for, say, setting the settee on fire.

"You were a big hit," said Alice.

I was surely not hearing straight. "Um, I wonder if you could run that by me again."

"Oh, John, everyone *loved* you. They thought you were a riot."

I couldn't believe my ears. Was she really saying that her friends had found my bad behaviour *amusing*? They thought I was a funny guy? Maybe next time I really should try setting fire to the sofa. That would give them something to laugh about. Wankers. What was the point of being a rebel and bad boy if everyone just cooed and chucked you under the chin?

For a while I was lost for words, which enabled Alice to bang on uninterrupted.

"Nick definitely wants you to come to the wedding, which is terribly convenient, because that way it'll be easier for you to make sure Georgina doesn't spoil it."

Ah yes, Georgina.

"You know what? I had a dream about her. I dreamt she was chasing me round the pond."

There was a pause, and then Alice said, "It wasn't a dream, John. She was there."

My heart went down like a lead-weighted yo-yo.

"Let me get this straight. Georgina Fitch was there? At the party last night? We're talking about the same party, right? Selina and Jolly's bash?"

"It looked as though she was trying to tell you something, but you kept running away," said Alice, and there was a shudder in her voice. "I don't blame you, John. I was kind of relieved she was leaving me alone and going after you. Now she's dead, she doesn't look the same. She doesn't look . . . *normal.*"

"Did anyone else see her?"

"I don't think so. Just us. Everyone else thought you were just fooling around."

No wonder I'd kept acting as though I were being chased. I was being chased. I heard my voice go up an octave as I said, "Why me? You're the one who's being stalked. Not me."

"I thought you were terribly brave," said Alice.

Brave, maybe. But any satisfaction I might have felt at hearing her say that was marred by the realisation that everyone else now thought I was barking mad.

"What about Nick?" I asked.

"He can't see her."

There was a pause, and then she added, "I don't think Nick can see anything. He's very firmly rooted in the real world."

I felt a disagreeable sensation welling up inside me—a sensation I hadn't felt for a long, long time and had hoped I would never feel again. It was a fluttery sort of panic mixed with a resigned awareness that what appeared to be the real world was just an optimistic front, and that the reality behind it was sordid, depressing and very dangerous.

I'd first felt it at the age of six, after I'd spent a good half-hour talking to a small girl who'd appeared on television during an episode of *Thunderbirds*. I'd thought at the time this was a little odd, since all the other characters on the show were puppets, but there she was, in the same room as Scott Tracy, so I'd simply assumed it was part of the programme. My parents had always discouraged me from mixing with other children, so I was thrilled to find a playmate of about my own age, albeit one who was on the TV screen in black and white while I was in living colour in the real world.

Despite our differences, we'd managed to play Cowboys and Indians and Doctors and Nurses, but then we'd played Hide and Seek, and she'd hidden so efficiently, somewhere on Tracy Island, that I hadn't been able to find her again.

After that, she made guest appearances on *Tales From Europe* and *Top of the Pops*, but it wasn't until I innocently mentioned her name to my father that I realised something wasn't right. In fact, something was horribly wrong, though for a long time I was unable to work out exactly what.

The little girl's name was Marion Tucker, though I could never remember how I knew this—I don't think she ever told me, not in so many words. But I do remember that my father, when he heard me say that name, had lost his rag and given me a damn good smacking.

"You're not to talk about it," he said. "You mustn't ever mention her again."

"Why not?" I asked.

"Because she's *dead*."

And then my dad had buttoned his lip and refused to say anything more, and I didn't want to get another smacking so I never asked what he'd meant, and the next day when I went into the living-room the TV set was gone and in its place was a round glass bowl containing a goldfish. I stared at the fish for hours on end, but it never seemed to do anything but swim round in circles. It certainly didn't play Doctors and Nurses.

I'd seen Marion Tucker just once more after that, on a visit to my uncle's, when *Crossroads* had been playing in the corner of the room, and she'd come right up to the screen and gazed out at me with big moist eyes, but only now did I see there was something not quite right about the way her head was joined to her neck, and her tongue seemed much too big for her mouth. This time, she tried to tell me how she'd died, but I didn't like what I was hearing, didn't like it at all, so I'd turned my back on her and that had been that, at least as far as Marion Tucker was concerned. Later on there would be others, but she was my first.

The rest of my childhood was a jumbled mass of strange impressions, and when I thought about it later I could never work out which were real and which imaginary. Our semi-detached house, so ordinary from the outside, always seemed on the inside to be full of strange shifting shadows and mysterious noises, and I always slept with a nightlight on. Once I thought I saw a mad scientist creeping across the landing towards my parents' bedroom, outsized syringe at the ready, and another time I thought I glimpsed a witch in a tall pointed hat digging in the rhubarb patch behind the garden shed. And I never let down my guard on the staircase, always remembering to tread softly lest the Hall Monster hear my footsteps and open a secret trapdoor in the stairs and drag me down into its lair, which was littered with the chewed bones of small children.

But my father's reaction when I'd mentioned the little girl I'd seen on *Thunderbirds* was the first time I truly understood that, sometimes, I could see things other people couldn't. It was also when I learned it was usually best to keep quiet about it.

Eventually Marion Tucker became nothing more than a suppressed memory, and though my father never bought another television I watched without incident at other people's houses. And so the years passed relatively uneventfully, and I managed to live a more or less normal life, with a more or less normal girlfriend, until it all went horribly wrong.

It later became clear to me that the break-up with Kate must have triggered something, and it was a bad few years after that. It was as though a door had burst open in my head, and all this mouldy old baggage came tumbling out.

Once I saw an old woman throw herself on to the tracks at Leicester Square underground station. The onrushing train split her head apart as though it were a melon, but by the time I'd raced down the platform to tell the driver, and they'd shut down the power and examined the line, there was nothing there. It was only by the skin of my teeth that I escaped being arrested for having held up the entire public transport system. So when, about a month later, I saw exactly the same thing happen at the very same place, I squeezed my eyes shut and counted slowly to a hundred and by the time I reopened them there was nothing at all on the tracks, not even the train, which had moved on without me.

Another time I was walking down High Holborn when I heard a sound like the slow flapping of giant leather wings behind me. I turned to see a large electronic billboard with vertical strips swivelling repeatedly between three different posters.

I stood and stared, hypnotised, as the image of a small Alpine village protected from an oncoming avalanche by the name of a large insurance company was replaced by that of a famous footballer balancing a well-known brand of soft drink on his forehead, which in turn was replaced by an accident victim with half his scalp hanging off, and don't even ask what he was supposed to be advertising.

I must have stood and stared at that hoarding for a good five minutes, and each time the accident victim clunked into place there would be more gory details, more brain and blood, and then eventually he began to speak to me, which was when I decided to call it a day and ran as fast as my legs would carry me up all the way up Red Lion Street, the sound of the giant leather wings still flapping slowly behind me.

As I said, it was a bad few years.

But at last, with a heroic effort, I put my shoulder to that door and forced it shut on all the demons and serial killers and half-scalped accident victims, so that nothing could come out. It was a close-run thing, but eventually I managed it.

And then I locked the door and threw away the key. Locked it, I hoped, for ever, and tried to live a normal life, behave like an ordinary man, which wasn't easy. How did normal men behave? I watched closely and tried to copy them. I gave it my best shot, even though sometimes I came perilously close to despising myself. Were other men really this desperate, this hopeless, this pathetic? Or was it just me?

And now Alice Marchmont was raining on my parade with her wretched snuff spam and haunted entryphones. With a queasy feeling in the pit of my stomach, I wondered if maybe it wasn't just telephones and televisions I had to be wary of. Maybe the whole of modern technology was a gateway to the netherworld. If that was the case, then I was well and truly up shit-creek without a paddle. Hell, I was up shit-creek without a *boat*.

I snapped to attention. Alice was saying something that didn't compute.

"Can you come round?"

I hesitated, a little confused. Another invitation was the last thing I'd been expecting after my behaviour at the party. Alice interpreted my silence as reluctance. Her voice took on a pleading tone. "She'll be there again tonight, I know it. She's been there every night this week, apart from yesterday, when she followed me to the party. She's stalking me, John, she's really stalking me. I don't feel safe."

The silence stretched on and on until I began to find it embarrassing, and I found myself saying, "This evening?"

Jesus! I felt like biting my tongue off. The words had popped out before I'd thought about them. In my current condition, I wasn't sure I was even capable of getting up from the sofa, let alone travelling halfway across town to meet a walking corpse. "On the other hand . . ." I began, but Alice didn't let me finish. All of a sudden, she was all snap and crackle and to the point.

"Around ten, then."

She gave me her address and hung up.

I didn't need to look her street up in the A to Z. I knew where it was; I'd been past it many, many times. Bloody Notting Hill again. Didn't anyone live anywhere else, for heaven's sake? How had I let Alice talk me into this? I threw down the phone and gazed dead-eyed at the clock. I had just under ten hours to get rid of this debilitating hangover. Ten hours to practise standing up without barfing. Ten hours to unblock my nose and scrub the disgusting mould off my tongue. I gazed at the clock so long that I drifted into a trance and lost thirty minutes.

Nine and a half hours in which to get rid of the hangover.

Gently, I extricated myself from Boris, who'd been winding himself around my neck like a furry boa constrictor with claws, and hauled myself to my feet and prepared the first of many, many industrial-strength black coffees to pour down my throat.

I needed to do some more work on Alice's case, but kept putting it off—in truth, I was having trouble deciding where to jump back in—and instead spent the rest of the morning trying to sort my scattered belongings into some sort of order. I would never be neat and tidy, but at least I could organise my affairs so I wouldn't have to spend half an hour rummaging through bags each time I needed a clean pair of socks.

But of course I got sidetracked and the barge ended up more chaotic than ever while I sat at the hub of the devastation, poring over the contents of an old biscuit tin I'd found buried in one of my innumerable bags. I had only to set eyes on the lid with its painting of sleepy Labrador pups to find myself instantly swept back in time. It was a tin full of treasures, and I sifted through them like a priest handling holy relics.

There was a *Ladybird Book of Bible Stories* in which the infant Moses was curled up in the bulrushes with a puff adder, while on another page Jesus's disciples were being menaced by a giant turtle that looked as though it had escaped from a Japanese monster movie. The book had never ceased to give me a thrill, even though my father had patiently explained how the pages had somehow got mixed up at the printing stage with the *Ladybird Book of Reptiles*.

I flicked through some photographs I'd taken of Kate. She was smiling at the camera, or possibly just screwing up her eyes because the sun was in them. Just looking at her gave me a painful feeling in my chest, as though my heart had been ripped out and the wound was still raw and palpitating. Wrapped around the prints was a letter that I set aside without unfolding since I already knew the contents by heart and reading them again would only have plunged me back into the slough of despond.

There was also a dog-eared black and white photograph of my mother, so small it wasn't easy to make out her features—photos had been a lot smaller back then. But she looked so young and carefree it could only have been taken before I was born, possibly even before she'd met my father, who was enough to put a frown on anybody's brow. She'd been so beautiful, back then, and to see her like that only reopened the wound in my chest. Why couldn't she have been more like other mothers?

I lingered over the photo for a while, then laid it carefully back in the tin, on top of another small photo, one that I'd never dared show anyone, and next to the skull of a small rodent, a dried orchid and a tortoiseshell pillbox containing a handful of green capsules that had long ago melted into a single gelatinous blob.

I examined all these objects carefully, feeling close to tears. What was the point of hanging on to these things? I felt no nostalgia for my childhood, and my sole remaining memories of Kate were distressing ones. As for my mother, the very thought of what she'd later become made me break out in a cold sweat. I would gladly have thrown everything away and started again from scratch, except that I couldn't shake off the feeling there was unfinished business in here somewhere, and that if I were to discard a single one of these items, it would be like disposing of an irreplaceable key, even if it was a key to something I almost certainly had no desire to unlock.

Eventually, when I'd spent the best part of the morning doing little but rearrange my belongings into a fresh config-uration of utter chaos, I forced myself to think about Alice's case again. Ever since I'd got Kevin's phone cut off by neglecting to pay the bill, I'd been forced to go elsewhere for my internet connection. So I took off up the Caledonian Road, shoring up my courage by calling in at a couple of pubs en route to Cyber-Bites in Copenhagen Street, where the Barnum brothers had arranged for me to have a massive discount in return for services rendered.

After about an hour, I finally located a newspaper article published a few weeks after Georgina Fitch's death, and though the scanning process had turned the accompanying pictures into little more than abstract smudges, I was hoping the text might give me some idea of what had happened.

The headline was TRAGEDY OF LONELY HEIRESS and then, underneath, in smaller type, POSH BINT SNUFFS IT or something along those lines. I shuffled through the pages, hunting for solid information, but it dribbled on in increasingly trivial fashion underpinned by the none too subtle subtext that although beautiful rich people might well have had lashings more dosh than you or me, it didn't mean they were happy.

What a crock. They always looked pretty damn happy to me.

As for Georgina's death, the article contradicted what Alice had said about drowning and instead reported she had died in a car accident, a mere five minutes away from Framptons. Drowning or car accident, which was it?

Then I read on and realised it had probably been both, because the car had somehow ended up in the canal. That it had happened after midnight and Georgina had been in her nightgown had been viewed as a tad suspicious, but there had been no indication that any other vehicle had been involved, nor had there been any shortage of 'friends' willing to testify that she'd always been the world's worst driver and had habitually used accelerator and brake like 'stop' and 'go' pedals on a dodgem car.

If it didn't cast much light on the incident, the article did lay one of my fears to rest. Nick had an alibi as tight as a duck's ass, with dozens of witnesses ready to swear that on the night in question they'd talked to him or bought him drinks or seen him chatting up women at Gnashers, in the heart of fashionable

Soho. It didn't sound like very gentlemanly behaviour, but at least it proved he'd been nowhere near his wife when she'd died.

I also read that Georgina had made a series of phone calls shortly before midnight. Two had been to her husband's mobile, but since he'd either turned it off or not been answering, she'd left messages on his answering service: the first had been a lot of hysterical babbling in which the only audible word was 'Fitch' or possibly 'bitch' or even 'witch', but in the second her voice had been surprisingly calm as she confessed to her husband that she knew he didn't love her, and that now she didn't love him either.

Then she'd tried, without success, to reach one of her girlfriends, but had ended up leaving just another barely comprehensible message in which the word 'bitch' had figured prominently. Then she'd called her parents, and though she hadn't said anything outright, they'd sensed immediately that something was wrong. *'She said she just wanted to hear our voices, and that she loved us.'*

Last of all, she'd called the Upper Wannell police station in a panic to say she was being stalked by some sort of animal and asking for help, though the sergeant in charge hadn't taken it any more seriously than any of the other calls she'd made to them with overwrought accounts of attempted break-ins or being followed.

(The writer of the article threw in his own two pennyworth here with the tidbit that Mrs Fitch had been addicted to books about real-life murder cases, which he suggested was maybe not the most sensible reading matter for a sensitive young woman with an overactive imagination spending a lot of time on her own in a big old house in the middle of nowhere.)

By the time the police got round to checking up on her, they found the house deserted and her car missing and it was assumed she'd gone to stay with friends. Only the next day, when someone finally managed to contact Nick in London and he'd listened to the messages on his answering service, did anyone bother to go back and search the house, the grounds and then, when she still hadn't been found, the surrounding area.

Afterwards, the shattered widower had issued statements to the press in which he'd threatened to sue the police.

In a sidebar, there were references to a local man called Tubby Clegg who a few days later been found dead in a ditch, clutching a shotgun, with a gold necklace (identified by Nick as a Fitch family heirloom) in his back pocket and an unfeasibly high level of alcohol in his blood. The shotgun had been fired, once, and the charge had taken part of his head with it.

No-one was actually *saying* he'd had anything to do with Georgina's death, but the inference was there, as was the snide suggestion (and here I was reading between the lines) that Georgina and Tubby were in fact well-acquainted, that she had been spending a lot of time in the village while Nick was down in London, that Clegg was her bit of rough and that the liaison had turned sour. The coroner's verdict in both cases was mis-adventure, though it was implied that Georgina's behaviour had been increasingly bizarre and unpredictable; only a few days before her death, she'd been spotted running down the lane with her hands clamped over her ears.

Case closed, though the report was frustratingly vague on pernickety but important details such as why the police had taken so long to find the submerged car, or what she'd been doing driving around in the middle of the night in her nightgown in the first place. It was as though everyone involved had been only too eager to tidy away the loose ends and get on with their lives.

I KEPT the mobile off in Cyber-Bites. On my way home, I switched it back on, and it immediately started throbbing in my hand like a sex toy, making joyful chirruping noises that were only marginally less annoying than the budgie ringtone. Something else that needed changing. One of these days I would find the time.

An envelope icon appeared on the LCD screen. Text alert.

This time the message was mercifully clear, with all the vowels present and correct.

CALL ME.

It was from Nick. So he was still talking to me. Or maybe he just wanted to give me an earful. I crossed my fingers and called him back.

"John!" he exclaimed before I'd even had a chance to introduce myself.

"Um, hello."

"Great seeing you last night!"

Was there a faint trace of sarcasm? Or was I being paranoid?

"Always cool, catching up with old friends," he went on. "Mustn't lose touch again. Now, about this evening . . ."

The finer points of this conversation were passing me by. "*This* evening?"

"Six o'clock, OK?"

Was this somehow connected to Alice's invitation, or not? I couldn't decide, and played for time. "You're talking about six o'clock this evening?"

"You do remember?" asked Nick.

I told the truth, but only because it required less effort than the invention of a lie. "Actually, no. Sorry, memory like a sieve. Brain cells destroyed. You know how it is."

"We're playing squash, old man."

"We are?"

"Court's booked. Can't wriggle out of it now."

I'd volunteered to play squash?

Fuck fuck fuck.

For Christ's sake, what had got into me? This was easily the stupidest thing I'd done in an entire evening's worth of stupidity. I hadn't touched a racket of any description for years, ever since I'd been suckered into a game of badminton against a woman twice my age who'd thrashed me so humiliatingly that afterwards I'd had to pretend I'd lost on purpose. I had little doubt my ball skills had not improved in the meantime, and that moreover I was so unfit I would probably collapse with a heart attack at the very first lunge.

"Six it is," Nick said, as though the proposal had come from me, and then added, "Fizz eek?"

There was no sensible answer to that, so I just said, "Sorry?"

"*Physique!* Fitness club just off Westbourne Grove."

"Ah well, you see, when I . . ."

But I'd already lost the thread, and before I'd managed to pick it up again, Nick was already saying, "See you on court," and before I'd registered what was happening he'd hung up. I stared at the silent phone.

I could have called him back and cancelled, of course. But I didn't want him thinking I was a lily-livered wuss who didn't do sports. So that was that.

I reached the barge, put on the kettle and tried doing some press-ups while it boiled. After only half a dozen I was so knackered that it was a relief when the phone trilled again, giving me an excuse to quit. I answered, hoping like mad it would be Nick calling to cancel. Talk about wishful thinking.

"Johnny?"

Oh no. "Not now, mum."

"Johnny my darling, I really need to speak to you. It's urgent."

"I can't, I really can't. Not right now."

As always, my mother started off sounding eminently reasonable, just like anybody else's mother. An eavesdropper would probably have wondered why I seemed so reluctant to talk to her.

"How are you, my darling?"

"I'm fine, mum."

"Are you keeping warm? Getting enough to eat?" Mothers. They all asked the same things, even mine. I had this hypothesis that as soon as women gave birth they were packed off to a special school where they were brainwashed into asking the same questions that every other mother asked.

I fumbled for the button to switch the phone off, but it was too late—the connection had been made, and the voice kept coming. "How's that nice girl? What's her name again? Kate?"

I sighed. "That was over years ago. You know that."

"No need to get snippy, John. It slipped my mind, that's all. Who is it you're going out with now? What's her name again?"

"I don't have a girlfriend at the moment, mum. Look, I've really got to go. I'm supposed to be playing squash . . ."

"Ah yes, with one of your exciting new friends. Well, don't get too comfortable there. You know they're just laughing at you behind your back."

"They're not like that."

"I really don't know why you can't patch things up with Kate. It's not every day you find a nice girl like that."

"It's just not possible, mum."

"What was the problem? Wasn't she good enough for you?"

"It just didn't work out."

"You frightened her off."

"I just told her the truth, mum."

"Why do you have to frighten everyone off? What did you say? I do hope you didn't tell her what your father did. You know that's a family matter. You know you're not supposed to share that with anyone."

"I've got to go, mum. I've really got to go . . ."

She took no notice. I stuffed the phone down the back of the sofa bed. I could hear her, muffled yet still audible, going on about my father, and about Kate, and about how I wasn't normal, but I didn't need to hear to know what she was saying; I knew it off by heart. I tried to stop listening and get on with my life, but it was only after I'd drunk my coffee, taken a shower and shaved that I found the phone had finally gone quiet.

SIX

THE SQUASH, predictably, was a fiasco, alleviated only by Nick being so understanding about the whole thing.

"That's OK," he assured me as yet again I swiped wildly at the ball and crashed into the wall. "No, really, I *like* winning."

It took only ten minutes for my shirt to be so thoroughly soaked in perspiration that it turned transparent, like some sort of trendy gay disco-garment. The game wasn't quite a white-wash, though I was uneasily aware that the few points coming my way did so only because my opponent closed his eyes or bungled his shots deliberately so as not to build up too embarrassing a lead. If it hadn't been so humiliating I might have been touched by his sensitivity, but I was too busy trying not to keel over and die.

"Are you sure you're all right?" Nick asked for the umpteenth time. "Your face is very red."

"I'm fine," I panted. "Bit out of practice, is all." I lunged forward, nearly snapping a tendon, and managed to scrape back one of his serves, only to watch him calmly place his return in the corner behind me, where I had an ice cube's chance in hell of reaching it.

"Never mind," he said. "I expect you'll clobber me once you're back on form."

I didn't like to say that even on form I wasn't likely to offer much in the way of a clobbering.

Afterwards we took a shower, studiously avoided comparing penis size and instead talked about manly things, like football. I'd expected Nick to support one of the glamour outfits, such as Manchester United or Arsenal, but to my amazement he turned out to be a fan of Luton Town, which was one of the few teams even more pathetic than my own. The bitter experience of watching your team lose, week in, week out, interspersed with the occasional relegation—it was another thing we had in common.

From what I could see without actually going so far as to stare openly, Nicholas Fitch was in excellent shape. He whistled as he towelled himself down. He didn't exactly have a six-pack, but by dint of sidelong glances I could see there was no trace of love-handle on his torso. I did, however, spot a tattoo on the inside of his upper arm. It was a skull surrounded by flames, which reminded me a little of Ghost Rider, and it struck me as odd, because he didn't strike me as the tattoo type, and particularly not a skull-surrounded-by-flames kind of guy.

I didn't have any love-handles either, but that was only because I was too puny. I guess if you were to half-close your eyes in a bad light, I might have passed for lean and mean, rather than weedy. And not just weedy—thanks to the unaccustomed burst of exercise I was now wobbly as well. I felt as though I'd been beaten by rocks until every last bone in my body had been broken. No, more like *pulped*. As I tried and failed for the third time to direct my foot through the leg-hole in my underpants, I realised my limbs were now working to rule. I was Mr Jelly.

When we'd finished getting dressed, Nick proposed I join him for a quick drink. I had time to kill before my rendezvous with Alice, and decided it would provide me with a useful opportunity to find out more about my squash partner, particularly since I'd been too busy concentrating on not being brained by oncoming squash balls to ask any of the questions I'd prepared.

"So long as it really is quick. I've got a date."

I thought it best not to mention the 'date' was with his fiancée.

Nick checked his watch. "No problemo. I'm supposed to be meeting someone myself. But it's just round the corner."

I thought 'it' would be a favourite pub, but it turned out he was referring to his swanky Bayswater flat, the one Alice had already described in dismissive tones as a 'bachelor pad'. I got the impression he was only inviting me up so he could show it off, but I didn't blame him; if I had a bachelor pad like that I'd have been inviting people up for drinks all the time so they could admire the leather upholstery and dimmer switches and shagpile and concealed audio system. I was especially impressed by the black and silver bar.

"Very James Bond," I said, stroking the mirrored counter and reflecting that it would be very handy for snorting lines of coke. If you were into that sort of thing.

"Handy for when I'm in town," Nick said, as though it were the sort of *pied à terre* anyone could cobble together out of an empty Squeezy bottle and a few lengths of string. I'd been toying with the idea of maybe one day inviting him to the barge for an aperitif—maybe he'd think living on a boat had a sort of bohemian cachet—but now I began to think better of it. The contrast would be too humbling.

While he was taking a slash in the bathroom, I scoped out his CD collection; much to my disappointment, it was all tasteful Miles Davis, Bryan Ferry and Bob Dylan, not a trace of Rainbow or the Sabs. I wondered if maybe he was concealing a stash of infra-dig vinyl somewhere where his friends wouldn't see it. That had to be the explanation. After all, why on earth would someone *pretend* to be a heavy metal fan?

On the shelf over the CDs was an arrangement of framed photos: one of Alice, looking stiff and posed in a studio, another of Nick and a couple of other blokes of around the same age, all looking matey and dishevelled, as though they'd just been playing squash. And there was a third photograph of a young woman in a green Barbour jacket, perched on a gate. It wasn't a great photo; I picked it up to get a better look, but her hair was blowing all over the place and partially obscured her face. Was this Georgina? She looked nothing like the horrifying vision I vaguely recalled from the party, but it was difficult to tell with the hair. This woman was very much alive, though she wasn't smiling. In fact, she looked rather unhappy. I felt a pang of sorrow on her behalf.

Just as I was restoring the photo to its original position on the shelf, my attention was caught by something in the background behind her. The depth of field was so shallow it was out of focus, but I could just make out a small brown and white dog. It was not unlike the one that had slimed all over my leg at the redhead's. Evidently, in this milieu, Jack Russell was the breed of choice.

Nick seemed to be taking an unusually long time to empty his bladder, so I crept out into the hallway to take a peek at the rest of the flat.

I'd taken two steps when I realised my host wasn't in the bathroom after all. He was talking on the phone in the bedroom—I assumed it was to Alice since my ears picked up the word 'sweetheart', though she'd obviously said something upsetting because he didn't seem at all happy.

"You mean you've been tarting around," he said.

In fact, the more I listened, the more I got the impression he was insanely jealous, and that she was trying to mollify him. I remembered how they'd behaved together in public the previous evening, and wondered what Alice could have said or done to make him so snarky and resentful now, but whatever she said next it seemed to work, because the conversation abruptly turned to things of a more intimate nature.

Blushing red, I stopped up my ears and slunk back into the living-room to lower myself into one of the squishy leather seats.

Nick came back into the room and began to fix drinks. His manner had changed. Whereas before he'd been welcoming, now he seemed a little brusque.

"I thought you said you had to be somewhere," I reminded him.

"That's right," he said. "We'll have to get a move on." Which I thought was a bit rich, considering it had been him who had suggested I stop by in the first place.

I nodded towards the photographs. "That must be Georgina. Sorry I never met her. She was quite a looker."

Nick followed my gaze. "Yes, she was lovely," he said, though without really paying attention to what I was saying. I wondered if he was still thinking about his lovers' tiff.

"But I'm sure she'd want you to be happy," I said. "I mean, life goes on."

"It does, doesn't it," said Nick. "It goes on and on. It's just . . . well, there are some things that are beyond our control. Smoke?"

I accepted the proffered cigar, which was as big as a Polaris missile, sank back into my chair and tried—not very successfully—not to inhale, which was when I realised Nick was staring at me with a rather odd expression, almost as though he were wondering what kind of noise my neck would make if it were to be snapped. But then he noticed me staring back and pulled himself together, instantly becoming so warm and charming that I decided I must have been mistaken.

"I've been thinking about what you do," he said.

Once I'd stopped coughing, I managed to gasp, "Oh yes?"

"It's not painting, is it?"

Had he found about my real occupation? I braced myself, prepared for the worst.

"I mean, this conceptual thing," he said. "What is it? It's more like . . . what? Lightshows? *Installations?*"

I relaxed. "Installations, yes. Lots of different things, really. *Objets trouvés* and all that."

"Not stuff you can hang on the wall, then?"

"Depends." I applied some thought to the matter. "I guess you could hang some of it. Though maybe not the litter trays."

Nick looked pleased. "Because you know, I'm always on the lookout for artwork to put up at Framptons. Rather too many gloomy old oil-paintings, if you ask me. A bit of modern stuff might be just the thing to brighten the place up, the wackier the better. It would be a terrific talking-point. Alice and I know lots of people in the art world. We might even be able to sell something. We'd have to take a commission, of course."

"Of course," I said, wondering how long I would be able to maintain this charade.

"Had many shows, John?"

"One or two."

"But you don't have a website, do you. I couldn't find one."

"Er no, I haven't got round to it yet."

"You really should get one of those. Maybe I can put you in touch with someone there. But of course you have photos of your work?"

"Of course."

"I'd really like to see them."

"Yeah, sure."

I was a little stunned at the speed at which my imaginary career was taking off. But why not? I was sure I could cobble something together to impress Nick and his cronies, maybe even dig up some of my old *chefs d'oeuvre* from my college days; I was sure I hadn't thrown anything away; those early master-pieces of mine were bound to be around somewhere, buried in one of my bags or boxes.

In fact, the more I considered it, the more my spirits rose. Maybe I had prospects after all. Maybe I'd always had prospects, but had just never run into the right people.

Until now. I'd forgotten that in Kate's world, in Alice's world, people's address books were always bulging with useful phone numbers and contacts and name cards of people willing to give you a leg-up or pass on an insider tip. Everyone knew everyone else, and they were always doing each other favours. *Quid pro quo*. If you were an outsider, forget about it, but if you were a part of that circle, even by proxy, you couldn't help but get along.

Conceptual artist, yes. Not a bad idea at all. Better than being a low-rent private detective. Maybe a change of career was in order.

All of a sudden, the future was looking rosy.

Nick handed me a Whisky Sour, clinked his glass against mine and said, "Tchin!"

NICK OFFERED to give me a lift, but I fobbed him off with some lame excuse about getting as much exercise as I could, and set off on foot to Alice's.

On the way there my nose began to drip blood, no doubt from all the unaccustomed exertion, so I dug around in my pockets for a hanky. I couldn't find one, but did turn up several other items of interest. My private investigator's notebook, of course—I never went anywhere without that—but also my passport, which I'd had to show to someone at the Post Office a few days earlier in order to pick up a registered letter; I quite liked the photo, which I reckoned made me look like a well hard East End gangster. I made a mental note to stow it in a safe place before I left it on a bus, though I knew only too well that stowing something in a safe place was no guarantee I'd be able to find it again.

I also turned up some ticket stubs, a name card and a matchbook. And something else. Something on shiny paper, folded in two.

A Polaroid.

I unfolded it and stared uncomprehendingly.

It was badly creased, so it took me a while to work out what was going on in the picture. It was me at the party. To judge by my commendable impersonation of a brain-damaged idiot, I was already very drunk. The image was soft, probably because I'd been swaying in and out of focus at the time, but my stomach lurched as I saw the figure standing behind me. A brunette in a black dress. She too had been moving as the shutter was pressed, darting forward, so her head was even blurrier than mine, and it didn't help that the crease went straight through her face, though she did seem to have her mouth wide open. I was thankful I couldn't see it any more clearly, but what I did see was enough to make me stop where I was on the pavement and close my eyes. I allowed several seconds to tick away before I dared open them and take another look.

No need to panic. No need to panic at all. It was only Alice. I'd been snapped in front of Alice Marchmont at the party, not some dead woman that no-one else could see. I told myself it was Alice in the picture, that it *had* to be Alice in the picture. It was a normal photo, that was all.

There was just one minor but inconvenient detail flitting around in the murky depths of my recollections of that evening. I tried to stop it swimming to the surface, but, slippery as a fish, it insisted on bobbing up.

Alice hadn't been wearing black. She'd been dressed in shimmering grey.

SEVEN

"YOU'VE GOT blood on your shirt," said Alice.
I mumbled something about having cut myself shaving, and she let it go. She was wearing jeans again, this time with an ethnic-looking blouse, though the effect was more chic-posh than baba-cool. I stood in the doorway, waiting for her to invite me in and offer me a glass of wine, cup of tea, drink of water—anything, I was panting with thirst after climbing five flights of stairs—but we stood facing each other awkwardly, as though I were a handyman come to fix her plumbing and she was worrying about how to direct me to the relevant pipe without letting slip any saucy *double entendres*. It struck me for the first time that for all her outward polish she was basically rather shy and unsure of herself, not like Nick at all.

I was finally forced to take the initiative. "So, do you want me blocking your entrance all night?" Which was a *double entendre* if ever I heard one.

She must have thought so too, because she laughed and said, "Come in," as though inviting me in was a novel idea that had only just occurred to her.

"I've just been playing squash with your fiancé," I said, following her down the narrow hallway.

"I was wondering why your face was all red. Did you have fun?"

"In a manner of speaking."

She glanced back over her shoulder. "You didn't tell him . . . you know, about my problem."

"Worry not," I said. "Your secret is safe with me."

She led me into what appeared to be a living-room, though I didn't see too many signs of life there. My hostess hovered uncertainly in the middle of the room, beaming expectantly at me as though this were my place and she were the visitor. I looked around, trying to spot something that might kick-start the conversation.

What had I been expecting? Family heirlooms, lovingly restored mouldings, a sprinkling of *Antiques Roadshow*? Alice Marchmont had no truck with any of that. The room seemed devoid of personal effects, and the few I spotted seemed carefully positioned, like artefacts in a museum. Complete sets of Dickens, Austen, Waugh, Forster. No vinyl, but the complete works of the Beatles, Bob Dylan and Puccini, including the early, funny operas such as *Edgar* and *Le Villi*. No heavy metal either, though to tell the truth I hadn't been expecting any. As Alice watched wordlessly, I lowered myself into a transcendentally uncomfortable armchair and started browsing the magazines on the coffee-table: *Bride*, *Bride & Groom*, *Weddings Monthly*, *Your Big Day*, *Planning Your Wedding*, *Weddings World* and *Weddings Weddings Weddings*.

Well, she was a completist, if nothing else.

I left the magazines in a neat enough stack, I thought, but as soon as I leant back Alice immediately swooped and started tidying them into an even neater pile.

I asked how long she'd lived there, and noticed how she hesitated before replying, "Oh, ages." Though it was only the briefest of pauses, it was enough to suggest she wasn't telling the whole truth. But why would she lie about such a trivial thing? What did I care how long she'd lived there? Unless it wasn't so trivial after all, not for her; I wondered whether to push it further, but she was so engrossed in tidying the magazines it seemed heartless to interrupt. Talk about OCD. When she judged the pile sufficiently shipshape, she perched on the arm of a sofa that looked every bit as uncomfortable as my armchair and fixed me with a stare, as though challenging me to contradict her. "My father bought this place for me."

It figured. Sometimes I seemed to be the only person in the world whose parents hadn't presented them with a sodding great slice of real estate for their eighteenth birthday. What meagre funds my father had managed to cobble together during his life as a working stiff were now being siphoned off to pay for the nursing attendants who wiped up his drool and changed his incontinence pads.

When I asked Alice what her father did for a living, she bristled as though it was an impertinent question.

"He's in finance," she snapped. "So what does yours do?"

Just thinking about what he'd done made me feel ill. "Not a lot nowadays. Alzheimer's."

She had the grace to look embarrassed. "I'm sorry, I didn't mean . . ."

I shrugged. "Doesn't worry him. He's beyond that now."

She smiled weakly. "It must be hard on you, though. And on your mother."

Uh-oh. Here they came, the inevitable mother questions.

I still had a hollowed-out feeling in my stomach from the phone call, and didn't feel like making it any worse, so decided to head her off.

"My mother is pretty scary," I said. "You wouldn't want to meet her."

Which wasn't a lie.

Alice laughed, but sympathetically, without malice. It was very different from the redhead's wicked chuckle. So different, in fact, that I caught myself tempted to try and make her laugh again, but then I remembered why I was there. Enough of this scintillating repartee. It was obvious we'd been putting it off, but now it was time to get down to business.

"Why don't you show me where she appears," I suggested. I didn't have to explain what I meant by 'she'. Alice sighed, as though I'd spoiled her fun, and stood up and led me back into the hall, to where the entryphone apparatus hung from the wall like an old-fashioned telephone. Perched on top was a moulded plastic creature with bulging eyes, ears like a Ferengi from *Star Trek* and a shock of hideous turquoise hair. I stared at it aghast; it was like something out of my worst nightmares, only smaller. A lot smaller.

"My troll," said Alice, a little embarrassedly. She picked the thing up and gazed at it fondly, as though it were a kitten. "His name's Moriarty. We all had them at school. We arranged troll marriages and so forth."

"Of course you did."

I had no idea what she was talking about. Troll marriages? What the fuck was that all about? The thing she called Moriarty was hideous, but it was the first sign I'd seen that a human being lived in that flat, as opposed to a Stepford Wife with a wedding fetish.

Alice replaced the homunculus on top of the entryphone where it crouched like an evil dwarf waiting to rip the heads off baby goats. Then, exaggerating her gestures like a flight attendant pointing out emergency exits, she lifted the handset and pressed a button and a fuzzy monochrome image flickered to life on a screen the size of a playing card. It was like the early days of black and white telly all over again, except that the image being relayed was even more bum-numbingly tedious than the test card. I squinted at it, the way you squint at arrangements of dots for detecting colour blindness, and was just able to make out the front doorstep. Not a lot was happening.

"That's the place," she said.

I wondered how she thought she could possibly identify any of her callers when the quality of the image was so poor you could have had Elvis decked out in full Las Vegas regalia and still failed to recognise him.

"You get sound as well?"

In reply, Alice pressed another button and I immediately got an earful of wild sound from the street. Actually it was more like white noise; it was hard to distinguish anything specific, though I could just about make out a swish that might have been a passing car, and, from somewhere a very long way off, a dog barking repeatedly, like a stuck record.

All the other noises receded as I found myself concentrating on the dog. In fact, it was more like yapping than barking. Obviously some ghastly little mutt that its owners allowed to run amok, crapping all over the pavements and disturbing the neighbourhood with its incessant yelping. I felt quite angry on Alice's behalf.

Yap yap yap

It was still a long way off.

Yap yap yap

But it seemed to be getting closer.

For some reason, I broke out in goose pimples.

And then, abruptly, the yapping stopped, leaving a dull, echoing void in its place. The sudden onset of heavy silence made my head spin. I leant against the wall, and Alice asked if I was OK, but I didn't feel up to answering. I groped my way blindly back into the living-room, slid one of the windows open and slumped across the sill.

The night air was clammy and cold compared to the stuffy interior, but I gulped it greedily into my lungs where it collected in slimy pools, like mist on a loch. My head stopped spinning, but I stayed where I was, gazing out into the night and experiencing an uncomfortable feeling of *déjà vu*. Clare Kitchener had lived in a house just like this one, not so very far from here, and I remembered leaning out of her window, gasping for air, just as I was doing now, which was when I'd looked down and seen a young woman impaled on the railings below. Of course the next time I looked she was gone, but that hadn't made me feel a whole lot better.

To begin with, the case had seemed straightforward enough; my old chum Graham had asked me to track down the scumbag who'd been selling copies of an alleged snuff video over the internet. What Graham had conveniently forgotten to tell me was that the house where the video had been shot was some sort of supernatural black spot, and by the time I found out, it was too late; I'd already made the mistake of looking into Clare's bathroom mirror, where in place of my own reflection I'd seen a dead man grinning from ear to ear, and his throat grinning too where he'd slashed it in some previous life.

After that, things had got a little out of hand. I'd seen other things, things I'd really had no desire to see, and heard rather too much as well; the flat had apparently once housed a psychedelic rock band called The Drunken Boats, and their music alone had been enough to make me want to run screaming for the hills when it had come blasting out of the walls at me some thirty years later. It wasn't long after that that Clare Kitchener had had some sort of nervous breakdown, and

I'd only narrowly avoided having one myself.

It wasn't the sort of thing that looked good on a person's CV.

But that was then and this was now, I told myself sternly as I forced myself to look down. There: no dead women, no slashed throats, just bumper-to-bumper BMWs. Over on the far side of the road a leafy communal garden was slowly turning the colour of rust behind metal railings. There were railings directly below me as well, fencing off the basement flat just like the ones in Clare's building, but the doorstep I'd seen on the entryphone was masked by the first-floor balcony, and I had no intention of leaning out further for a better look. As it was, the ground seemed such an awfully long way down that I began to feel giddy all over again, experiencing the same zoom-in-and-track-back effect as James Stewart in *Vertigo*.

Vertigo. Now there was a movie.

I straightened up abruptly and banged my head on the window frame.

"You sure you're all right?"

Alice was right behind me. I was feeling sweaty and claustrophobic, and her proximity didn't help. Didn't she have any concept of personal space? I tried to back away from her but the window was in the way.

I tugged at the collar of my T-shirt and laughed weakly. "It's hot in here."

She stared at me. "No, it's not hot. It's actually rather chilly. In fact I was thinking of turning the heating up. Why don't you take your jacket off, make yourself comfortable?"

I kept my jacket on and looked at my watch. It was a quarter past ten. "And your, er, unwanted visitor appears when, exactly?"

"Usually around midnight."

"She might not show up while you have company."

"You didn't exactly put her off last night," Alice pointed out.

I started feeling resentful in retrospect, as though Alice had deliberately lumbered me with a boring and obnoxious friend that she had brought to the party.

"Why didn't you come over and join us? You could have had it out with her there and then, woman to woman, as it were."

Kicking and hair-tugging? The idea of a catfight between Alice and her stalker no longer fired my erotic imagination. In fact, it didn't bear thinking about.

"I don't know," said Alice. "There always seems to be this distance between us, and it's not like I'm in a hurry to get any closer. You saw what she looked like. She frightens me, John."

I didn't want to admit that she frightened me too, nor did I want to own up to having less than perfect recollection of her due to having been blind drunk. It hadn't been very professional, and I wasn't exactly proud of myself.

"How do you know we were the only ones seeing her?"

Alice frowned. "Of course I can't be sure. There were too many people there and I couldn't exactly go round asking them."

I started babbling. "But Georgina hasn't actually *done* anything to you, right? What can she do? Not a lot, not if she's dead. Dead people aren't up to much."

"You're sure about that?" she asked uneasily.

I said, "Absolutely," but in fact I wasn't sure at all. I'd encountered more than a few dead people in my time, but I still had no idea what their limitations were, or even if they had any. Maybe they didn't *need* to do anything—they'd certainly managed to fuck me up without raising so much as a spectral finger. It wasn't as though I'd researched the subject, though maybe that's what I should have done, all those years ago when things had first started to fall apart.

Instead, I'd closed my eyes and pretended there was nothing wrong, clinging to the idea that I had only to keep the door locked for all the unpleasantness on the other side of it to vanish and allow me to get on with a normal life.

I'd wasted so much time. But maybe it wasn't too late to start . . .

Only not now. Not right now. Maybe one day soon, when I was feeling more robust, when I didn't have a hangover. Maybe one day . . .

Maybe never.

Once again, my legs were threatening to let me down, and now it wasn't just the effects of the squash. Coming back to

Notting Hill had been a mistake. Remembering the Clare Kitchener case had been a mistake. This was what happened whenever I started thinking too hard about the past. Now I was on the verge of a full-blown Existential Crisis.

My palms were sweaty, my brain was hurting and I couldn't afford to have a client seeing me in this state. Hell, I needed a drink to steady my nerves. If this dead broad really was going to turn up on the doorstep, the last thing I needed to be was completely sober when I saw her.

Hair of the dog. Dutch Courage. That would do it.

As if drawn by an invisible force, I began to drift towards the door.

Alice followed me into the hallway. "Where are you going?"

"Just popping out for a recce. Back in a jiff."

"Oh."

She sounded so disappointed, and was looking so lost, with an expression so exactly like Boris's when he realised I was about to go out and leave him, that I sensed some sort of reassuring gesture was required. I rooted around in my pockets. Passport, Polaroid, matchbook . . . I located the dog-eared business card, crossed out the outmoded phone number, scrawled the new mobile one in its place and handed it to her with a flourish.

"But I already have your number."

"You don't have my *card*."

"No, but . . ."

"Well, here you go. If anything happens while I'm out, give me a call."

"John Oliver Croydon," she read out loud. "Discretion guaranteed."

She flipped it over and continued reading. "Carlsberg. Miaowmix. Pringles."

"Old shopping-list," I said quickly, making a mental note to carry clean cards with me at all times. I really needed to get my act together. I started down the stairs, leaving Alice still staring at the list as though she expected further items to materialise on it at any second.

Outside, the night air felt cold on my moist forehead, so I

didn't hang around; I headed straight for the warmth of the Saddleback Arms and ordered a pint of bitter.

I spent an agreeable half hour ogling a young Australian with a stud through her eyebrow and no bra, but she melted away before I had a chance to introduce myself. Then last orders were called and since I was still feeling distressingly sober I transferred my custom to a nearby drinking club called Mondial. I wasn't a member, but Russell the barman was an old chum from my Royal College of Art days. I hadn't actually succeeded in getting into the Royal College of Art, but had somehow managed to fritter away a sizeable chunk of my early twenties hanging out in the bar there, hobnobbing with people who had. Rather sad, now that I looked back on it, but I'd met some interesting people that way. Russell had been a print-maker, and we'd struck up a lasting friendship based on a mutual disdain for middle-class punkettes, shared enthusiasm for *The Beano* and a masochistic passion for Crystal Palace FC, whose execrable results had regularly plunged us into states of despair.

I sipped Jack Daniel's, and we discussed Crystal Palace's imminent relegation and reminisced about all the middle-class punkettes who had broken our hearts, and at some point I glanced at my watch and realised that midnight had come and gone, and I hadn't even noticed.

"Blimey," I said. Russell watched, amused, as I fished the mobile out of my pocket and realised I'd forgotten to switch the bloody thing on. Waiting for me were six text messages, all exactly the same.

SHES HERE. WHERE R U?

Oh Lord. So Alice had been trying to get hold of me all this time. I quickly settled my bill—which even with Russell's generous discount turned out to be a lot heftier than I'd anticipated—and hurried out of the club and around the corner, back into the cul-de-sac where Alice lived. The air was misty with drizzle. The road surface gleamed dark and wet. The doorstep was deserted. I crossed the road and peered up at Alice's window.

While I stood there, racking my brains in search of a plausible excuse for not having come back sooner, big drops of water fell from overhead branches and splashed down my neck. The water was icy, like dead people's fingers, and I sneezed once, twice, thrice. That did it. If I didn't get back inside and dry off, I would catch pneumonia.

I looked up at Alice's flat again, and this time saw her framed in the window. She seemed to be gazing down at me, but the light was behind her and she was too far away for me to see her expression. Was she cross with me? What could I say?

The solution came to me in a flash. No need to confess I'd missed her call because I'd been knocking back Jack Daniel's and talking about football; I could say I'd been down here, scoping the front of her building all along. She couldn't see everything from her window; she need never know the difference.

Buoyed up by this thought, I waved cheerfully, and she waved back. Or rather she signalled frantically, flapping her arms like a desperate semaphorist.

I screwed up my eyes, trying without success to get her into focus. She appeared to have changed into a big old bathrobe with enormous wide sleeves, like the sleeves on a kimono. Even from that distance, it looked a bit scruffy, the sleeves trailing uneven lengths of thread like lines of vapour from a passing jet. It didn't strike me as an Alice type of garment at all, but maybe it was a comfort thing, like the Ronnie James Dio T-shirt I couldn't bring myself to throw away even though repeating washings had reduced the black fabric to the colour of old grey dishcloth.

Maybe Alice was one of those people who dressed down for bed. Still, I thought she was overdoing the flapping, just a little.

The night seemed unnaturally quiet, as though traffic lights all over the city had simultaneously jammed at red. With a view to breaking the silence as much as anything, I crossed the street, climbed the front steps to Alice's building and jabbed at the bell labelled *Marchmont*.

By now I was shivering so violently that my finger almost missed the button. It was colder than a penguin's popsicle, so cold that the instant my breath came into contact with the night air it turned into mist.

I waited. Not a peep. Maybe I hadn't pushed the button long enough. I pressed it again, long and hard this time, wondering what kind of bedraggled mist-wreathed figure I would be cutting on the entryphone video. Maybe Alice would think I was a ghost. Maybe that crappy camera made *everyone* look like ghosts.

The metal box gave out an electronic crackle, unnaturally harsh against the silence. I interpreted it as the word, "Yes?"

"It's me," I said, gazing beseechingly into the lens. "Can I come in? I'm going cryogenic out here."

Another crackle. No, not a crackle—more like a scrabbling sound, like fingernails against slate.

I said, "Hello?"

"John?" The sound quality was dreadful. I could barely make out what she was saying.

"That's me."

"John *Croydon*?"

"That's my name," I said, thinking it odd that she needed to repeat it.

"Stop it."

"What?"

"You have to stop it."

Stop what? But then the lock clicked and I pushed it open and hauled myself once again up the five sodding flights of stairs, wondering what I was supposed to be stopping. Apart from Georgina, that is, and I thought that went without saying. My drinking, perhaps? Though there was no way she could know where I'd been.

Those five floors gave Alice plenty of time to get to the door but when I finally staggered up to it, gasping for breath, it was still closed. I rapped on it with my knuckles and then, when there was no response, rapped again. The seconds ticked away. I shifted my weight. She really needed to take hostess lessons. This time I didn't bother rapping—I pounded, so hard that it bruised my fist.

At long last, she opened the door, and I stumbled gratefully into the warmth.

"Sorry," she said. "I was on the phone to Nick. Have you been there long?"

"Only about an hour."

"Why didn't you press the buzzer?"

I stared at her, still rubbing my bruised knuckles. "I did."

Alice shrugged. "Must have got the wrong bell."

"But you . . ."

My voice died away and I felt cold all over, even colder than I'd felt outside. I'd just noticed that Alice hadn't changed into a scruffy old dressing-gown after all. She was still wearing jeans and an embroidered blouse.

Trying to keep the panic out of my voice, I asked, "Is there someone here with you?"

She giggled, as though I'd made a saucy suggestion.

"You know there isn't." Then realised I hadn't been joking and peered at me more closely. "What's wrong?"

"Nothing," I said, but what I really meant was *everything*.

My legs were feeling wobbly again. Whoever I'd spoken to over the entryphone, it hadn't been Alice. While I was trying to get to grips with this realisation, she grabbed my arm and said, "You look as though you could do with a drink."

There didn't seem much point in telling her I'd already had a drink. Or two, or three, or half a dozen. All I knew is I needed another one.

I followed her dazedly into the living- room, where a stainless steel cocktail shaker and a couple of glasses sat ready and waiting on the mirrored shelf of an Art Deco cabinet. The front of the cabinet was unprepossessing, which was probably why I hadn't noticed it earlier, but with the flap down and the lights on, it was transformed into a glittering fairyland of glass and mirrors and crystal. It transformed the room as well—now, instead of looking like an anonymous hotel room, it bore a striking resemblance to Santa's Grotto.

"Oliver Twist?" she asked.

"Um, I prefer Bleak House myself," I said, wondering where this was leading.

"*Olive. Or. Twist*," she said. "Of *lemon*."

"I'm easy," I muttered, feeling foolish.

She decanted a quantity of greyish liquid into one of the

glasses, added a curl of lemon peel and handed it to me.

"Cheers!"

I said "Cheers!" back, took a sip and almost gagged. It tasted like neat gin.

"You did it!" she was saying.

I started guiltily. "Did what?"

"This is the first night in over two weeks that I haven't seen her," Alice said, almost bubbling over with relief. "She's gone. I *know* she's gone. And she's not coming back. I can feel it."

She was so happy and carefree it seemed almost criminal to spoil the mood. But spoil it I had to. It was my job. Professional mood-spoiler.

"I don't get it. If you didn't see her, why send the messages?"

She frowned. "What messages? When?"

"The text messages." I was about to add *the ones you sent while I was getting ratfaced in Mondial*, but bit my tongue just in time.

"What are you talking about?" She burst out laughing. "I did try calling, but you'd switched off your mobile again. Why do you keep switching it off?"

"I don't like phones," I babbled. "Too many people trying to get hold of me." *My mother, for example.* "If I could get by without a phone, I would."

Alice stared at me as though I'd told her I'd been frightened by a horseless carriage. "But how would you get by without a phone? How would your friends get hold of you?"

I didn't tell her my friends didn't care for phones any more than I did. There was Sol, who was deeply suspicious of modern technology and believed that all telephones, not just mobiles, deep-fried the brain. And there was Dennis, who had an uncanny knack of knowing which pub to find me in without need of prior consultation, especially when I owed him money. And then there were Benny the Mackerel and the Barnum brothers, and you never had to get in touch with them; they always knew just where to find you, more's the pity . . .

"I didn't leave a message," she said, biting her lip.

"Someone did."

I took out my phone and showed her. SHES HERE. WHERE R U?

"That wasn't me," said Alice. "Oh my God . . ."

And she clutched my arm as though her high heels were suddenly just that little bit too high.

That was it. Mood thoroughly spoiled. She sank into an armchair and stared gloomily into her drink.

"You think *she* sent it?"

"I'm keeping an open mind," I said. "There's something else: before I came up here, I saw someone standing by that window. And it definitely wasn't you."

Alice cast a frightened glance at the offending window. "You're sure?"

"Positive," I said, wishing I wasn't.

"I told you already," she said in a small voice, "I was the only one here."

I nodded grimly. "Don't you ever close the curtains?"

"Not five floors up. There doesn't seem much point."

"Maybe it's time you started drawing them."

I refrained from adding that there were few things worse than seeing somebody peering in through your window when you lived on the fifth floor, without a balcony. Unless it was seeing someone peering in when you lived on the nineteenth.

Alice stared at me for a few moments, as though digesting all this unwelcome new information, before leaping up, running over to the window and drawing the curtains like a woman possessed.

Then she folded her arms tightly across her chest and peered warily around the room, as though dreading what might be lurking in the corners. "You think she's still here?"

"I'll take a look around."

I was putting up a bold front, though in truth I was trying not to let her see how frightened I was. It wouldn't do for me to be more of a nervous wreck than my client. At least fifty per cent of this job, I knew from experience, was putting people's minds at rest. Frightened people had a tendency to see more than they needed to. I'd said all the wrong things to Clare Kitchener, for example. I wasn't going to make that mistake again.

Alice made a sound I took to be assent, and so I left her there while I prowled around her flat like a VIP's bodyguard checking for hidden assassins. I wandered from room to room, pausing every now and again to test the air. Once or twice I thought I glimpsed something moving at the edges of my vision, but this was almost certainly due to fatigue.

In the end, I rather relished having an excuse to poke around Alice's bedroom which, apart from an unruly pile of shoes and sandals and a battered teddy-bear propped up against the perfectly plumped pillow, was as preternaturally tidy as the living-room, as though she was expecting photographers from *Hello!* to barge in at any second.

I ended up in the hallway, opening all the cupboards, expecting to find them crammed to bursting with hurriedly stowed belongings, but they were as empty as the rooms, and what objects they did contain—a shopping bag, shoe polish, a vacuum cleaner—were ranged as neatly as items in a show-flat.

As I closed the last of the cupboard doors, having found nothing that might have clued me in as to the details of Alice's everyday life, I caught sight of the blue-haired troll perched on the entryphone. It seemed to be watching me. Whereas before I had found it hideous, now its deformed sneer seemed downright sinister. But if there had been some sort of supernatural presence in the flat earlier on, I sensed nothing now. Alice and I and the troll were on our own.

I went back into the living-room to find Alice standing where I'd left her. She looked at me hopefully.

"Nothing," I said. "You can sleep easy."

She didn't look reassured. "I don't know if I *can* sleep, not after what you said. You really think Georgina was here?"

Since I was beginning to regret having told her what I'd seen, I decided not to report the short exchange I'd had on the doorstep via her entryphone, though I was already rationalising that away with the explanation that I really had pressed the wrong bell.

The fact that whomever I'd spoken to had known my name was not something I wanted to think about.

"Well, if she was here, she isn't here any longer," I said brightly. "I would sense it. And I'm always right about such things. I have highly developed feelers."

She managed a smile. "I guess I could take a sleeping pill. That ought to knock me out, especially if I have another Martini . . ."

She gestured with her glass, but I declined seconds. It was a rare day when I said no to alcohol—but I was already feeling more than a little blurry around the edges, and there was still a formidable cross-town trek looming between me and my bedtime.

Besides, I'd never been a big gin fan.

Alice excused herself, and, knowing that women never spent less than five minutes in the bathroom, I took the opportunity to extend my snooping to her handbag, which she'd left on the floor.

Actually it was more kitbag than handbag; I had the impression her whole life had found its way in here, rather than being spread around the flat. I found a small fortune in Chanel cosmetics, a collapsible umbrella, a paperback copy of *Howards End*, a large bunch of keys and a small bottle of mineral water, as well as a wallet and a leather-bound address book.

I flicked through the latter; it was nothing like my own battered address book, which was patched together with Sellotape and contained about two dozen entries and several hundred crossings-out, as well as a lot of my trademark skull-and-crossbone doodles. Alice's contacts extended into infinity, like the listings in a universal telephone directory, all inscribed in handwriting so neat it was almost like printing. God, but she knew a lot of people. Surely she couldn't be friends with them all?

I had plenty of time to scribble down some of the names and numbers before the sound of the flushing toilet alerted me to the imminence of my hostess's return.

By the time she arrived, my notebook was safely back in my pocket and I was sitting innocently on the sofa, finishing off my drink.

"I've taken half a Diazepam," she announced, gliding across to the cocktail cabinet to mix herself another drink. "I'm going to sleep like a baby tonight."

I interpreted this as a hint that I should take my leave. I drained my glass and got to my feet and said, "I'll be off, then."

She had her back to me, so I couldn't see her expression when she said, ever so casually, "You could always stay here."

I froze. Did this mean what I thought it meant? Or was I letting my imagination run away with me?

"I'd feel a lot safer if you were around."

She turned round. She looked exhausted and a little squiffy and just the tiniest bit naughty.

My instinct told me to back away, but my legs, which had already been through a lot that evening, refused to obey. I sneezed violently, several times in succession. She took that as an excuse to close the gap between us and place a hand on my brow. The hand was cool from where she'd been holding her glass, but a comforting cool, so I closed my eyes, wanting it to stay there forever.

After what seemed like an aeon she removed it, and I opened my eyes, feeling as though I were awakening from a dream. Everyone was the same, yet it had changed. Alice was staring at me as though willing me to say or do something.

"You have got a bit of a fever," she said at last.

Back off, I thought. *Back off.*

She was definitely standing too close. I took a step back. But now she mentioned it, I did feel rather shivery, and there was a prickling in my limbs. I suddenly wanted to curl up on the floor and go asleep right then and there, but that would have been madness. I needed sleep, and I needed it badly, but I needed to sleep alone.

I said, "I should hit the road."

"Mm yes," she said sleepily. "Maybe you should go."

Was that disappointment I was sensing? Or just my imagination again?

I checked my watch; I'd almost certainly missed the last tube. Alice offered to call me a cab, but I told her I would pick one up on the street, too embarrassed to admit I'd drunk most of my cash away and wasn't sure I could muster enough for a taxi fare. It was the adult version of spending your bus-fare on gobstoppers. Then again, maybe it wasn't so very adult.

She followed me to the door and said, "What do we do now? About Georgina, I mean." Her speech was ever so slightly slurred.

"We've still got a week." I sounded more confident than I felt. "We'll sort it out, don't worry." No matter what was going on here; Alice had to *feel* safe, that was the main thing.

In a sudden dipping movement she leant forward and kissed me. It was very different from her elegant social smooching at the party; it seemed to me she'd been aiming at my mouth, but at the last moment I jerked my head and her lips brushed my cheek.

"*Thank you,*" she whispered.

And then I was outside and she'd closed the door on me. I stared at it for a few seconds before stumbling downstairs in a daze. I could still feel the cool imprint of her hand on my forehead.

She couldn't possibly have been coming on to me. Could she? She was getting married in a week's time, for heaven's sake. I just wasn't used to women being nice to me; it didn't mean I should read too much into it.

But I was on treacherous ground here; if she was coming on to me, it wouldn't do to egg her on. On the other hand, I couldn't afford to offend her.

THE JOURNEY home was epic. And wet. And cold. The tube station was indeed closed, so I walked most of the way along the canal towpath, wishing fervently I could summon the barge to come and collect me, the way Batman summoned his Batmobile.

The silence of the canal was a bit unnerving; there was a strange echo to my footsteps, which kept making me think I was being followed, but whenever I glanced over my shoulder, just to check, there was no-one there, though I did pass a couple of night-time strollers heading in the opposite direction, and once or twice thought I heard a dog barking a long way behind me, which made me feel uneasy because it reminded me of the yapping I'd heard earlier.

To take my mind off that, I began to whistle Dio's greatest

hits, and eventually the opening bars of *Don't Talk to Strangers* metamorphosed into that same musical phrase that had been bugging me for the past twenty-four hours. I whistled it repeatedly, sounding like a stuck Roger Whittaker record, but still couldn't put a name to it. But I didn't think it was by Dio. I made a mental note to ask Nick if he recognised it.

It wasn't until I'd finally made it back to base and lit the stove and peeled off my wet clothes and wrapped myself in Kevin's towelling bathrobe and downed a generous measure of whisky and draped Boris around my neck as a sort of muffler that my muscles finally stopped going into spasms.

I was so exhausted that I couldn't sleep, so I reached for my usual soporific—the Scott-Moncrieff translation of *Swann's Way* by Marcel Proust. It would surely have impressed anyone who wanted to know which book I kept on my bedside table, providing they didn't ask the question too often, because I wasn't progressing very rapidly. I'd been dipping into it nearly every night for the past six months and was still only on page sixty-three. But as a sleeping draught it worked like a charm. This time I managed eight lines—about half a sentence—and boom! Out like a light, swayed into oblivion by Marcel's prose and the almost imperceptible rocking of the boat.

I WAS WOKEN by the weight of Boris sitting on my chest. He had a habit of doing that. I opened my eyes, tugged at the lamp-toggle and squinted at the clock—I'd been out for no more than an hour. I was still summoning the energy to rear up and throw my cat off the bed when I realised I was mistaken and he wasn't there at all.

There was a soft scrabbling noise behind my head. I turned over, expecting to catch him in the act of commandeering the pillow, which was another of his favourite tricks.

But he wasn't there either.

"Boris?" I sat up in bed and looked around and saw him curled up in his tartan cat-basket. He peered at me through slitty feline eyes, still half-asleep but ready to rouse himself if food was in the offing.

"Never mind," I told him. "Go back to sleep." I turned off the light and waited for sleep to reclaim me.

This time the noise was louder. I eyed the small curtain covering the porthole by the bed. I knew now it couldn't possibly be Boris, but it nevertheless reminded me of the sound he made when I'd inadvertently shut him outside and he wanted to come back in.

After all the effort it had taken to warm myself up, my blood froze over again, this time so solidly that Torvill and Dean could have gone out and skated their Bolero routine on it.

There *was* someone—or *something*—outside, only a few inches from the top of my head. The only thing separating us was the hull.

There it was again. More scrabbling. No question about it now. Someone, or something, was scratching at the window. Someone, or something, wanted me to open it up and let them in.

There was nothing for it. Either I could stay ignorant and scared to death for ever, or I could take some form of action. I told myself not to be such a wuss and, in a movement so swift it took even me by surprise, yanked the curtain aside.

Nothing.

I pressed my face against the reinforced glass and tried to peer past the reflection of my nose into the darkness beyond. There was nothing to see but the still black waters of the canal, not even a trace of froth on the surface.

Nor could there have *been* anyone outside, not unless they'd been treading water. And only a fool would tread water around here, because the canal was filthy and almost certainly riddled with Weill's disease since all the local rats, and most of the local drunks as well, used it as a toilet. Not that a dead person would have to worry about Weill's disease. And would a dead person need to tread water? Wouldn't they just walk on it, like Jesus? Or under it, like Godzilla?

I shook these toxic droplets from my mind. There was no-one out there, alive or dead. I let the curtain fall back into place and tried to snuggle back down, only now my skin had once again erupted into goose pimples and I had to get up and grab Boris and carry him back to bed for company. After one or two burbles of protest he settled back into his feline dreams, twitching and pawing at imaginary mice, or rabbits, or whatever it was cats dreamt of. How I envied him. How I wished I could have had dreams like that.

But this time, even with Boris curled up beside me, it took three whole pages of Proust before I was able to go back to sleep.

EIGHT

A S FAR back as I could remember, I'd been having this dream. It wasn't my only dream, by any means, but it was the only one I had repeatedly. I'd be in my bedroom, surrounded by small model Cowboys and Indians, or Native Americans as we must call them now. These weren't just any old Cowboys and Native Americans either; they were Swoppet deluxe moulded plastic figurines with interchangeable heads and limbs, which meant that with a modicum of creative imagination you could construct a culturally integrated, sexually liberated version of the Old West in which squaws wore the trousers and white men wielded bows and arrows.

But in my dream, it was even better than that—the figurines moved around of their own accord, like tiny robots. Imagine really having toys like that! This part of the dream, at least, was bliss.

And then I would hear my mother, calling from her room across the landing. "Johnny! Come here, Johnny . . ."

At the sound of her voice, I would lose interest in the game and start moving towards the door, which all of a sudden seemed miles away, and my route would be strewn with precious Swoppets I had at all costs to avoid stepping on. And all the time my mother's voice would be calling softly, insistently, "Johnny, Johnny, come here Johnny, I've got something to tell you. Something important . . ."

Finally, after several aeons of gingerly picking my way like a tender-hearted giant over this Lilliputian Wild West, I would reach the door and cross the landing to my mother's bedroom, though in my dream it would seem less like a bedroom and more like an echoing vault smelling of incense and scorched herbs. I could hear the howling of wolves in the deep dark forest outside, even though I'd actually grown up in a part of Exeter that had been noticeably lacking in trees.

And ranged beyond my mother's bed would be a line of cowled figures, and they would be chanting, voices rising and falling like an ocean swell. I could never quite make out the words, but one thing I knew for sure—it wasn't Latin.

In the dream, my mother's bed would be hung with flimsy muslin drapes that made everything hazy and indistinct. I would approach it stealthily and pull the muslin aside, and as soon as she saw me she would struggle to sit up, smiling sadly in that way she had, repeating, "Come here Johnny, I've got something important to tell you."

This was my mother as I preferred to remember her—young and ethereal, not yet the frightening creature she would later become. And she would put her cool arms around me and draw me to her bosom, and I would bask in that perfume I'd never been able to identify, no matter how many hours I spent loitering in perfume departments, asking bemused and some-times downright suspicious salesgirls to squirt samples of their product on to my wrists.

And she would whisper into my ear, as though imparting the secret of the universe . . .

"Johnny . . . *we're dead.*"

At which point I would always wake up.

It varied. Sometimes, instead of, *we're all dead*, she would say, *she's dead*, or, *you're dead*, or, *they're dead*. But *someone* was always dead, no argument there.

The night after my visit to Alice's flat, after finally getting back to sleep, I had the dream again. The Cowboys and Native Americans part was much expanded, incorporating surprise guest appearances from forgotten friends and elements from *The Godfather* as well. My mother's voice, when she finally called me, was accompanied by a scrabbling sound, like a pack of small rodents trying to scratch their way through the taut fabric of reality, and when I lifted the muslin drapes I'd found it wasn't my mother after all. It was Alice. Looking pale and ethereal and just the tiniest bit disgruntled.

"Johnny," she said crossly, "I'm dead."

And then she opened her mouth and screamed. Even in my dream, it was a sound so ear-splittingly ghastly that I felt wrenched out of my sleep as painfully as a medium snatched out of an ectoplasmic trance. I immediately began to sneeze. I sneezed on and off for several minutes, after which there was no point in trying to get back to sleep. Every muscle in my body was punishing me for the squash, and if ever I could have done with a long soak in a hot tub full of soothing bubbles it was now. Unfortunately, all Kevin's barge could muster was a dribble of tepid water from a hand-held shower attachment.

Even after my coffee and bagel, shreds of the dream stayed with me, clinging like strips of torn polythene to my slowly dawning consciousness. What did it mean, Alice telling me she was dead? She'd seemed very much alive, but you could never be too sure, not where I was concerned. I'd seen *The Sixth Sense*, like everyone else, except that for me it hadn't so much been a spooky fictional yarn as a fly-on-the-wall documentary that was a little too close to some of my own past experiences for comfort, though of course I wasn't a neurotic screw-up, like the little boy in the film. Or at least that was what I kept telling myself.

All the same, maybe my subconscious had spotted something unnoticed by the rest of me, as one's subconscious is wont to do, and had been trying to tip me off. I thought about it as I sipped my second cup of coffee. The ghosts in *The Sixth Sense* hadn't know they were dead. Maybe Alice was dead, only she didn't realise it . . .

No, that was absurd. Nick would have noticed if he'd been engaged to a dead woman. And I'd seen her interacting with loads of other people at Selina and Jolly's party. But wait a minute . . .

I paused in mid-sip as an even more alarming thought occurred to me. Hadn't some of those guests seemed just a little strange? *Maybe they'd all been dead.* Maybe I'd stumbled into *a dead people's party*, with me the only living soul present. Anything was possible. Maybe everyone in London was dead, and I was the only living person left. It was like *The Omega Man*, only with ghosts instead of vampires . . .

I reined in my galloping imagination. I needed to get a grip. Besides, the redhead had been real, no question. I'd touched her, smelled her, kissed her ... What else had I done to her? Not a lot, apparently, but I could always remedy that next time we met. Then I remembered there wasn't going to be a next time, because I didn't know her name or telephone number.

I slopped around the barge in my dressing-gown, seized by a temporary attention deficit disorder that prevented me from getting down to anything useful for more than a few minutes at a time, and gulped cup after cup of bowel-scouring coffee in a desperate effort to disperse the fog clouding my brain. The greyness of the sky did little to alleviate the gloom that had moulded its contours around me like a heavy blanket, and the canal wasn't much help either. Even in summer, when jaunty barges chugged past throngs of amateur anglers jostling with dog-walking families for pole position on the towpath, the water always looked dark and unpleasant and impenetrable to shafts of sunlight, as though unmentionable things were festering just below the surface.

It wasn't just this canal, I reckoned, it was all of them, canals as a species. No cleansing tide. Things were just left to moulder. I had troubled memories of stagnant corners lapped by greasy water and rotting leaves. But it was on gloomy autumn Sundays like today that my section of the Regent Canal really came into its own—wreathed in mist, grey sky reflected in even greyer water, like a charcoal sketch rattled out by some manic-depressive Belgian symbolist just before he'd been carted off screaming to the asylum. If the oceans were the cradle of life on earth, then canals were the open coffins. Nothing wholesome could possibly have existed in the murk below that oily surface. It amazed me that anglers ever hooked anything, but I'd seen them winch odd wriggling shapes out of the water and plop them into jars or plastic bags. I only hoped for their sakes they never ate what they caught.

I started sneezing again. I felt prickly with fever, and when I yawned I could hear the phlegm crackling in my ears; with all that going on, it was little wonder I'd been hearing strange noises in the night.

I got dressed and pulled on the baggy brown jumper that Boris had been using as a nest all summer, trying as best I could to remove some the accumulated cat-fluff with lengths of sticky tape.

Outside, the mist thinned out, leaving a wispy trelliswork on the surface of the water.

And Sol came round.

I'm not sure I would ever have described Sol as my best friend, but that's more or less what he was. On more than one occasion, he had also, bizarrely, acted as my muscle. Despite a frame even weedier than mine, he was adept at a comically inelegant martial art, a customised blend—or so he claimed—of Brazilian *capoeira*, Thai boxing and Irish pub-brawling.

Sol's own origins were equally diverse; sensing a *soupçon* of Hispanic, I'd once asked if his mother had named him after the Spanish word for sun. He'd said nah, it had been her favourite brand of lager.

So we smoked and listened to Black Sabbath and talked about computer games and discussed the latest version of *Mortuary*, with additional zombie gore factor, and eventually I steered the conversation round to what was really on my mind.

Sol listened, rapt, as I related the events of the past few days. He was a firm believer in the supernatural—if *The Sixth Sense* seemed like a documentary to me, Sol always talked about *The X-Files* as though it were a current affairs programme—so I didn't expect him to scoff, and sure enough, he had no problem at all believing that Alice Marchmont was being stalked by a dead woman.

"So what are you going to do?" he asked when I'd finished telling him about the figure I'd seen at Alice's window and the voice on the entryphone that hadn't been hers. I'd decided not to mention the scrabbling in the night; the more I thought about it, the more it just seemed like part of a dimly remembered dream. Maybe it had been a dream, or maybe this was just wishful thinking, but either way, it seemed to me that describing it to Sol would have given it way too much credence.

"I guess I need to find out more about Georgina," I said.

"Maybe she's searching for peace. Maybe there's a way of

laying her to rest."

"You mean like exorcism?" *The Exorcist* was one of Sol's favourite movies, though once again I wasn't sure he realised it was fiction.

"I'm not a priest," I said. "I'm not even a believer."

"You believe in the Devil."

"No, I don't," I retorted hotly. Sol was one of the few people I allowed to wind me up. "I don't believe in God or the Devil."

"But you believe in ghosts," he pointed out.

"That's different. That's not a matter of faith; I don't have any choice in the matter."

He shrugged. "Maybe you should think more about religion."

I told him I'd already been there, done that. With mostly catastrophic results. Religion only complicated things that were complicated enough to begin with. It was best left alone.

"But you believe you can get rid of her, all the same?"

"I have to believe that. Otherwise I might as well just call it quits."

"You don't sound very confident, John."

"Well duh," I said. "This isn't a Hollywood movie, where all you have to do is psychoanalyze the spook and bingo, it ascends to a higher plane or moves into the light with a serene expression, leaving everyone in peace. Sometimes ghosts do things for no reason. Sometimes they're just plain evil. Sometimes they just want to fuck with you."

"I don't agree," Sol said earnestly. "I think they're basically people, just like the rest of us."

"They're *not* people!" I raised my voice more than was strictly necessary, and my friend flinched. "They're not people any more. The man I saw in the mirror at Clare's—he wasn't human. He was just trying to mess with my head."

Sol knew all about the Clare Kitchener case; being able to talk to him about it had probably been the one thing that had saved my sanity.

"But didn't Mirror Guy commit suicide? He must have had a really unhappy life to have done that."

I snorted derisively. "From what I've heard, he was even more of a psycho while he was alive. Did I tell you he once put his girlfriend's eye out with a fork?"

Sol started to roll another joint. "Many times."

"The point is," I continued, "that ghosts don't know what they want any more than the rest of us. They're just emotional cancer, amorphous little blobs of malignancy looking out for ways to infect other people with their unhappiness."

"Have you spoken to Alice about this?"

"Good grief no, and I'm not going to. I just have to find some way of making sure that Georgina doesn't spoil her wedding. That's all she's worried about—that her fiancé will think she's barking mad and get cold feet and dump her."

"Not much of a fiancé," said Sol.

"Oh, he's quite charming," I said, amazed to find myself sticking up for Nicholas Fitch, who obviously had no need of my help in that or any other department. "He's just . . . conventional, I suppose. Just wants to get hitched to someone normal, not another bipolar fruitcake, like the first wife."

"And you reckon Alice Whatsername is normal?"

I shrugged. "I guess so."

Sol chuckled. "You think it's normal to make a pass at a guy who isn't your husband-to-be just a week before your wedding?"

"Hang on," I said, regretting having told him about that bit, "I don't even know if it was a pass. She was very tired, and very frightened."

Sol raised his eyebrows. "Precisely."

"I don't know what's precise about it," I muttered.

"So how are you going to get rid of her?"

"Alice Marchmont?"

"No, the other one. The dead bird."

"I don't know," I admitted.

"But you've got rid of ghosts before?"

I hesitated. "I guess so."

"So what did you do then?"

He had me there. "I honestly don't know. They were there, and then they were gone. I'm not even sure I had anything to do with it."

"It seems to me," said Sol with one of those bursts of lucidity that he sometimes had, "that the answer lies in your past.

Maybe you should try and think about what you did or didn't do, and take it from there."

"Maybe you're right," I agreed glumly. The idea of dredging up those memories was far from appealing.

Sol held out the joint, but this time I turned it down; I needed to keep a relatively clear head if I was going to get any work done.

My friend suddenly remembered he'd arranged to go and talk to Benny about replacing a hard drive. When he'd left I switched on my mobile and read the latest collection of text messages, each consisting of a single word repeated dozens of times, like a typewriting exercise:

ITS COMING COMING COMING COMING COMING CLOSER CLOSER CLOSER CLOSER CLOSER

OK right, I get the idea, enough already.

I tried to suppress the cold chills that were zipping up and down my spine like small electrical charges. The number wasn't listed. Was this Georgina again? And if so, what the hell did she mean? That she was coming closer? She was already more than close enough, it seemed to me.

But I dutifully recorded each message, together with the precise time it had been sent, in my notebook.

Time to have another talk with Alice. Calling her was dead easy; hers and Nick's were the only numbers I'd got round to entering into the phone's memory.

"John?"

She sounded harassed, and there was a lot of wild sound in the background. I got the impression she wasn't at home.

"How are you today?" I asked.

"How am I? You mean apart from being driven insane by bridesmaids? *Oh, we can't possibly wear pink . . . oh, that length skirt is going to make my ankles look thick . . . oh, I have to have mine shorter . . .*"

This wasn't at all the sort of thing I'd had in mind when I'd put the question. "I mean, how *are* you? How are *you*? No more sightings of Georgina? Did you sleep OK?"

"Christ, yes. Like a log."

She sounded very different from the frisky filly of the night before. Her brisk tone reminded me that, Sunday or no Sunday, she had a wedding to plan, a whole new life to organise, and she obviously hadn't made a pass at me after all. What had I been thinking? Of course she hadn't made a pass at me, and I could only thank my lucky stars I hadn't got carried away and responded as though she had; not only would it have led to acute embarrassment, it would have got me fired.

But just in case there was still a lingering suspicion, I decided to demonstrate beyond a shadow of a doubt that my attentions had always been directed elsewhere anyway.

"Hey, remember the redhead I was talking to the other night?"

The silence went on for so long that I began to wonder if she was still there. But at last she said, a little huffily, "I don't know who you're talking about."

Whoah. No mistaking that edge to the voice. She was jealous. I was torn between feeling flattered and dismayed. "The redhead? At the party?"

"I know several redheads," she said. "You'll have to be more specific."

"Green eyes," I said. "Red dress. Foxy."

There was a long cool pause, then she said, "You must mean Ginny."

Her voice was flinty and accusing. I was left feeling as though I'd made a faux pas.

"I, er . . ."

"Listen, John, I'm in the car. It would be better if you came round again."

"Right now?"

"Good Lord no. I'm supposed to be meeting Janie in half an hour and I'm running late . . . Could you make it . . . let's see . . . tomorrow morning . . .?"

"Well," I stalled. "I don't know if . . ."

"Sorry, roundabout coming up . . ."

"I'll let you get on," I said. "Call me back when you reach dry land." And I broke the connection.

Christ, she sounded pissed off. But at least now I could put a name to that red hair. I reached for my notebook and looked through the details I'd copied out of Alice's address book. There was no Ginny, but I did find a Virginia Fisher.

I took a deep breath and called her.

Hers wasn't the only number I called that afternoon. What Sol had said about looking into my past made a weird kind of sense, so I picked up my ratty address book and opened it at the Gs.

GRAHAM WAS sitting at a corner table in the Landrace Inn, knocking back Mojitos with his Italian girlfriend, who was a hot babe if ever I saw one: ripe figure, glowing chestnut-coloured hair, gleaming wet-look lips. I'd never understood Graham's success with women; he was basically a New Age hippy who tended to wear infra-dig things like bead chokers, and spoke in a soft, almost feminine murmur, the very opposite of alpha-male. The term 'slacker' might almost have been invented to describe him—he was so incredibly lacking in ambition it was a wonder he found the motivation to get up in the morning. He'd never had much money, he wasn't particularly good-looking and his personality was, well, a bit too tree-huggy and save-the-whaley for my tastes, but as long as I'd known him he'd managed to attract a stream of uncommonly gorgeous women, of whom Isabella was only the latest.

I ordered a pint for myself and another round of Mojitos for my friends, we exchanged pleasantries and I got down to business and asked after Clare.

"Didn't you hear?" said Graham. "She and Miles got back together. Shacked up together, in fact."

I said, "I don't think I ever met Miles."

"Sophie's ex," said Graham. He glanced at his companion. "Bit of a wanker, actually."

I already knew Miles was Sophie's ex, but I was surprised to hear Graham being so hostile. Normally he was all peace and love and everybody's super.

"Miles can be very charming," purred Isabella, who seemed to find everyone charming but me. Or maybe she just sensed that she made me nervous. It didn't help that her father was rumoured to be a big cheese in his local *cosa nostra*, which made me worry what might happen if one day I were to accidentally piss her off, the way I somehow managed to accidentally piss off a lot of people.

"A *charming* wanker," said Graham, who evidently never lost a moment's sleep about such matters. "Didn't seem particularly upset when she died. Bounced back pretty rapidly. But charmingly, of course." He bared his teeth at his girlfriend.

"He was upset," she retorted. "Why else do you think he's been so patient with Clare? Do you think she would have stood a chance with a cool guy like him if he hadn't been feeling guilty?"

They started to bicker pointlessly, in that way couples have, about the precise degree to which Miles had been upset by what had happened to his ex-girlfriend, and if, indeed, Sophie really had been his ex, or they had in fact got back together just before her death, as Isabella seemed to think.

My attention wandered across the room, which is how I noticed someone staring at me from the other side of the bar, where he was propped up next to an anxious-looking brunette. The brunette was talking to him intently, yet somehow not noticing that he wasn't paying her any attention at all. He had big jowls and a slightly incongruous tan and looked vaguely familiar. But I couldn't for the life of me place him, so in a bid to avoid dropping a social clanger, I waved cheerily and smiled. He waved back, albeit a little woodenly, but didn't return the smile.

Maybe I didn't know him at all. Maybe I'd just gone and waved at a total stranger. Or, oh Lord, maybe he thought I was trying to pick him up.

I deliberately shifted my chair so my back was towards him. But then Graham said something that made me forget all about the jowly man.

"She's very grateful, you know."

"Who?"

"Clare. She would never say it to your face. She's too embarrassed about the whole business. But you really did help her out."

"Poor Clare," Isabella said, a little bitchily I thought. "She didn't have much luck with that apartment."

The memory of Clare's flat made me feel as though spiders were scampering all over me. "Who's living there now?"

"TV presenter and her husband," said Graham. "They gutted the place—turned it into a sort of mini-loft. The bathroom as we knew it has apparently ceased to exist."

"Thank God for that." I relaxed a little. "So there's no more . . . er . . .?"

"Not that I'm aware of," said Graham. "Maybe that's all it takes—exorcism by interior design. Remove the walls and you remove the emulsion on to which the bad memories are printed."

"What's emulsion?" asked Isabella, whose English was pretty perfect but whose vocabulary obviously didn't extend to obsolete pre-digital photographic processes. While Graham patiently explained it to her, I racked my brains trying to think of how I could apply his *aperçu* to Alice's situation. I couldn't very well start knocking down the walls of her flat, but there wasn't a whole lot of point anyway since it wasn't the only place I'd seen Georgina, who unfortunately didn't seem to be confining her appearances to one specific location. Yes, radical alteration of the site of the haunting would have been a terrific idea—if only I could work out where the haunting was.

"Mind you," said Graham, "it might just be that the TV presenter and her husband are about as sensitive as slabs of concrete. If there was something there, they're certainly not the types to pick up on it."

"I liked her," said Isabella.

"My darling," said Graham, gazing at her fondly. "You like everyone."

"But not equally," she said, snuggling up to him in a way that made me want to look away in embarrassment. "I like you *better*."

"But you reckon it's resolved," I said, trying to reclaim Graham's attention. "Though I still don't see why Clare should be grateful. I didn't have anything to do with it."

Graham gave me an odd look. "Oh but you did, buddy. Clare said you acted like a sort of lightning conductor, drew it away from her. You saw everything she'd seen, didn't you?"

I nodded, shuddering at the memory. I'd seen a lot more than I'd wanted to see and, unlike Clare, I'd seen it all at once. *Bam bam bam.*

"Well, she said she never had any problems after your visit. It was as though you'd somehow drained the poison."

"Then why did she move out?"

"Oh, don't be ridiculous," said Isabella. "She'd seen her best friend die there, for heaven's sake. And then once she'd split up with that guy she really didn't want to stick around. It was his place, not hers."

"By *that guy*, you mean the throat-slitter," I said.

"Though I have to say he was pretty cute," said Isabella.

"I wouldn't say they *split up*, exactly," said Graham. "It wasn't as if they had a lot in common to begin with. I mean, he was dead and she wasn't."

"I met him, you know," Isabella said excitedly, as though she were talking about a film star. "And you know what? I had no idea he was dead! I was seeing him as clearly as I see you now; there was absolutely nothing *spettrale* about him. He was quite charming. He offered to introduce me to Brian Jones."

"Brian Jones is dead," I said.

"Exactly," she said, and began to rub Graham's back. Graham half-closed his eyes, like a cat.

"You should have taken him up on it," he murmured. "He might have introduced you to Jimi Hendrix as well. Maybe even Jim Morrison."

"Or Elvis," said Isabella, digging her thumbs into his shoulders in a way that made me want to look somewhere else.

"You could have sold your story to the tabloids," I said, wondering why I never encountered famous dead people, just the rotting *hoi polloi.*

By now Isabella's administrations had moved further south, Graham's eyes were almost completely closed and I was feeling like a third wheel. After one last glance at the jowly man, who appeared to be saying something to the brunette that was making her look more anxious than ever, I said goodbye to Graham and Isabella, but since they were no longer aware of my presence I don't suppose they noticed me leaving.

*   *   *

I WALKED SLOWLY up the road, wondering whether my talk with Graham had been a waste of time. So I was a 'lightning conductor'? In other words, I attracted all this stuff away from people? I was a sort of supernatural fridge magnet? Why me? What had I done to deserve this? It didn't seem fair.

But maybe, just maybe, that would explain why Alice wasn't seeing Georgina any more. Maybe that pleasure was now all mine. Except that I didn't want it. I would willingly have given Georgina back to Alice, if only I'd known how.

I felt the need to think, so I took a detour and then of course I found myself walking along Talbot Road, going right past the flat I'd once shared with Kate. As far as I was aware, she still lived there, though I'd stopped asking after her a long time ago. I found myself wondering what she looked like now, whether she'd changed, whether she looked any older, whether she still wore her hair in that cute boyish cut.

I even contemplated loitering in the vicinity, keeping a watch on the doorway to see if she emerged. But then I realised I really didn't want to fall into that trap of thinking about her as it never failed to depress me, and so I backtracked to Ledbury Road and quickened my step towards the woman I hoped would help me put Kate back where she belonged, in the past.

I headed towards the future, and Virginia Fisher.

NINE

"WELL HELLO, Mr Barnes-Wallis. How delightful to see you again."

She was dressed in baggy denims, high-heeled mules and the sort of droopy cardigan favoured by the skinny whinging girls in Eric Rohmer films. The red hair was pulled back into a ponytail and her face had a well-scrubbed look that radiated natural health. She'd obviously taken no trouble at all with her appearance, and yet still managed to look trouser-tighteningly sexy.

"Virginia Fisher, I presume?"

She took one look at me, and said, "You forgot my name, didn't you."

"Of course not! I just never . . ." I trailed off, not knowing what else to say.

"Nobody calls me Virginia. It's Ginny."

"Hello Ginny."

"Do come in." Here there was no awkward standing in the doorway, like at Alice's. Instead, she melted aside as though in sweet surrender to my vastly superior will. I patted her on the bottom and headed straight for the kitchen, which was just as I remembered it, complete with Jack Russell parked in its favourite spot beneath the table. As soon as I sat down the animal began sniffing at my leg. Gently, I tried to push it away, but whatever it smelt there was far too interesting for it to want to stop and pretty soon I could feel clammy canine mucus seeping through the fabric of my jeans. I gritted my teeth and told myself I could put up with it. Just as long as it didn't start snuffling around my groin. Now that would have been embarrassing.

"Coffee? Wine? Beer? Whisky?"

Attagirl. I opted for beer. Ginny opened the fridge.

"Why do I get the impression this is not purely a social call?"

I couldn't be bothered to lie, chiefly because I couldn't remember what fibs I'd already told her and I didn't want to contradict myself. "I haven't been entirely straight with you."

She placed a tumbler and a can of Heineken on the table in front of me before pouring herself a glass of white wine. "Is that so?"

"Remember I said I was a conceptual artist?"

She threw back her head and roared with laughter. "How could I forget? Of course I knew that was bullshit."

I exhaled slowly, trying not to take offence. "I did go to art college, actually." I didn't think it worth mentioning I'd dropped out before the end of the course. For personal reasons.

Ginny eyed me sceptically. "You? An art student? Don't make me laugh. You're the least artistic person I've ever met."

Lord, but she knew how to bust a fellow's balls. This was not turning into the passionate reunion I'd had in mind, but it was hard to stay vexed with her for long. I decided to throw caution to the wind and hit her with the truth. "In actual fact, I'm a private eye."

That shut her up. For all of two seconds. She sat down and leaned across the table to give me a spectacular view of her cleavage. "You mean like Sam Spade?"

This was more like it. I could tell she was intrigued.

"Maybe not quite as cool," I admitted, trying to tear my eyes away from her *décolletage* because I was keenly aware that women preferred men to look at their faces while conversing. "But kind of like that, yes."

She smiled seductively. "So tell me, Mr Detective—do you have a gun?"

I wanted desperately to say yes, but now that I was cruising comfortably along Honest Avenue the idea of doing a U-turn and heading back towards the City of Lies seemed counterproductive.

"This is England, not South Central L.A."

"Doesn't mean you can't have a gun," she said. "I know lots of English people with guns."

I failed to conceal my shock. "You hang out with criminals?"

She laughed and shook her head. "Shotguns, you oaf! Shotguns—for killing small birds and animals, maybe the odd burglar."

"Well, I don't altogether approve of guns," I blustered, "and I'm not *that* kind of private investigator anyway."

I didn't see any point in confessing that I didn't think I was terribly good gun-owning material. The last thing I needed was such a handy way of putting myself out of my misery.

"So what kind are you?"

"Paper-shuffling and phone calls. Occasionally a bit of fieldwork. Last year I went undercover as a junkie."

"Undercover, eh?" She propped her chin in her hands and gazed at me thoughtfully. "You are full of surprises. So tell me— what kind of thing do you investigate? Divorce? Insurance fraud? *Murder?*"

"Bog-standard stuff. Things the police don't have time for. Low-grade extortion, petty swindles, missing teenagers, that sort of thing."

"So was it always an ambition of yours to be Sherlock Holmes?"

"I'll let you into a little secret." I was beginning to find all this truth-telling curiously addictive. "I'm only a private eye because I was so fucking hopeless at everything else. I've had every job going at one time or another, but this is the only thing I've been able to stick with." The "fucking" just slipped out, but she didn't seem offended.

"Ever been a shoe salesman?"

"No."

"Secretary?"

"Of course not."

"Then don't exaggerate. There are loads of jobs you've never tried. I bet you're only a private dick because you're too lazy to do a proper nine till five job, like a regular working stiff. You just want to slob around in your houseboat all day, listening to music."

Boy, she certainly liked to get stuck in.

"It's a *barge*. And who told you where I live anyway?"

"Alice."

So they'd been comparing notes after all, despite Alice's little fit of pique.

"I'd never have guessed you two were such pals," I said. "You weren't exactly thrilled to see each other the other night at the party."

"Nonsense," Ginny said briskly. "We're *huge* friends. We were at the same school. I'm one of her bridesmaids."

I felt my eyebrows shoot up. I'd always had a soft spot for bridesmaids. I suspect all redblooded men had.

"Really? How many of you are there?"

"Just the three. Ginny, Finny and Janie."

"Finny?"

"Fiona," explained Ginny. "We called her Finny at school, and it kind of stuck."

"Ginny, Finny and Janie," I echoed, trying to remember if I'd copied any Fionas or Janes from Alice's address book. "Sounds like a nursery rhyme."

"Three little maids from school," Ginny said with what sounded like heavy irony.

"It's funny," I mused, "but I seem to remember you giving me the impression that you didn't know Nicholas Fitch."

She was all innocence. "Did I? When?"

This was rich considering we'd met only once before, but I let it pass. "You acted like you didn't know he'd been married before."

Her face was an expert mask of surprise. "I *did*?"

"Yes you did."

She shrugged it off. "I really don't remember. I don't know him *that* well, you know. I'm *much* more friends with Alice. But you were probably confused. You were very hungover, my darling. Very *very* hungover."

I couldn't argue with her there, nor did I want to; the casual yet affectionate way she'd slipped the word 'darling' into the conversation had completely disarmed me. That, and the way she was gazing at me through those big green eyes of hers.

"By the way," I said, sipping my beer and trying not to think about my erection, "What do you call Alice?"

"Excuse me?"

"Nicknames. Ginny, Finny and Janie. Three little maids from school, all in the same class. Don't tell me you didn't give Alice a nickname as well."

"Well, yeah." For the first time, her forthright gaze wavered. "We just don't use it any more."

"Why not?"

"Doesn't seem right." She let slip a sudden nervous giggle. "And she'd kill us if we called her that now."

My curiosity was piqued. "Called her what?"

Ginny opened her mouth, but at the last minute decided against telling me and smiled apologetically, shaking her head. "No, I can't."

Her teasing was getting me all excited again. "I'll tell you mine if you'll tell me hers."

"Go on, then."

"Jock." I was lying. The nickname I'd acquired at school had been something I had no intention of divulging, not ever, not even if she were to pull my fingernails out with red-hot pliers.

"Jock?"

"Acronym. John Oliver Croydon. Name's not really Barnes-Wallis, as you might have guessed. Right, that's my side of the bargain. Now it's your turn. What did you call Alice?"

Ginny's smile wavered.

"Pongo."

I stared at her. I'd been expecting Allie, or Marchy, or Monty. But Pongo?

"*Pongo?*"

"Afraid so."

"Isn't that the name of the dog in *101 Dalmatians*? Why on earth would you call her that?"

What remained of Ginny's smile became even more sickly.

"Because she was smelly."

I'D THOUGHT I had Alice Marchmont all figured out, but now I listened, mouth agape, as Ginny set me straight. About how Alice had been the odd one out at their posh public day school. About how she'd been shunned by the other girls, just because she'd been less than scrupulous about personal hygiene and had worn sensible lace-up shoes and carried a second-hand satchel, just because she had flyaway hair and wore big knickers and was too embarrassed to take showers with the other girls after gym. About how they'd whispered about her behind her back, and held their noses as she walked by . . .

"Alice was *smelly*?" I was profoundly shocked. This didn't mesh at all with the sweet-smelling vision who'd stepped on to my barge two days earlier.

Ginny made a wry face. I suspected she was getting a kick out of puncturing my illusions.

"Hard to imagine, isn't it? Oh, we all knew she was a scholarship kid, and that her family didn't have much dosh, but none of us had the imagination to understand what that meant in practical terms. You know, she told me later that she'd had only one school blouse, and it was made of something ghastly like nylon, and she'd had to wear it every day and only ever got a chance to wash it at weekends. Can you imagine what that must be like? The problem was that we couldn't, and even if we had done I don't suppose it would have made much of a difference. Adolescent girls can be brutal, you know, and we were such spoiled brats. We had no idea what it was like to be poor, or to have strict parents who would make you wear ugly shoes when all the other girls in your class were skipping around in cha-cha heels with pointy toes."

A dreamy look drifted across Ginny's face, as though she were having a pleasurable footwear flashback.

"Let me get this straight," I said, still trying to wrap my head around this new information. "Alice is *poor*?"

"Oh, not *now*," said Ginny. "She's rolling in it *now*. Whatever she did while she was away, you know, all that time she told you she spent in *Paris*, it must have paid extraordinarily well." She gave me the sort of look that said, *Yes and we know the word Paris is just a euphemism, don't we*, though I couldn't for the life of me imagine what it might have been a euphemism for. Surely she couldn't be implying that Alice had been a prostitute or a *poule de luxe*. Could she?

"But the reason we gave her such a hard time wasn't because

she was poor," Ginny continued. "It was because she was *different*. We hated her for being *different*."

Alice? *Different*? My beer went down the wrong way and I almost choked. My hostess got up to thump me between the shoulder-blades, and then started to walk in circles around the kitchen, apparently loath to sit back down and look me in the eye as she described how she and her friends had committed small acts of sabotage and then blamed them on Alice, just for laughs. How they'd got her into trouble by spray-painting her name on the back of a lavatory door. How they'd made her late for lessons, or tricked her into doing the wrong homework.

It hadn't been malicious, Ginny said unconvincingly. It was simply a Darwinian fact of life—the strongest members of the species picking on the runts. It hadn't really been bullying, not *proper* bullying. It was just the way things were.

I felt like a priest listening to confession, and wondered whether she expected me to absolve her with a couple of Hail Marys.

Ginny sat down again and said, "And then one day everything changed."

It had begun as the usual thoughtless prank, of the sort they routinely played several times a day. They'd stolen Alice's pencil case shortly before a double-geometry lesson, hidden it behind the radiator, but this time, obviously, they must have pushed her too far because she'd broken down in front of the whole class—collapsed into shuddering great hiccups that had convulsed her body and torn howls of anguish from her throat.

Ginny said she had never seen anyone weep like that before; she still seemed shaken by the memory. The teacher's efforts to calm her howling pupil down had failed, so Alice had been escorted to the sick room, which is where she'd spent the rest of the day until her mother could be contacted to come and take her home.

It was nearly a week before they saw her back at school, but by then everything had changed. Ginny, Finny and Janie had been so racked with guilt they'd undergone a collective Paulene conversion. When Alice returned, she suddenly found herself showered with invitations to birthday parties and picnics, barbecues and gymkhanas. The sniggering and nose-holding had been replaced by peace offerings of cast-off designer clothes. She must have waited suspiciously for the other shoe to drop, but it never did.

According to Ginny, the upshot was that, after a couple of terms of this privileged treatment, Alice ended up ten times snootier and more designer conscious than her classmates. Ginny shook her head at the memory. "Look what we did. Did you ever meet such a frightful snob? But it's not her fault, Johnny. She's our Frankenstein monster. We *made* her that way. And you know what? She's *really* good at it, even better than the rest of us."

She suddenly looked coy. "We've all hooked big fish at one time or another, but she's the only one who's actually managed to reel one in."

I had a sudden mental image of the anglers fishing small squishy things out of the canal. "You mean . . .?"

"Nick." Ginny's eyes were glowing again, like a cat's in the dark. "Everyone always fancied him, but as soon as Georgina was out of the way it was *Alice* who got her hooks into him. He's the real deal." She paused, giving me just enough time to digest her admission that she did, in fact, know Nicholas Fitch a lot better than she'd been letting on. She'd known him well enough to fancy him, for starters.

"Oh, I know Finny married Justin. But let's face it, he's an also-ran."

"With a name like Justin?" I marvelled. What chance did a mere John have?

"He's a sweetie. We all adore him. But oh my God, what a loser."

"What does he do for a living?" I inquired, thinking he had to be a rubbish collector or sewage worker, at the very least.

"Commodities broker, I think." Ginny wrinkled her nose delicately, as though what Justin did was too sordid to contemplate.

"Exactly how well *do* you know Nick?" I asked.

Her response was to lean over me and plant a long lingering kiss full on my mouth. Her lips were slightly dry and tasted of

Chardonnay and cigarettes, and it was divine.

"You think I'm lowlife, like Justin?" I murmured as she finally disengaged.

"You are *so* low," she whispered. "You are so totally beneath me, John Croydon. You have *no idea*."

"How low can you go?" I asked, getting to my feet.

She took me by the hand and led me into her ocelot-patterned bedroom, where she proceeded to show me the answer to my question.

It was very low indeed.

TEN

I WAS CAREFUL to keep my phone switched off while I was at Ginny's. The last thing I needed was my mother interrupting while I was in bed with a woman. And so it wasn't until I got home later, much later, that evening and turned it back on that I found a lot of missed calls logged, and a text message from Alice.

OFF TO FRAMPTONS TOMORROW MORNING. WANT TO COME?

Framptons? Oh yes, Nick's country house in Norfolk. I fed Boris and fixed myself a nightcap. Of course it would be helpful to go and see where Georgina had died, but just as I was debating whether it was too late in the evening to call Alice back, my mobile started tinkling out the theme from John Carpenter's *Halloween*; as a ringtone it wasn't perfect, but it was less irritating than the budgerigar noises, and had the added advantage—rather unexpected considering it was adapted from the soundtrack of a seminal slasher movie—of not making me jump out of my skin every time I heard it.

Talk of the Devil I didn't believe in.

"I've been trying to get hold of you all evening," said Alice. "Where've you been?"

Pongo, I thought, fighting back the urge to say it out loud.

"I was with a client."

There was a stunned pause. "You have other clients?"

"Several," I said airily, then quickly added, "But don't worry, I'm giving you priority. The others are ongoing cases, nothing urgent."

"Good," she said. "I'd hate to think you're not giving me your full attention. Now about Norfolk—I don't see any reason why you shouldn't come along, do you? If you haven't got a prior appointment with *another client*, that is. Nick likes you; he'd be thrilled if you came over for dinner, and we can easily find you a bed."

"Nick's going too?"

I was so pleased to hear that he liked me it was pathetic. I was keen to prove I was more than just an embarrassing drunk and a lousy squash player—that I could, on occasion, be witty and urbane, and that I was, in fact, a serious and eminently collectible modern artist and therefore someone worth having as a close chum.

"He's already gone on ahead. Oh, and he really wants to see some of your art. Can you bring your photos?"

"Of course!" I said, and quickly changed the subject.

"Which station do I go from? King's Cross?"

I heard Alice chortling as though I'd cracked a joke. "Oh, don't even think about the train; it's a complete nightmare. You'll be going up in the car with me."

Three, four hours alone with Alice in her car? I had mixed feelings about this. It would be a useful opportunity for me to squeeze more information out of her, maybe try to get her to talk more about Nick and Georgina, or maybe her school days and what she'd been up to in 'Paris', because she sure as hell hadn't told me everything there.

On the other hand, the last thing I needed was her getting it into her head to make another pass at me. Unless, of course— and this is where it got delicate—I was again reading more into the situation than was warranted. I still wasn't sure what had happened between us the previous evening. If, indeed, anything *had* happened.

Oh Lord, why did women have to be so complicated? Why couldn't they say what they wanted and have done with it?

On the other other hand, she would be busy driving. So at least that meant her hands would be occupied.

A sudden loud bleating at the other end of the line made me leap out of my skin. It was like one of those small round boxes that made animal noises when you turned them upside down, only a hundred times louder.

"What the . . .?"

"The entryphone," Alice said in a small, shocked voice.

I checked my watch. Nearly midnight.

"Leave it. Don't even look."

"I have to. What if it's Nick?"

"Alice," I said sternly. "You know perfectly well who it is."

I heard the bleating again, then a series of muffled thumps and clicks, and then Alice saying, "Hello?" though not to me. I wanted desperately to hang up. What could I do from this distance anyway? I had a sensation of impending doom.

More clicks. Then I heard Alice say, "Oh."

"Alice?" I yelled into the phone. "Are you all right? Talk to me!"

I heard her say, "No problem," and then her voice was back in my ear, giggling with relief.

"Someone pressed the wrong buzzer."

"Right," I said.

But the sensation of impending doom didn't go away. Just as lightning conductors don't make the lightning go away.

They just force it to take another route to the ground.

ON MONDAY morning I packed my overnight bag and left keys to the barge with Sol, who was a rabid animal lover and would sooner have chewed his own leg off than forget to feed Boris.

It had been such a long time since I'd last ventured further north than Crouch End that I'd completely forgotten there was a very sound reason why I didn't venture into the countryside more often, and by the time I remembered, it was too late and my fate was sealed. I'd failed to bring insect repellent. As soon as Alice's BMW, with me in the passenger seat, broke through the safety zone of the M25 and into the wide world beyond, the call went out nationwide in the insect world.

Prime target approaching.

And maybe not just the insect world, I thought with a ripple of dread.

In the end, we didn't talk much in the car. Alice apparently found it hard to talk and drive at the same time, so my initial attempts at gentle cross-examination petered out. I stole sidelong glances at her profile and resisted the urge to call her Pongo. It wasn't so bad a nickname, I decided. Affectionate, even charming. Though I reckoned it probably hadn't sounded so cute coming from Ginny and her friends.

Ginny. Instead of mulling over the case or probing my client, as I should have done, I started thinking about what we'd got up the night before. It was tricky staying professional where Ginny was concerned, though at least I had prodded her into providing me with potted histories of her fellow bridesmaids as part of our cosy post-coital chat.

Well, not post-*coital* exactly, because we hadn't actually got as far as having sex, not *technically*. But as far as I was concerned it had been pretty damn near enough.

"And Jeremy," she'd said. "You watch out for Jeremy. He's so possessive where Nick's concerned that if I didn't know better I'd have said he's gay. All the same, if I were you I wouldn't turn your back on him."

"Who's Jeremy?" I tried to summon a mental picture of Alice's address book, but couldn't remember any Jeremys.

"He's the Best Man," said Ginny. "I expect you'll run into him at some point. You are coming to the wedding?"

"I hope so."

"Of course Alice will want you there," Ginny said, propping herself up on one elbow and gazing at me curiously. "Your being such good friends and all."

"Yes, we *are* good friends."

Ginny had peppered me with questions about my work, my sordid past and—in particular—the exact nature of my relationship to Alice. It was no use pretending I wasn't flattered by a gorgeous young woman taking such an interest in me, but alarm bells started going off in my bed—she was just that little bit *too* curious—so I played the mysterious card, dropping what I hoped were juicy titbits without giving anything concrete away. If that made her jealous, the way Alice had been jealous, then so much the better.

We'd had such a rollicking time that evening, both in and out of bed, that I'd dropped heavy hints about staying the night, but she wasn't having any of it, insisting she had to get up early for a photo shoot. She slid out of bed, pulled on a baggy T-shirt and began to rub cream into her face.

"You're a model?" I asked, gazing at her in awe, and thinking, *I've just been to bed with a model!*

"You've got to be kidding!" she said scornfully, as though calling someone a model were the biggest insult possible. I waited for her to elaborate, and at last she said, "I'm a stylist. And the plane's at half six in the morning, which is why I'm chucking you out."

"Plane?"

She muttered something about Amsterdam and started rummaging through her dressing-table drawer.

"Amsterdam!" I exclaimed. "I love Amsterdam! Particularly the coffee shops!"

"See you later," she said, without looking up.

See you later. The most depressing phrase in the English language. Because it didn't mean 'see you later' at all. It meant, "Bugger off and die, you boring bastard".

But just as I was about to slink off with my tail between my legs, she looked over her shoulder at me and smiled a smile so dazzling that, even though she almost immediately turned her attention back to her dressing-table drawer, the afterglow continued to warm my cockles all the way back to the barge.

ALICE'S CAR, like her flat, was airless and overheated; it didn't do much for my blocked nose and stuffed-up head, which seemed to get worse with every second that passed. After a while, the straightness of the road, the throb of the engine and the inability to clear my sinuses properly so I could take a deep breath all combined to lull me into a sort of fugue state.

I gazed out of the window, only half aware of the countryside flashing past. Fields. Trees. Road, and yet more road. And then a muddy brown canal that seemed to come racing across the fields to meet us before running alongside the road, faithfully reproducing every last kink and bend, like a slow wet shadow that refused to be shaken off.

It was only as we turned off the main road that Alice broke the silence.

"He seems a bit depressed."

"Who?" I was staring uneasily at the canal, which seemed

even gloomier than the one I lived on.

"You know when you and Nick played squash? Did he say anything? About how he was feeling, I mean. He seems a bit down, don't you think? Do you think he suspects something?"

"Actually, no." I managed to tear my gaze away from the water. "Seems chipper to me. More than chipper, in fact. And he damn well should be—he's about to marry you . . ."

Alice appeared not to notice the clumsy compliment. "I suppose you don't know him like I do. There's definitely something wrong."

"I'm not engaged to him, it's true."

She must have thought I was suggesting that being engaged to her was enough to give anyone the blues, because she dropped the subject. Or maybe it was because we were approaching our destination. There was a sign up ahead.

WELCOME TO LITTLE YAWNING

And then, in smaller letters:

HOME OF THE WORLD FAMOUS CHEESE-TRAMPLING FESTIVAL

I did a double-take, but the sign was already behind us.

"Did that really say *cheese-trampling*?"

"Just a stupid stunt to bring in tourists."

I was curious about the cheese. What kind of cheese, and how would you set about trampling it?

But Alice had already begun to fill me in on the evening's arrangements. I'd assumed I would be staying the night at Framptons, but she had evidently decided my keen detective's senses weren't required so long as her fiancé was present; she told me I'd been booked into a room at something called The Stumps, which I hoped wouldn't turn out to have been named after a local dismembering: a farm worker, say, whose legs had been torn off by a combine harvester.

But the inn sign, when we drew up beneath it, depicted nothing more grisly than a cricket bat and bails. We sat in silence, Alice obviously trying not to look at me, until I realised she was waiting for me to get out.

"So I won't be staying with you," I said, eyeing the building before me with trepidation. It looked like the pub that time forgot. The roof was shedding its thatch, and several of the windows had been boarded up.

"Oh no, there's still too much to straighten out," said Alice. "Anyhow, this place isn't so bad." She laughed, and I laughed back, though it didn't seem terribly funny to me. How would she know how bad it was? It wasn't as though she'd ever had to *stay* there.

"Well then," I said, opening the door, but before I'd had a chance to clamber out she'd leant across and kissed me. It wasn't a passionate kiss by any means, but the fact it was mouth-to-mouth and her mouth lingered there slightly longer than it should have done made me nervous. I tried to extricate myself without actually pushing her away and fell, rather than climbed, out of the car.

"Around seven, then," she said briskly, as though nothing had happened. She pulled the door shut and sped off, leaving me staring after her open-mouthed. I stood there long after the car had vanished, and then I turned and walked into The Stumps like a condemned man walking to the gallows.

The bar was deserted, almost devoid of natural light and about as welcoming as an undertaker's parlour, but I cheered up considerably when I saw it served Black Monk, an unfashionably flat bitter I hadn't tasted since my student days.

I had to shout, "Hello?" several times before a hunch-backed crone in fishnet stockings and showing several acres of wizened cleavage came hobbling out from a back room, grumbling and rubbing her neck. She confirmed the reservation and handed me a key.

"Second floor. First on the right."

I climbed the stairs, which were uncommonly steep and winding. My room appeared to be a converted attic, and it seemed I would have to share the first floor toilet facilities on the first floor with the pub's clientele. Nice.

I dumped my bag on the narrow bed, opened the window and leant out, getting a panoramic view and a noseful of loose thatch. Down to my right was a village green, actually more brown than green, a bench stippled with birdshit, an old-fashioned red telephone booth that had all but disappeared beneath a gaudy montage of graffiti and stickers, and a small pond containing two or three seedy-looking fowl. The finishing touch was a small, scruffy gang of disaffected adolescents yelling obscenities at each other as they kicked a crushed beer-can back and forth.

Ah, country life. I hung as far as I dared out of the window, trying to spot any big old houses that might be Framptons, but beyond village limits there seemed to be nothing but the odd wizened tree and the canal cutting through the countryside like a faded scar.

I returned downstairs and snacked on pork pie and Black Monk before setting out for the churchyard.

I'd been expecting a cracked and gloomy sepulchre, maybe a couple of ravens and a carved inscription on Georgina's grave saying, *I'll be back.*

But it wasn't like that at all: the grass was neatly mowed and there were fresh flowers on most of the well-tended plots, and while it wasn't somewhere you'd choose to have a picnic, it was a long way from the Hammer horror notion of a churchyard.

Georgina's grave was marked by a tasteful grey marble headstone with name, dates and no mention at all of the circumstances of her death. Not that I'd expected a tombstone to display the pathologist's report. But I did learn something: the late Mrs Fitch's middle names had been Laetitia and Rosemary.

Laetitia. What had her parents been thinking? Bet she'd kept that one quiet at school. They'd have called her Lettuce. Or Titty.

I snapped away with my disposable camera, taking pictures of the grave and its surroundings from every conceivable angle. Despite Ginny's scepticism about my artistic credentials, I really did have a good eye, but I'd sold my old Olympus SLR because the photos I'd taken with it had had an unnerving tendency to show things that hadn't been there. Not shadowy figures, either, but people who appeared so solid you might never have guessed they weren't flesh and blood had they not been missing important body parts, such as legs or heads.

And then there were the animals—mostly cats or dogs, though once it had been a big lizard—sitting or lying quietly at someone's feet as though they had every right to be there.

I'd had to vet all those photos pretty thoroughly, and even so I'd once had a lot of explaining to do to Kate's parents, who'd wondered what kind of sick sense of humour had compelled me to add a naked, bleeding man to the background of what was supposed to be their silver wedding celebration.

Right now, however, I was actually hoping Georgina would show up in one of the photos, so I'd have a clearer image than the one in the crumpled Polaroid. Towards the end of the film, I even started to enjoy myself, pretending I was a professional taking photos of scantily-clad supermodels and calling out things like, 'Smile!' and 'Looking *good!*' which got me some funny looks from an old biddy who was waddling past with a bunch of flowers.

When I'd used up two-thirds of the exposures I decided to explore the village, which took all of five minutes. There were a couple of pretty stone cottages and a quaint old school that had been converted into flats, but mostly it seemed to consist of council houses and a rather grim parade of shops. Villagers could tuck into sausage and chips in Sally's Teashop, drool over old Airfix magazines in Patel's, have their hair snipped in Di's Tresses, fill their larders with tinned soup from Ronnie the Grocer, or furnish their homes with 'quality Danish' coffee tables from Vern's Antiques.

The last shop in the parade, and the only one I felt an urge to explore, was a dusty old bookshop called *Yawning Pages*, which contained stacks of Georgette Heyer and Barbara Cartland, a large selection of hymn books and shelf upon shelf of ancient tomes that were not so much slightly foxed as dipped in mould and nibbled by worms.

The proprietor was engrossed in the *Daily Telegraph* cross-word and barely glanced up as I entered, and since the only other customer reeked of stale cigarettes and kept muttering unintelligibly to himself, I chose to browse as far away from him as possible.

As I browsed, I spotted a familiar-looking spine. I pulled it out—as I'd suspected, it was *Murder Is My Business* by Dilbert Jenkins, former FBI agent and veteran investigator of some of

America's most notorious serial killings. The copy I had at home was less battered than this one; it had been given to me as a birthday present by a well-meaning friend who'd thought it might come in useful in my line of work, although so far the only corpses I'd come across had been of junkies who'd shot up once too often, or of teenage runaways who'd frozen to death in doorways. All very tragic, but somewhat lacking in mystery. I flicked through it, wincing, as usual, at the ghastly photographs of ruined heads and rotting flesh.

As I was sliding Dilbert Jenkins back into place, my eye was caught by the next title along: *Old Egbert's Almanac of Eerie Things*, stamped in faded gold on tatty red leather. I nearly sprained my wrist pulling that one out. I opened it at random, unleashing a cloud of dust and, when I'd recovered from a coughing fit that made even the storeowner glance up, found myself gazing at the name FITCH.

Blimey, what were the chances?

Old Norfolk family with bloodline dating back to pre-Norman times. Tobias Fitch (1710-65) one of the co-founders of The Sulfur (alt. orthog Soul Fire) Society, said to have exceeded the notorious Hellfire Club in its depraved amorality . . .

There was more, but the text had been printed in a typeface so ridiculously fancy that trying to decipher it in the gloom of the shop threatened to give me a migraine. I made a mental note to ask Nick about this ne'er-do-well ancestor of his, but now the stale cigarette smell was making me feel queasy, and my ancient bookshop allergy was kicking in, making my bowels contract alarmingly, so I was forced to leave the book where it was and sprint back across the green and up to the first floor of The Stumps.

In the middle of relieving myself it occurred to me that *Old Egbert's* might come in useful, but by the time I'd made my way back to the shop, the place was in darkness and the door locked.

I looked at my watch. Barely five-thirty. Typical provincial opening-hours. I retraced my steps to the pub, which was already filling up with customers—chain-smoking pensioners, unwashed criminal types and what looked like a couple of boisterous 12-year-olds quaffing from vast tankards of cider. It seemed only natural to see the proprietor of Yawning Pages there as well.

The barman was, at a guess, in his late twenties, clad in a grungy sleeveless knitted tank top that showed off over-developed biceps and the tattoo of a parrot with plumage that matched the incongruous streak of turquoise in his otherwise oily black quiff. I installed myself at the bar and knocked back a pint of Black Monk, feeling the eyes of the pensioners drilling into my back. I was obviously the most exciting thing that had happened around here since, well, since Georgina Fitch had been killed in a mysterious car accident and Tubby Clegg had been found dead in a ditch with half his head missing.

When I'd finished my drink I went up to the attic to change for dinner—not a habit that came naturally, but I was deter-mined to make an effort, and so I swapped the brown jumper with cat-fluff trim for a crisp-ish white-ish shirt. Alice had suggested I turn up for drinks at seven, but it was still only quarter past six, so I stopped off in the bar for another pint. By the time I set off, half an hour later, I was feeling pretty mellow. But not drunk, not by a long chalk.

At the edge of the village green was an old-fashioned wooden signpost with arms shooting off in all directions, as though Little Yawning had elected itself centre of the known universe.

I set off, as instructed, in the direction of Upper Measle.

ELEVEN

U P CLOSE, this canal looked even murkier than the one I lived on. I didn't think I was in any danger of falling in, but gave it a wide berth all the same, keeping more or less to the other side of the lane, which was flanked by a vicious-looking hedge that became taller and more unruly the further it got from the village. It wasn't long, in fact, before it stopped being a hedge altogether and started being a closely-packed thicket of the sort the prince probably had to hack his way through in order to get within kissing distance of the Sleeping Beauty.

Alice had assured me Framptons was only twenty minutes away, and I was soon enjoying the stroll, trying to draw clean air into my blocked pneumatic tubes and humming a country tune. It was only after I'd been walking for about half an hour that I began to wonder if she'd been talking about twenty minutes *by car*. I tried calling on my mobile, but it came as no great surprise when I couldn't get even a whisper of a signal; it was already clear that Little Yawning and the countryside around it were one big Dead Spot.

As the light bled slowly out of the sky, the lane became increasingly wreathed in shadow and started to remind me, rather disconcertingly, of one of Gustave Dore's etchings for Dante's *Inferno*. Perhaps I'd misread the signpost. Or maybe the local yobs had tampered with the arms and were even now shrieking with laughter at having directed a wet-eared city oik towards the bottomless sucking bog whence no traveller returned. To make things worse, the insects were emerging in force; I already had half a dozen bites in places it wasn't considered polite to scratch in public.

I was on the point of turning back when there was finally a welcome variation in the surroundings: the canal abruptly stopped hogging the road and tore off across some fields like a dog let off the leash. A little further along, I spied a gap in the thicket. Had it been any darker, I might have missed the rough track winding away into the dusk. Alice had spoken of a 'driveway', which this patently was not, but I decided to give it a try, and sure enough, once I'd rounded a small clump of scrawny alders, I was rewarded by the sight of a big house about a hundred yards up ahead.

It was the first country mansion I'd ever visited that didn't belong to the National Trust, but at first sight I was underwhelmed. It wasn't what you'd call an architectural treasure; it was an ugly bugger, more a hotchpotch of styles and materials all tacked together willy-nilly, as though half a dozen mad architects had been struggling to impose their will on one other. The walls were an unsightly patchwork of brick and stucco and pebbledash, the roof a thicket of chimneys and gables and sticky-out things that might once have been gargoyles but were now so eroded they resembled half-formed foetuses.

But Alice's BMW and Nick's battered Saab were parked out front, so this had to be it. Framptons. As I mounted the front steps towards a massive door surmounted by a disproportionately large architrave, I felt as though I was being swallowed by a many-windowed beast.

The bell set off an absurd carillon of tinkly bells somewhere inside, and after a foot-shuffling wait of only about half an hour, the door was opened by Alice. She'd changed into a long blue dress that in London might have looked frumpy; here, where trendy London garb would have seemed outlandish, it harmonized perfectly with the surroundings.

"Thought you'd got lost," she said, leaning towards me, and I was afraid she was going kiss me on the mouth again until she suddenly let out a shriek and shrank back, flapping her hands.

"Omigod, what's that on your nose?"

I felt with my finger and found a hot little bump that had probably been glowing red in the gloaming, like a tail-light.

"Insect bite."

Alice laughed. "Poor John. Living creatures don't like you much, do they?"

I didn't much care for this turn of phrase, but just then Nick came barrelling up and greeted me like the old chum he evidently still believed I was, with a warm handshake and a manly pat on the shoulder. "Hullo there, squash partner!"

"Not just squash," I said, stepping into a hallway as lofty and echoing as a cathedral. "There's a whole range of other activities I regularly fail at."

Nick roared with laughter. "Don't do yourself down. I've a feeling our little art venture is going to be a stonking great success. You did bring photos?"

"I did indeed," I said, patting my pocket.

Alice wanted to know what we were talking about.

"Just a little money-making project John and I are hatching," Nick said with a wink in my direction.

Alice scowled at me, as though I had no business fraternizing with her fiancé in matters not directly related to her. "I'd better keep an eye on dinner. You'll give John the guided tour, won't you darling?" And she slipped quietly away.

I'd somehow never pictured Alice toiling in the kitchen. "She cooks?"

Nick looked almost apologetic. "You're right, we should have hired someone, but the expense . . . you know."

I didn't know, and I wasn't entirely sure that Nick did either. How on earth could someone talk about 'expense' when they owned not just a swanky flat in Bayswater but a house the size of Wembley Stadium? I gazed up the beams on the vaulted ceiling, oh, about five miles above my head, half-expecting to see clouds scudding around, and said, "Nice little place you have here. Sure it's big enough for the two of you?"

Nick seemed pleased, as though I'd complimented him on the size of his manhood. He asked what I wanted to drink and I said, "I'll have what you're having," which is how I ended up with a disgusting Italian aperitif that tasted like cough mixture. Even in my student days I had never been that desperate. As Nick showed me round the ground floor, I quietly slopped small quantities of it into each potted plant we passed.

There seemed to be no internal logic to the layout of the rooms—parlour, lounge, living room, games room, laundry room all led into each other with neither rhyme nor reason—and I soon lost track of where I was.

We ended up at the foot of a broad wooden staircase. On the wall above the stairs was an enormous oil painting so dark I had to squint to make out the cluster of figures at its heart: centre-stage was a tall man with a nose just like Nick's, lording it over a seated woman, a horde of children and a dog. They were all posed in front of a big house that I assumed was meant to be Framptons, though it was hard to tell through the gloom. The sky was overcast, almost black in places, but streaked with white lightning.

How odd, I thought, that these people should have wanted their portrait painted with a stormy backdrop instead of, say, a nice sunny one.

Nick saw my interest.

"Tobias Fitch," he said. "One of my ancestors."

"Tobias Fitch? Hey, I was just reading about him."

Nick frowned. "Oh yes?"

"In your local bookshop. Dusty old tome, *Old Egghead's* or something."

Nick's frown deepened. "Oh yes, we are mentioned in a few local histories."

I felt like kicking myself for not having snapped up the book when I'd had the chance; it would obviously be full of interesting information about Framptons and the Fitches.

As we reached the landing I glanced back at the painting. "Aren't there rather a lot of children?"

"Oh, that's his third wife. Or was it his fourth? He was very free with his seed. Thoroughly disreputable type."

"I trust you don't take after him," I said waggishly.

"Actually I do," Nick said with a laugh so short it was practically a bark. "Can't help it, old man. Runs in the family. What are you doing over New Year, by the way?" He asked the question so abruptly I wondered if it was a deliberate ploy to change the subject. "Alice is already planning some sort of gigantic house party. I'm sure she'd love for you to come."

"I'll have to check," I said, not wanting to give the impression I would be short of invitations.

"Of course," said Nick, as though it went without saying that my social calendar was a tangled growth of double bookings. I had to scamper to catch up with him; he was already striding down the passageway, flinging doors open and apologising for the state of the rooms within.

"There's so much that needs doing, I hardly know where to start. It's all in such rotten repair."

I dutifully poked my head through each doorway as we passed. Each room was kitted out with the same sort of utilitarian bed and chest of drawers and hung with doleful paintings of sad-eyed women or slabs of mouldering cheese. The place didn't look in such bad repair to me, but then I was accustomed to sleeping in flats decorated with patches of damp and half a dozen different species of fungi.

I was backing out of yet another of these bedrooms, unable to tear my eyes away from a minutely rendered slice of Roquefort, when my ears picked up a strange scraping sound from somewhere above our heads. I tilted my head back to eye the ceiling. Well, more of a scrabbling, really. A scrabbling that reminded me of the sound I'd heard on the barge two nights ago.

"Um, did you hear that?"

Nick didn't break stride, but laughed dismissively as he reached for the next doorknob. "These old houses, full of odd noises. Probably the wind."

It hadn't sounded like that to me, unless the wind had sprouted fingernails, but before I could start brooding he'd opened the door and I found myself standing on the threshold of a bedroom very different from the others.

There was more furniture, for a start—maybe even too much. The bed was large enough for three, maybe four people, and so high that anyone shorter than me would have needed a stepladder to climb in. It was the most hideous thing I'd ever seen: a ghastly knicker-pink quilt topped off by a heavy black wood bedhead carved into the shape of a large snake tightening its coils around a small mammal that might have been an otter, or possibly a stoat. Either way, it was doomed.

"My room," Nick said with a note of pride.

"Nice," I said, unable to suppress a shudder.

"What? Oh, the bedhead. I guess it must be pretty grotesque if you're not used to it. Georgie always claimed it gave her nightmares, and I have to say Alice doesn't seem very keen on it . . . Probably should chuck it out, replace it with something from IKEA, but hey, I was born in this bed, all my ancestors slept here and consummated their marriages in it, so it kind of has historic value."

"Midwife must have been on stilts," I remarked, and he chuckled.

But if Alice didn't sleep here, where *did* she sleep?

I soon found out. The first thing I saw when Nick opened the next door along was her bag on the bed, a small four-poster hung with floral drapes that matched the curtains and bedspread. Unlike Nick's, this bed was so compact I found myself wondering what position a woman as lanky as Alice could possibly sleep in. Scrunched up sideways? Or flat on her back, with her feet sticking out of the covers?

But imagining Alice in bed was making me uncomfortable. Even as a passing thought it was more intimate than I had any desire to get with her. She just wasn't my type—not to mention the fact she was about to get married to the man currently standing only a few inches away from me.

We moved on. We'd had our fun; the remaining rooms were all furnished in the predominant minimalist style. And then, at the end of the passage, Nick opened a cupboard, stepped inside—and was instantly swallowed up by the darkness. I was hanging back, wondering if there would be room enough for the two of us, when his muffled voice reached my ears. "Come on."

I stepped in and found myself, not in a walk-in closet, nor even in Narnia, but at the bottom of a narrow stone staircase. My host was already at the top, waiting to show me the second floor, though it turned out there wasn't a lot to see—just a series of interlocking attics lit by bare bulbs and devoid of even the most basic furnishing.

"Just look at all this space," said Nick, waving his arm, "waiting to be filled with art. And it's up to you to fill it, John. I can give you *carte blanche* . . ."

I looked around doubtfully. There was a lot of space, it was true, but the ceiling was low and the windows little more than narrow slits, and it all seemed a bit bleak. I couldn't really imagine these unwelcoming rooms thronged by chattering art collectors. Still less could I imagine the chattering art collectors flocking up the narrow staircase that led there.

Our footsteps were dulled by the thick layer of dust coating the floorboards, apart from one or two places where it looked as though someone had been trying to write on the floor with a rolled-up carpet. I wondered if the marks were connected with the scrabbling I'd heard earlier. Might there be someone hiding up here in the attic? Did Nick have a mutant relative, or was it simply infested with rats? Rats was bad enough. Rats were too intelligent for comfort. I'd once seen an episode of *Doomwatch* in which they'd invented a rat version of the wheel before chowing on down on a lady scientist.

Nick saw me staring uneasily at the floor. "You're right, old man. Needs a good clean. No-one ever comes up here."

"It would be a great place to play sardines," I said, trying to forget about rats, but regretting the word *sardines* as soon as it was out of my mouth; I still had unpleasant memories of a classmate's birthday party when I'd found myself sharing my hiding-place with something that hadn't been on the guest list.

"Funny you should say that," said Nick. "There's an old family legend about a small boy who hid up here during a game of hide and seek, oh, centuries ago. And no-one ever found him until, years later, someone popped open a trunk and lo, a tiny skeleton. Yet another family tragedy. We Fitches don't seem to have had much luck."

There was an awkward silence which I broke in the clumsiest possible way.

"Don't you ever feel like selling up and moving out?"

Nick stared at me. "Why would I want to do that?"

"You know." I felt the blood rushing to my face. "After all these tragedies. After what happened to . . . Georgina."

For a moment I thought Nick was going to plant his fist in my face. He turned away so I couldn't see his expression, though from the way his voice cracked it wasn't hard to picture it. "It wasn't here that she died."

"I'm not suggesting it was," I blustered. "I just got the impression that, you know, she spent a lot of time here alone, maybe too much time."

"What are you trying to say?"

"Oh, I don't know," I said, blundering all over his feelings like a big fat bull charging around in a very small and delicate china shop. "It's just the sort of place where . . . Well, if you were an imaginative type . . ."

"Shouldn't believe everything you read in the papers," Nick said, and then added in a voice that was barely audible, "I never stopped loving her, you know." As though I might have been thinking otherwise. "I couldn't set foot in the place for months afterwards. Had to get rid of her stuff. I couldn't stand seeing it around."

"By *stuff* you mean . . .?"

He shrugged. "Books and things. Clothes. Sewing-machine. Some furniture. But you're wrong about the house. She loved it here, she really did. She spent all her time running up curtains, making covers for chairs, turning it into a home."

He started to say something else, but changed his mind. We walked on in silence, each of us sunk in our own private thoughts, until the attic ended in a blank wall and we were obliged to retrace our steps. I was wondering how best to broach the subject of Georgina's accident when I sensed him looking sideways at me. I pretended not to notice, but after a while he said, "I know why you're here."

"Alice invited me."

"Yes, and I know why." He patted me on the back. "No need to keep it bottled up any longer. I know everything."

My heart did a little hop and a skip. Everything? Had Alice finally decided to confess to Nick about her stalker? She might have bloody well warned me. Now I was going to be left with egg on my face . . .

Nick said, "I don't mind *at all* that you and Alice once stepped out together . . ."

Whoah. What the hell had she been telling him?

Nick patted me on the back again. He was patting me so

regularly I was beginning to feel like his dog. "It's only natural you should still have feelings for her. She is a splendid piece of work, isn't she? You don't meet many women like Alice Marchmont nowadays. Not at her age."

"What do you mean?"

"Well, you know . . . In this day and age . . . Now that kids are having sex as soon as they can walk . . ."

Alice was a virgin?

I stared at my feet, struck dumb with embarrassment, until Nick mumbled something I didn't catch and I had to ask him to repeat it. He said, "So your relationship with Alice isn't a professional one?"

My heart, which had never really recovered its rhythm after the last shock, now went into freefall, like a lift after the cables had snapped. All these emotional ups and downs were beginning to make me feel seasick. I struggled to keep a clear head and concentrate on the matter at hand.

"We don't . . . no, of course not . . . *What do you mean, professional?*"

"She didn't, er, hire you to do some sort of, say, detective work?" he asked, rather too casually.

I managed to stay calm, but he was peering at me so intently that I knew I was going to have to make this good. "Detective work?" I chuckled. "You've got to be kidding. Whatever gave you that idea?"

"Oh, just something Jeremy said. But I wouldn't worry about it. Your word's good enough for me. Bit of a drama queen, is Jeremy. Always trying to stir things up."

Jeremy. I growled inwardly. This was no doubt the same Jeremy on whom Ginny had advised me not to turn my back. My God, I had yet to meet the guy, and already he was sticking the knife between my shoulder blades and twisting it, hard. I needed to have a serious talk with him when I got back to London. I also needed to stop Nick thinking about what Jeremy might or might not have said, and I needed to do it fast, which is why I ended up saying, "I might as well come clean. The truth is that I still love Alice. I've always loved her, always will. But please don't think of me as a rival, because

I'm not. She's nuts about you."

There. I'd said it. I squirmed with embarrassment and prayed that Nick wouldn't repeat what I'd just said to Alice. Christ, what if he did and she took it seriously? Hell no, I would just have to tell her the truth—that I'd been trying to throw Nick off the scent.

Nick took out a packet of Marlboro and paused to light one. I wanted a cigarette too, desperately, but he wasn't offering and I didn't trust my voice to ask.

He calmly drew smoke into his lungs and asked, "So you wouldn't want to, say, stop us getting married?"

"Stop you . . .? You're kidding. I couldn't be more delighted for you both. Um, it's what Alice wants, and of course I want what's best for her."

Nick smiled affably. "That's good. Just so we understand each other."

Something had just passed between us, though I wasn't sure what. I had kept my end up and not given too much away, but at what cost? Now Nick thought I was in love with his fiancée and, knowing my luck, she'd end up thinking it too, and next thing you knew Ginny would get to hear of it, and then . . .

My thoughts were in such turmoil that I completed the tour in silence while Nick filled in for the both of us with a running patter about the glory days of Framptons. I listened with half an ear to tales of fugitive priests, murderous spouses and The Sulfur Society, a dodgy-sounding outfit that sounded as though it had been invented for the sole purpose of enabling Tobias Fitch to indulge in prodigious amounts of extra-marital rumpy-pumpy.

"They used to have orgies in these very attic rooms," Nick said, "though of course back then they were properly furnished. Wives were never allowed up here, of course. Only maidservants. Lots of maidservants . . ."

Somewhere among those interlocking rooms, I'd got all turned around, so when Nick opened a door and led me down a narrow staircase, I naturally assumed it was the same one we'd climbed earlier. But to my surprise, instead of emerging into the first-floor hallway we stepped straight out into the kitchen, where Alice the Virgin was serving up dinner.

It didn't smell good.

TWELVE

Alice had decided we were going to do things properly and eat in the dining room, which required much scurrying back and forth from the kitchen with tureens and covered dishes and weird-looking silver cutlery so old it was almost black; I could see why one would need servants. So it was that the three of us eventually found ourselves huddled around one end of a dining-table big enough to seat the entire membership of the Sulfur Society, their wives, mistresses and a couple of excommunicated priests as well.

Despite the logs smouldering in the fireplace, the dining room had a damp, unlived-in air and the fire only succeeded in filling the room with a thin effluvium of smoke that made my eyes leak. I was seated with my back to the window and even with the collar of my jacket turned up there was a cold draught on my neck, and the thought of all those empty fields stretching out behind me didn't exactly help.

On the wall over the fireplace was the portrait of a youngish woman who might have been beautiful had she not been so incredibly gloomy; her expression was that of someone resigned to suffering, like a terminally ill mother-to-be who'd decided to forgo chemotherapy so as not to endanger the life of her unborn child. It was one of those portraits where the eyes seemed to follow you round the room, gazing out at you accusingly.

"Mary Ann Fitch," said Nick. "Old Jebez's second wife. Or was she his third? Quite lovely, isn't she?"

"But terribly sad," I pointed out.

"That's us Fitches for you," said Nick. "A laugh a minute."

There weren't many laughs during dinner. I found myself breaking rules I hadn't known existed. I sawed my bread into little cubes and dropped them into my soup, which to judge from Alice's expression was absolutely not the way to go about it. I also used the wrong spoon, but since the cutlery resembled a set of gynaecological instruments for operating on mutant women in a David Cronenberg film, it was hardly my fault. Nick dispensed vinegary Bordeaux from a dusty bottle and prattled on about people called *Strathers* and *Knobsworth* as though we were mutual friends. Since I couldn't work out whether or not they were people I would have met during our fictional past acquaintance, I restricted myself to nodding sagely.

Worst of all was the food. Alice had obviously gone to some trouble, so I tried to look as though I was enjoying the dry grey meat which bore only a superficial resemblance to chicken. I had to drink more wine than was prudent, just to wash it down. It came with a mountain of indifferently mashed potato and a hillock of dull green peas. I began seriously to doubt she had ever lived in Paris; no-one who had even a passing familiarity with French food would have dreamt of cooking up a meal like this. I spilled some of the peas on the table and for a tense few moments it was like a vegetable version of the wild west with the little critters rolling in all directions, but I finally managed to head most of them off at Wineglass Gulch. Nick was so busy shovelling food into his mouth he didn't notice. Alice almost certainly did, but pretended not to.

"This is excellent, darling!" Nick exclaimed. "Isn't it, John?"

"Delicious!" I tried to sound jollier than I felt, but if this was the best she could do, Nick really would have to think seriously about hiring that cook.

Alice looked down at her plate with a small, shy smile, which is when Nick made a face at me and stuck two fingers in his mouth. I was horrified. What if she saw? I immediately launched into an anecdote about Boris in a bid to distract her. It worked—she started watching me rather than her husband-to-be, and even though I was aware my skills as a raconteur left a lot to be desired, she giggled and looked goofy in all the right places.

Dessert was a nest of dry meringue smothered in sickly chocolate sauce. I wondered if Alice had found her recipes in *The 1950s School Canteen Cookbook*, and struggled through the meringue the way an explorer wades through a leech-infested swamp, trying not to let revulsion show on my face, and on tenterhooks lest Nick should start making faces at me again.

"Well now," he said suddenly. "What do you think of the house?"

I thought it was a lugubrious monstrosity, but sensed an honest response wasn't likely to endear me to either of my hosts.

"It's . . . spectacular," I said, searching for words.

"But too big," said Nick. "In fact, I'm thinking of having part of it demolished to make it cheaper to run."

Alice looked shocked. "Oh, you mustn't do that."

"Just kidding, darling. I couldn't anyway, bloody thing's listed. And I can't sell it; no-one wants to buy, there's too much that needs doing. Costs a fortune to run. It really is a bit of a millstone."

"But so much history," I said.

"You're right there," sighed Nick. "Sometimes I think it's rather too much history. You know, I quite fancy the idea of living in an ordinary semi-detached, like everyone else."

I thought it best not to point out that even though I'd grown up in a semi-detached house, I didn't know a single person who lived in one now.

"So many portraits of sad-looking women," I said, looking at Mary-Ann.

"Not much fun being a woman in the days before Women's Lib," said Nick. "Always getting pregnant, always dying in childbirth while their husbands were off gallivanting with their mistresses."

"Thank God for progress," laughed Alice.

I thought her smile looked a little forced. I was tempted to call her Pongo, just to try and cheer her up. *Poor Pongo*. Was she going to end up as just another sad-faced women, staring down at us from the walls?

Nick pushed his chair back and got to his feet.

"But enough of this doom and gloom! We're going to have to have parties, artists-in-residence, literary festivals! Bring a bit of life to the old place! Anyhow, time for cheese and brandy. Shall we take it in the kitchen?"

Without waiting for a reply he stacked up some of the dirty plates and carried them out of the room. The dish-stacking was a good sign, I thought; at least it showed he was willing to help out on the domestic front.

I wondered whether the remark about artists-in-residence had been directed at me. Would I really want to be 'in residence' in a house like this?

Alice didn't say anything, nor did she show any signs of wanting to follow her fiancé into the kitchen. Her eyes were wide; at first I thought she was staring at me and diligently refused to look back at her, but after a while I saw her gaze was actually directed past my shoulder. I turned to look for myself, but couldn't see much beyond our reflections in the window.

I turned back and saw her face was drained of colour. You couldn't even have called it white—it was the exact same shade as her own mashed potato. I asked if she was OK.

She murmured, "I thought I saw something."

Oh Lord, not again. Surely Georgina couldn't have followed us all the way from London? On the other hand, it would probably make sense if Framptons turned out to be the base of her operations; it did seem to be Ground Zero, so to speak. Maybe it had been a mistake for Alice to come here.

I got up and went over to the window and slid it open and poked my head outside. The air was cold but fresh after the smokiness of the room. I couldn't see anything much, but stayed like that for a moment or two, trying to accustom my eyes to the darkness.

No Georgina. Nothing. Not a thing.

Thank you, God.

I waited a couple of beats before closing the window and rejoining Alice at the table. She was trembling, but that might have been due to the cold night air I'd let in.

I said, "Please don't tell me you saw Georgina."

She shook her head. "An animal, I think. It had yellow eyes."

I didn't know whether to laugh or cry. We were in the country. *Of course* there would be animals. But I wished she'd told me about the yellow eyes before I'd stuck my head through the window and given whatever it had been a chance to bite my nose off.

"Maybe a fox," I said, wondering if foxes ever attacked people. I knew they sometimes ate cats, which was bad enough.

"I guess."

"In any case, Georgina didn't have yellow eyes, did she?"

Alice shook her head again. "I really don't know what it was. Maybe nothing, maybe just a reflection."

"This house is enough to give anyone the willies."

"I'm scared, John."

She placed both hands palm down on the table in front of her and I watched in horrified fascination as the fingers of the left one began to creep, almost imperceptibly, towards my own. My first instinct was to snatch my hand away before she could make contact, but I was afraid that any sudden movement on my part might trigger a grabbing motion on Alice's.

I was trying to work out a diplomatic way of distancing myself when Nick started bellowing from the kitchen. "Where the hell *are* you chaps?"

"The cheese . . ." murmured Alice, and as though Nick's yell had plucked her out of a dream, she rose and hurried out. I was left staring out of the window into the darkness beyond and contemplating the close shave I'd just had. This time it hadn't been my imagination; she really had wanted to touch me. Jeez.

I decided a large brandy was definitely in order.

THE KITCHEN table was heaving with a dozen varieties of sticky, smelly cheese. They ranged from off-white through toenail orange to mouldy old blue, but every last one of them was oozing.

"Help yourself," Nick said jovially.

I picked up a water biscuit and poked it into the nearest deliquescent wedge. There was a small sucking sound as I drew it out again. I nibbled apprehensively. It tasted like a sumo wrestler's jockstrap. Or what I imagined a sumo wrestler's jockstrap might taste like, since of course I'd never gone so far as to put one in my mouth.

Nick had barely finished pouring the brandies when Alice

grabbed hers and gulped it down as though she were glugging lemonade. Nick didn't raise so much as an eyebrow. He leaned back in his chair and lit a cigarette. This time, I didn't wait for him to offer; I leant across and helped myself from his packet, not so much because I wanted to smoke as to provide myself with an excuse not to eat any more cheese.

"So, said Nick. "Let's see what you've got in the way of masterpieces, old man. Let's see your art."

Ah, the photos. Happily, I'd come prepared. I reached into my pocket, pulled out the Polaroids snapped in the early hours of Monday morning with Sol's ancient Land Camera, and slid them across the table. Nick and Alice spread them out and studied them intently, as though they were museum curators and I'd presented them with artefacts from Tutankhamen's tomb.

"Interesting," Nick said at length. "This one with the baby and the snake . . ."

"*Moses in the Bulrushes with a Puff Adder*," I told him. "And that one's *Twelve Disciples Menaced by a Giant Turtle*."

"Hmm," said Nick. "I like it."

Alice didn't say anything, but continued to stare at the *Skull of a Rodent with Orchid and Pillbox* as though trying to decipher the hidden message. Of course, she was well aware I wasn't really an artist, but she was doing a damn good job of acting as though she thought I was.

"You're very quiet, darling," said Nick. "What do you think?"

Alice looked up with shining eyes. "I think he's a genius."

I had a feeling she wasn't kidding. She was staring at me as though I were Rembrandt.

"These are great," enthused Nick. "Can I hold on to them?"

"Be my guest."

I finished my brandy and waited for Nick to pour me another, but instead he looked at his watch. I checked my own and saw it was only five past ten.

Nick started fiddling with a slice of Emmental. "Sure you'll be all right on that road, this time of night?"

I could take a hint, but it did seem ludicrously early. At this hour, Londoners would only just be shining their shoes and powdering their noses in preparation for going out on the town. I guessed the countryside was different and everyone had to get up at the crack of dawn to milk cows and stuff. But I wasn't looking forward to the walk back. I hoped that whatever Alice might have glimpsed through the dining-room window was long gone.

She placed a hand on Nick's arm. "Couldn't he stay?"

I almost felt like kissing her, though naturally that would have sent out entirely the wrong message. But of course I could stay. Framptons might not have been the most welcoming place in the world, but bunking down in one of the bedrooms would be infinitely preferable to walking back to The Stumps in the dark.

"Afraid it's not five-star," said Nick.

"Just don't put me in the attic," I joked, adding mentally, *or anywhere near that freaky snake headboard.*

"He can have the room next to mine," said Alice. "I'll go sort out some blankets. I think there's a spare quilt in one of the boxes Janie brought up." She smiled at me in an oddly encouraging way as, a little unsteadily, she got to her feet. I looked back at her with what I hoped was a non-encouraging smile, wondering if I would be forced to lock my bedroom door.

"There's an extra reading lamp in the study," she said, as though putting someone up for the night was the most fun a person could possibly have. "And I think we may even have a spare hot water-bottle."

I didn't really need a hot water-bottle since the brandy had already done a thorough job of warming me up, but I said, "That's very kind of you," anyway, and then the devil got into me and I added, "*Pongo.*"

Even before the word was all the way out, I knew I'd made the biggest tactical blunder since Adolf Hitler had insisted on laying siege to Stalingrad. I tried to gulp it back, but it was already too late. The word was too big to be recalled. The damage was done. The city lay in ruins.

Alice was already halfway out of the door, but she froze in mid-step and stood unmoving for a few seconds, as though she'd forgotten something, before turning and walking back to the table and sitting down again. All this without giving the slightest indication she'd heard what I'd said. I couldn't help marvelling at the studied neutrality of her expression.

But she'd gone pale again.

Nick looked up from a slice of Gorgonzola-like substance that was threatening to slip off the plate and ooze across the table.

"What was that?"

"Nothing," said Alice, and surely it was my imagination that picked out that faint tremor in her voice, because Nick didn't appear to notice anything amiss. She stared accusingly at me. "Actually, John, I don't think you can stay after all. I'm sorry; it wouldn't be practical."

"No really," Nick persisted. "What was that you called her? *Pongo*?"

"Just a nickname." I looked at her beseechingly. "Wasn't it, Alice? Didn't they used to call you Pongo at school?"

"Pongo!" Nick sat up and beamed like a schoolboy who'd just won an extra-big conker. "How delightful! You don't mind if I call you Pongo, darling?"

"Actually I do mind," she said. "I mind a lot."

Her eyes were shining again and I realised with a sharp little stab of regret that she was trying not to cry. She was still staring at me accusingly, as though she were my girlfriend and I'd just told her she was fat. I began to feel horribly guilty.

"Alice," I said, inadvertently dipping my cuff into one of the runnier curds as I reached across the table to touch her arm, "I really didn't mean to . . ."

She pulled away and murmured, "You'd better be going, John."

I felt like kicking myself in the head. Now I had to walk back to the village along that dark lane, being stung to death by insects, and possibly chased by foxes as well, with the world's worst bed and breakfast waiting for me at the end of the road.

Well, it probably served me right. I should have realised Alice would still be sensitive about her nickname. I'd behaved like a cad.

"I'll give you a ride," said Nick, lurching to his feet.

"You will not," Alice said sternly. "You're drunk."

He surrendered without a fight—now that Alice had mentioned it, he did seem awfully squiffy—and started rummaging in a nearby drawer.

"*Voilà!*" he said at last, brandishing a torch. "You're going to be needing this, old man."

I examined it doubtfully; it was covered in dried mud. It looked as though it might have done service at the Somme. But it was better than nothing. No-one said a word as they walked me to the front door, Nick whistling tunelessly and Alice stubbornly refusing to look me in the eye.

Boy, that *Pongo* must have really hurt.

"I'll be off then." I hovered on the doorstep, still hoping for a last-minute reprieve. "So long."

"You'll make your own way back to London, then," she said as though it was an option we'd just been discussing.

"Yeah, sure," I said. "No problem."

"See you back in the smoke, old man," said Nick, sending me on my way with a slap on the back so hearty that it almost pitched me face-forward down the steps.

"Goodbye, John," Alice said as though she really meant it.

And I set off down the driveway, gravel crunching beneath my feet. Several times I looked back to where Nick and Alice were standing framed in the doorway like some fairytale couple, orange light spilling out around them on to the drive. He had his arm around her, and even though my feelings towards Alice were not, and would never be, of a romantic nature, I wished I could have swapped places with him, so that it was me standing in the doorway with my sweetheart, and Nick faced with the long and lonely trudge through the dark to a cold and empty and incredibly uncomfortable bed.

Hell, I would have settled for being in that doorway with my arm around *Nick*.

Then they stepped back inside and shut the door behind them, and darkness fell, leaving me with nothing but the pale oval of light from the torch. It was better than nothing, but as I turned into the lane, even that flickered and died. I considered returning to the house to demand fresh batteries, but the thought of once again having to face Alice's withering gaze was just too discouraging.

So I set off up the lane. The canal gleamed black and slightly sinister in the night, so once again I stuck to the hedgerow. I wondered exactly where it was that Georgina had met with her accident, but then decided I didn't want to think too much about that as I walked alone in the darkness. For this was not the sort of darkness I knew and loved—a fusion of nightclubs and music and neon-lit bars, clubbers and scrubbers and dealers rubbing shoulders on greasy pavements against a backdrop of grumbling traffic. This was real dark, unalleviated by street-lamps or brightly-lit buildings.

As I walked, I had the impression I'd somehow slipped into another dimension where I was the only human being, and where every sound was magnified: the flutter of nocturnal insects circling my head as though it were a light-bulb, a slight rustling in the hedge to my right, the soft tread of my shoes against the surface of the road and the even softer echo just behind me.

I tried to look on the bright side. Didn't everyone say there were advantages to real dark? That you could see the stars, for example? I tipped my head back and walked for a while with my face tilted towards the night sky, trying to make out sights that were normally eclipsed by the bright city lights, though tonight most of them seemed at least partially obscured by cloud. *That* was the Great Bear, or the Saucepan, or was it the Big Dipper? *That* had to be the North Star. Or was it Venus? But then what the hell was *that*? Orion's Belt? Or the Mad Snake?

Uh-oh. The thought of snakes inevitably started a stream of association that ended with Nick's ghastly headboard. I shivered, and not just from the cold night air. *Snakes! Why did it have to be snakes?* It was the one thing I had in common with Indiana Jones; we were both ophiophobes. I tried to draw comfort from the knowledge that there was only one venomous species indigent to the British Isles, that it wasn't very big and that, in the event of my encountering one, it would be even more frightened of me than I of it.

I glanced down anyway, just to make sure I wasn't about to

tread on any stray reptiles, and saw I'd been veering diagonally across the road in the direction of the canal. Not that I was likely to fall in, what with the earthen bank between me and the water, but you never knew; I could be remarkably clumsy at times. Star-gazing was all very well, but it paid to look where you were going.

I walked until I began to lose track of time, until it seemed that my feet had been pounding the same stretch of crumbling macadam for hours on end. It was as though Alice had cast some spiteful curse, condemning me to walk the lane until the end of time. And then, oh joy, my eyes picked out a slight alteration in the sky up ahead. Very faint, barely discernible in fact, but a definite shift in the darkness, like velvet giving way to silk. A reflected glow of light. The sight lifted my spirits and I picked up my pace. Somewhere, a dog began to bark. Little Yawning at last. Five minutes away, at most.

There, that hadn't been so bad. I felt almost cheerful. Somewhere up ahead, somewhere not so very far away, was a pint of Black Monk with my name on it. Maybe even two pints. The thought spurred me on. A couple of pints and I would sleep like a baby, even if that stupid dog continued to bark all night.

That was it then. That was my plan for what remained of the evening. I was nearly there. I started whistling *Balls to the Wall* by Accept and the barking stopped, but before I knew it, the melody had shifted into another key and damn me if it wasn't that tune again, the one that reminded me of the beginning of *Don't Talk to Strangers*. What was it? It was driving me nuts. I whistled that same blasted phrase over and over again, trying to put a title to it.

In retrospect, maybe I shouldn't have repeated it quite so often. Certain musical phrases, I've since realised . . .

I must have been whistling for a few minutes before it dawned on me that I was no longer entirely alone.

I'm not sure what first tipped me off. Maybe the sudden realisation that the insects were gone; normally, their departure would have cheered me up, but now all it did was make me apprehensive. Why had the insects gone? What did they know that I didn't?

The lights of Little Yawning were now positively glowing against the sky up ahead. I walked faster. Any minute now I'd come to that bend. Any minute now.

But the lane stretched on. It seemed longer than before, and straighter than I remembered. I wondered if it was a Roman road. When had I last encountered a bend?

Which is when I made the mistake of looking back.

The figure was about a hundred yards behind me. In a flush of optimism, I hoped it might be Alice or Nick, haring after me to say it was OK, I could stay at Framptons after all. Or maybe—a less welcome but still tolerable prospect—it was one of the surly youths I'd seen hanging around the village. Maybe he'd been tailing me all evening, waiting for an opportunity to pounce and help himself to the thirty pence in loose change in my pocket. Thirty pence and a crumpled tenner and a maxed out credit card. Even supposing it was a mugger, I reckoned I could easily beat him to the bright lights of Little Yawning. I had a healthy head start of at least a hundred yards . . .

I blinked, and looked again and saw with a disagreeable jolt that the distance between us had dwindled. Now it was more like eighty yards. Whoever it was, they were moving fast, but now I saw there was something odd about the movement. It wasn't so much walking as *gliding*, like someone on one of those automatic walkways you get in airports.

Each time I blinked, the distance seemed to diminish.

Now it was seventy yards.

Coming closer.

COMING CLOSER COMING CLOSER

I didn't waste any more time staring. I didn't even stop to think. The terror welling up inside me was primal, a thing born of dark caves and limitless forests and strange shadows shifting beyond the comfort zone of the campfire. I began to run . . .

And ran headfirst into the hedgerow.

In my blind panic, I didn't feel the thorns clawing stripes across my face, but found myself hitched up as securely as if I'd been stuck on a *Texas Chain Saw* meathook. I was forced to sacrifice precious flesh and blood tearing myself free. As I set off again I risked another backward glance, which is when I ascertained beyond all doubt that whoever was behind me was definitely not one of the village delinquents, a last desperate hope to which I'd been clinging. Not unless the village delinquents went in for cross-dressing. Because the figure behind me was clearly wearing a dress, a long dress with long sleeves trailing uneven lengths of cotton, as though the fabric itself were starting to unravel . . .

A dress—*or what's left of a dress after it's been rotting beneath the earth*, said a pesky little voice in my head.

I ordered the voice to shut the fuck up, but it kept pestering me.

Run, it urged. *Run! You don't want it to catch up. You really don't want that to happen . . .*

So I kept running and ignored the other, more reasonable voice, the one that was saying, *So what if she's dead? What can she do? Flap her fraying sleeves in your face?*

It was all very well for the voice to say that, but I didn't know if it was true. The problem was, dead people could do things. They could scare the shit out of you, that much I knew from experience. Maybe they could scare you to *death*. Maybe all they wanted was for you to join them in the cold, damp earth . . .

Sixty, no, fifty yards.

Getting closer. Closer all the time.

I ran and ran, but it was like a nightmare in which the formerly flat ground now seemed to be sloping upward, ever steeper. The faster I ran, the less ground I seemed to cover, until it seemed to me that I was running on the spot while whatever was behind me glided nearer.

I couldn't remember ever having been this scared before. Not when I'd seen Marion Tucker for the very last time, on *Crossroads*, and she hadn't looked so nice, and she'd said things about my father that had turned my blood to ice. Nor even when I'd made the mistake of getting stoned at that party in Archway, in a house where—I found out too late—a serial-killer had once boiled pieces of his victims in a Le Creuset casserole. I hadn't *seen* much that night, but I'd heard and smelled plenty. That had been scary, that had been a *really* bad night.

But it was nothing compared to this.

I had the feeling this was personal.

Another quick look over my shoulder.

Thirty yards.

Coming closer

COMING CLOSER

She was even darker than the surrounding darkness. She was a black hole in the night, an inkblot of nothingness that ate up the light, and life, and laughter, chewed it up and spat it out again as deep-dyed despair. I knew I couldn't let her catch up with me. I knew that would be the end of everything, so I put my head down and kept running, even though my legs now felt like shapeless lumps of lead and my lungs felt as though they were being ripped apart and my heartbeat was skittering all over the place like a skinny dog on a frozen lake. But I ran, because I didn't have a choice.

And then—praise be to the God I didn't believe in—I finally came to that famous last bend, the bend that I knew would lead to safety, and I tore round it like an Olympic sprinter on steroids, and there, *there!* was the first of the local authority housing, windows lit up and a white Ford Fiesta in the driveway and light spilling out and WELCOME TO LITTLE YAWNING at the side of the road.

As soon as I clapped eyes on the sign I stopped running. I had to stop, I was all run out. I leant forward, bending almost double, trying to suck great draughts of air into lungs that had long since thrown in the towel and were now twitching feebly, like punctured balloon animals. I was dimly aware of a hideous wheezing coming from somewhere in my chest.

It seemed to me that long minutes ticked away, and after I'd recovered some semblance of breath I turned back to see if she was still there.

She was still there, all right.

She was right on top of me.

THIRTEEN

T HEY SAY that fear, *real* fear, is primarily fear of the unknown, of amorphous possibility, of things that *might* or *could* happen, and that as soon as something takes tangible form, as soon as reality takes over from your imagination, it loses its power.

Well, they're wrong.

This was a thousand times worse than anything I could have imagined.

She swooped down on me like a cruel-beaked kestrel lunging on a fieldmouse, hands stiffened into claws, fingernails yellow and broken, her mouth stretched open in a scream so shrill I could never afterwards be sure that I'd actually heard it so much as felt it through my molars, and I was transfixed, unable to move. In that instant I had a glimpse of black holes where there should have been eyes and pale skin like rotting parchment and lips peeled back to reveal a blackened tongue and oesophagus and the skeletal vault of a throat that yawned impossibly wide, threatening to swallow me up, and I felt a strip of tattered cloth brush across my face and a blast of air so fetid that I couldn't breathe and I think my heart stopped, *actually stopped*, and my mouth was flooded with poisonous ink and I tried to close my eyes but couldn't, it was as though the lids were glued open so I was forced to look into that abomination of a face, only it wasn't a face any more, and I remembering actually wishing I could pass out and that this was it, this was Hell . . .

. . . and then—*blam!* Hell was split down the middle by a dazzling beam of light and the ear-splitting blare of a custom-ised klaxon. *Do Ya Think I'm Sexy?* unless I was very much mistaken, and the very sound of heaven to ears still echoing with the shriek of death.

I managed to wrench myself free from whatever spectral glue had nailed me to the tarmac and hurled myself to one side as the car flashed past, so close I was buffeted by its slipstream. I caught a glimpse of a fleshy neck hunched over in the driver's seat. He wasn't even watching the road. To judge by the medley of rock, folk and metal, he was trying to tune into a radio station. It was sheer good luck he hadn't ploughed into me.

The driver finally found the station he'd been searching for, and accelerated into the darkness, trailing tepid U2 behind him. I turned my head to follow his progress and just for an instant glimpsed the beam from his headlights connecting with a rippling black shadow in the road. It was there and then it was gone, and the headlights had swept on, and then they were already half a mile away, and all was calm.

All except my stomach, that is. I lurched towards the hedge, and Alice's supper—chicken, mashed potato and ghastly sucking cheese—came spurting out of me in three long and increasingly painful torrents of steaming lava.

Afterwards, I turned weakly to stagger the rest of the distance into Little Yawning. My ears were ringing as though I'd spent the last three hours pressed up against the speakers at an Iron Maiden concert, and my legs felt as though they'd been fractured in several places and then reset, badly, but I made it as far as the birdshit-spattered bench on the village green.

As I sat there, head in hands, trying to gather my wits, three of the local delinquents rolled up and called me a wanker, possibly as a prelude to kicking the shit out of me. But when I raised my head and they saw my face they backed off in a hurry.

Eventually I stopped trembling and became aware not just of the vile taste in my mouth that wasn't just attributable to vomit but also to a raging thirst. My trousers seemed to have adhered to the bench so I had to peel myself off to negotiate the short distance to The Stumps.

I made it just in time; the tattooed barman was calling last orders. I ordered two pints of Black Monk and then, as an afterthought, shelled out for a bottle of cheap Cabernet as well. I yearned for oblivion, but wasn't too sure how to achieve it short of banging my head against a wall until I lost consciousness.

I installed myself on a stool at the shadowy end of the bar. The barman watched curiously as I drained the first of the glasses in one gulp.

"Expecting company?" he asked. His voice seemed to come from a long, long way away.

"Lord, no!" I laughed bitterly. "I've had more than enough company for one evening, thanks very much."

The barman wasn't put off. "You're staying upstairs, ain't ya."

"Not for long," I muttered.

"Come again?" The barman leaned forward. I couldn't place his accent, but it seemed to have originated somewhere in the Midlands.

I shifted sideways to avoid his gaze, but only succeeded in moving into a round patch of light cast by one of the spots in the ceiling. The barman let out a loud whistle. "Your face is bleeding!"

I sensed a stir in the room behind me. Gingerly I touched my face, wincing as my brain registered several raw stripes of pain across my left cheek. There was blood on my fingers. "Bumped into the hedge back there."

"Back there . . ." The barman's eyes narrowed as the penny dropped. "Ooh, you *didn't*."

I was still busy mapping the pain, so he tried again. "You came up from Framptons, didn't ya?"

Once again I failed to respond, which only confirmed his suspicions. He bobbed down behind the bar and came up with a couple of paper napkins and a bottle of TCP. I soaked one of the napkins in antiseptic and dabbed blindly at the scratches, wincing like a wuss and trying not to worry about the tetanus germs I had no doubt were already burrowing like evil little moles into my torn and bloodied flesh.

As I dabbed, the barman searched my expression for further clues. "You didn't . . . *walk?*"

I couldn't be bothered to reply to that one either, but he seemed to be making up some sort of picture all on his own.

"Bloody hell! You *walked?* You walked up *Fegs Lane? After dark?*"

There was an outbreak of twittering behind me. *The blighter walked.* This time I turned round and saw the cluster of pensioners ranged around the tables behind me, ears flapping like African elephants' as they eavesdropped shamelessly. This was just great. Rhubarbing yokels in horror movies always warned the ignorant traveller not to go near Dracula's Castle before he'd set out for it. I'd somehow stumbled across the only set of villagers so retarded they issued the warning after the event. They'd all seen me in that bar earlier on, and clearly I'd made an impression. Why the devil hadn't anyone said anything then? There should have been notices pinned up: FEGS LANE AFTER DARK—NOT A GOOD IDEA.

The barman was shaking his head. "You walked that road on your own." He couldn't seem to get over it. Normally I wouldn't have given him the time of day, but in my current state I welcomed any sort of human interaction, however inane.

I snapped. "Well, I wasn't on my own, was I."

The barman clapped his hands together. "Black Shuck! I knew it!"

"Black . . .?"

"Shuck! The Devil Dog!"

"Oh, for God's sake . . ."

"Black Shuck takes many forms," said the barman, leering like a child-molesting raconteur at a Halloween bonfire party. "Usually a hound, but sometimes a cow . . ."

I lost patience. "Well, unless it also takes the shape of a dead woman, I'm not interested."

"A woman?" The barman wrinkled his brow. "First time I've heard that one."

"Whatever it was," I muttered to myself, "it scared the shit out of me."

Unfortunately, thanks to the ringing in my ears, my muttering came out rather louder than I'd intended, and the barman heard. His gaze dropped to my trousers as though he were expecting to see the stains. "You were so scared you wet yourself."

Too late, I remembered the sticky stuff on the bench. "It's not what you think. I sat in something."

"I won't tell," he grinned.

"*I did not wet myself!*" I said. "Some asshole spilled something all over your bloody village bench, and I sat in it, didn't I."

I explored the dark patch with my fingers. They came up red and sticky.

"My God," breathed the barman. "*Blood.*"

"It is *not* blood," I said crossly, sniffing my fingers and then offering them to him so he could do likewise. He declined with a convulsive shake of the head. "It's Cherry Zinger or Raspberry Beezer or some other brand of tooth-rotting pop."

The barman couldn't have been less interested in which brand of fizzy drink I'd sat in. All of a sudden he drew himself up to his full height and started reciting in a doomy voice. "Like one along a lonesome road that walks in fear and dread, And having once turned round walks on, and turns no more his head, Because he knows . . ."

"That's enough." That poem had always given me the creeps.

"A frightful fiend . . ."

"That's *enough!*"

" . . . doth close behind him tread. Coleridge."

"I *know* it's Coleridge," I snapped, irritated beyond measure by the idea of a rural bartender thinking he could give me lessons in culture.

"It was his lordship's bit on the side left that book of poems behind."

"By his lordship you mean . . .?"

"Fitch, yeah. I'm being ironic. We provincials do like to use a bit of irony now and again."

"When you say his *bit on the side . . .?*"

"Posh bint with big feet."

"She's *not* his *bit on the side.* She's his *fiancée.*"

"Whatever. She was here every other weekend. Same room you're in now. Hardly ever came downstairs, of course . . ."

"She stayed *here?*" I couldn't imagine Alice hanging out in The Stumps, though, come to think of it, hadn't she told me it wasn't so bad? How would she know if she hadn't actually stayed here?

Then again, it *was* that bad, so she obviously knew nothing.

"Waiting until the coast was clear, I reckon."

"Well, the coast is clear now," I said. "They're getting married on Saturday."

The barman nodded. "Yeah, heard he was getting hitched again. Just goes to show it pays to hang on in there. All things come to those who wait, and heaven knows she's waited long enough."

"Not as long as all that."

"Nah, years."

I wasn't sure I'd heard right. "You're saying Alice has been coming to Little Yawning for *years?*"

"That her name? Alice? Yeah, she was getting it on with old wanky-pants. Every other weekend, right under the wife's nose."

"I think you're wrong," I said, remembering what Nick had said about Alice a few hours earlier. "She's not that kind of girl."

The barman snorted. "Could have fooled me. She would be in that room upstairs, the one where you are now, and his lordship would pop in and go straight upstairs without so much as a hello, how are you and I'll have half a pint of bitter, no manners at all. Couple of hours later, he'd go straight out, never saying a word to anyone, but you had to be blind not to see what was going on. Snotty-nosed git."

So was Alice a virgin or wasn't she? I tried to think back. Had Nick actually *said* she was a virgin? Or had I simply jumped to conclusions? After all, you didn't find many women of her age who had never had sexual intercourse, unless of course they were nuns. But what about all that bullshit she'd given me about having met Nick at a dinner party six months ago? All that crap about the whirlwind romance? But I'd suspected straightaway that was bollocks. And I could imagine her not wanting to tell me she'd been having an affair with Nick while his first wife was still alive. It wasn't the sort of thing that nice girls got up to.

Or maybe she wasn't such a nice girl.

"He was an idiot to treat his wife like that," the barman went on, warming to his theme. "Lovely lady, she was, lovely. Bloody awful driver, though. Nearly knocked *me* over once or twice. Can't say I was totally surprised when I heard what happened. But it was a crying shame."

I saw my chance and grabbed it. "What *did* happen?"

"You don't know?"

"Would I be asking if I knew?"

He shrugged. "Guess not. She crashed into the canal."

"How come?" I asked.

"Odd thing." The barman shrugged. "No other traffic. No reason to go off the road like that."

"She crashed into the canal," I repeated dazedly, picturing the earthen bank and wondering what kind of speed a car would have to be going in order to jump it. "You think it wasn't an accident?"

The barman lowered his voice. "Of course Fitch wasn't around when it happened. He'd fixed himself up with the perfect alibi, but there were rumours he'd tampered with the brakes, that sort of thing. Not that faulty brakes would be enough to take you over the bank."

I looked him directly in the eyes. "What do you think?"

"I think she was going too fast. *Way* too fast, like she thought she was on a motorway or something. Maybe she fainted and her foot got stuck on the accelerator. Maybe she swerved to avoid an animal. Maybe she ran into *Black Shuck*."

"Oh do shut up about Black Shuck." I thought about Georgina, all alone in that big empty house. "Had she been drinking?"

"Definitely." He leant forward conspiratorially. "But personally, I reckon she was running away."

"Leaving Nick?"

"Yeah, I reckon she'd had it up to here with him. The way he treated her . . . She wasn't a doormat, you know. She wasn't stupid. It was obvious she adored him at the beginning but, I dunno, there was probably a tipping point when his behaviour got too much and she decided she wasn't going to put up with it any more."

"But then why would she have been in a nightdress?"

"Oh, so you *do* know about it," said the barman, but I ignored him.

"Was there any sign she'd packed a suitcase to take with her, something like that?"

"Not that I know of," said the barman.

My brain was going into overdrive. "Could someone have been trying to stop her from leaving? Or might they have been chasing her?"

"Someone," said the barman, "or some*thing*. Black Shuck, the hell hound . . ."

"Will you please stop this hell hound nonsense."

He stopped, and looked at me, and said, "I'll stop if you tell me what happened out there tonight?"

"Wouldn't dream of it."

The barman held out his hand. "Name's Clint, by the way."

Numbly, I shook it.

"Go ahead," I said glumly. "Make my day."

IN ORDER to postpone the dreaded moment when I would finally be left on my own, forced to face up to whatever it was that had happened to me, I spent most of the night playing at being drinking buddies with Clint. He locked the pub doors and we polished off my bottle of Cabernet and a large part of what he maintained was his personal collection of Single Malt, and we talked and talked, and I probably told him more than I should have done, though since he seemed even drunker than me, I was fairly confident he wouldn't be able to remember too much of it afterwards, and anyway the prospect of him hooking up with one of Nick's set and spilling the beans was about as likely as Crystal Palace winning the Premiership.

Besides, he turned out to be a metal fan, so we spent at least half an hour exchanging fond memories and reenacting highlights from *The Last in Line* video, which led naturally into the subject of *Don't Talk to Strangers* and the tune that kept bugging me, the one I'd been whistling in the lane shortly before . . . but I didn't want to think about that. Not while I was still so close. Not until there were a hundred miles between me and the spot where it had happened.

All the same, I hummed the tune for Clint.

He stared at me as though I were stupid. "*Don't Talk to Strangers!*"

"I just told you," I said, exasperated, "it only *sounds* like

Don't Talk to Strangers."

I hummed it again. "Listen, it goes off on a tangent . . ."

Clint was concentrating so intently, one of the blood vessels in his temple began to throb so hard I feared it might burst. "Run that by me again," he said.

So I started to hum the tune again, but this time broke off before I'd finished because the air in the bar was starting to feel oppressive and the light flickered and it seemed to me there was a branch or something scratching at one of the shuttered windows . . .

Luckily for me, Clint killed the deepening mood by breaking in with, "I know what that is! It's an old folk song!"

"Are you sure?" I asked sceptically.

"It's some old wives' tale about meeting the Devil," said Clint, making Dio's horned devil sign with his fingers.

The Devil. Great. Just what I needed to round off the perfect evening. Not that I believed in the Devil, of course.

"Does it have words?"

"I imagine so," said Clint. "Just don't ask me what they are. I'm not from around these parts, as you may have noticed. I prefer the Van Halen version."

And he began to yodel, "*Aaaagh! Runnin with the Devil! Aaagh-haa, yeah! Whoo-hoooo!*"

It curdled my blood all right, but for aesthetic rather than diabolical reasons, and I forgot all about the tapping branch, and began to list out loud all the reasons why Ronnie James Dio was a far, far better vocalist than either David Lee Roth or Sammy Hagar.

MY DRINKING session with Clint had the desired effect: as soon as my head hit the pillow, I was out like a light. The main problem was that I was woken by a dog barking—doubtless the same dog I'd heard earlier—only a couple of hours later.

I opened my eyes, feeling as though I'd only just closed them, and wondered why I felt so battered and exhausted. It wasn't just the late night; it took me a few moments to remember *a)* where I was and *b)* what had happened in the lane. Oh and *c)* Alice had lied to me.

Christ, yes—everything was completely different now; I could no longer take refuge in denial. What I wanted, what I really wanted, was to take refuge in some far flung place where neither Alice and Georgina could find me—Buenos Aires, maybe, or Brisbane.

I lay and listened to the barking dog for a while, cursing the owner who had tethered it to a gatepost or whatever negligent dog-owners did to make their animals bark that much, and finally decided it was time to get up, more or less. I slid out of bed and into my clothes, feeling about as refreshed as an unwashed sock, and went downstairs to settle up with the hunchbacked crone. Much to my surprise, I found I'd run up quite a tab; evidently the Single Malt we'd been drinking hadn't belonged to Clint after all.

The night's carousing hadn't done much to alleviate the head-cold that was rapidly gaining ascendency over my system; my nose was packed with solidified mucus and the nether side of my brainpan was being systematically pummelled by armies of Wagnerian narns swinging large mallets. Naturally the village didn't boast anything as sophisticated as a pharmacy, though I daresay Ronnie the Grocer stocked some sort of primitive paracetamol. Ronnie the Grocer had yet to open for business, however, and I had no intention of hanging around in Little Yawning any longer than necessary, but there was one more thing I wanted to check up on before hitting the road.

IN THE misty morning light, the village green looked almost picturesque, the sort of thing you might see on a postcard of Ye Olde Englande, with nary a trace of can-kicking delinquent, so I used up some of the remaining exposures on my disposable camera, then snapped the outside of The Stumps, as well as the front of Sally's Teashop, where some of the locals seemed to be breakfasting on bacon and eggs.

I salivated a little over the idea of a fry-up, though when I pressed my face up to the glass for a closer look, the tuck didn't look quite so appetising—actually it looked like pigswill—so I decided to give it a miss. Otherwise the village seemed deserted, so I walked quickly to the end of the parade of shops and, when

I was sure the coast was clear, ducked round the corner.

I found myself in a sordid little cul-de-sac chock-full of rubbish bins overflowing with varicoloured plastic bags, most of which appeared to have been eviscerated by cats. So much for Ye Olde Englande.

Using one of the bins as a rudimentary step-ladder, I hauled myself over a brick wall and landed in a grubby concrete no-man's-land between the back of the shops and a row of makeshift garages cobbled together from corrugated iron and plastic sheeting. Still no sign of intelligent life, so I wrenched open what I took to be the back door to the bookshop and found myself confronted by a wall of tinned vegetables.

Shit, I'd hit Ronnie the Grocer's by mistake.

Maybe I should have gone in and hunted around for that paracetamol, but instead I backtracked to what, this time, had to be Yawning Pages. The door wasn't locked but the jamb was so swollen by damp it yielded only after protracted and noisy kicking and (after I'd twisted my knee doing the kicking) loud cursing.

I took another look around, but the only witness was a stout ginger tom eyeing me from several walls away, so I stepped inside, crossed a storeroom-cum-office and pushed through a heavy curtain of malodorous velour into the main body of the shop.

The weak morning light filtering through the smeary front window was barely enough for me to see my way around. It was a strain even to read the titles near the back of the shop, but I didn't dare switch on the lights. So it was only after much shin-barking and inhaling of ancient dust that I finally located what I'd come for.

Old Egbert's Almanac of Eerie Things.

I carried it over to the front window, the brittle binding leaving shreds of old red leather on my fingers. Who exactly was Old Egbert, I wondered as I leafed through fragile pages that threatened to disintegrate as I turned them.

Oh yes. Here it was. This time I kept reading, even though the effort once again threatened to give me a serious migraine.

FITCH. Old Norfolk family with a bloodline dating back to pre-Norman times. Tobias Fitch (1710-1765) one of the co-founders of The Sulfur (occasionally spelt Soul Fire) Society, said to have rivalled the notorious Hellfire Club in its depraved amorality.

First reports of the so-called FITCH CURSE *appear in Little Yawning parish records during the latter half of the sixteenth century, but the unusually high mortality rate amongst females marrying into the bloodline is now thought to have its origins in the unhygienic pregnancy and childbirth rituals once commonly practised in this part of the country, sometimes involving the sacrifice of wild animals, birds or snakes . . .*

I had a sudden thought and turned to the title page. There it was in black and white, in loopy, sinuous, almost childish handwriting.

A signature. *Georgina Rossiter.*

Rossiter? I vaguely recalled having seen the name on Georgina's tombstone, as in 'beloved daughter of Ralph and Jacinta'. So this must have been one of the things Nick had got rid of after her death.

Numbly, I slid the book back into place on the shelf before having second thoughts, pulling it out again and tucking it into my bag. Hell, I needed it more than the proprietor of Yawning Pages—or any of his other customers, come to that. It was blindingly obvious that from now on I would be needing all the help I could get.

I half expected burglar alarms to go off as I passed through the back door, but they didn't.

I WAS FORLORNLY examining the timetable at the bus-stop (a bus could apparently be glimpsed passing through the village at 14h05 on alternate Mondays and Thursdays) when an ancient Golf pulled up alongside me, and an old geezer with iron-grey hair peered out.

"Want a lift?"

I recognised one of the pensioners from the pub. I didn't

bother to ask where he was going—it was all too clear that just about anywhere would be better than Little Yawning—but climbed gratefully into the passenger seat.

"Arnold Huffington," said the pensioner as he somehow managed to change noisily into second and then third gear while at the same time offering his hand for me to shake. He peered at me through gimlet eyes, though I would have felt more comfortable had he been directing them at the road ahead. "You're a detective, aren't you?"

"Um," I said, taken aback. "Kind of. Um, have you, er, seen that . . ."

"I can tell," said Arnold, narrowly avoiding, as much by blind chance as anything, a large woolly dog that was padding lazily across the road. I wondered whether it was the one that had woken me up, but it looked too laid back to be much of a barker.

"Used to be a copper myself," Arnold added.

I glanced guiltily downward, to where a corner of *Old Egbert's Almanac* was visible through the unzipped opening of my bag. He couldn't possibly know I was a shoplifter. Or could he? Had the offer of a lift been a set-up? Was he planning to drive me directly to the police station?

Arnold was still staring at me. "Someone go at you with a razor?"

I forced myself to ignore the bag at my feet. "Walked into a hedge." I fixed my eyes on the road, as though I might be able to make Arnold follow my gaze through willpower alone.

"Oh yeah, you were the one came up from Framptons last night."

It was obvious he'd overheard every last thing I'd said to Clint. But I also had the impression that he was sharper than he looked. Which was just as well, since he looked like a slack-jawed retard who should never have been allowed behind a steering wheel.

I sighed and decided that if I were going to die in a car accident, I should at least go out while attempting valiantly to do my job. So I asked, "Do you remember Georgina Fitch's death?"

"Course I remember. I was one of them that helped fish her out. Funny thing, her eyes were wide open, and so was her mouth. Like she'd had a surprise, or something. And it wasn't a nice surprise, neither. Never saw a look like that in all my years on the force, and I've seen some things." He seemed keen to itemise them, and it was with some difficulty that I steered our conversation back on course.

"Probably could have got out if she'd kept her head," he said. "You have to wait for the water to rise, you know, before you can open the door; no good trying when all the pressure's bearing in on you. She probably panicked. Most people do, you know."

"Yeah, well so would you if you were trapped in a sinking car," I said.

"Matter of fact, it did happen to me once, when I was younger, and I didn't panic at all," he said. "Mate of mine downed a few too many whiskeys and we ended up in a harbour. I got out, and then I dived back in and got him out as well."

I looked at Arnold Huffington with new respect, concluding he had to be blessed with some miraculous survival gene. Maybe I wasn't going to die in a road accident after all.

"Perhaps Georgina banged her head," I suggested.

He scratched his head noisily. "Verdict wasn't drowning, in fact. Coroner said it was anna . . . phil . . ."

"Anaphylaxis?" I suggested. Acute allergic reaction leading to potentially fatal restriction of the airways.

"I reckon."

"And Tubby Clegg?"

"Funny you should say that. He had the exact same expression when we found him."

"I thought he shot himself in the face?"

"That he did. But there was still enough left to piece his expression together, if you get what I mean." He shook his head. "Tripped and blew his own head off. That was Tubby Clegg all over—what you might call a hopeless case. Though of course if you talk to his son, he was a blinking hero. Charlie maintains his dad tried to save Georgina Fitch, not burgle her. He was taking a slash in the lane when he heard her go in. Jumped straight in after her."

"He jumped into the canal?" I said, impressed despite myself.

"Yeah, but according to Charlie, he couldn't get her out, cause of what was in the car with her."

I sat up. "What was it?"

Arnold shook his head. He wasn't going to be drawn. "Depends who you're talking to."

"What did Clegg say? Or his son?"

"According to Charlie his dad said it wasn't a person. Was a *thing*. An animal."

I felt my scalp prickling. I wasn't sure I would have described the creature I'd seen in the lane as an animal, but it sure as hell hadn't been human.

"What did it look like? Was it wearing a dress?"

Arnold shook his head. "Charlie seemed to think it was Black Shuck. But then Charlie's always been a few skittles short. According to Charlie, his father had seen something he wasn't supposed to see, and after that he was scared shitless, said he was being followed, though if anything was following him it was pink elephants, if you get my drift. According to Charlie, of course, they whacked him."

"The pink elephants?"

"God knows. The FBI, probably. Or the RSPBC. Tubby did a roaring trade in rare birds' eggs, and I suspect he was single-handedly responsible for killing off all the adders in the region. Wore their skins on his hat. He was always on our list, but he knew his way around. We never could catch him red-handed."

Single-handedly responsible for killing off all the adders in the region?

At least that was one thing less I had to worry about. I offered a silent prayer of thanks to Tubby Clegg, wherever he was now.

FOURTEEN

ARNOLD HUFFINGTON dropped me by the main road, from where I hitched to the nearest railway station to catch a southbound train. It wasn't easy; drivers were reluctant to stop and pick up a hiker who looked as though he'd gone *mano a mano* against Freddy Krueger and his razor-fingered glove.

Merely getting to the station took the better part of two hours, and then I had to change trains twice before finally alighting on one that went within shunting distance of King's Cross. But the further I got from Little Yawning, the more my mood lightened, as though I had managed to shrug off all the heavy stuff and leave it behind in the village. Now I'd seen Georgina up close and personal, the worst was surely over. London welcomed me back with open arms, I embraced the city in return and, by the time I reached the barge, I was feeling almost euphoric.

That in itself should have been enough to tip me off that something was not right. As it was, I was a little upset by Boris' behaviour. Normally when I came back from somewhere he would be all over me, miaowing and threading himself around my ankles. This time, though, he gave me a wide berth, and only deigned to touch his food when I'd retreated to a safe distance from the feeding bowl. I spent twenty minutes trying unsuccessfully to coax him out of his sulk before giving up and striking out for Cyber-Bites.

This time I knew exactly what I was looking for, and found it without too much difficulty. After that I made a lot of calls on my mobile—calls to old friends, contacts, people who owed me favours—which is how I ended up knowing a number of things about Alice Marchmont that left me feeling rather cross and incredibly stupid.

Finally I headed west, to a lesser known branch of the Royal Borough of Kensington & Chelsea library, to plug some gaps that the internet just couldn't fill. I spent a couple of hours rummaging through the archives, a slow and frustratingly lo-tech process since little of it had been computerised or even recorded on file in the old-fashioned way.

Eventually I managed to track down a clutch of Fitch-related items in the society pages: pictures of Nick's mother and grandmother as beaming debutantes, pictures of Nick's rakish-looking father and even more rakish-looking grandfather accompanied by medleys of glamorous women who were clearly not their wives. Berkeley Square, Monte Carlo, Cape Town: it was another world.

Even the causes of death were exotic; Nick's mother had perished in a yachting accident, his stepmother had drowned in the swimming-pool of an Etruscan villa belonging to an Italian aristocrat, and his grandmother had succumbed to a lethal combination of too many Martinis, a gentleman friend's Hispano Suiza and an inconveniently sited clifftop.

There had been a lot of untimely death in the Fitch family, though like many nobs they did seem to invite catastrophe by leading peculiarly reckless lives. For example, I found that Nick had had an uncle called Lucas who had shuffled off his mortal coil approximately three and a half minutes after having been stung on the eyelid by a large winged insect while on an expedition for some mythical cancer-curing herb. Well, what did he expect? That would teach him to go trekking through the Amazon jungle.

But where was all this getting me? I spread the photocopies I had made all over the desk and stared at them, as though they were pieces of a jigsaw. The problem was slotting them all together to form the Big Picture. I continued to search until the dusty silence of the library was disrupted when my mobile, even though it was supposed to be in discreet mode, started throbbing so stridently in my pocket that heads turned disapprovingly in my direction.

I scooted outside to answer. It was Nick.

"Got back all right, then?"

Was it my imagination, or was he expecting me to say *no*?

"Actually, it was easier than I expected. You?"

"Just got in." He sounded breathless, as though he'd run all the way back from Norfolk. "You got plans?"

"Depends," I said cautiously.

He proposed an early evening game of squash. Apparently his designated partner had dropped out at the last minute, leaving him with a court and no opponent.

"I don't know." I saw in my mind's eye the pile of fiches that still had to be sifted through. Plus there was the considerable thought I needed to apply to the events of the past twenty-four hours, but which I kept postponing, because I knew the process would make me break out in a terrified sweat. Plus I needed to have a serious talk with Alice. "I've got a lot on my plate right now."

"Come *on*," said Nick. "All work and no play, you know? You can take a couple of hours off, can't you? Humour me, John, wedding's looming and I'm a bag of nerves."

He didn't sound like a bag of nerves to me. In fact, if anyone was a bag of nerves, it was me. I mumbled that I had no time to go home and get my kit, but he assured me it wouldn't be necessary; he could lend me a T-shirt, an old pair of jogging pants and some socks, and the club kept a selection of old plimsolls on hand for occasions such as these.

It was a done deal. Nick made me feel as though his life wouldn't be complete unless I agreed to play squash with him. I felt steamrollered into doing something I didn't really feel like doing, but decided to make the best of it; at least it would provide me with another opportunity to question him about his wretched family.

I checked my watch. There was just time to run one more errand before setting out for the torture chambers of Fizz Eek. I went back inside and tidied my desk and handed the fiches back to the librarian. He looked at me as though I was one of the Kray twins, but by this point I was getting used to people flinching when they saw my face.

"Can I just ask you," I said. "This mark here . . ."

I pointed to an indecipherable squiggle next to an entry on

one of the file cards.

"That means we don't have it," the man behind the desk hissed in his special librarian's whisper.

"Then why the hell is it listed in the first place?"

The librarian lent across the desk towards me to give the impression he was raising his voice, though it was still that same soft and even pitch. "It means we did have it, but it's gone missing. Misplaced, or stolen."

"I see," I said. "Thank you."

I wondered who would want to steal information on The Sulfur Society, and why.

GINNY HAD told me Jeremy worked in a shop just off Portobello Road. What she hadn't told me was that he *owned* the shop.

To someone like me, who didn't get out very often, it was an Aladdin's Cave crammed with carved coffee tables, sequinned cushion covers and chuckling soapstone Buddhas that Jeremy obviously snapped up for a couple of rupees and then sold on to wealthy Trustafarians at a two zillion per cent profit. The air was thick with the smell of rip-off and sandalwood. A dozen or so customers, mostly couples, were milling around as though they had nothing better to do on a weekday afternoon, examining the outrageous price tags with unfathomable expressions.

I recognised Jeremy straightaway, and gave him the chance to acknowledge that he recognised me back by greeting him with, "Haven't we met somewhere before?" The Landrace Inn was one of his local bars; he'd had every right to be drinking in there on a Sunday night, with or without anxious-looking brunettes, though I was curious as to why he'd been staring at me the night I'd been in there with Graham and Isabella.

To my surprise, he shook his head. "No. But hey, I do feel as though we're old friends. Nicky's barely stopped talking about you."

That still didn't explain why he should have been staring at me, nor why he was now acting as though he'd never laid eyes on me before. The scratches across my face were a new addition, admittedly, but it wasn't as though I would need to replace the photo in my passport, which I remembered now, was still in my pocket and needed to be safely stowed.

He proffered his hand. "I won't shake," I said, backing away and nearly knocking over a tin incense holder. "I think I'm coming down with flu."

It was true I was sounding even more bunged-up than ever, but Jeremy kept coming and fearlessly crushed my fingers in a pincer-like grip. "I've been dying to meet you."

I studied his expression warily, but it seemed he wasn't being ironic. Maybe, with Jeremy, what you saw was what you got. A *does what it says on the tin* kind of guy. Pleasant-looking, with big jowls and crinkly wayward hair that had a mind of its own. Shabby corduroy suit. A tan that seemed slightly incongruous, because the rest of him was so English. He reminded me of a comfy old sofa, or a much loved and somewhat battered teddy-bear.

He ushered me into what he called his 'office', but which turned out to be a small windowless area that doubled as a stockroom. He invited me to take a seat while he poured generous slugs of rum into a couple of waxed paper cups, even though it was barely three o'clock in the afternoon. "Medicine," he said, "To fend off your flu."

My kind of guy. In fact, one of the most amiable fellows I'd ever encountered, though he did have a disconcerting habit of reacting to things I said by raising one eyebrow. "Are you sure we haven't met before?" I persisted, giving him another chance to come clean. "Last Friday, perhaps? Selina and Jolly's bash?"

He shook his head "I was in Goa. Only got back Saturday."

"Very nice," I said. "Holiday?"

"Nah, hunting and gathering." He nodded back towards the shop. "Emporium's a hungry beast. Needs constant feeding."

"You must travel a lot," I said.

He scrunched up his face in a quasi-comical manner.

"Ye-e-es. But quite frankly it's a colossal bore. Only a few more years of this drudgery, and I'll be able to flog the wretched business and retire. Then I can collect cars, breed Arabs, something droll like that." It took me a few beats to realise he was talking about horses, not people.

He made importing furniture sound so easy. I couldn't

understand why I hadn't thought of it, except I'd never travelled further than Western Europe, had never been in an aeroplane without picking up with some sort of virus, and broke out in a rash at the very thought of *India*, where death lurked around every corner in the shape of king cobras and pneumonic plague and dodgy vindaloo. In a perfect world I would have stayed at home, sealed into a germ-proof chamber, eating tinned tuna with sterilised cutlery. Sometimes I felt as though I had a lot in common with Howard Hughes, though obviously not the money.

I took another sip of the rum and felt it zipping through my system like a magic bullet.

"One of my assistants comes in, just pretend it's tea," said Jeremy. "Now, what can I do for you?"

What *could* he do for me? Caught off balance, I found my gaze alighting on a stack of carved teak coffee tables. "Just trying to pick up a few ideas for a wedding present." Not bad, and even partially true. "One of those, for example."

Jeremy raised his eyebrow and lowered his voice, though the nearest customers were well out of earshot. "Good grief, you think Nick would stand for tack like that? This junk is for cheap suckers who want to give the impression of being well travelled but can't be arsed to go further than the end of their street."

I felt chastened, though personally didn't think the table was so bad. I wondered whether the happy couple might appreciate a complete set of Proust instead. Even if Alice never got round to reading it, it would look cool on the shelf between Dickens and Puccini.

I lobbed the ball back into Jeremy's court with, "What kind of gift do you reckon, then?"

He snorted. "Tricky, very tricky. Everything you think Nick might like, he already has. Though I know there are a couple of things he wishes he *didn't* have."

"Like what?"

"Family obligations." Jeremy shrugged. "The house."

"Expensive place to run," I said.

"Oh, not so much the expense," Jeremy said. "It's like the Emporium. Needs constant feeding."

I assumed he was speaking metaphorically. "How long have you and Nick known each other?"

"Alice didn't tell you?" He shot me a meaningful glance, though the actual meaning of it escaped me. "Seems like I've known him for ever. I just can't imagine *not* knowing him, you know?"

I nodded sagely.

"I once dropped his guinea-pig out of an upstairs window, but he didn't seem to mind, which was pukka. Another time, I whacked him in the face with a French window. Accident, of course. The glass shattered and cut his lip and there was blood everywhere. You've seen the scar?"

I couldn't remember having seen any scars, not on Nick's face nor anywhere else, but nodded anyway. Jeremy was now looking at me so searchingly that I began to wonder if he was testing me, or maybe he was just wondering what had happened to my face.

Or maybe there was no scar . . .

"I don't know about the scar," I said brightly. "But I've seen his tattoo."

The eyebrow went up again. "Tattoo?"

"Skull against a backdrop of flames."

"You mean like this?" Jeremy rolled up his sleeve and gave me an eyeful of his inside arm. Skull and flames. The exact same tattoo as Nick's.

I chuckled. It seemed like the thing to do.

"What is this? Some sort of club?"

I was closer than I realised.

"We go way back," Jeremy offered, as though that were explanation enough. "Quaffed rather too much ale one evening. I'm sure you know the sort of thing."

He gave me another meaningful look, though this time I grasped the meaning all too well. But how did he know about my drinking? And the name etched into my backside? It wasn't hard to work out why I'd ended up with that. I wondered what kind of crazy drunken thought process would have resulted in skulls and flames.

There was a pregnant pause before Jeremy added, "And you?

How far back do *you* go?"

"I'm more Alice's friend than Nick's."

"Of course."

He seemed to be waiting for me to go on so I added, "We used to step out together." Might as well stick to the same old lie.

Jeremy chuckled. "Step out. Now there's a quaint old-fashioned term. But how sweet you stayed in touch. That's very unusual."

"I guess I do still carry a torch for her."

I thought this sounded convincing, particularly because I was sure that if I *had* stepped out with Alice, I *would* still be carrying a torch for her, the way I continued to schlep around a bloody great blazing brand for Kate, but now I could see there was something wrong with Jeremy's smile. It was going on too long, and there no longer seemed to be any warmth in it. Alarm bells should have been ringing in my head, but all of a sudden I was preoccupied with strange, unfamiliar emotions; my imagination was busily whipping up such a giddy past relationship for Alice and myself that I started to feel almost wistful it wasn't true.

"Of course the flame's gone out," I said, still pumping that torch metaphor for all it was worth. "But the wick's still smouldering, as it were."

An eyebrow shot up. "Is it, now?"

Maybe wick wasn't the best word to use, in the circumstances.

"But I'm so glad she's found Nick," I added hurriedly. "She seems really happy."

"Of course she's happy," Jeremy said. "It's a match made in heaven. Like Fred Astaire and Ginger Rogers. He gives her class, and she gives him . . . Well, I'm not entirely sure, but I daresay she's bringing *something* to the party."

I was startled by his lack of gallantry, but he went on, "No, I have to say Nick was lucky to find her. Girls like Alice are jolly hard to come by these days. We had to search high and low."

He smiled again, and this time there was no mistaking the malice in it. What did he have against Alice? Maybe he was gay, despite what Ginny had said, or maybe he simply resented the fact that his best mate was getting married.

And what exactly did he mean by *we*?

"What do you mean you searched?"

"We couldn't let old Nicky pine away," said Jeremy. "He's been a good friend to us over the years; it was time to do something for him in return. Only natural really."

I'd opened my mouth to quiz him further on his matchmaking role when he brought me up short with, "And pray tell me, John Croydon, what do you do when you're not playing at being Marcel Duchamp?"

Some instinct told me he would be a lot harder to bullshit than Nick, so once again I decided to stick to something like the truth.

"Not a lot."

Jeremy nodded thoughtfully, as though this were precisely the answer he'd been expecting, and I was just beginning to relax again when, without warning, he came out with, "You know Clare, don't you? Clare Kitchener?"

Talk about knocking someone for six.

I gasped like a goldfish that had flopped out of its bowl and was now flapping around on the carpet. Jesus H. Christ. How much did he know about Clare? More to the point, how much did he know about *me*? When I'd seen him in the Landrace Inn, he'd been too far away to have been eavesdropped on my conversation with Graham. But what if he could read lips? The subject of Clare Kitchener was a minefield, and I would have to pick my path through it very carefully.

"Clare? Haven't seen her for ages. How is she?"

"I hear she's doing just fine, though I imagine the therapy sessions will have helped." Jeremy was smiling in a way that allowed me to see all his teeth at once. "She's doing better than Robert Jamieson, anyway. Robert's not doing so well these days, though I guess you don't need me to tell you that."

Robert Jamieson was the name of the dead man I'd seen in Clare's bathroom mirror.

"You knew Robert Jamieson?" I asked weakly.

"We never actually met, though I heard you did have that

pleasure." Jeremy leant forward, still with that smile. "And you do know, don't you, that Nick had nothing to do with Georgina's death. He was nowhere near Framptons that night."

I reeled, thrown off-balance by the direction this conversation was taking, and unsure where it was headed. "So I've heard."

"It's true. He was with *me*. And about two hundred other witnesses. All of us prepared to swear on our mothers' graves."

"I'm sure you were." I took a running jump into the void. "You and the rest of the Sulfur Society, I imagine."

Jeremy's smile vanished so abruptly it was as though he'd flicked an off-switch. "I just want to make sure there's no ambiguity here. Because I hear you're in the business of death. I hear that where death is concerned you're something of a *connoisseur*."

The word rolled off his tongue like the name of some particularly virulent poison. I gulped noisily, and the sound of it bounced off the opposite wall and hung in the air between us, like a frozen ping-pong ball.

"Where did you . . . hear, er, that?"

"Let's just say I asked around. It's a small world, this part of London. Bit of a village, really. Everybody knows everybody else. We all eat in the same restaurants, drink in the same bars, shop in the same shops. So if I were you, I wouldn't go round asking questions about Georgina. Nick's kind of sensitive about it."

Don't turn your back on Jeremy.

Ginny had been dead right to warn me, though I'd foolishly disregarded her advice and let myself be lulled into a false sense of security. This man wasn't a teddy-bear at all; he was a shark, circling round and round while I thrashed helplessly in the water. I was supposed to be the one asking the questions, but somehow he'd managed to twist them round so now I was the one in the hot seat.

"I didn't mean to upset anyone," I said, deciding to play it safe. "I was just curious."

"Curiosity killed the cat," said Jeremy, touching the side of his nose with his finger in a way that reminded me of Marlon Brando in *The Godfather*. I remembered the scene with the horse's head. Oh Lord, was this a threat to decapitate Boris?

"That's good," he said, and then the moment had passed and his smile was totally reassuring again, leaving me wondering how it could ever have been anything else. I was being paranoid. *Of course* there was a strong chance that anyone living in this part of West London would have heard about Clare Kitchener. It was a small world, just as Jeremy had said. It didn't necessarily mean that everyone was out to get me.

I hadn't finished asking everything I'd been meaning to ask. In fact, I hadn't even got started, but I didn't much feel like it now. I had the feeling Jeremy had wiped the floor with me and was only now rinsing out his mop prior to putting it away in a bucket. He drained his paper cup and got to his feet. I recognised this as my cue and got up too.

"By the way," he said, "My sister's a minx. I wouldn't believe everything she tells you."

I stared at him uncomprehendingly. "Your sister?"

"Virginia."

I stared at him in surprise. There was perhaps the faintest of family resemblances, a gingery tint to his hair, freckles. But she was foxy and he was not.

"Half sister," he said, as though reading my mind. "Different dads."

"So you're not . . . Jeremy Fisher?"

"No." He didn't even crack a smile.

"I'm sorry," I said, without knowing why I was apologising. "I didn't realise."

Did he know I'd slept with her? I started thinking about *The Godfather* again, and now *Scarface* as well. *You sleeep with my seester, focking fock you focker, say hello to my leeetle friend . . .*

"She'll make a super bridesmaid," I said, summoning my most innocent expression.

"Yes she will." He looked fierce. "And I will make a super Best Man." He made it sound like a challenge.

"Wouldn't have it any other way."

"You're seeing Nicky tonight, aren't you." A statement, not a question. My God, but this man knew everything.

"That's right." I moved towards the door. I needed air.

Jeremy gave me one last warm and extra-cuddly smile.

"Give him my regards."

"GOOD GOD, man," Nick said when he saw my scratches. "Whoever she was, I hope she was worth it." He burst out laughing and nudged me in the ribs.

"Who was . . .? Oh, I see. Oh yes. Absolutely."

This time, I managed to give my opponent a run for his money, which left me feeling unusually upbeat, though I couldn't help thinking he'd deliberately cocked up some easy opportunities with the express purpose of making me look good.

Afterwards, I repeatedly tried to prod our locker-room chat towards his genealogy (without, of course, letting on that I'd just been swotting up on it) but each time he skilfully skipped around the subject without truly broaching it, and then threw me off by asking complicated questions about my career in art, so I was kept busy trying to think up credible comments about litter-tray display or *The Sermon on the Mount with Crocodiles*.

I did manage to squeeze in a few questions about the Sulfur Society; Nick deflected most of them with the same skill he'd applied to my feeble squash returns, though he did tell me, with a chuckle, that the society had been outlawed since the Thirties, when high society had been rocked by (unproven) rumours of human sacrifice and (rather less unproven) Hammer horror-style orgies, many of them held in the attic at Framptons. But the Fitches had been relatively minor players in all this, he told me—the gossip had mostly centred on a cross-dressing politician and a couple of high-court judges.

After getting dressed, we went for a Bloody Mary in one of his neighbourhood bars, which I judged would be a fine opportunity to continue our little chat. So the Bloody Mary turned into two Bloody Marys, then three Bloody Marys, then a whole coven of the sanguinary bitches, but I did find out the following: *1)* That Georgina had attended the same school as Alice and Ginny; *2)* That Ginny and Jeremy were sometimes known as the Evil Twins, even though they were neither twins nor, Nick assured me, particularly evil; *3)* That the skull and flames tattoo had originally been inspired, as I'd suspected, not by Ghost Rider but by an ancient Sulfur Society symbol, though Nick insisted he and the others had only had it done for a drunken lark. And before I knew it the evening was over and he was patting me on the back in that one-man-and-his-dog way he had, and saying, "See you Thursday."

"Thursday?"

Nick looked at me incredulously.

"My stag party!"

He seemed shocked that it had slipped my mind. Though, in all honesty, I couldn't remember having been invited in the first place. But he stood over me while I jotted down the details, and afterwards I stumbled off towards the tube, feeling pleasantly tanked, already looking forward to getting even squiffier on Thursday night, and completely forgetting that time was running out and that the afternoon and evening had passed without my having made a whole lot of progress on the Fitch family history front.

I WAS AWARE that something was not right, but, other than the whole world and Boris ganging up against me, and an obscure sense that I'd missed something very obvious and very important, I couldn't put my finger on what it was. But I was feeling increasingly uneasy, as though the weight I'd thought I had left behind in Little Yawning had followed my scent, hitching a lift and catching a train to King's Cross, where it had followed my trail up the road to the canal and was even now loitering outside, waiting for an opportunity to crawl on to the barge and clamp itself back on to my shoulders.

That night, I double-locked all the doors and windows and made sure all the curtains were drawn. I left all the lights burning—there was no way I was going to risk the darkness again—and instead of taking Proust to bed with me, I took *Old Egbert's*, propping it up on my chest so I could look through it. I flicked back to the entry for Fitch, reread it and this time forced myself to tackle the eyesight-destroyingly minuscule print of the footnotes.

The first read as follows:

FITCH possibly corruption of FETCH (qv)

I flicked back through the entries, through FIR DARRIG, FIRBOLG, FIN BHEARA, FIGGY BOTTOM, and a great many other entries beginning with FIG or FIN or FIDDLE, until I came to FETCH. What I read there made my blood run cold.

FETCH. Spectral figure, shade or other type of super-natural manifestation, sometimes known as a WAFF or, more rarely, a CO-WALKER. While ghosts in the traditional sense of the term tend to colonize specific locations or, on occasion, objects, the FETCH is said to haunt a particular dynasty or bloodline, passing from one member to another like an inheritance, occasionally benign, but more frequently ill-starred or malevolent. To see one's FETCH is said to be a portent of death.

I reread it, just to make sure I'd understood.

To see one's FETCH is said to be a portent of death.

Oh boy. I flicked back to FITCH . . .

First reports of the so-called FITCH CURSE appear in Little Yawning parish records during the latter half of the sixteenth century, but the unusually high mortality rate amongst females marrying into the bloodline is now thought to have its origins in the unhygienic pregnancy, childbirth and deflowering rituals once commonly practised in this part of the country, sometimes involving the sacrifice of animals, birds or snakes . . .

Wraiths?
Sacrifices?
Snakes?
Oh boy, oh boy.

Whatever was going on, I didn't like the sound of it. But one thing was clear. If Alice went ahead and married Nick she would be letting herself in for a whole world of trouble.

I had to stop that wedding.

FIFTEEN

O N WEDNESDAY morning, after a dispiritingly shallow sleep punctuated by a series of exhausting dreams in which I was running around like a madman, trying to keep appointments or look up names in telephone directories so I could phone up and say I was running late, the now familiar ragged throat and bunged-up nose were joined by a Bloody Mary hangover. I cursed myself for having fallen under Nick's spell the night before. What had I been thinking? I'd had work to do. Anyone would have thought he'd been trying to stop me doing it.

The post arrived—mainly bills, but also, to my excitement, a picture postcard from Ginny, though she'd scrawled what I thought was a needlessly sarcastic message: *To the biggest dick in town.* I turned the card to look at the picture and felt something clench in my stomach; it was a painting from Amsterdam's Rijksmuseum and even as I looked I felt a couple of geese, or more likely an entire flock of them, waddling portentously over my grave, pecking at it querulously as they went.

Odd choice of painting, I thought, though despite the severed head of Holofernes dripping gore in the foreground, I concluded it could still be interpreted, at a pinch, as a come-on. OK, so Judith was waving a bloodstained sword, but she still looked pretty damn sexy, and one of her nipples was showing. Plus she had red hair, like Ginny.

Call me wacky, but I got turned on just looking at it.

NOT A single ray of sun pierced a sky that was incessantly grey and glowering, as though saving up a shitload of rain to dump on my head in a single cranium-crushing downpour. With every tick of the clock bringing me closer to Saturday, my former certainties were leaking away like sand. I couldn't get rid of the memory of Georgina's blackened tongue and oesophagus and the skeletal vault of a throat yawning impossibly wide, as if to swallow me up. Supposing that car hadn't come along. What would have happened? How far would she have taken it? I couldn't help thinking I'd escaped a fate worse than death, though I couldn't shake off the feeling that far from having got clean away, I was still being followed.

Like one along a lonesome road
That walks in fear and dread

I didn't believe for one second in Tubby Clegg's hitman story, of course, but as I nipped down the road to get a pint of milk and a packet of bagels I thought I knew just how he must have felt. I kept looking back, expecting to see cadaverous women in black, ghouls with flapping scalps, black beasts with yellow eyes dogging my shadow—and yes, why not, sinister-looking FBI types in dark suits and shades. But all I ever saw were regular folk pretending not to notice the jumpy neurotic who was looking over his shoulder so often it was starting to resemble a nervous tic.

Alice rang, and sounded unfeasibly pleased to hear my voice. I was tempted to let her know right off the bat what I thought about her lies, but decided it might be more prudent to hang fire, maybe even give her a chance to come clean. I didn't blame her for not telling me; it was kind of embarrassing. But in the end all I said was, "You've forgiven me, then."

Pause.

"For what?"

"The Pongo thing."

Another pause, then laughter.

"Oh, *that*. That was just some nickname they used to call me at school. No big deal, John. No problem at all."

I couldn't believe my ears. She was pretending that nothing had happened, that she hadn't got all uppity and chucked me out into the night, thus causing me to be subjected to the singularly most horrific experience of my horror-filled life.

Women. They were so . . . *changeable*.

She sounded tired. I assumed it was due to pre-wedding

pressure until she told me she'd had a wild night out on the town with the bridesmaids.

"I thought your pre-nup bash was this evening."

"It is. Though quite frankly after last night I'm not sure I'm up to it."

"But are you up to lunch?" I asked.

"Lunch?"

"We need to talk, Alice."

She agreed so eagerly it made me feel guilty again. She probably thought I was proposing a romantic tryst, whereas all I wanted to do was spoil her day, her week—maybe even her life. I felt like the heel of all time.

No sooner had I signed off than the *Halloween* ringtone started tinkling again, as though someone had already been trying repeatedly to get through. I half expected it to be Alice again, but it wasn't. It was Ginny. I thanked her politely for the postcard.

"You really think I'm a dick?"

"It was a joke," she said, laughing. "I adore you. Isn't it obvious? So what are you doing for lunch today?"

"Erm, already taken," I said, fulminating silently about the bad timing—a cosy *tête-à-tête* with Ginny would have been infinitely preferable to what was sure to be an awkward and upsetting confrontation with my client—and momentarily even considered calling Alice to put her off, but guilt—not to mention the memory of my dodgy bank balance—won out, as well as a desire to close the case. After what I'd seen and read, there was a moral imperative as well. It was obviously my duty as a citizen to talk Alice out of marrying into a family afflicted by a wife-killing curse. Rudimentary ethics.

"Call it off," urged Ginny.

I gritted my teeth. "Can't."

"Oh go on," she wheedled. "I'm feeling oooh so horny, just talking to you."

I started feeling horny too. "I can't. It's business."

"Who with?"

"None of your beeswax."

"But it can't go on all afternoon, can it? You can still come and see me afterwards, can't you?" She lowered her voice so it sounded all hot and breathy, and I could almost feel her lips against my ear. "Just thinking about you makes me feel moist," she whispered.

Thinking about her was making me feel moist too. "I've got a ton of work," I protested feebly.

"Oh, come on," she wheedled, and then added, "I've got something to tell you. Something you really need to know. About Nick's family."

I sat up. "What?"

"Not on the phone. I need to see you . . . *in the flesh.*"

I didn't need any more persuading. If Ginny had something to tell me about the Fitches, then I could easily justify time spent with her as being part of the investigation.

So that was all right, then.

ALICE AND I met in one of the upstairs rooms at Gnashers, where she picked her way through a selection of gourmet salad leaves while I tucked into a plate of steak and chips. She made the expected solicitous comments about my facial injuries, then added, "You're looking a little peaky in general. Are you all right?"

"Virus," I said, and promptly sneezed into my napkin. Alice looked away politely and started to perform some sort of triage operation on her lettuce. I eyed her surreptitiously. If she didn't look exactly carefree, then at least she looked like someone who had her whole future ahead of her. I had a delicate task to perform, and wasn't looking forward to it, but I wanted to preserve that future for her. We talked about everything and nothing, anything other than what was really bugging me. I was so nervous about broaching the subject I'd got halfway through my sticky toffee pudding before I finally plucked up the courage.

"About the wedding . . ."

"Oh God," groaned Alice. "What a nightmare. The bridesmaids' dresses still aren't finished. And half the choir's come down with gastric flu. We're having to draft in replacements from the next village . . ."

I took a deep breath. "You're going to have to call it off."

She stopped toying with her kiwi delight and looked me straight in the eye. "Oh John . . ."

Oh no. Anything but that. She thought I was trying to sabotage the wedding because I had *feelings* for her.

"Truth is," I said, "Georgina is still a bit of a problem." Understatement of the year.

Alice looked at me as though I'd rained all over her parade. "You said she was gone."

"*No I didn't.*"

"But I haven't seen her since the party."

"I have," I said.

That shook her. "*When?*"

"Monday night. After I left Framptons. She followed me down the lane. And this wasn't just a fuzzy over-the-entryphone visit, Alice—this was one on one, in my face. *Right* in my face. She was right in front of me, closer than you are now. It wasn't pleasant."

I indicated with my spoon exactly how close Georgina had been, and Alice looked suitably horrified.

"Oh John," she said again before leaning across the table and placing her hand on my arm. "It must have been awful."

"It was." I eyed her hand and wondered what it was planning to do next and whether I could possibly forestall it. I said in a rush, "Which is why I think you should postpone the wedding, just to be on the safe side."

Alice stuck her chin out. "But that's just what she wants!"

"I didn't say cancel, just put it off. You can always reschedule . . ."

She sighed and to my relief withdrew the hand. One thing less for me to worry about.

"You don't understand," she said. "You can't reschedule weddings just like that. The church has to be booked months in advance and I'd still have to pay for the catering and the choir and the invitations. It'd cost a fortune, and quite frankly I couldn't afford it, not now. Besides, Nick wouldn't stand for it. He's so impatient . . ."

"Alice," I interrupted gently. "There's a Fitch family curse. Georgina wasn't the first. Nick's mother, as well. And grandmother. All the Fitch women die young, in mysterious circumstances."

"I know." She stared at the tablecloth, biting her lip. "Everyone knows about that. But it's a joke. Nobody takes it seriously."

"Georgina took it seriously," I said. "And so should you."

She shook her head emphatically. "I'm nothing like Georgina. I'm down to earth. And I don't drink and drive."

"That's not the point!" I said, louder than I meant to. Several diners turned to stare at us, so I forced myself to calm down. "Look, you came to me for advice, didn't you? Well, I'm advising you now—call the wedding off."

"It wasn't your advice I wanted," she protested. "It was your *help*. There's a *difference*. And you *did* help, John. She's not stalking me any more."

"Maybe not *you*," I said, "but she's still out there. I think she's just biding her time, waiting for the right moment. You know, even just seeing her is bad, bad luck. *Really* bad luck. You don't even want to *see* her, Alice."

She looked preoccupied, and I began to hope that she was seriously considering what I'd been saying about postponing the wedding. Alas, no. When she finally spoke, it was to change the subject altogether.

"I know you're sweet on Ginny and I don't want to sound catty or anything, but I think you should watch your step. It wasn't my idea to go out last night, you know; it was hers. And you know what? I got the impression she arranged the entire evening purely because she wanted to make sure I didn't see you. And she was asking an awful lot of questions about you."

Despite my frustration at not getting through to Alice, my heart gave a little skip of pleasure, and I couldn't help asking, "What kind of questions?"

"How we met, how long we've known each other . . ." Alice shrugged. "She's jealous of our relationship, I guess."

Jealous? Of our relationship? Our *relationship*? For God's sake, we didn't *have* a relationship, at least not in the way Alice seemed to think. Hell, I had more of a relationship with *Georgina* than with Alice. But the news that Ginny had been asking questions about me jiffed my mood up no end. It suggested she wasn't just looking on me as a two-night-stand, or a one-night-one-afternoon stand, or whatever it was. On the contrary, she was obviously intrigued and wanted to know more about me. My romantic life actually seemed to be on track, for once. Now if only my professional life could fall into step as well, everything would be hunky-dory.

I gathered my energy to make another attempt at persuasion, but Alice was looking at her watch. "I'm sorry John, I really do have to get going." She reached into her bag and pulled out a cheque book, and I thought she was going to signal for the bill, but instead she filled out a cheque and solemnly presented it to me.

"That's what I owe you."

As I took it I caught sight of the amount she'd entered. "This isn't what we agreed."

"It's for other stuff as well. It's for everything."

I felt sleazy, like a male escort. "But I haven't done anything. And it isn't over. I don't think you should . . ."

"It's over as far as I'm concerned," Alice said firmly. "I'm not seeing her any more—that's what I wanted. You did exactly what I hired you to do, and I'm grateful. I know it sounds crazy, but I'm even grateful to Georgina—if it hadn't been for her, I would never have met you. I just hope . . ."

She looked me in the eye again. "I just hope you can look on me as a friend, now, rather than as an employer. I know that's been a bit of barrier between us . . ."

I wanted to yell, *No! it wasn't a barrier at all! There* is *no us! You're out of your mind!*

But I didn't. It would have sounded so . . . melodramatic. I watched unhappily as she put her chequebook away. She asked if I'd booked my room for the wedding. "Because if not, I'm sure we can squeeze you in at Framptons. It's not as though we're short of space."

So now I was welcome? *Now* I could stay at Framptons? *Now*, when it was too late? The steak and chips were sitting in my stomach like soggy indigestible cardboard.

"You're determined to go through with it?"

"Of course." She smiled wistfully. "Though I can't help feeling it's rotten timing. If only we'd met a few years ago . . ."

I didn't like the direction this conversation seemed to be heading in, but felt powerless to stop it.

" . . . or even six months ago, before I got engaged."

"But if you're not in love with him . . ."

She sighed, so heavily I could almost feel the depth of her longing. "But I do love him . . . in a way. It's just that I'm not *in love* with him, the way I'm in love with . . . you know. Try to understand—marrying Nick Fitch is my dream. My whole life has been building up to this. I can't turn my back on it now. I'm so terribly sorry . . ."

I should have kept on trying to talk her out of it, but it would only have reinforced her belief that I was wildly in love with her, so I chickened out and settled for making a non-committal noise in my throat. I looked again at the cheque and wondered how much there would be left in her bank account. Of course she couldn't postpone the wedding—in a matter of weeks, maybe even days, she would be skint.

Skint.

It was worth a shot. Time to spill what I'd found out. I looked straight at her and said, "I know all about you, Alice."

She frowned prettily.

"I made some calls," I said. "I called French *Vogue*, and you know what? They'd never heard of you."

She laughed, but I could see a hint of panic in her eyes. "Of course not! They wouldn't even remember my name—I was nothing but a gopher, lowest of the low, the office dogsbody . . ."

"Give it up, Alice," I said. "You weren't anywhere near Paris. You were staying in Portsmouth with your aunt. Working as a secretary, wasn't it? I spoke to Ian Roker."

She opened her mouth to say something, then thought better of it and shut it again.

"And then last year, your mother won some money on the Lottery; she gave most of it to you and you spent it on setting yourself up as someone you're not, someone Nick might want to marry, and now it's nearly all gone. Your father didn't buy that flat for you—you rented it, and your lease expires at the end of the month, which is why you're so determined not to postpone the wedding. In two weeks' time you'll either be moving in with Nick, or out on the street, homeless."

For a moment I thought she was going to burst into tears and make a scene, but then she seemed to change her mind and merely shrugged. But she wasn't finding it easy to meet my gaze; she stared down at an unused teaspoon, every now and again reaching out to adjust its position by a fraction of a centimetre.

"It's OK," I said. "I don't give a shit what you told your friends, and I have no intention of telling them the truth, though quite frankly if they really are your friends they wouldn't give a shit either. But you hired me to do a job and now I have to see it through. I kind of feel responsible for you. It's a pain, but I can't help it. I'm like that."

Alice swallowed noisily and raised her eyes to meet mine. They were shining. Oh Lord, I'd only gone and made things worse; now she was gazing at me as though I were Sir Galahad.

"What can I do?" she asked.

"You have to make a clean breast of it to Nick. Have it out with him, before it's too late. If he ends up thinking less of you, then I'm afraid that means he's just not worth it."

"I can't do that," she said. "And he *is* worth it. You know he is. You like him, don't you? Everybody likes Nick."

"He's very charming," I said, but for the first time started wondering how deep the charm actually went. Maybe he was nothing but charm. Or maybe the charm was a dazzling mask for something else—something that wasn't quite so enchanting.

And there was another topic I needed to broach—a topic even more delicate and embarrassing than all the other topics of discussion laid end to end, but I had to ask it, because I was formulating a theory about the Fitch Curse, and there were things that needed to be confirmed.

"There's something I have to ask," I began haltingly. "Don't take this the wrong way, but . . . Have you ever had boyfriends before?"

She bristled. "Of course I have! You surely don't think Nick's the first man I've ever been out with!"

"Um, when you say *been out with* . . .?"

"Yes?"

"I wondered if it might possibly be a euphemism."

"Euphemism for what?"

"What I mean to say is, well ... Did you ever, you know, sleep with anyone before Nick?"

Instead of slapping my face, which is probably what the occasion demanded, she snapped, "Of course I have!"

But she'd gone bright red. And by now I knew her well enough to know when she was lying.

There was a long and embarrassed silence. She seemed chastened, like a child who'd just been subjected to a telling-off and a slap on the wrist. She toyed with the strap of her bag, and then finally asked, "I suppose you're going to his stag thing?"

I nodded. It was too good an opportunity to pass up. "You needn't worry, my lips are sealed. But I'll keep my ear to the ground so I can report back to you."

"Please don't," she said primly. "I have absolutely no desire to know what Nick and his buddies get up to when they're left to their own devices. It's bound to be laddish and disgusting."

All the fight seemed to have gone out of her, but I didn't feel as though I'd come even close to presenting my case in a persuasive manner.

I picked up the tab for lunch. It was the least I could do.

GINNY DIDN'T give me the sort of welcome her come-hither phone call had led me to expect. She didn't offer me a glass of wine, nor even a cup of tea. Nor did she inquire after my health, though it was obvious from my scratches that I'd been the victim of some sort of violent assault. I couldn't help feeling a little peeved, and wishing there could have been some way of transplanting Alice's feelings into Ginny's body.

We sat facing each other. I couldn't help but notice the carved sandalwood casket in pride of place on the table between us. It looked as though it might have come from Jeremy's emporium. I asked what was inside. She smiled and said, "Take a look." So I lifted the lid, and saw: a cigarette lighter decorated with a recurring leaf motif; a number of matchbooks bearing the names of cafes and bars; a variety of cigarette papers, some of them fruit-flavoured; a booklet of roaches decorated with a recurring Jimi Hendrix motif; a selection of sticky black and brown substances wrapped in cling-film. The substances were giving off an earthy herbal smell—a smell familiar to me from my younger spliff-smoking days.

I chuckled. "Is that what I think it is?"

Ginny pointed out varieties of hash like a salesgirl selling bonbons. "Afghan Dipstick. Indian Chewbacca. Morocco Chocco . . ."

"Souvenirs from the coffee shops of Amsterdam, by any chance?"

She grinned like a naughty schoolgirl. I was impressed. "You smuggled all this into the country? But how?"

"In my fanny," said Ginny. "No, just kidding. Waltzed through customs, no problem. It's goodies for Alice's girly bash tonight. Want to try some?"

I hesitated. I was accustomed to smoking joints, but this looked like strong stuff. And was getting stoned such a smart idea when I still had things to do, information to dig up, weddings to stop? And mightn't it make me even more paranoid than I was already?

"Go ahead, roll away," Ginny said, leaning forward so I could see down the front of her blouse. She was wearing a scarlet brassiere.

That settled it. I glued three leaves of liquorice-flavoured paper into a T-shape, split open a cigarette and sprinkled the contents over the paper. "What was it you wanted to tell me about Nick?"

"Later," she said.

"No," I said. "Now."

"OK," she said. "Nick doesn't love Alice. He's marrying her for her money."

I looked up from my cigarette papers. This wasn't exactly news. I'd pretty much come to the same conclusion already. Oddly enough, it didn't make me think any less of Nick, though it was despicable. But it was also, in a way, poetic justice, since it wasn't as though Alice was marrying for love either.

I asked cautiously, "How much money does he think Alice has?"

"She's loaded," said Ginny. "You've seen her flat?"

"It's not much bigger than yours," I pointed out.

"You think I paid for this?"

"No, I think Daddy paid for it."

Ginny burst out laughing. "That's one way of putting it. Though I don't suppose he'd be thrilled to hear himself referred to as my father."

I felt a surge of jealousy. "Who?"

"Mind your own beeswax," she said. "Have a joint." She refused to answer any more questions, but came round to join me on the sofa and watched closely as I peeled open one of the cling-film parcels. The smell hit me in the face and immediately made me giddy. The contents were so soft they didn't even need to be cooked. I broke a small morsel off and started to shred it over the tobacco.

"You'll need more than that," said Ginny.

"Better not overdo it," I said, remembering all those times I'd got so out of it I'd had to lie down on the floor. My friends and I had always referred to it as needing to be *close to the earth*. Sometimes I'd felt the need to be *close to the earth* in the presence of total strangers, who'd inevitably been alarmed by such behaviour.

"It's just like you," Ginny whispered as I lit up. "Pungent, but not that strong."

And, fool that I was, I believed her.

SIXTEEN

W HAT GINNY and I did together wasn't so much lovemaking as animal rutting—or at least it might have been animal rutting had she ever let it get that far.

The foreplay took us all the way from the living-room into the bedroom, where we graduated to . . . yet more foreplay. To paraphrase Steve Martin in one of his films, it was the best sex I'd almost had. In fact, it was so very *nearly* sex that only the fact that I'd already *nearly* had it twice before was beginning to tip me off to the fact that Ginny Fisher was a tease, albeit such an accomplished one that only a churl would complain. I certainly didn't stop to wonder why she didn't go all the way. I never once stopped to ask myself why her definition of sex was so . . . Bill Clintonesque.

And then afterwards we sat back on her ocelot-print bedspread and I rolled another joint, and Ginny propped herself up on one elbow and, in that way she had, scrutinised my face with a bemused expression, as though she had no idea how she'd ended up in bed with such a weird yet endearing form of wildlife.

"Why?" she asked.

"Why what?"

"Tell me why you love me."

I hadn't yet told her I loved her. I considered it jumping the gun. But neither had I been expecting the Spanish Inquisition, so I really didn't have an answer prepared. "Um, the colour of your hair?"

"What about it?"

Christ, she was demanding. "It's the colour of Dubonnet. Or maybe Whisky Sour."

She chuckled. "Very romantic. And?"

"And?"

"That's pretty superficial. There's got to be more."

I rummaged around in my head for a bit. What was it that Kate had once said? That I made her laugh?

"Because you laugh at my jokes."

She laughed again, and I felt satisfied that I'd proved my point until she said, "Actually I'm not laughing at your jokes. I'm laughing at *you*."

I wondered how seriously I was supposed to be taking this. "You're heartless."

"I try hard," said Ginny. "What else?"

Was there no end to this cross-examination? The truth was I thought she was sexy and sophisticated and smart, the kind of woman I'd always hankered after but had generally been too shy to approach, the kind of woman who I thought might help finally erase memories of my ex, and I had no intention of owning up to *that*.

"Go on," Ginny urged.

"Um," I said, racking my brains and managing to come up something vaguer but somehow even more embarrassing.

"Because as long as I'm with you, you make me forget."

"Forget what?"

I couldn't very well say *Kate*, so I improvised.

"Death." It came out sounding a lot less flippant than I'd intended. "You make me forget that we're all going to die," I said, warming to my theme. "That we're halfway to death already, more or less, and it's downhill all the way."

"Wow," said Ginny. "Heavy."

"Now it's your turn."

"To do what?"

"Tell me why you love me."

"But I . . ."

She trailed off, smiling a small, secret smile. She started absent-mindedly plucking at the hairs on my chest. At the last count there had been seventeen, but at the rate she was going I was going to end up smooth as an Olympic swimmer. "I guess I've never met anyone quite like you before," she said.

This was good. This was the sort of thing I liked to hear.

"You're so quirky," she said.

I didn't care so much for that. "I'm not quirky."

"Yes you are, you're like one of those TV detectives. Holmes, Morse, Cracker—they're all quirky. They all like Mozart, vintage cars, things like that."

"Holmes isn't a TV detective," I protested. "And Mozart isn't a quirk. You can't like or dislike Mozart. He's a cultural given, like Martin Scorsese."

"I don't like Martin Scorsese," she said, which started us squabbling about the madonna/whore dichotomy in the screenplays of Paul Schrader. Actually, after an initial spirited attack by Ginny, she faded into silence and it seemed to be me doing most of the talking. Me and the Afghan Dipstick.

Ginny finally hauled me back on track with the observation that Hercule Poirot had quirks.

"Hercule Poirot has an *accent*," I said, vexed at what I saw as an attempt to lump me in the same bracket as an Agatha Christie character.

"You live on a houseboat," she said. "That's pretty damn quirky."

"It's a barge! And it's not mine! And please don't say *quirk* or *quirky*. It's an ugly word, like *irk*."

"Like jerk," she said.

"No, jerk's OK."

"And you've got a cat."

"So what? You've got a dog."

I braced myself for the counterthrust, but she was looking blank.

"No I haven't."

"Oh *please*," I said. "Then what do you call that hairy little mutt than keeps sliming all over my leg?"

We looked at each other.

It seemed to me that many minutes passed. Entire lifeforms evolved, whole species became extinct in that pause.

And then the truth struck me like a hammer-blow. Or it might have done if I hadn't been so stoned.

Instead I just reiterated feebly, "You don't have a dog?"

She shook her head, a slow smirk spreading across her face.

Smirk. Irk. Quirk.

"*Never* had a dog?" I asked, obviously thinking it best to make absolutely sure.

She went on shaking her head.

Uh-oh. "So you've never had a Jack Russell."

The smirk vanished. "That's not funny."

"What's the matter? Don't like Jack Russells? Tenacious little buggers. Never stop yapping. Georgina had one too."

Ginny looked at me as though I really were full of shit. "No she didn't."

I rubbed my eyes, trying to make sense of this new information. Now that I thought about it, there had been something not quite right about that dog. I could still feel its slimy doggy snot against my calf, only now it occurred to me that even doggy snot wasn't generally that slimy. Instinctively I reached down now and wiped my leg with a convulsive gesture.

"What's the matter?" asked Ginny. "Got an itch?"

Belatedly I realised that throughout this last conversation she had been putting her clothes on, and was now completely dressed, apart from her shoes.

Feeling at a disadvantage, I tried getting up to get dressed in my turn, but my head started spinning and I had to sit back down again. Only now did I reflect that it had been me doing most of the smoking; Ginny had made a great show of sharing but now it seemed to me once again that she'd been taking Bill Clinton as her role model. She hadn't inhaled.

I groped groggily for my underpants and tried to put them on without raising myself up from my supine position on the bed, which was easier said than done.

"Well now," she said, "I did hear you had a vivid imagination."

"I suppose you've been talking to your brother."

"Stepbrother, please." She pouted and lit a cigarette. "Oh, let's not squabble, John. It's just . . . I just don't feel you're being honest with me."

Instead of snapping back with, "And I don't think *you're* being honest with *me*," as I should have done, I pounced on her words as a golden opportunity to show her just how honest I could be. "Ask me one question, go on, any question at all, and I'll give you an honest reply."

She looked me right in the eye and asked, "Have you and Alice had sex?"

"No!" I said, shocked.

Ginny looked relieved and for a moment there, I felt good about that.

"Why did she hire you?"

Technically this was a second question, so I wasn't really compelled to answer, but I was so stoned I wasn't counting. I felt constrained to tell the truth, the whole truth and nothing but the truth. More truth than any one man should tell.

"Alice had a stalker."

Ginny nearly dropped her cigarette. Evidently this wasn't the answer she'd been expecting. "She didn't hire you to look into Nick's background, something like that?"

"Why? Is there something about Nick's background I should know?"

"Well, you know. The Sulfur Society and all that. All those poncey public school larks."

"What do you know about the Sulfur Society?"

"Only that it provides certain people who shall remain nameless with a grand excuse to behave like jerks." She waved her hand impatiently. "Yes, *jerks*. But what were you doing in Kensington and Chelsea library anyway?"

It was my turn to drop something, only in my case it was a sock. "And how would you know about that, Miss Fisher?"

"Let's just say I have friends in low places." She waggled her fingers, as though that absolved the need for further elucidation. "So now Alice thinks she's being stalked, just like Georgina?"

Up until this point I hadn't really connected Alice being stalked with Georgina's claims of being followed. But now Ginny had pointed it out, it seemed obvious.

"She's more flaky than she looks, isn't she," Ginny was saying.

I'd promised Alice I would never tell. But, deep down inside me, there was a lurking imp that reckoned it might be worth a shot, that thought that maybe, *maybe* if I told Ginny the truth, she would tell her stepbrother, who would then pass it on to Nick, and it would be he, and not Alice, who finally called the wedding off. Because he didn't want to marry someone who was 'flaky'. Nick or Alice? I wasn't fussy about who postponed it, just as long as it was postponed. So while I was pulling on the rest of my clothes, I told Ginny everything: why Alice had hired me, what I'd seen on Fegs Lane, Georgina's ghost . . . Everything.

So much for investigator-client confidentiality. And, since even to me it all sounded a little far-fetched, I threw in a potted history of my career as well, complete with Marion Tucker, Clare Kitchener and the rest.

Thank you so much, Afghan Dipstick.

Ginny listened open-mouthed. Her hair was tousled, there was a faint pink flush to her cheeks, and I remember thinking she had never looked more beautiful. Had she been the Devil, I would have sold my soul to her, then and there. In fact I would probably have handed it over for free.

"Jesus," she said when I'd finished. "*Jesus.*"

She stood for a minute, trying to digest what she'd heard, before suddenly seeming to make her mind up about something and swivelling on her heel and disappearing into the living-room. I wondered whether I'd made a mistake in being so honest and open.

Christ, *of course* I'd made a mistake—now she would think I was insane. I followed meekly and caught her midway through dialling a number. As soon as she saw me she broke off and dropped the handset back in its cradle.

"Don't mind me," I said.

I couldn't find my shoes. I knew they couldn't be far away, but I couldn't see them anywhere. I sat down on the sofa to survey the room from that angle and instantly found myself distracted by the sandalwood box and its contents. I forgot all about shoes and instead pulled out a grape-flavoured cigarette paper.

Ginny was looming over me with her arms folded. "You should go."

I had no intention of going anywhere, not just yet.

"But we haven't finished . . ."

"I mean now," she said. "I've got things to do, John. Important things."

"Relax," I said. "Take a pew.

She changed her tune. Now she was all big eyes and pleading. "Look John, I'm sorry I have to chuck you out. But I'll make it up to you, I promise."

"When?"

"How about tonight?"

I finally located my shoes under the table, where I'd kicked them in the early throes of passion. In the struggle to put them on and do up the laces, I had a nagging feeling there was something I'd been meaning to ask, but I'd completely forgotten what it was. Then I remembered, or thought I did. "Wasn't Alice having her pre-nup bash this evening?"

Ginny looked a little surprised, as though it had slipped her mind. "Well, I don't suppose it'll go on that late. We can meet up afterwards. If you haven't got plans, that is . . ."

I shook my head emphatically. "Hey, what do you know? I'm free. What kind of bash is it anyway? Seventies disco? Lesbian lap-dancing?"

Ginny snorted derisively. "Hardly Alice's style. Janie's playing hostess, which means it'll be ladylike and decorous."

"Janie?"

"Fellow bridesmaid."

"No male strippers?"

"No male strippers." A wicked gleam appeared in her eye. "Unless, of course, you fancy filling in . . ."

"You're kidding."

"Yes, of course I'm kidding. Besides, we don't need male strippers. There'll be entertainment aplenty when I tell everyone what you've just told me."

I felt the blood draining out of my head. "No!"

"What's the matter? You don't want everyone knowing that you're some sort of crazy psychic?"

"I'm not a psychic!" My ears were burning.

"What do you call it, then? You see dead people, don't you?"

"Not that often. Hardly ever, in fact . . ."

Her gaze softened, and so did her voice as she sat down next to me. "Relax, lover," she murmured, tickling me under the chin. "I won't tell."

The casual way she called me 'lover' reassured me, and I kissed her on the mouth. She responded magnificently.

"You promise?" I said when she finally pulled away.

"Promise."

"You won't tell Alice or anyone else what I told you?"

She pulled an imaginary zip across her lips. "Your secret is safe with me, darling."

Again with the darling. "Not even your stepbrother?"

She snorted again. "The last person I'd tell."

"OK then." I got to my feet.

"I'll call you later," said Ginny, plucking one of the cling-film packets out of the casket and thrusting it into my hands. "Here, darling. Present. Now get the hell out of here, you crazy psychic loon."

I STUMBLED HOME with the hash burning a metaphorical hole in my pocket and the tube journey transformed into a paranoid ordeal. I reflected that it would be just my luck to run into a pack of sniffer-dogs.

The thought of dogs reminded me of the Jack Russell. Even several days and two pairs of jeans later, I could still feel its snout leaving a trail of slime across the bottom of my leg. Instinctively I reached down to wipe the wetness away, found of course that the fabric was dry as a bone, and then had to clamp down on the almost irresistible compulsion to repeat the gesture ad infinitum. I didn't want the other tube passengers thinking I had some sort of twitchy obsessive-compulsive disorder.

So the Jack Russell hadn't been real. Big surprise. It wasn't the first time I'd seen animals that weren't really there. But I'd also seen it, or something that looked very much like it, in a photo with Georgina, so if it hadn't been her dog, whose was it?

Back on the barge I took even more notice than usual of Boris. In the normal run of things, my cat had only to spot a distant canine presence on the towpath for him to start spitting like a deep fat fryer, and it was true he wasn't as affectionate as usual. But he seemed to have got over his sulk and approached warily as I put food in his bowl. I settled down on the sofa and resisted the urge to roll a joint; now was as good a time as any to get down to the disagreeable business of reflecting on everything that had happened in the past few days. Boris finished foraging in his bowl and curled up beside me as I opened my notebook and picked up a pen.

THIS TIME it wasn't Cowboys and Indians on the bedroom floor, it was small grey snakes with black zig-zag markings. Adders. They weren't much bigger than earthworms, but they wouldn't stop writhing and squirming, making it difficult to pick my way across the room, because I had at all costs to avoid stepping on them. Not only would squashing them make a mess on the bedroom carpet and risk calling down the wrath of my father, but I wasn't wearing shoes or socks. I wasn't so much afraid of being bitten as of getting pulverised adder innards stuck to my bare soles.

And all the time my mother kept calling, "Johnny! Come here, Johnny . . ."

After what seemed an age, I finally made it to the door and crossed the landing to my mother's room with its familiar smell of incense and scorched herbs but when I reached to pull the muslin aside she reared up like a hooded cobra, mouth stretched open to reveal a blackened tongue and oesophagus and the skeletal vault of a spectral vulva yawning impossibly wide open to swallow me up, and the unearthly noise emerging from this hellish cavern was . . .

. . . a rinky-dink digital version of the theme music from *Halloween*.

I opened my eyes, feeling sweaty and feverish. The barge was all shadows. Boris protested as I pushed him aside and sat up on the sofa, rubbing my eyes. Christ, how long had I been out?

I groped for the nearest light switch, but the feeble glow of the lamp did little to dispel the darkness that had crept up on me while I'd been asleep. I was shivering, and not just from the fever; the temperature seemed to have plummeted.

Damn Ginny and her drugs. And damn me for having

smoked so many joints. Little wonder I'd passed out. I switched on all the lights I could find, found my mobile and, without thinking, answered the incoming call.

Big mistake.

My mother immediately picked up where she'd left off, and once she was in full swing nothing could stop her, not even trying to turn off the phone, which naturally enough refused to be switched off no matter how many buttons I pressed. Even burying it under a pile of cushions wasn't enough to stifle that pleasant, utterly reasonable voice, the sort of voice you hear over teacups and biscuits at a meeting of the Women's Institute, which kept seeping into my head, filling me with nameless but now familiar dread.

"Oh, Johnny, what did I tell you about talking too much? And to that redheaded girl as well . . ."

"I've told you before, mum." I was addressing the pile of cushions. "This is my life, and you need to keep out of it. I know you mean well, I know you think you have my best interests at heart, but this is something I have to sort out for myself."

"You keep saying that, Johnny, yet you never learn. It's very clear to me—and I do have some experience in the matter, you know, I'm not the old fuddy-duddy that you think I am—that you need to keep away from her . . ."

I sighed. I could tell she was working herself up into one of her lathers.

"You let them take advantage of you. Your father was right, you need to toughen up, be a man, but I know it's not your fault, you're a freak of nature, and you keep forgetting that, keep getting ideas. But you're not as clever as you think you are, Mr Detective. Do you honestly think a girl like that would give you the time of day if she wasn't after something? What possible reason would there be for a girl like that to be interested in a gutless spineless pusillanimous slob like you? Could it be your money, oh no I forgot, you don't *have* money. Or your prestigious job good looks charming personality self-confidence, call yourself a detective, you don't even have the gumption to face up to what you are . . ."

I'd heard this one before.

"And what *am* I, mum? And whose fault is that?"

"You're a damn a skin dah you know why Kate left you don't you Johnny? Because you're pathetic! That's right, a dead loss you should be ashamed of yourself. You live among the dead people because you're too weak to face up to reality, because dead people don't talk back . . ."

Not true, I thought miserably.

" . . . might as well end it all, jump into the canal or off a high building or cut your throat like the man in the mirror, damn run a skin duh lammy lammy lammy . . ."

She started sounding like someone who'd had a stroke; her speech devolved, as it often did, into gobbledygook and finally dwindled away into silence, leaving me feeling wiped out.

As soon as I thought it was safe, I dug the mobile out from beneath the pile of cushions and scowled at it. It glowed back at me maliciously. There didn't seem any point in switching it off now—it would have been like nailing the coffin shut after the corpse had already got up and spat in your face.

It took several straight whiskies before I was able to work out that my stomach was churning more from hunger than fear. I fixed myself a sandwich and a beer. It was eleven fifteen. I tried to forget about my mother's ravings by fantasising about Alice's hen party, conjuring an Ingres-like vision of soft-skinned houris lolling indolently around, sipping from goblets of glowing green absinthe, puffing aromatic Turkish cigarettes, occasionally rousing themselves just enough to run fingers over each other's creamy flesh . . .

Mission accomplished. My mother's words were duly relegated to the basement of my memory and fenced off behind yellow tape with a sign saying "Do not disturb'. I started thinking about what Ginny might be doing at that very moment, but the perfumed fantasy soon gave way to the thought that she was probably repeating everything I'd told her that afternoon, humiliating Alice in front of her friends and ensuring that I would never be able to show my face in public again.

Despite all that, and despite my mother's warning, I was still looking forward to seeing Ginny again and having some more of that almost-but-not-quite sex. I hadn't forgotten her promise to call; in fact, it had probably been the one thing that had saved me from sinking into a depression.

I riffled through the various menus of my phone, hoping to find she'd called or left a message while I'd been asleep, but the only listing was the no caller ID from my mother.

It was now eleven thirty. If the party was as ladylike as Ginny had predicted, surely it would have been over by now? Maybe she'd forgotten. Maybe she needed reminding. Maybe she'd got confused and thought *I* was the one who was supposed to call *her*. Maybe she was drunk. Ha! *Maybe she was so drunk she would go all the way with me.* Maybe she was on her way home right at that moment. Maybe I could leave a message; she *had* promised to call, after all, so it wouldn't necessarily seem desperate.

I spent about ten minutes dithering over whether or not to take the plunge, and then finally succumbed to temptation and tapped out her number, though not without opting for the *no caller ID* option, just in case she wasn't there and I needed to call several times, in which case I wouldn't want her coming home to find her machine clogged with needy messages from me.

I'd thought of everything, except what actually happened.

"Hello?"

Someone answered. But not Ginny. A man's voice. Obviously a misdial. Obviously. I hung up and tried again.

And got the exact same response.

This time he said, "Ginny? Is that you?"

It was a voice that was all too familiar. I felt my testicles shrivel.

And then, in my best Gorbals accent, I said, "Sorry, wrong number," and hung up and poured myself another whisky. A giant one.

Well, what had I expected? It wasn't as though I had any rights in the matter. I'd known her less than a week, and neither of us had so much as mentioned the words *exclusive* or *monogamous*. I couldn't exactly accuse her of not being faithful when we hadn't established anything for her to be faithful to.

But it hurt, all the same, in particular because it meant that my mother had been right. How could I ever have imagined that a classy chick like that would have been interested in a slob like me? She'd been using me all along. How could I have been so blind?

I thought back to the party, and to the way she'd zeroed in on me like a guided missile seeking its target. Fool that I was, I'd kidded myself that she'd been attracted to me, but now I asked myself whether she mightn't have had a hidden agenda from the very beginning. Hadn't Alice felt as though she were being followed? What if it hadn't been *Georgina* following her? What if someone else had followed her to the barge, that first day, and then that someone had told someone else, and then that someone else had told Virginia Fisher to keep an eye on me, to get into my trousers as a way of finding out how much I knew, what Alice was up to . . .

My head was spinning. Maybe I was reading too much into this. I'd smoked too much dope and now I was seeing Seventies-style conspiracies everywhere. Just because Nick Fitch had answered Ginny's phone didn't mean the two of them were having an affair. She was a bridesmaid, after all; maybe he'd gone to see her about a wedding-related matter.

Yeah, right. At a quarter to midnight. Maybe they'd been discussing the colour of the confetti.

But at least now I knew who Ginny's oh-so-generous Daddy was.

I drowned my sorrow in yet another whisky, then tried to take my mind off Ginny by immersing myself in the mouldy old prose of *Old Egbert's*. Even thinking about my mother seemed preferable to thinking about Ginny now.

On a whim, I looked up the word 'mother', hoping that maybe I'd find an entry headed MOTHER, HOW TO ESCAPE FROM that would enable me to put a stop to those infernal phone calls, but all I could find were references to MOTHER EATING and MOTHER WITCH, neither of which were much help.

I searched for 'telephone', but the entries skipped straight from TEMPLARS to TEZCATLIPOCA. Then, as much as to while away the time as anything, I tried looking up some of the meaningless drivel my mother was always coming out with. At least I'd always assumed it was meaningless. What was it she was always babbling? *Lammy*?

I looked it up, and hit, if not paydirt, then a few crumbs of rich soil.

> LAMIA *Queen of Libya who according to Greek mythology was transformed into a vampiric monster by vindictive Hera. Her victims were mostly said to be children, though in some versions she ate men. Sometimes portrayed with the head and breasts of a woman and the body of a snake, and often said to possess the ability to pluck her own eyes out. See also John Keats' poem Lamia.* LAIMOS = *gullet. See* LAMIAE, LAMIDAE, EMPOUSA.

Ate men? I thought of Georgina's horrible gaping mouth. And body of a snake? Snakes! I thought about Nick's bedhead, and my dream. There was definitely a snake motif slithering through this. Maybe my mother was more on the money than I'd realised. What was that other thing she was always banging on about?

damn run a skin duh

Damn run? A damn close-run thing? Dammerung? *Gotter-dammerung*? Maybe it was that. I could hardly expect my mother to speak German with a perfect accent, particularly when she was raving. I looked it up, not really expecting to find it, and of course it wasn't there; whatever she'd been going on about, I was almost certain it had nothing to do with opera. But I knew *Dammerung* on its own was German for twilight, so, for want of anything better to do, I gave that a whirl.

Bingo. Or very nearly. There was nothing for Dammerung. But there was an entry for DAMMERUNGSKINDER.

damn run a skin duh

I adjusted the lamp so the light fell directly across the page.

> DAMMERUNGSKINDER *(literally: children of the twilight) generally assumed to refer to the issue of the coupling between thanatoid and athanatoid. See* AMBROSIAL, THANATOID.

Thanatoid. Oh yes, I already knew that one.
Just one of the many things I'd been trying to forget.
The thing I'd been trying to forget, in fact. Oh hell.
I forced myself to remember it now.

SEVENTEEN

"**B**UT WHY won't you introduce me to your parents?"

It was the same demand she'd made a thousand times already, but this time, I sensed, something was different. There was something in her tone suggesting that she wasn't going to be fobbed off with one of my feeble excuses, not this time.

Kate's mum and dad had always made me feel welcome. They were a sweet couple who lived in a nice little village near Oxford. She liked gardening, he was a member of the local cricket team. Each time we went to see them, I mentally compared them to my own parents, and told myself once again that I could never let Kate know the truth.

"But *why* can't I meet them?"

As usual, I made excuse after excuse until she finally lost her temper. But this time, instead of us both retreating into a sulky silence, she persisted.

"You're ashamed of me, is that it?"

"Anything but. You're the best thing that ever happened to me."

"You're ashamed of your background."

"It's not like that at all."

"So what is it? Don't you love me?"

"You know I do," I said, though it was true I had always found it a bit embarrassing to actually say those three little words out loud.

"Then why can't I meet them?"

"It's complicated."

Her voice softened. I could tell she was trying hard to be understanding. "Maybe less complicated than you think. Maybe talking about it will help. Try me, John. Have faith."

I owed her something, though I thought I could maybe get

away with not telling her absolutely everything. Maybe I could get away with just a small part of the truth. So I steeled myself and said, "My father's a psychopath."

She smiled and shrugged. "So what? So is mine."

"No," I said. "Mine really *is* a psychopath."

She stared at me for a moment before saying, "I'm sorry. I didn't realise. Why didn't you tell me earlier? Did he hit you?"

Is that what she thought? That it was about hitting? I felt like laughing out loud, but instinctively knew it was not the sort of reaction that would go down too well.

"Worse," I said gloomily.

"What then?" She cast around for ideas. "He killed your dog or something?"

I shook my head, and clammed up again. I couldn't see how telling her would help. On the contrary, it could only make things worse. But she was visibly near the end of her patience and making a gigantic effort to be compassionate. She crouched down in front of me and took my hands and tried to make me look directly at her.

"Whatever it is, it'll be better if you tell me about it. But if you carry on keeping it bottled up, John . . . *we can't be together*. Do you understand? What's the point of loving someone if you can't share your deepest, darkest secrets with them? What kind of relationship is that? It's not real. It's not honest. If you love me, *really* love me, you *must* tell me."

I really loved her, but still I hesitated.

"I'm afraid that if I tell you, you'll leave me."

She looked at me sternly and said, "Let's get one thing straight, John. I'll leave you if you don't."

So there it was. She couldn't have made it any plainer. I was left with no choice.

But I couldn't look her in the eye. Looking off to one side, I said, "My father killed a little girl."

I must have been muttering it under my breath, because she said, "What?"

I repeated what I'd just said, louder this time.

She tried not to gasp, but when I looked back at her I could see she was reacting as though I'd just slapped her face.

Eventually she recovered just enough to be able to ask if he was in prison. How I wished he was; my father being behind bars would have explained everything. Everybody knew that people with parents in prison didn't like talking about their families.

"He buried the body in the rhubarb patch behind the garage," I said. "He was never caught."

Kate went white. Even her lips went white. "What did you do?"

"What could I do? I was just a little kid. And there wasn't any proof."

"They could have dug up the patch . . ."

"It wasn't that simple."

"Maybe you got it wrong . . ."

I shook my head, but didn't tell her how I knew I was right. I didn't think she was ready to hear it was because the dead girl herself had appeared on TV and told me.

But I could tell what Kate was thinking.

Do you take after him?

She moistened her lips. "I'm thirsty. Want a beer?" I nodded—when did I not want a beer?—and she disappeared into the kitchen for longer than was necessary. When she finally returned with the beers it was clear she'd taken the opportunity to think about what she should ask next.

"Do you still see him?"

"Now and again. Not often. There's not much point—he doesn't recognise me."

Her face asked the question.

"He's in a nursing home," I explained. "He's older than your dad. He was already quite old when they had me. And the Alzheimer's doesn't exactly help."

I knew what she was going to ask next. I could see it coming from a mile off, like a cricket ball descending in a slow arc out of a cloudless sky, and I also knew that however much I shuffled around and squinted into the sun, getting into position and cupping my hands in preparation, the ball would still end up clobbering me on the head.

"What about your mother?"

I riposted, "What about her?"

It was a stalling tactic, pure and simple and painfully ineffective. All it succeeded in doing was to rile Kate even further.

"*Did she know about it?*"

I thought about lying, but instead said, "Yes."

"She didn't go to the police?"

"She couldn't."

Kate mulled this over for a while, with an expression like someone who'd just bitten into a lemon. "She wasn't his . . . you know, his accomplice? Like Myra Hindley, or Rosemary West?"

"No!" I answered with some relief. Even my parents, bad as they'd been, had never been *that* bad.

"Then what . . .?"

I was trapped. I couldn't see any way out. I could have refused to answer, but that would have meant it was all over between us. Kate was waiting for an answer. She was expecting an answer.

"My mother couldn't do anything," I said, knowing that this would be where it got *really* difficult, "because she was dead."

Several expressions passed over Kate's face in rapid succession: surprise, pity, suspicion, irritation . . .

"And what? Your father married again?"

"No, he and my mother . . . stayed married."

She tried to get her head around this, and failed. I didn't blame her; I had trouble with it myself. But she obviously wanted to take me by the shoulders and shake me. I knew I was being annoying, drip-feeding information like this, but each word was a painful effort, yet another barefooted step along a road of sharpened knives.

"I don't understand. He must have married again."

"I wish."

Kate let out a squeal of frustration. "Then who is it you're always talking to on the phone? The woman you say is your mother? The one who's always calling you? What's going on here, John?"

Dark suspicion clouded her face. "You're not having an affair, are you?"

I gulped at my beer. I was too emotionally wiped out to

think of any halfway plausible lie.

"I'm afraid that is indeed my mother."

Kate slapped her forehead in frustration.

"You just said she was dead!"

I remember at this point feeling quite ill. I wasn't sure whether I wanted to lie down in a darkened room or run to the bathroom and throw up. Instead, I swallowed another mouthful of beer.

"OK," I said quickly, before I could change my mind, knowing that every word was another poisoned pin in the beating heart of our relationship, but still hoping against hope that maybe, just maybe, my confession would end up bringing us closer together.

"Here it is: my mother is dead. My mother has always been dead. My mother died before I was even born."

I paused, not for dramatic effect, but really not knowing how to continue. Kate said nothing, didn't even make a noise, and I didn't dare look at her, so I went on, "Don't ask me how that works. I'm not even sure myself. Apparently I'm a . . . a *Thanatoid* . . . I think that's the word, but obviously there's not a lot of call for it. Half-human, half-dead. Physically I'm exactly the same as everyone else but mentally," I tapped my head, "it's another story. I mean, there's so much I haven't told you. You remember how we met? That party where you lost your grandma's ring in the garden? Well yeah, obviously you remember that, but I never told you how I found it. Well, it was your grandma herself who told me where it was, and so I just . . ."

I broke off because I'd just caught sight of Kate's face, and I knew right away it was over between us, though I went into denial for a while, and kept telling myself things were still salvageable even though I was aware, deep down, that they were nothing of the sort. I told her I'd been joking, that what I'd said was a bad joke, in terrible taste, but the damage was done and she didn't believe me, any more than she believed what I'd just said about my parents. She probably thought I was mentally disturbed, which I guess wasn't so far from the truth. Just try having a background like mine and not being mentally disturbed.

In the end, though, I don't really know what Kate thought, I could only ever guess at it, running the suppositions through my head again and again until they grew blunt with over-familiarity, because I never got another chance to talk to her properly. She was staring at me with a mixture of hurt and revulsion, and the knowledge that it had been me who had inspired such feelings made me want to kill myself or, at the very least, knock back the rest of my beer and then open another one, and then another . . .

As it happened, I did end up drinking all the beer in the fridge that evening, because Kate, after giving me that look, had gone straight into the bedroom and packed a bag and had then announced that she was going to her sister's, and that she expected me and all my possessions to be out of our flat by the end of the week, and that she never wanted to see me again.

I thought it was unfair, but what could I do? Apart from spending night after night hanging around outside the flat we'd used to share, gazing up at the bedroom window, that is? Apart from bombarding her with phone calls, and then answering-machine messages and then, when she finally changed her number, long and exceedingly heartfelt letters? Apart from loitering outside her office so I could try and talk to her? Apart from laughing bitterly in the face of threats of physical violence from some of the guys she worked with, and getting into a stupid punch-up with her new boyfriend?

It wasn't just Kate. I'd been forced to find myself a whole new set of friends. I'd stumbled into the detective business by accident, when one of my new acquaintances had asked me, I suspect more out of pity than any real expectation that I'd actually be able to help, to track down his missing brother. But I'd found him. And, bit by bit, I'd managed to cobble together a whole new life for myself.

There had been setbacks, of course, such as the Clare Kitchener case.

But right up until the meeting with Alice Marchmont, things had been working pretty well.

EIGHTEEN

W HEN I turned on my phone the next morning, there was a
single text message waiting.

KEEP AWAY FROM ALICE.

No caller ID, of course.

Nick? Ginny? Georgina? I could only guess.

That was it, then. The gloves were off. But if they thought an
anonymous text message would be enough to make me keep my
distance, they were wrong.

The wedding was still two days away.

And a lot could happen in two days.

JANIE CARRUTHERS lived in Shepherd's Bush, which from what I'd
gathered from Ginny and Alice was several social notches down
from Notting Hill, but it enabled her to live in a house as
opposed to a flat, which was probably why she'd been selected
to host the hen party.

I knocked on her door with trepidation, expecting her to
collapse into snorts of derisive laughter as soon as I introduced
myself, but instead she was straightforward and friendly, though
the lazy eye gave me a few bad moments. I kept thinking she
was winking at me and had worked myself up into a froth of
paranoia, imagining she knew all about me and my not-so-
brilliant career, before I realised it was probably a birth defect
and not in the least bit deliberate.

"So how did it go last night?" I asked, a sour taste in my
mouth as I remembered my misguided vision of the hen party; I
no longer saw it as an assembly of odalisques—more a coven of
harpies gathered together to plot my downfall.

Janie's reply was to groan, and when I saw the cartons of
empties stacked up by the door, I wasn't surprised. Nor would

she be the only girl in town currently suffering from colossal dehydration, a thumping headache and a digestive system that threatened to regurgitate anything that was put into it. I knew the symptoms only too well, though it was a refreshing change to see them in someone else.

"Did you, er, have fun?" I asked, fishing for details. Surely Ginny couldn't have gone the whole evening without spilling at least a few of the beans?

"It was a blast," said Janie.

"What did you talk about?"

She screwed up her nose. "Everything and nothing. Mostly, though, we just drank."

"So I see. But . . . you didn't talk about, er, men?"

Janie let out a whoop. "Of course we talked about men! We tore them to pieces. We told Alice she was insane to get married . . ." She lowered her voice. "Especially to Nick. But she wasn't having any of it."

"Really?" I asked, interested. Maybe the hens had done my job for me. "You tried to get her to call off the wedding?"

"Duh, no!" said Janie. "We weren't being *serious*."

She was leading me to her kitchen when I spotted the photo on the wall. It was one of those panoramic jobs about three feet wide, framed and hung in the hallway for no reason I could think of other than to let visitors know their hostess had once attended a posh public day school as opposed to, say, a comprehensive on a sink estate. I stopped and stared fascinated at the serried ranks of uniformed jailbait.

"Happiest days of your life?"

"They were OK," said Janie. I glanced sideways and saw her winking at me, making me think that what she really meant was, "Yes, and we had masses of schoolgirl lesbian sex as well." I tried to think Zen and concentrate on the picture.

Even in that sea of faces, it wasn't hard to spot Ginny and Janie, standing on either side of a thin girl I deduced had to be the third bridesmaid, Fiona, who Ginny had described as having a face like a pair of ballet shoes. It was true; she did have, though even in two dimensions and on a tiny scale, all three of them were emitting a sort of glamorous aura that transformed their school uniform into an erotic instrument expressly designed to torture the hapless male onlooker.

"Ginny, Finny and Janie," I said.

"Everyone called us The Three Graces," sighed Janie, who had the grace to sound embarrassed. "I guess we were sort of a clique. *The* clique. Everyone wanted to be friends with us."

As I peered closer at the ranks of tightly packed schoolgirls, I thought I recognised younger versions of some of the well-groomed women I'd encountered at Selina and Jolly's party. But it took me a long time to find Alice, so radically had she been transformed since the days of the photo. I finally located her in the back row, trying to disguise her height by hunching her shoulders. Her hair looked like an exploding nebula, her eye sockets were black pits, and she was scowling fit to bust. In fact, she looked downright scary. If the other three were Graces, then she was a Gorgon.

"This was before you and Alice were friends?"

Janie hummed and haahed and eventually decided the answer had to be yes. "Otherwise we would have been standing together," she explained. "Once we'd started being nice to her, we were inseparable. Everyone called us The Four Marys."

Three Graces. Four Marys. Whatever next? Maybe The Four Marys could take on extra members and be upgraded to Five Easy Pieces, Six Proud Walkers or the Seven Per Cent Solution.

"Alice was kind of clingy," Janie recalled as we stepped into her cavernous kitchen. "Once she'd attached herself to us, it was impossible to shake her off."

The kitchen was filled with the aroma of something baking. I took a seat, and Janie started filling the kettle.

"It doesn't sound as though you were too fond of her."

"What? No, I adore Alice," said Janie serenely, hugging the present tense as though that could wash all past unpleasantness away. "She was a bit of a pain at school, that's all."

"But you were beastly to her. Remember when you hid her pencil case?"

Janie whistled, though the incident didn't appear to be nibbling at her conscience the way it seemed to have been gnawing at Ginny's.

"Alice told you about that? Oh, *Ginny* told you. Christ, I'd forgotten all about it. She made such a terrible scene. But you know what?" She winked meaningfully, and I wondered if this time it might be deliberate. "I always thought . . . Don't quote me on this, for Christ's sake, but I always got the impression we were being manipulated. There were only the four of us there when she left it out on her desk, and then she left the room, almost as if she were *challenging* us to steal it."

"Why would she do that?"

Janie shrugged. "Alice was always rather passive-aggressive. If you ask me, she knew exactly who'd taken the wretched thing, but waited until all the rest of the class had turned up before putting on her show. It was all rather cringe-making, especially when teachers got involved and the three of us got detention."

"Alice snitched?"

"No, Ginny did. I was mad at her at the time, but we did deserve to be punished. We were so heartless. You know how you are at that age."

I did know, but not in the way Janie meant. At school I'd been more of an Alice than a Ginny or a Finny or a Janie, a misfit rather than one of the gang. But I'd managed to avoid being a victim, principally because the other boys had been scared of me and thought I might do a Carrie and set their hair on fire or something. I knew they talked behind my back, but none of them had ever dared say anything to my face.

In fact, I felt new stirrings of respect for Alice, for the way she had turned the tables on the erstwhile bullies and ended up with them eating out of her hand. And now the icing on the gateau—inviting her former tormentors to be her bridesmaids must have seemed a juicy revenge for all those slights in the past. I was beginning to understand why she was so determined that nothing should spoil the wedding. For her, it would be the ultimate triumph, a day when old scores would finally be settled and she would be able to take her rightful place as Top Girl.

Always provided that Georgina didn't mess things up by rematerialising at an awkward moment, such as halfway through the ceremony.

She screams, she swoops, she stops the wedding.

Not such a bad thing, now I thought about it.

"But Alice is one of you now, isn't she?" I pointed out. "Especially now she's getting married to Nick. When did she first meet him?"

I paused, then added, "When did *Ginny* first meet him?"

I couldn't tell if it was mention of Ginny that made Janie frown. "Nick? We've all known him since forever. Since Sixth Form, really. Let's just say he's already broken Alice's heart more than once. Like when he got engaged to Georgina. Alice was devastated, but Georgina was prettier and wealthier, so it was no contest."

"Alice was jealous of Georgina?"

Janie looked at me as though I'd said something incredibly stupid. "Of course not! They were best friends! Until the pencil case incident, she was Alice's *only* friend. They were inseparable!"

Oka-a-y. This was news. There I'd been, thinking Alice and Georgina had always been deadly rivals, which might have explained why Georgina's ghost was haunting her now.

"But they fell out later?" I suggested hopefully.

Janie shook her head. "No-one was more upset than Alice when Georgina died."

I kept at it. "But it didn't exactly stop her throwing herself at Nick."

"Actually, we had a few heart-to-hearts about that," Janie said. "She did worry about it. But I told her she should go ahead, if that was what she really wanted. And boy, did she want it."

She looked thoughtful. "You know what? Don't tell anyone I said this, but I don't think Nick even knew Alice existed until last year, when she came into money . . ."

"So Nick knew about the lottery . . ."

"Lottery? I thought it was an inheritance."

"Yeah, of course." I felt like kicking myself. Of course Alice wouldn't want the true source of her sudden wealth revealed. I tried to remember whether I'd said anything about it to Ginny, and concluded that I hadn't. Trying to distract Janie from my *faux pas*, I asked, "So you've all known Nick Fitch for ages?"

"*Known* is pushing it. We sometimes ran into him, but he was older than us. He probably thought we were silly little girls.

But we knew all about him, we were all a little in love with him at one time or another. I think Alice even kept a scrapbook—Nicholas Fitch, his life and times. He was always cropping up in diary pages and stuff. She kept all the cuttings. She even staked him out a couple of times, you know. I guess you could call it stalking. Nothing serious, but she made sure we all got invited to the same parties."

Janie got up and crossed over to where she'd left the tea brewing, which was just as well, because I was struggling not to look too gobsmacked. So Georgina wasn't the only stalker in town; Alice had done her fair share of stalking too. The idea made me uncomfortable. Given the way she seemed to feel, I just hoped she never got it into her head to start stalking me.

Janie set two steaming mugs of tea down on the table.

"In other words," I said, "Alice targeted Nick a long time ago."

Janie chuckled. "You could say that." Then she added, "Hold on," and left the room. She returned a few minutes later with a Callisto Rodriguez shoebox, flipped the lid off and started rifling through a sheaf of letters and certificates. "Ah, here we are . . ."

She slid a sheet of paper across the table. It was lined, with a margin and an uneven edge as though it had been torn out of an exercise book.

TEN THINGS TO DO

1) Do something about hair. Highlights? Streaks? But subtle.

2) Lose weight and get a tan.

3) Do NOT slump. Stand up straight, shoulders back. Posture VERY important.

4) Stop biting nails. Get a manicure. And NEVER go out of the house without mascara.

5) Never wear lace-up shoes with flat heels again. EVER.

6) Read all of Jane Austen, Evelyn Waugh, Ronald Firbank.

7) Bone up on opera eg Puccini, Mozart.

8) Live in Notting Hill or Holland Park.

9) Marry Nicholas Fitch or near equivalent.

10) Get rich and live happily ever after.

I said, "Alice wrote this?" But I already knew the answer; the writing was the same anally retentive printing I'd seen in Alice's address book.

"We all made lists, all the time," said Janie. "Kind of a party game. I think this one was our ten-point plan for success, or something."

"Does Alice know you kept it?"

"Christ, no. She'd die if she knew. I thought about reading it out last night, at the hen party, but . . ."

"It was good that you didn't," I said.

She looked down at the paper and shook her head, and said, "It's a bit sad, you know?"

I nodded. I knew what she meant. I made a mental note to go through my own papers and destroy any leftover adolescent lists I turned up. It wouldn't do for them to fall into the wrong hands.

"I bet *Ginny* wouldn't have thought twice about reading it out," I remarked, just a little too vehemently.

Janie gave me a searching glance. "Funny you should say that. I was half expecting Ginny to behave like a bitch last night, but in the end she was good as gold. Really sweet."

"She was? That's a relief."

I suddenly felt a twinge of guilt. Maybe I'd misjudged Virginia Fisher. Maybe there was an innocent explanation for everything after all. *Maybe there was still hope for us.* However, I forced myself to prod a little harder, and asked, "Does Ginny often behave like a bitch?"

Janie waved her hands around. "Well, you know, she can't stand anyone being prettier than her. Which was why she never got on with Georgina. I mean, you did see what she looked like, didn't you?"

I had a sudden flashback to Fegs Lane. What did Janie know? Had Ginny told her something after all?

"See her?" I echoed.

"In the school photo?" Janie prompted.

Oh, so she was talking about the photo. No, I hadn't seen Georgina in the school photo, so when it was time for me to leave and we passed through the hallway on our way to the front door, I paused to have a look.

"There she is," said Janie, smudging the glass with her finger.

I peered closer and saw her. Standing right next to Alice the Gorgon. I couldn't think how I'd missed her the first time round; I must have been so shocked by the way Alice had looked back then that I'd been blinded to everything else.

But Georgina was quite lovely, not in a knowing Lolita-esque way, like the Three Graces, but open-faced and honestly beautiful. Despite the reduced size, it offered a much clearer view of her face than the photo I'd seen at Nick's. It was hard reconciling this vision of teenage pulchritude with the shrieking hag I'd encountered in Fegs Lane, but I had no doubt it was her. Something about those cheekbones.

But if she and Alice had been such close chums, why did Georgina's ghost have it in for her now?

NINETEEN

I PHONED ALICE, but there was no answer on either her land line or her mobile, so against my better judgement—now she would definitely think I had a crush on her—I left the first of what would shortly be a long string of messages, begging her to ring me back.

But she didn't. It was as though she had fallen off the face of the planet.

I couldn't help feeling a little miffed—if she really did fancy me, the least she could do was call—but also increasingly worried. Where was she? Was someone, or something, preventing her from getting in touch? Granted she would no doubt be busy with last-minute preparations, but it wouldn't have taken more than a minute to phone, just to let me know what was going on.

I remembered what she'd said about Ginny taking her out on the town, and also remembered how insistent Nick had been that I play squash with him. Was this just part of a concerted effort to keep Alice and me apart? What were they afraid of? Did they know I was going to try and talk her out of getting married?

Forty-eight hours to go before the ceremony, and I wasn't making much progress. I knew Ginny was an evil she-bitch from hell, but oddly enough this just made me fancy her all the more. I knew the Fitch family was bad news, but where did that get me? And I knew that if I couldn't stop Alice from getting married, she would meet an untimely death, just like all the other Fitch women.

... the FETCH is said to haunt a particular dynasty or bloodline, passing from one member to another like an inheritance, occasionally benign, but more frequently ill-

starred or malevolent. To see one's FETCH *is said to be a portent of death . . .*

Well, Alice had already seen her Fetch. The Curse already hanging over her, like the Sword of Damocles. The question was, at what point would it fall? It couldn't be immediately after the wedding ceremony, or the Fitch bloodline would have died out long ago. After having children? No, Georgina had been childless, so I ruled that one out. Maybe there was something the Fitch women did, presumably unwittingly, that brought the Curse down on their heads. But what could it be?

I spent the rest of the afternoon in Cyber-Bites, frantically surfing the net, but failed to come up with anything new. Time was running out. No, time was positively *galloping*. But I still had a card up my sleeve—maybe not an ace, but a colourful court card nonetheless.

I still had Nick's stag party.

THE WHOLE point of holding the stag party on Thursday night was to give the groom enough time to recover for the wedding on Saturday.

That was the theory, anyhow.

Around Friday lunchtime, however, I awoke with the sort of hangover that threatened to last all weekend and well into the following week as well. I couldn't say what time I'd gone to bed, but dimly recalled streaks of light in the sky as I'd lurched back to the barge. Apart from that vignette, there was a deep dark void where the Thursday night stag party should have been, and an empty space in my head where millions of brain-cells had been annihilated, much as the population of Princess Leia's planet had been wiped out by the Death Star.

Star Wars? Hmmm. Not my favourite film, not by a long chalk.

And why did the thought of Princess Leia make me feel so uneasy?

I fixed myself a glass of Alka-Seltzer. Then followed it up with another.

To judge by the raging thirst, I'd drunk what even by my standards must have been prodigious quantities of alcohol. The phlegmy cough and fur-coated palate indicated I'd been smoking too much as well.

But this was as far as my investigative abilities got me. Beyond the smoking and the drinking—and, let's face it, what else was new?—nothing. A mystery. Thursday evening was a blank.

So I reluctantly gave up on the past and started thinking about the future, namely what would happen tomorrow, Saturday, at three o'clock. Unless I'd actually murdered the groom at some point during the blank space that had been Thursday night, I assumed the wedding would still be going ahead and when it did, the curse would be irremediably triggered, unless in the meantime I could somehow find a way of reversing it, which wasn't looking too likely since I still didn't really know how it worked in the first place.

It was more urgent than ever I made sure Alice understood this, but once again she was proving impossible to get hold of. I tried both her numbers repeatedly, but now she'd even turned her answering machines off. Or someone had turned them off for her. Or I'd filled them up with so many messages they just couldn't take any more.

If I couldn't get hold of her in London, I realised, I would just have to travel up to Norfolk to get the wedding stopped. It was a last-ditch plan, but better than nothing. Wasn't there a part of the service when the vicar asked if anyone knew of any reason why the bride and groom shouldn't be joined in holy matrimony? If the worst came to the worst, I thought bitterly, I could always leap to my feet and yell, "Stop the wedding! He's shagging the bridesmaid!"

But that in itself threw up questions. If Nick wanted to shag Ginny so much, why in hell wasn't he marrying her? She was free, wasn't she? Why would any woman settle for being a mistress when the role of wife was up for grabs? It didn't make sense.

Unless, of course, Ginny knew all about the Fitch Family Curse and had absolutely no intention of putting herself in the line of fire.

For want of anything more constructive to do, I reached for my phone to try calling Alice again, which was when I found the text message from Nick.

YOUR NO LONGER WELCOME AT THE WEDDING CHUM. IF I SEE YOU THERE YOUR DEAD. FUCK OFF BACK TO WHERE YOU CAME FROM.

I had to read this two or three times before it sunk in. Surely some mistake. This wasn't Nick's style at all. It had to be a stupid joke. I called his number.

"Oh," he said. "It's you."

"You bastard," I said jovially. "You had me going there for a while."

There was a frosty silence.

"You *were* having me on?"

The silence grew icicles.

"Hey, I'm all ready to come up to Norfolk tomorrow and rock and roll . . ."

He had the grace to sound embarrassed. "Well, you see, we can't really have you there. Not after last night."

Last night? I already knew it was no good trying to remember, but what on earth could I have done that was so terrible? How could anybody possibly do anything terrible at a *stag party*, for heaven's sake? Surely the whole point was to get wrecked and find ingenious new ways of behaving badly? And anyway, how could it have been worse than what I'd got up to at Selina and Jolly's? I'd behaved appallingly, yet still been hailed as the star performer of the evening. So what could have gone wrong this time?

Finally, I said, "I don't know what you mean."

When Nick spoke, it was with maddening calm. "Seen those photos yet, old man?"

I wanted to yell at him to stop calling me 'old man' in that patronising manner. Who did he think he was? The Great Gatsby? But instead I said, "Say what?"

My jacket was draped over the back of a chair. I turned out the pockets and found a half-empty book of matches, a creased Polaroid, my passport, a couple of ginger nuts, a lot of crumbs, some ticket stubs and scraps of crumpled paper and a disposable camera in its torn foil wrapping, the counter set at thirty-six exposures.

"Oh, those photos," I said, as though I'd known all along what he'd been talking about. "Haven't had a chance to get them developed."

"I suggest you get that done, old man. Maybe they'll help you realise what an asshole you are. And then if I were you I'd burn them. With your track record, you shouldn't find that so difficult."

He let out a horrible hollow laugh.

"Frankly, John, I don't want to see you anywhere near Little Yawning tomorrow, and Alice is in complete agreement. I'm sorry, but consider yourself uninvited."

"No, wait," I said, but he'd already hung up.

Wow. I felt as though someone had split me open and scooped the marrow from my bones with a metal spoon.

Oh boy, what *had* I done?

I DASHED STRAIGHT out to Poppity Pix, but was informed that—due to industrial action—the pictures wouldn't be ready until ten o'clock the next morning. Not so poppity, in fact.

I did some sluggish mental arithmetic; if I called round on the dot of ten, I would be able to study the photos, work out whatever it was I'd done on Thursday night, and then still have enough time to drive up to Norfolk and thrash things out with Alice before she got to the *I do* stage.

THE REST of Friday turned into a Kafkaesque nightmare in which I had been tried and found guilty of a crime I had no recoll-ection of committing. My nerves were playing up; I didn't so much have butterflies in my stomach as an entire nest of angry wasps. Alice still wasn't answering either of her phones. The barge seemed to shrink to the size of a doll's house as I paced up and down in it, so I caught the tube to Notting Hill Gate, and before I knew it my feet were taking me round to Alice's flat.

There was no answer when I rang the bell, but then I hadn't really been expecting one. I stood on the opposite pavement and gazed up at her window, just as I'd gazed up at it a few nights earlier. But there was no sign of life up there now.

Where the hell was she?

Maybe Nick's friends had kidnapped her, though when I thought about it logically there didn't seem much point; she more than anyone had been determined that the wedding should go ahead. But surely she couldn't have left for Norfolk already? She would want to be immaculately groomed for her big day, and I couldn't see her trusting her coiffure to Di's Tresses of Little Yawning as opposed to, say, Teasy-Weasy of Kensington.

I gave up and struck out for Ginny's place, though wasn't surprised when I didn't get a reply there either; she, like Alice, would probably be up to her neck in seaweed wrap in some beauty parlour or other. But I rang her bell again, just for the hell of it, and then, because I couldn't think of anything better to do, pressed the bell a third time, long and hard, directing all my frustration and bitterness into that one finger.

The entryphone finally crackled into life.

"Will you *stop* it, John."

No-one could say persistence never paid off.

"How did you know it was me?"

"Who else would it be?"

I had an answer to that, but instead just asked, "Can I come in?"

"No you cannot."

Angrily, I pressed the buzzer again. "Why not? Is he in there with you?"

I sensed I was making a fool of myself but was powerless to stop.

"I'm busy, John," she said. "I'm a *bridesmaid*, remember?"

"I'm going to keep pressing this buzzer till you let me in."

There was a long silence followed by a grudging click from the lock. I pushed my way in, climbed the stairs to her flat and rapped sharply on her door. The instant my knuckles made contact with the wood, a dog started yapping on the other side, but when Ginny finally opened it—and she wasn't in a hurry— there was no sign of the Jack Russell, or indeed of any other animal.

She positioned herself in the doorway, as though she thought I might try and force my way past, so I was forced to shuffle around on the landing, feeling like an unwelcome floor-polish salesman.

She seemed shorter than I remembered, though it might have been because her feet were stuffed into slippers instead of perched on the usual heels. Had I run into her anywhere else I might have had trouble recognising her—not that she would ever have gone out looking like that in the first place. She was wearing an old dressing-gown. Her head was wrapped in baking foil, her face slathered in pale green mud and there was a strange earthy smell hanging in the air. I wondered if she'd been smoking a joint. It was her appearance, more than anything, that impressed upon me the scale of the rift between us. No woman would ever have allowed herself to look like that in front of a man she was seeking to impress.

It was obvious now that she didn't give a fig about me, never had.

"What's with the Bacofoil turban?"

"Henna," she replied. I must have looked blank because she added, "Hair colour."

These two words astonished me more than anything else I'd heard that week. "You're not a natural redhead?"

"No, John," she said tartly. "I'm not a natural redhead—as you might have seen for yourself if you'd ever taken the trouble to go down and look."

The rush of disappointment was so overwhelming I could taste it in my mouth. It was the final humiliation. And now, just to make me feel even shittier, I could feel the Jack Russell wiping its slimy muzzle on my leg as well; I couldn't see it and neither, of course, could Ginny, but my downward glances and vain attempts to kick it into touch were enough to lend me an air of shiftiness I could probably have done without.

I tried making conversation, to distract her. "So how's the bridesmaid thing going?"

"Oh, just dandy." She scowled. "We're being forced to wear these abominable frocks. Alice is doing it on purpose, so we'll look like pink meringues and she'll look all the more glamorous."

"It *is* her big day," I pointed out.

She shook her head wearily. "Look, John, I really don't have time to stand here and chat. Say what you've got to say and get lost."

"You're Nick's mistress, aren't you," I said. "You've been his mistress for years. Even when Georgina was still alive, you were going up to stay in the village and the two of you were carrying on right under her nose. You're the Camilla Parker-Bowles of this sweet little rom-com."

She said, "There's no need for insults."

I tried to read her expression but her face was, quite literally, a mask.

"So what happened? Did Georgina find out about you? Did you arrange to have her killed?"

She looked scornful. "Christ, no."

"No, of course not," I said. "You didn't have to, did you."

"That's right," she said.

"You've been playing me," I snarled. "All this week, you and Nick have been going out of your way to keep Alice and me apart. You were terrified I'd find out what was going on, and tell her."

"I wouldn't say *terrified*," Ginny shrugged. "I just wanted to make sure she didn't get it into her head to call the whole thing off. After all the trouble we'd gone to."

"Why? What is it to you?" Ginny didn't reply. "Did he buy you this flat?"

"Think what you like, but nothing can change the way Nick and I feel about each other."

What had I been expecting? That she would suddenly have a change of heart and declare that it was all over between her and Nick and invite me inside and we'd be friends again? But when, really, had we ever been friends to begin with? And how could I hope to compete with a lover who showered his mistresses with real estate?

"If you're so damn keen on him," I said, "why are you letting him marry Alice? Why don't you marry him yourself?"

This time she smiled, and her mask cracked into a hundred thousand tiny fissures, like the cracks in the baked wall of an adobe hut in New Mexico.

On the other hand, it might not have been a smile, not exactly—with all that stuff on her face, it was hard to tell.

She said, "Duh."

"Because you don't want to die, is that it? You *do* know about the curse. And you don't give a rat's ass what happens to Alice."

She was growing restless. "I have a shitload of things to do, John. Thanks for stopping by. Now get lost and leave me alone."

"How do I stop it?"

The door was closing. I thrust my foot into the gap.

"Where *is* Alice?"

The mask cracked again. "Somewhere you're never going to reach her, so don't even bother trying. Let's face it, John, it's a done deal. All you can do now is throw confetti as they come out of the church."

"Actually, I had my invitation revoked."

She laughed the laugh I had once thought deliciously wicked. Now it just struck me as cold-blooded.

"Is that so? Can't say I'm surprised, not after last night."

"That's just it," I said. "What *did* happen last night?"

She was applying pressure to the door. Not wanting a crushed metatarsus, I withdrew my foot, and said, "Don't forget to feed that dog," as the door closed definitively in my face.

I WANDERED UP and down Portobello Road, trading obscenities with the market stallholders and elbowing my way through crowds of tourists before stopping off at the Saddleback Arms for a pint, then at the Boar's Head for another, and before I knew it I was doing a full-blown Notting Hill pub crawl.

At some stage, I decided it would be a good idea to stop off at Jeremy's shop and see if he was there. Jeremy would know what had happened at the stag party, if anyone did. Jeremy would be able to tell me where I'd gone wrong.

Had I been sober, of course, I would have known better than to go within a hundred miles of Jeremy.

*   *   *

THE SHOP was crowded. I asked an assistant if he was in, and my sunken spirits lifted as I saw him barrelling out of the back office, holding out a hand in welcome, face lit up with a friendly beam. I completely forgot that Jeremy had it in for me, and took this as a good sign. At long last, someone seemed pleased to see me.

"How are you?" He shook my hand warmly and invited me back into his office, which seemed smaller and stuffier than ever.

"How are you feeling?" he asked, leaning back in his chair.

"Bit rough, actually. Had too much to drink last night."

"Of course you did. It was a stag party. That's what stag parties are for."

I relaxed. Everything was going to be all right. Jeremy was on my side. Maybe he could even get me reinstated on the guest-list. He produced his bottle of rum and poured out the usual measures and handed me one of the paper cups. I sipped gratefully. Then he sat back and put his feet on the desk and asked how much I remembered.

"Oh," I said vaguely. "You know . . ."

He sniggered. "It was a gas, wasn't it? That snake dancer!"

Snake dancer? I must have looked horrified, because he burst out laughing.

"But of course you don't remember! Because it never happened! Know what I mean?"

Once again I cast my mind back, trying to salvage some sliver of memory, but it was as though the entire evening had been smothered in an impenetrable fog, the sort of pea-souper in which the only sounds emerging from the murk would be the rattle of wheels over cobblestones and the occasional scream of an eviscerated prostitute.

"Listen, Jeremy," I said, searching for the right words. "Did I . . .? Do you know if . . .? Did I do anything to offend anyone? Nick, for example?"

Jeremy threw back his head and roared with laughter, so loudly I saw customers peering at us curiously through the open doorway. I thought he was never going to stop, but finally he calmed down enough to ask, "You really don't remember? You don't remember anything?"

I finished my rum. "Not . . . as *such*."

He began to laugh again. "Oh, excuse me," he said, dabbing at his eyes with a handkerchief. "It's just so . . . so . . . Oh, I'm sorry . . ."

"Just so *what?*" I was beginning to wish I hadn't stopped off to see him. But too late now.

He stopped laughing abruptly, like a TV sitcom laughter track cut off by a sound engineer, and leant across the desk and lowered his voice, as though letting me in on a grand secret.

"You thought you were well in there, didn't you? Thought you could worm your way into Nick's inner circle? Thought you could be his *best friend*? Well, let me tell you—he thinks you're a despicable sleazeball and a detestable freak, always has done. All I did was confirm his worst suspicions. The only reason he tolerated your creepy presence as long as he did was that he thought Alice was still sweet on you. But he didn't realise you were a fraud, that you'd only just met her, that you were trying to screw things up royally for him, for them. Until last night, when you went too far. Boy, did you go too far! You went all the way to Timbuktu!"

He started laughing again.

There's nothing quite like a powerful blast of contempt to sober a person up. I pushed back my chair and stood up and walked back through the shop with as much dignity as I could muster. When I was halfway to the door, Jeremy poked his head out of the office to yell at my departing back. "You do realise you caused about ten grand's worth of damage? You're bloody lucky no-one was hurt! Bloody lucky no-one was killed!"

I kept walking without looking back. Customers and assistants were staring at me curiously, wondering what I'd done to merit such derision. I smiled weakly, as if to say, *Well, you know what we hellraisers are like . . .*

"You're goddam lucky we didn't get you picked up by the cops!" shouted Jeremy. "You've got Nick to thank for that. Nice guy, Nick. Me, I'd have had you strung up by the balls."

Cops? Damage? What the hell? But everyone was staring, so I didn't like to hang around. My face was burning scarlet as I pushed the door open and escaped into the street.

What the hell had I done?

I SLOUCHED HOMEWARD, feeling numb and slightly unreal. I'd sinned and been cast out of Eden. But maybe there was still a way of sneaking back over the garden wall while no-one was looking. I still couldn't get hold of Alice—she had been whisked out of my reach by Nick or his cronies, that much was clear— but I had at least one advantage. I knew exactly where she was going to be at three o'clock on Saturday afternoon. And unless Nick was planning to post armed guards around the church, he wouldn't be able to keep me away.

Three text messages awaited me.

STOP THE WEDDING

STOP THE WEDDING

STOP THE WEDDING

Not a lot of ambiguity there, then.

When Sol popped round for coffee and spliffs later on, I showed him.

"So who's sending them?" he asked.

"Georgina, I guess."

"But why would Georgina want to *stop* the wedding? Wasn't she supposed to be the portent of doom?"

"What's your point, Mr Spock?"

Sol took another long toke of the joint. He was just about the only person I'd ever met who made more sense stoned than when sober.

"OK, so she's the ghostly manifestation of this Fitch Curse. So presumably she can't wait for Alice and Nick to get married so she can get down to a-cursing in earnest. That's her *raison d'être*, isn't it? So why would she try and put herself out of a job by trying to get the wedding stopped? It doesn't make sense."

I thought about it. Sol was right; it didn't make sense. I looked at the text messages again.

"Maybe it wasn't Georgina who sent these."

Sol shrugged. "Yet who else would it be? You said yourself that Nick and Ginny are eager for the wedding to go ahead. So who would that leave?"

I couldn't think of anyone else, and neither could Sol.
"Maybe Janie," I said doubtfully. "Or Jeremy."
"Does not compute," said Sol.
And he was right again. It didn't.

TWENTY

I WOKE UP to find my head wedged in Boris' basket, the taste of old underpants in my mouth and *Stargazer* repeating itself endlessly on the sound system.

My biscuit tin was open, its contents strewn across the floor. Glued to my palm was the tiny photograph of my mother's grave, a photograph I'd never dared show anyone, because anyone who knew my date of birth would spot straightaway that the dates didn't tally.

I tried to smooth out the creases, but eventually gave up and laid it carefully back in the tin, like the precious relic it was. I wondered whether I'd been stupid enough to show it to Sol, or whether I'd got it out after he'd left. I hoped it was the latter—I never shared the contents of my biscuit tin with anyone—but my memories of the evening were blurry. Not as blurry as Thursday night, of course, put pretty hazy all the same.

Next to me on the floor were an ashtray overflowing with stubs and a bottle of Famous Grouse with a couple of inches left in the bottom. Was this a new hangover or simply a continuation of the old one? Still, I decided, it could have been worse: I could have finished the bottle.

I looked at my watch: it was ten to ten.

Cowboy time.

What day was this? Oh yes, Saturday.

And why should the thought of Saturday weigh down on me like an extra brick on top of a man already being pressed to death?

Oh yes, today was the day of the wedding.

I sat up.

Alice and Nick!

The curse!

The wedding!

And I had photos to collect.

Not moving as fast as I would have liked, I hauled myself into the shower and rinsed away the thick mat of cat hair adhering to one side of my face before pulling on some clothes and careering down the road to Poppity Pix. I handed my yellow slip to a chinless youth who flipped through a drawerful of packets before chewing his lip for a moment and then asking if I wanted the other packet as well.

"Other packet?" I turned the words over in my head, trying to decipher their hidden meaning.

"You dropped another disposable camera off a couple of days ago."

My memory of the past few days had more holes than a lace doily, but this bloke obviously remembered me, so I decided to wing it.

"OK. Might as well take that one too." I held out my hand.

Chinless shook his head. "I'll need the slip."

I blinked in disbelief. Wanker! Why had he mentioned the other photos in the first place if he was going to be difficult about handing them over? Was he trying to be annoying on purpose? I felt like grabbing him by the ears and mashing his face into the counter, but he was bigger than me so I mumbled incoherently and emptied my pockets.

A small queue built up behind me as I pulled out passport, matchbook, ticket stubs and several scrunched-up balls of paper. I'd apparently eaten the ginger nuts I vaguely remembered had been there the last time I'd looked, but there was a plentiful supply of crumbs. I unballed the wads of paper and smoothed them out on the counter top. Two receipts from the off-licence. One receipt for cat food. And oh yes, hallelujah, one yellow slip from Poppity Pix. I handed it to Chinless Wanker, who'd been looking as though he expected me to cough up frogs.

I counted out my money and got the two packets in return. I resisted the temptation to tear them open there and then. To judge by Chinless Wanker's snotty-nosed expression, he was already well-acquainted with the contents, and the last thing I wanted was to give him the satisfaction of hearing my shrieks in horror as I confronted the awful truth.

So I loped back to the barge, where I sat and stared at the stag night packet and realised I wasn't sure if I wanted to open it after all. As Dana Andrews (or was it Peggy Cummins?) said at the end of *Night of the Demon*, maybe it's better not to know.

But I was the only thing standing between Alice and the Fitch Family Curse. I was her only hope. I was the only one who *cared*.

I ripped open the seal.

The photos were more effective than any madeleine. Random dribbles of memory started trickling back. I remembered just enough to be thankful they weren't any more coherent.

NICHOLAS FITCH'S stag party had begun in Gnashers and ended up in Hell.

But if Nick knew that I knew he'd been shagging Ginny, you would never have guessed, because he started off as friendly as ever. And, because I didn't want him to know how much I knew or cared, I tried to look as though I were enjoying myself, all the while silently urging, *Go on you bastard. Do your worst.*

Because nestling in my pocket was my secret weapon—a disposable camera. How thrilled would Alice be if she were to see photos of her precious fiancé getting arseholed and shagging a stripper? Would *that* be enough to persuade her to call it off?

FLASH!

The first photo is harmless enough. We're in an upstairs room at Gnashers. Everyone's a little stiff and self-conscious, for no-one has yet had much to drink. Nick and Jeremy are here, and so is Jolyon, the chef whose party I'd crashed, as well as the pink-cheeked man who'd punched me in the face. To my surprise, I find I know his name; it's Simon Knowlesworth, but for as long as he can remember his friends have called him *Knobsworth*.

I reflect that it's not just girls who saddle each other with stupid nicknames.

Now my memory has been jogged, it seems to me that the first part of the evening, at least, is relatively clear in my head. Yes, it's coming back to me now. I think I'm being smart by avoiding the first couple of rounds of Dry Martinis and sticking to lager. All this does, however, is make me over-confident, so that when a photographer called Rupert Strangeweather (whom everyone calls *Strathers*) produces what a handful of what look like bright red Smarties, I do what everyone else is doing and eagerly gulp a couple of them down.

Not the smartest move, in the circumstances.

Flash!

To judge by the next photo, we're no longer in Gnashers, though I have no clear memory of switching venues. Now it's a basement drinking club fitted out to resemble a grotto with polystyrene stalactites. Bit of a fire-trap, in other words. The barman is hovering solicitously in the background, but he doesn't have much to do; someone has ponied up a shitload of cash so we stags can have the place to ourselves, and we seem to be mixing our own drinks. The red neon sign behind the mirrored bar reads SOUL FIRE, which rings a bell somewhere in my increasingly fuddled brain. Isn't that a brand name, maybe one of those ready-mixed alcopops? Whatever, we revellers have no need of prepackaged tat like that—we're making up our own recipes as we go along.

Flash!

Ah yes, the drinks. I groan at the memory. As if gulping pills and lager weren't enough, we're also inventing cocktails. It's a challenge to see who can come up with the ghastliest. Nick goes first. He whips up a little something he calls Slow Death in honour of a depressing Swedish rock band called The Leather Nun. The ingredients include absinthe, gin and a swirl of something black and viscous that might possibly be Marmite. I take a sip, shudder with horror and pass the glass to Justin Carver, who's sitting next to me.

But wait. Nick's asking me what it was like. I assume he's seeking my verdict on his cocktail, and try desperately to think of something complimentary to say, but it turns out he's talking about something else entirely. Dan Barclay, a TV producer even shorter than me (and whose attempt to disguise his lack of height with stacked heels makes me feel morally superior) tells me Nick is asking about the hen night. Everyone's theorising about what the chicks get up to without the civilising influence of their hunters and gatherers.

All of a sudden, everyone's looking at me. What makes them think I have the faintest idea of what went on at the hen party? Do I *look* like a hen? Do they think Janie gave me a slide-show? It doesn't matter—what does matter is they've got it into their heads that I'm somehow privy to the arcane mysteries of female behaviour. So I say the women snogged each other. I know instinctively this kind of comment will go down well in all-male company, and I'm right. Cheers and whistles. There are exclamations of *lesbians!* and someone, maybe even me, starts yelling about witchy rituals and seances. An American called Charles Hooper, who's over in Europe to research the Great American Novel he will never write, asks if they succeeded in summoning any spirits, and if so, which ones.

I'm ratfaced. I say the first thing that pops into my head, which just happens to be about the Fitch family banshee. I mention her as a joke, but even through the fug of liquor, I can sense a chill in the atmosphere.

Hooper either seems not to know the history of the Fitch curse, or knows it perfectly well and simply wants me to screw myself up the arse. He asks if the banshee was a babe. Aware that everyone's listening, but wholly unable to rein in my runaway mouth, I start theorising about Georgina's death, about how she thought was being stalked, about what happened to make her crash her car into the canal, and why she might now have turned against her former best friend. Willy the gardener is doggedly trying to distract Nick with an argument about whether the definitive death-knell of Sixties cinema was sounded by *Easy Rider*, *Night of the Living Dead* or *The Sound of Music*, but Nick isn't paying attention to him. He's listening to me. And frowning.

Hooper lets out a long, low whistle, like an old-fashioned kettle coming up to the boil. All eyes are still on me and I take this as a signal that it's now my turn to invent a cocktail.

Flash!

Someone else must have got hold of the camera, because here I am, in position behind the bar, knocking up a saucy blend of Guinness and Tia Maria. I dub it a Black Fingernail, after Sid James' character in *Carry On Don't Lose Your Head*. Dan Barclay, who declares that Sid James is his hero and role model, adds the finishing touch by gobbing into the mixture. Strangely enough, this doesn't seem to deter anyone from tasting it.

I ask Dan Barclay if he's *the* Dan Barclay. He nods, flattered at having been—he thinks—recognised. I tell him the wedding is all his fault, or maybe not, depending whose story one wants to believe, and not surprisingly he looks baffled. I ask rather aggressively if he actually remembers having introduced Alice to Nick, which was just one of the tall stories she'd spun to me. Dan Barclay chews thoughtfully on a toothpick and tells me it's possible, since he does remember Nick being keen to meet her.

Jeremy chips in, and says Nick had been keen to meet Alice's bank balance.

Raucous laughter.

Dan says something about Nick having a hungry mansion to feed, and I reply that in that case the joke's on him since Alice is stony broke. I'm confidently expecting everyone to burst out laughing again, but the bar goes dead quiet and I realise I've made a bit of a gaffe. Nick calls me an asshole. He's pissed off at me . . . but not that pissed off. He doesn't believe for a second that I might be telling the truth.

Then Jolyon—or maybe it's Hooper—unfolds a small paper packet and tips a quantity of off-white powder into a pile on the mirrored surface of the bar. He chops it up with a razor-blade and divides it into neat lines.

There's no photo of this, of course, but I distinctly remember it happening.

This time it occurs to me to ask what I'm getting. To which Jolyon—or maybe it's Hooper—asks if it really matters, since no-one gives a fuck.

Which is evidently good enough for me, because I go ahead and hoover up a couple of lines anyway. After that I start smoking someone's Marlboro. I smoke so many that I have to go to the machine and buy a replacement packet. I end up smoking most of these as well and have to go back for more, several times.

Flash!

Which is probably why the cigarette machine gets a photo all to itself.

Willy the gardener, who I learn is Janie's boyfriend, calls his cocktail a Flayed Member. Among the ingredients are grenadine and a dead earthworm he's brought along in his pocket.

Someone's throwing up on the floor of the gents' toilets. I think it might be me.

Flash!

We seem to have been joined by a group of women. I didn't see them arrive, but they're here now. In fact, one of them is sitting on my lap. She's wearing a tight red leather mini-skirt and laddered stockings, and I have an erection as big as the Eiffel Tower, even though I can clearly see she's equipped with an Adam's apple and a chinful of stubble. Come to think of it, she looks not unlike Dan Barclay's hero, Sid James.

I grumble that her tits aren't real. She assures me they are.

Flash!

A man dressed in a spangly Nehru jacket and turban is playing the flute. I recognise the tune straightaway—it's that same Ronnie James Dio song I've had on the brain this past week. I sing along happily, though my attempts at air guitar are hampered by the girl in my lap.

Next to the flautist is a large laundry basket. I ask the woman straddling my groin what the basket is for. She leans forward, revealing a Grand Canyon of cleavage, and her stubble tickles my ear as she whispers that the flautist is a snake charmer and that inside the basket is a snake.

I feel a panic attack coming on. I tell her I don't like snakes, to which Sid James replies that's odd because I seem to have an anaconda of my own. She wriggles provocatively, and my hard-on upgrades from Eiffel Tower to Empire State.

I look over to where Nick is sandwiched between two women. Both seem larger than average but neither, as far as I can see, possesses anything resembling an Adam's apple, at least not in the gullet region. Nick is smoking a cigar the size of the Graf Zeppelin. One of the women has unzipped his flies and is busily foraging within, but Nick isn't paying attention; he's staring over her shoulder towards the basket and asking who's in it. Knobsworth sniggers that it's for him to find out.

The lid falls off the laundry basket and rolls across the floor like a hubcap after a car crash.

Flash!

Emerging from the basket are long tanned fingers covered in jewelled rings. The fingers are attached to a hand, which is attached to a bare arm. The arm is attached to a surprisingly muscular shoulder. Next, a leg emerges from the basket. There's a gold chain around the ankle. The feet are enormous, toenails lacquered in glimmering mother-of-pearl.

The head and torso emerge last of all; they either belong to a gymnast or to an anatomically incorrect freak. The lower half of the face is veiled in yellow chiffon. The eyes are deep black and ringed with kohl. She's wearing a gold bikini that inevitably reminds me of the one Princess Leia wore in *Return of the Jedi*. As far as I can remember, though, Princess Leia didn't have a thick black snake draped around her neck.

I hate snakes. *Really* hate them.

I begin to feel nauseous with fear.

I take another look at the Snake Dancer.

Omigod. It's Ginny.

This is too freaky. Quickly I look away, but too late, because she has seen me looking at her, and now she's fixing me with an unblinking stare as she uncoils and starts to move sinuously towards me. Surely she's not going to make a play for me right in front of her lover? The snake raises its small head lethargically as she advances. Maybe it's drugged. But I can see its forked tongue flickering.

My hard-on withers away. I make a strangled noise in my throat and try to shift my chair backwards, but my weight combined with that of Sid James is too much. The legs creak, but the chair won't budge.

The snake is coming closer.

COMING COMING CLOSER CLOSER

I shrink back.

Then someone shouts at the Snake Dancer to change direction.

In a single sinuous movement, Ginny swivels and glides away from me, towards Nick. He immediately tips the two women off his lap and greets his mistress with open arms, though without getting up from his chair. She slips out of her gold bikini bottom and straddles him and he grips her buttocks with both hands as she begins to move up and down in his lap. I stare in disbelief. They're doing it? They're actually *doing* it? *In front of people?* The cigar is still clamped between his teeth. He blows a cloud of smoke in her face, but she takes it in her stride.

Don't even ask what the snake is doing.

Some of the photos are missing. For example, I clearly remember taking a photo of Strathers peeing into a beer-glass, but there's no record of that here. And I clearly remember someone lying on the floor, and me not being able to identify him because there's a semi-naked woman sitting on his face. I remember framing this scene in an artistic, almost abstract way, but that seems to be missing too.

Sid James has long since found another lap to sit on, so I saunter over to where Jeremy is hunched over the mirrored bar, hoovering up another line of powder. I prop myself up next to him and ask him, pointedly, where they found the dancer. I tell him she looks familiar.

Jeremy bursts out laughing and slaps me on the back and I look over to where the Snake Dancer is jogging up and down like a big kid on a bouncy castle. Nick's cigar has gone out, but he's still chomping down on it like a man biting a piece of wood while a backwoods surgeon saws off his arm and I realise, too late, that Jeremy is Saint-Just to Nick's Robespierre, which unfortunately would probably make me Marat, destined for an early bath. Or maybe Jeremy is Dean Martin and Nick is Sinatra and Ginny is Shirley MacLaine's evil id. So what would that make me? Sammy Davis Jr?

I try to express these thoughts out loud, but Jeremy remarks that I'm even more arseholed than he is and invites me to snort another line, creep. I tell him not to call me that, but go ahead and snort a couple more lines anyway. Hell, why not?

I look back at where Nick and the Snake Dancer are getting it on.

How could I ever have thought she was Ginny? She looks nothing like Ginny. She looks as much like Ginny as I do.

Flash!

I've taken a photo of the dancer and Nick. Together. Just for the record. (So where is it? Because I sure as hell can't find it here.) As I press the button and the flash goes off, Nick looks round, blinking, trying to pinpoint the source of the dazzle, and asks me what the fuck I'm doing. His speech is slurred. I lower the camera and tell him it's one for the record books. He tells me he'd rather I didn't. I notice his face is distorted, as though he's having to concentrate on not ejaculating. I'm glad to see someone else has that problem.

I demand to know why he's marrying Alice. He says, *What?* His fingers are digging into the Snake Dancer's rump. She stops moving, paused like a tiny fishing-craft on the crest of a wave. She's wearing way too much make-up.

Why Alice, I ask. Why not Ginny?"

What? Nick can't believe his ears.

But I've started, and so I'll finish.

Why not Ginny? I tell Nick that he and Ginny make the perfect couple, and he lets out an incredulous laugh. Actually, it's more of a short, sharp yelp. And then he asks what it has to me with me, buster.

I tell him he's not the only one who's been fucking Virginia Fisher.

Nick looks taken aback, but not for long. His face cracks wide open in a vicious grin and he says that wasn't what *he* heard, that according to what *he* heard there hadn't been any fucking at all, just a bit of schoolboy fumbling.

I can't help it. I start yelling. I yell that his fiancée is only marrying him for social status, but that now she's madly in love with *me*, she's going to call the wedding off so she can marry *me* instead. Nick can't stop laughing. I totter a couple of steps in his direction, intending to sock him one in his smug patrician jaw, but at the last moment I notice the snake and lose my balance and have to concentrate on not falling over. And as I'm doing this, someone grabs my upraised arm. I lash out at Nick again, but now Jeremy has got me around the waist and my arms aren't long enough to reach their target. I keep on swinging anyhow. I imagine the effect must be quite comical.

Jeremy tells me I've gone too far. I tell him I always have had trouble judging distances. I squirm free of his grip at last, turn my back on Nick and brush myself down.

I can feel everyone's eyes on my back as I slope off to hunt for my jacket. Slip it on and defiantly light a cigarette and stand there, smoking furiously. I'm playing at being Marlon Brando in *The Wild One* again, but one by one the other stags lose interest and get back to doing whatever it was they were doing before they were distracted by my tantrum.

Nick has taken up where he left off with the Snake Dancer. Jeremy has gone back to chopping up powder. Strathers is lying naked on the floor, being jerked off by Sid James, or maybe Barbara Windsor, I can't tell the difference any more, but I can see that Strathers has a skull tattooed on his inner arm. Willy the gardener and Charles Hooper appear to be entangled in some sort of threesome, or maybe a foursome, and I see they have skull tattoos as well, and Dan Barclay is puking his guts out into the empty laundry basket, though since his arms are covered I can't see whether he has one as well.

And all the while someone is chanting in a weird and rather disturbing falsetto: *May the meat of my bones be eaten by worms, May my eyes be plucked out with pincers and crushed beneath the hooves of fire horses, The bones beneath the flesh The skull beneath the skin May my gums be seared with red-hot irons My teeth be ground to dust . . .*

I can't tell which direction this singsong voice is coming from—maybe it's just the CD-player behind the bar—but I don't much care. I don't care about anything much any more.

Except maybe my cat. My cat Boris, whom I'd rescued from a sack in the canal and who has rewarded me with unconditional affection ever since.

Well, I guess it was unconditional if you discounted the food thing.

Time to go home and give my cat some kitty-nibbles. Time to quit this hellhole.

At least I'm not coming away empty-handed. I pat the pocket where the camera is stowed, and saunter unsteadily towards the bottom of the stairs. I take one last defiant puff on my cigarette and toss what's left of it towards an ashtray.

But I've never been much good at ball-games. My aim is way off target.

Out of the corner of my eye, I see the butt rolling off the table and landing plop in the middle of the Snake Dancer's discarded gold bikini bottom.

Which is where I leave it, gently smouldering.

TWENTY ONE

I FRITTERED AWAY precious minutes by calling Poppity Pix and demanding to know what they'd done with the missing photos.

"They were obscene," said a whiny nasal voice I recognised as that of Chinless Wanker.

"It was a *stag party*. Those pictures were an irreplaceable record of an unrepeatable occasion."

"They were pornographic."

I felt anger bubbling up inside me. "What is this? A police state? Who said you could censor people's private photos?"

"We here at Poppity Pix have a moral duty to protect the public."

"I *am* the public, you asshole."

I rang off, feeling as though someone had just severed my feet at the ankles. All that anguish and humiliation, and fuck-all to show for it. Now I didn't even have visual proof of Nick's bad behaviour. I could tell Alice all about it, of course, but would she believe me? Would she *want* to believe me?

My distracted gaze fell upon the second Poppity packet. I remembered now; it was the film I'd taken the day of that awful dinner at Framptons.

I wasn't expecting anything much—just a few arty compositions of the graveyard, but what I saw when I opened the packet made my blood run as cold as an Alpine stream in winter.

I was able to get a good look at Georgina because she was in every single photograph, shadowy and yet distinct, darker than the rest of the frame, so that if I hadn't known better I might have accused Chinless Wonder of doctoring the prints, of pasting in a figure from an older picture, but doing it badly, so that the lighting on her was all wrong and parts of her were missing. It reminded me of that kiddy book in which you had to find Wally, who was hidden somewhere in each picture, except that Georgina wasn't so very hidden, and you would never have dreamt of inflicting a face like that on children; their parents would have sued you. She was standing behind the telephone booth, or perched like a crow on the village signpost, or looking out of the attic window of The Stumps or, most alarmingly, peering out from the window of Sally's Tea Shop, a mere few inches away from the lens.

She was everywhere. It was obvious she'd given up stalking Alice and had started to stalk me instead. I was obviously way more fun to stalk than Alice had been.

I wondered if Georgina was watching me right now. I hurriedly stuffed the photos back into their packet. The barge suddenly seemed an awful lot smaller. And full of shadows. I sought out Boris to say goodbye, but he was hunkered down at the back of a cupboard, and refused to come out, even when I rattled a packet of kitty-nibbles. When I reached in to get him, he hissed at me and tried to back away.

Which wasn't like my cat at all.

BENNY'S PANDA stalled halfway between Cambridge and Ely and refused to start again, so I left it on the hard shoulder with a scribbled note on the dashboard, grabbed the carrier bag containing *Old Egbert's*, planted myself at the side of the road and stuck out my thumb.

Nobody stopped. No-one was going to be dumb enough to pick up a wild-eyed scruff who was hopping up and down like a flayed soul frying on a hotplate in hell. How were they to know it was from anxiety at the approaching deadline, and not because of an urgent need to use the lavatory?

The words *three o'clock* were scorched like a brand into the soft tissue of my brain. I checked my watch so regularly I could feel the beginnings of repetitive strain injury in my wrist. Little more than an hour to go, and I was still a world away from Little Yawning. Little more than an hour, and the minutes were ticking away and I could feel the overture from *William Tell* pounding away in my temples.

I was on the point of hurling myself in front of a car—giving the driver the choice of knocking me down or picking me up, it didn't seem to matter any more—when finally, miraculously, a large bronze-coloured Jaguar coasted to a halt a hundred feet or so along the road.

I stared after it in disbelief, half expecting it to take off again without me as soon as I made a move, but it stayed where it was, engine idling, until I'd caught up. The nearside back door popped open, all by itself.

"Little Yawning," I said, clambering in as though it were a London taxi. "I'm late for a wedding."

The driver grunted without turning round. He was completely bald. I slammed the door shut and he started off without a word. He didn't speak once on the journey. I stared at the prominent veins in the back of his head and thought of The Humungus in *Mad Max 2*. Though fortunately my driver was wearing a grey suit rather than a skimpy black leather S&M outfit.

I checked my watch. Fifty minutes to go.

I MUST HAVE dozed off, because the next thing I was aware of was the car braking more sharply than was necessary—as though the driver wanted to jolt me awake and thus spare himself the trouble of having to open his mouth and actually say something.

Where was I? Oh, yes. We'd drawn up alongside the sign.

WELCOME TO LITTLE YAWNING

We couldn't go any further, not in the Jag, because the road was blocked by sloppily parked cars. Only pedestrians could get through. Were all these people going to the wedding, I wondered, because this line-up of battered Fiestas and rusty Seats didn't look at all like the sort of vehicles that Alice and Nick's friends would have been seen dead in. I'd expected something more along the lines of BMWs and SUVs.

I glanced at my watch. Ten to three. Still on schedule, just, but I had to look sharp.

The bald man pressed something on the dashboard and my

door popped open. I climbed out and shut the door and prepared to thank the driver to his face, but before I'd taken more than a couple of steps in his direction, he'd already stomped on the accelerator and the Jag did a smooth U-turn and sped back down the lane. And I'd never even seen his face. Why had he picked me up? Was he some millionaire philanthropist who routinely gave lifts to anxious-looking strangers?

But what the hell, I was working to a deadline here. I checked my watch again.

Eight and a half minutes to three.

I realised I was standing right on the spot where Georgina had caught up with me on Monday night. I didn't hang around there. I turned and started to jog up the road.

THE FIRST hint that it was not business as usual in Little Yawning was the sound of amplified Eminem that almost drowned out the peal of church bells. The closer I got to the village green, the more I became aware of a fetid smell that reminded me of my gym-socks after I'd played squash. Then I saw the green itself was all but obscured beneath a large marquee, a semi-circle of market stalls and a milling crowd of, oh, about thirty or forty people, some of whom I recognised as regulars from The Stumps. There was a lot of semi-hysterical yelling and screaming, but I didn't have time to worry about that now. I jogged straight past the parade of shops.

The door to Sally's Teashop was wedged open with a telephone directory, but the place was as deserted as the Marie Celeste, even down to several platefuls of half-eaten food. Patel's, Ronnie the Grocer and Yawning Pages, scene of my recent misdemeanour, had all shut up shop. There was a handwritten notice taped to the grocer's door.

CLOSED FOR CHEESE-TRAMPLING FESTIVAL

The combination of music and bells was threatening to give me one of my headaches. But the seconds were ticking away. Aiming directly for the church tower, I started to cut across one corner of the green, craning my neck as I went to try and see what it was that the villagers were finding so hilarious.

Through a gap in the crowd I glimpsed half a dozen squealing children and several of the local delinquents leaping up and down on something large and squishy that made wet farting sounds as it was trampled. I was unable to identify the cheese, but it was the size of a small paddling pool, with the texture of Brie and the colour of dirty Caerphilly made even dirtier by the repeated impact of scuffed trainers. The spectacle was so grotesque it left me with no desire to see any more than I had to.

Four minutes to three . . .

And then—disaster.

Someone grabbed my arm and before I realised what was happening I was being hauled away from the church and into the crowd.

"No," I protested. "Wait . . ."

I dug my heels into what remained of the grass, but to no avail. My abductor was bigger than me.

And he had a turquoise quiff.

"Thought you'd never make it," said Clint as he dragged me away from my goal. He was a caveman, and I was his bitch. I tried to prise myself loose, but he had a grip like a pitbull. "Come on, I know where there's a nice slice of Double Gloucester waiting to have the shit kicked out of it."

"Got to . . . stop the wedding . . ." I gasped, but my voice was drowned out by the sounds of merrymaking. Someone thrust a can of lager into my free hand. The tug of the crowd succeeded where my own efforts had failed and loosened Clint's grip, but too late. I was hemmed in on all sides, and jostled and spun until I couldn't tell which way was up.

In mounting despair, I checked my watch. Three minutes to three, but the church was no longer in view. So near, and yet so far. My nostrils were filled with the smell of overripe curd mixed with stale body odour. I tried pushing in what I thought might be the right direction, only to find myself tipped sideways, and lifted, and then the ground itself gave way, and my feet were sinking into something soft, and I had to keep bobbing up and down on the spot, just to stop myself from being swallowed up.

I was trampling cheese.

"No!" I yelled, "*Noooo!*"

I caught sight of Clint grinning at me from over the tousled head of a runny-nosed small boy.

"Ain't this fun?"

"*The wedding . . .*" I mouthed, trying to step down, but three or four arms were wound tightly around my torso, holding me securely in place, and my efforts to disengage were hampered by my having to hang on to my bag and the can, which disgorged a thin geyser of lager with each downward lurch until the front of my jeans was soaked.

"The wedding!" smiled Clint, who seemed to be having no trouble making himself heard over the din; maybe yelling *Time, gentlemen please!* every night was good training for the larynx. "Wacky local tradition! Each time one of those bastards gets hitched his lordship has to treat the village to a truckload of cheese."

Two minutes to three.

I yelled at the top of my lungs. "*I've got to go!*"

This time he heard me. "What's up, mate?"

"*I have to get to the church!*"

"OK, mate." He was mildly offended but trying to hide it. "If you'd rather hang out with the nobs, go ahead. No worries . . ."

I wanted to tell him that, in the normal scheme of things, I would have preferred to stay out here, trampling cheese with the unwashed masses, but felt myself pitched brusquely out of the huddle, and the can was jerked out of my grasp so roughly that more of the lager splashed out and soaked my sleeve.

I was on my knees, surrounded by a forest of legs. I got up and tried to push my way through the throng, which now seemed to have swollen to Old Trafford proportions and was making a noise to match.

One and a half minutes to three, with the church tower once again in my sights, but now I was being sucked sideways into the maw of the marquee.

The hubbub bouncing off the canvas like shouts in an indoor swimming-pool, the greenish lighting and suffocating smell of sour milk made it feel as though I were trapped in some sort of dairy limbo. Villagers were busily enacting a low-rent version of the stock exchange, yelling and waving slips of paper in the air. Rosy-cheeked women chalked complicated sums on black-boards and traded cans of lager for pink cloakroom tickets. Big men in white aprons rolled outsized truckles into place and small children squealed like piglets.

For what seemed like an eternity I bobbed like a cork in the ocean, swept first one way and then another, until the tide carried me clean across the tent and I found myself crushed against a trestle table loaded with several tons of uncut Wensleydale. I ducked beneath the table, scrambling on all-fours until I emerged into an area piled with empty wooden trolleys. There was no crowd here; the only trouble was that I couldn't see any way through the canvas either and I was forced to follow the wall of the tent until I came to a slit wide enough for me to squeeze through.

Free at last! Free, and breathing in great draughts of lactose-free air. I was now on the far side of the village green, and after the mayhem of the marquee, the silence was deafening in my ears. *Too* deafening. Something was missing.

The bells! The bells had stopped.

I started running again, until there was no longer anything standing between me and the church. It was there, right ahead, and no crowds in my way.

Only a couple of minutes past three o'clock. Surely they couldn't have started on time? It would be typical of Alice to be the only bride in history to reach the altar ahead of schedule. I could hear faint organ music, but the doors were already closed. I flung them open with a crash and stood there on the threshold, blinking uselessly, trying to adjust to the relative darkness within.

The organ music paused in mid-arpeggio, leaving the notes hanging in the air. I shifted my weight from one foot to the other, still virtually blind. For all I knew, I was poised on the edge of a sheer drop. But it was now or never.

I took the plunge.

I broke into a run.

"Stop!" I yelled. "Stop the wedding!"

It wasn't the scene I'd had in mind, which I suppose was the one at the end of *The Graduate*, because even though I was yelling at the top of my voice, the sound was instantly absorbed by booming echo and the loud slap of my soles against the stone flags.

Gradually my eyes adjusted and as I raced up the aisle the scene in front of me developed slowly, like a Polaroid. I doubt anyone could have understood precisely what I was shouting, but I was making an unseemly racket, and they'd all turned to stare. Some of the faces I recognised, others were unfamiliar, but as I raced towards the altar, I just had time to register the little group clustered in front of it. It was as though the entire cast of my recent life-story had been assembled in front of my eyes, ready to mock me.

I saw Ginny and Finny and Janie, all trying desperately to look fetching in ruched pink taffeta, and Jeremy with his smug bastard smile, and a vision in frothy white lace that I knew had to be Alice even though her face was veiled, and standing next to her was an older man who didn't look anything like the Mr Marchmont I'd been expecting, which I suppose was a sort of hand-wringing careworn Bob Cratchit type in a chequered suit. This Mr Marchmont was grey-haired and distinguished-looking, like a lawyer or bank manager.

Everyone's mouth was open—a row of perfect *O*s. I might have laughed, if I'd had time.

Nick's was the only mouth that wasn't an *O*. His was set in a grim line.

Last of all, I recognised Nick's fist, which was coming up to meet my face. I didn't have the space to slow down, and I couldn't raise my own hands in defence, because I was still clutching *Old Egbert's Almanac* to my chest.

The velocity of Nick's arm combined with my hurtling onslaught added up to the impact of a small train wreck as his knuckles made contact with my head.

Bang!

Everything went black.

TWENTY TWO

SOMEONE WAS moaning with pain. I concluded it was probably me.

Where was I? *When* was I?

It was so dark I had to bring my watch right up to my nose to see the hands. Five o'clock. But am or pm? Impossible to tell.

All I could see were flowers, flowers everywhere, arcing over my head like dark blooms in a midnight bower, strange and flat and two-dimensional, though maybe this was because I was seeing it through only a single eye. The other eye was blocked by something cold and wet, which was strange because the rest of me was sweaty and overheated. Breathing was a laborious business; not only was there a weight on my chest, but the air had a stuffy and over-familiar feel to it, as though it had already been recycled through my lungs too many times.

Over and above the moaning, which now I thought about it probably wasn't me after all, my ears were picking out a muffled *ker-chunk ker-chunk*, as though someone in an adjoining room were hammering nails into a coffin.

That would be mine.

I couldn't move my arms and legs. Obviously a form of paralysis—someone had slipped me a Mickey Finn, and a mad surgeon was even now sharpening his scalpel prior to removing my kidneys for sale on the black market before burying the rest of me alive.

But no, I wiggled my toes and raised my chin; I appeared to be immobilised beneath a tightly tucked-in floral-patterned quilt. I struggled to free my arms, and the cold, wet object that had been covering my eye slid off. This didn't do much to improve my vision, though; I was still half-blind.

I twisted round and, with the eye that worked, saw a small

plastic bag of melting ice on the pillow next to my head. Gingerly I probed the unseeing orb with my fingers. The socket was puffed up, lids swollen shut, and so tender that even the lightest touch made me wince. I wondered whether the damage was irreversible. Maybe I would end up with an involuntary wink, like Janie Carruthers. There seemed to be a dull throbbing pain coming from the back of my head as well. I explored it with my hand and discovered a raw swelling, like the tip of a soft-boiled egg embedded in my skull.

I struggled to loosen the quilt still further. My shoes had been removed, but otherwise I was fully clothed and tucked into a four-poster draped with chintz; no wonder I was hot and sweaty.

I poked and pulled at the drapes until they parted. In the room beyond I saw a dressing-table covered in little pots and tubes and fearsome black plastic instruments of torture that might have been hairdryer attachments. On the chair in front of it was an open bag disgorging a froth of wispy lingerie and half a dozen pairs of ridiculously flimsy shoes.

The bag looked familiar. So did the room.

Ah yes, this was Framptons. The bag was Alice's.

I was in Alice's room.

Bloody hell. It was all coming back to me. I'd dreamt Nick and Alice were getting married, and that Nick's family was cursed, and Alice was doomed, and Ginny had been using me and I'd behaved so unspeakably badly at Nick's stag party that I was now a social pariah.

Oh wait, it hadn't been a dream.

The realisation was so demoralising that I rolled over on to my side and tried to go back to sleep, but the noises got in the way. The hammering wasn't DIY, I realised now; it was bass, leaking up from somewhere down below. As for the moaning, it sounded as though someone were being tortured.

Or having sex.

Yes, that was it. Sex.

I listened as the sounds increased in urgency, getting more high-pitched, until finally they erupted into a flutter of little gasps and cries.

Oh oh oh oh.

In the normal run of things, I might have found it arousing, but now it just made me all the more depressed. Someone was having fun, and it wasn't me. I would never have fun again.

I closed my one functional eye. The moaning stopped, but the beat of the music pursued me into a fitful slumber. Every so often the thudding would pause, only to resume a few seconds later. The rhythm never varied; it was so insistent and monotonous that my heart tried to beat along in time to it and failed, so that I was left breathless, forever lagging behind and trying in vain to catch up. I dreamt I was on the barge, and that water was leaking in through gaps in the floor, and that I was hammering boards across the leaks, but the water kept on coming in . . .

At some point I rolled over again and saw that one side of the canopy had been drawn all the way back. Alice was standing next to the bed, silently gazing down at me. I couldn't tell how long she'd been there; it made me uncomfortable to think that she'd been watching me sleep, the sort of intimate observation normally reserved for lovers. She was dressed in palest green, barefoot but carrying her shoes, or what passed for shoes in her world—a fantasy of silver filament and diamante trim.

Even I had to admit she looked lovely.

But sad, so sad.

My heart did an excited little flip. Of course she was sad—I'd gone and spoiled everything. I'd arrived at the altar in the nick of time and shattered her lifelong dream just as it had been on the point of being realised. So of course she was sad, it was only natural. But she was also safe. She would be mad at me to begin with, but soon she would come to realise I'd been right, and thank me.

If only I could have expressed all that in words. I opened my mouth, but all that emerged was a pitiable croak.

"Oh John," said Alice. "You just *had* to go and do it."

But she didn't look as cross as she ought to have done.

I managed to say, "Sorry," but I wasn't sorry at all, I was weak with relief. I'd finally managed to do something right, and a fist in the eye was a small price to pay. I felt a triumphant grin threatening to break out on my face and struggled to hold it back; partly because it would have been inappropriate but mostly because even the smallest facial movement was excruciatingly painful.

"I ruined it, didn't I?"

Slowly, Alice shook her head. "Actually no, you didn't."

The urge to grin promptly deserted me.

"A couple of the boys carried you out," she said. "And then the ceremony just took up where we'd left off."

She waited for this information to sink in, or maybe she was just waiting for me to say something. But I was tongue-tied with dismay.

"I'm *married*, John."

I finally found my voice, but all it said was, "Oh no."

It all came pouring out of her in a breathless rush.

"Don't think I don't recognise the bond between us, John. It's special, it really is. I know how you feel about me, and I'm flattered. And you must be aware I have feelings for you too. You're a wonderful person, and I love you, I really do, but you must understand it's just not possible. It's Fate, or maybe Karma. Maybe at another time, in another place, another lifetime, it might have been different and we could have got together and there would have been something truly beautiful between us, but this is the real world. I'm *Mrs Fitch* now and I'm afraid you have to respect that."

"No," I groaned. "No, no, no. That's not the problem *at all.*"

"We can still be friends," she said, "but who's to say that friends can't be passionate, and romantic, and loving? Just not passionate and romantic and loving in the way a husband and wife can be."

She leant over and for an excruciating moment I thought she was going to kiss me, but instead, she plonked something on the bed, next to the pillow. I twisted my neck and saw a small slice of wedding cake on a paper napkin.

She continued to gaze down at me like a compassionate nurse wondering how to break it to a patient that both his legs had been amputated.

"I'll never forget what you did for me."

"That's just it." I struggled to sit up. "I didn't do *anything*. And now you're Mrs Fitch. Have you any idea what that means?" My voice was thick, as though my breathing passages had been pumped full of tar. "Can you hear what I'm saying, Alice? Nick married you for your *money*."

Alice laughed bitterly. "Of course he married me for my money. That was the whole idea. Do you think someone like Nick would marry me for *love*? Isn't he in for a shock when he finds out, poor baby. But it's too late."

"It's not too late," I burbled. "You can get a divorce. You can't stay married. You *mustn't* stay married."

This was music to her ears of course. She couldn't get enough of what she imagined was me telling her how much I adored her.

I tried to get out of bed, but my head began to whirl, and she had no difficulty pushing me back down. "Oh no, you stay there. The doctor said you needed rest . . ."

Doctor? What doctor?

"He gave you a shot to help you sleep."

Or a Mickey Finn to shut me up.

But I suddenly remembered I had proof. I had the book, I had photos.

I got as far as placing one foot on the floor before a shockwave of dizziness indicated that getting up wouldn't be such a good idea.

"Where's my jacket?"

Alice found it draped over the back of a chair.

"The pockets," I said.

She slipped her hand into each of the pockets, all the while beaming at me as though humouring a batty old relative.

"No, no. Give it here." I grabbed the jacket and turned the pockets inside-out on to the bedspread. A matchbook, a couple of ticket stubs, some scrunched up receipts, my passport and . . .

Eureka! The packet from Poppity Pix! I thrust it at her.

"Look! *Just look!*"

I watched, hardly daring to breathe, as she opened the packet and scrutinised the contents.

"Well?"

"You look like you're having fun," she said at last, a little uncertainly. "What's that ghastly muck you're drinking?"

I grabbed the photos and shuffled through them in dawning disbelief. Knobsworth. Jeremy. The cigarette machine. *The stag party*. Shit, I'd brought the wrong set.

I'd left the photos of Georgina on the barge.

But all was not lost.

"The book," I muttered. It was all I had left now. "Where's my bag?"

Alice went through the motions of looking around the room. "What bag?"

"The plastic carrier bag I had with me. There was a book in it."

She shrugged. "Probably downstairs."

"You have to find it," I gasped. "You have to bring it to me. There's something I must show you . . ."

I launched into a garbled version of what I'd read in *Old Egbert's*: Fitch women had a tendency to die suddenly, *Fitch* was a corruption of *Fetch*, and the *Fitch Fetch* was probably lurking nearby even as we spoke, ready to pounce and . . . well, I wasn't sure what was going to happen exactly, or when, but I did know Alice's clock was ticking.

Fitch Fetch

Even to my own ears it sounded like the babbling of a certified lunatic, and it was clear Alice wasn't really listening, that she didn't really want to listen. I made a feeble attempt to grab her arm. She took my hand and squeezed it before gently laying it back to rest on the quilt.

"You poor dear," she said.

"We have to talk," I persisted, but she was already picking up her bag, moving towards the door, opening the door . . . I made a last-ditch attempt to sit up, and it very nearly killed me. "Wait," I said. "What about the reception?"

She looked surprised. "Almost over. Only a few diehards left."

"But we can still talk?"

"Of *course* we can talk," she answered serenely. "Just because I'm married doesn't mean we have to stop seeing each other.

Nick's pretty pissed off, but I'm sure he'll forgive you, whatever it was you did, and you can come and see us any time you want. I mean, it was a *stag party*. Everyone behaves badly at stag parties."

Then she smiled one last smile and said, "See you later."

See you later.

The most depressing phrase in the English language.

I had no pride left. I opened my mouth to beg her to stay. I was prepared to tell her I really did love her, to swear she was the only one for me, to propose marriage, offer my body, whatever it took, but the door was already closing behind her. I tried climbing out of bed to follow, but my legs still weren't working properly and I somehow got snarled up in the bedclothes and ended up in a heap on the floor.

I closed my eyes, trying to work out what to do next, which limb to untangle first, though my brain wasn't functioning too well and I think I may have passed out for a while.

I WAS ROUSED by a sudden turmoil rising from somewhere beneath me—screams and shouts and slamming doors, followed by more yelling and a great deal of scrunching and scraping and clanking. The good news was that the thudding dance music had stopped.

The bad news—well, it didn't bear thinking about. That was it, then. The reception was over. And I'd missed it, which was a shame. I'd always loved a good reception. But at least now I felt just about capable of making my way downstairs, and at least now I could talk to Alice halfway coherently, and without being interrupted by speech-giving or cake-cutting.

I struggled to my feet and this time managed to stay upright. There was an unpleasant gurgling in my stomach—I'd had nothing to eat since a snatched breakfast of greasy croissants. I devoured the slice of wedding-cake in two bites, but all it did was whet the edge of my appetite. I was parched with thirst as well. Maybe I could find some leftover refreshments downstairs.

I stumbled out of the room and along the corridor to the landing, where I was forced to stop and recover from all this sudden activity. As I tried to regulate my breathing I took another look at Tobias Fitch and his family, all lined up in front of Framptons as lightning split the heavens behind them. I found myself focusing on the dog. I peered closer. I'd never been this close before; I could see all the little cracks in the paint, and the brushstrokes, and the effect was almost abstract. The oils were so murky it was difficult to be sure of anything. But I thought it looked just like the Jack Russell I'd seen at Ginny's.

And it had eyes. Small yellow eyes.

I nearly fell backwards down the stairs. This had to be more than just a coincidence. Maybe I'd be able to find out more about the painting if I knew who the artist was. I dipped to one side to try and decipher the spidery signature in the corner of the frame, but the spooky thing was that, squinting sideways like that, I saw something in the picture I hadn't seen before. It was like that painting *The Ambassadors* by Hans Holbein the Younger in which you could make out a skull—but only if you looked at it from a certain angle.

From my angle now, the house in the painting stopped being a house and started being a face. It was a face I'd seen before, with black holes where there should have been eyes and pale skin like rotting brickwork and the front door gaping open like to reveal a blackened hallway that threatened to swallow me up.

I closed my eyes to block out the vision and thought I felt a strip of tattered cloth brush across my face, and when I opened my eyes again I forced myself to turn my back on the painting and carry on downstairs.

Halfway down I couldn't resist one last glance back, and now it looked just like a house again, just Framptons against a lightning-streaked sky, and I couldn't be sure that what I thought I'd seen hadn't been a trick of the shadows, but I had no intention of climbing back up to check. I hurried the rest of the way down. Framptons, for all its vastness, suddenly felt airless and claustrophobic, and I didn't want to spend any more time here than I had to. I already wasn't sure that it had been such a good idea to sleep in one of the rooms, allow it access to my dreamlife, give it a foothold in my subconscious—not that I'd had much choice in the matter. I'd been out for the count.

The ground-floor looked as though it had been hit by a

hurricane. Never in my life had I seen such a litter of empty champagne bottles, party poppers and cigarette butts. I spied one or two unconscious guests as well as I lurched from room to room, searching for Alice and hoping at the same time to find a leftover morsel of flan or cake or pie that didn't have a cigarette stubbed out in it.

At long last I found my way to the kitchen. Janie Carruthers was sitting at the table, alternately taking puffs from a cigarette and gnawing at the corner of a large slab of wedding-cake as she perused the pages of *Old Egbert's*. She was spilling crumbs into it as she ate, which made me itch to dart forward and brush them away. She looked clean, and cool, and makeup-free, and Willy, her other half, was nowhere to be seen. She'd changed out of her bridesmaid's outfit and into a little black dress, but her feet, resting on a neighbouring chair, were bare as Alice's had been.

She looked up as I came in and said, "Hi."

I squinted and said "Hi" back.

At least now we were equals in the eye department.

I asked, "Where's Alice?"

Janie paused in mid-nibble. "She left."

I still wasn't with the programme. "Left?"

"Honeymoon," said Janie. "They'll be halfway to Venice by now."

Halfway to Venice.

So that was it. I sank defeated into the nearest chair. The cacophony of slamming doors I'd heard earlier hadn't just signalled the end of the party—it had also marked the newly-weds' grand send-off into the night.

Janie offered me a cigarette and even though I would have preferred food, I took it and lit up.

Lord, I'd messed up royally. Alice was still in deadly peril but now she was also a thousand miles away, or soon would be.

"Suite at the Di Lusso," Janie said through a mouthful of cake, so that it came out more like *Wheat udder loose oh*, and I had to ask her to repeat it, several times, and then explain to me what the Di Lusso was.

She caught sight of the expression on my face and asked,

"Who's died?"

"No-one," I said. "Yet."

The thought cheered me up a little. Alice was still alive, wasn't she? And where there was life there was hope? Maybe the situation wasn't as dire as all that. Maybe it still wasn't too late. Maybe nothing could happen to her while she was so far away from Framptons. How far did this curse reach? Wasn't it just the house that was out to get her? Mightn't she be safe just as long as she wasn't anywhere near Little Yawning? Mightn't it be just a *local* curse?

This spark of relative cheerfulness lasted for all of thirty seconds as I ticked off what I knew. Georgina's car had gone into the canal. The mother had died in a yachting accident, the stepmother in a swimming-pool. And the grandmother . . .

How had the grandmother died? I couldn't remember, but what was the betting it had something to do with water?

Water! Oh for Christ's sake, Venice was full of the stuff! She could hardly have gone anywhere wetter.

"Oh God," I said.

"Interesting book, this," said Janie through another mouthful of cake. "You know it's full of info about Nick's ancestors? What a shower. You know they used to sacrifice dogs, just to get their jollies?"

"You know about the curse?"

"Of course," Janie chuckled. "Everyone knows about . . ." She put on a mock declamatory voice. " . . .*The Legend of the Deadly Bed.*"

"The Legend of the . . .?"

"Deadly Bed," said Janie. "That's in here too. Somewhere."

I sat up straight. "Bed?"

"Oh you know, that baroque monstrosity with the snake headboard. Tobias Fitch's father died a slow lingering death in it, and ever since it's been cursed. Tobias had only to roger one of his wives in it, apparently, and she'd have an unfortunate accident."

"In the bed?"

"No, at sundown the next day. One of them drowned in the bath," said Janie, barely stifling her mirth. "Another was skating on a frozen lake and fell through the ice . . . If you ask me, it's all a bit suspicious. Where's Miss Marple when you need her?"

Where indeed? I asked her to show me the relevant section and had to stifle the urge to lean across and snatch the book out of her hands as she licked her fingers and riffled through the pages, crumpling many of the edges as she went. Finally she found what she was looking for and slid it across the table to me.

"If it was my bed, I'd burn it," she said. "Even if it isn't really evil, it doesn't half look evil."

And there it was, in black and white, under the heading BED LEGENDS, with a reproduction of an Eighteenth Century engraving. I recognised the bedhead straightaway.

The infamous bed adorned with the Fitch family crest—a small animal, possibly a dog, trapped in the coils of a snakelike creature—dates back to the death of Tobias Fitch's father JEBEZ, who died therein of a mysterious wasting disease, rumoured to have been the result of poison administered by his second wife, Mary Ann. The latter was alleged to have been a witch who had cuckolded her husband with the Devil in Jebez's own bed, but this may well have been a calumny later propagated by Jebez's surviving relatives. With his dying breath, Jebez condemned her and all other wives having carnal relations in that same bed to a hideous death before the next sunset . . .

"So the bed's the trigger?" I said, struggling to sound as amused by this whole business as Janie was. "Then that's OK, then, isn't it? Because Alice hasn't slept in Nick's bed, has she? She always slept in the four-poster . . ."

I tailed off. Oh yes, I realised. That four-poster I'd been tucked up in earlier. The four-poster where I'd lain and listened to the sounds of lovemaking from next door . . .

Janie snickered. "I shouldn't think she's *slept* in it, no."

"But . . .?"

Janie winked at me, and this time there was no mistaking it for anything but a wink.

"Nick was very eager to consummate the marriage. Didn't even have the decency to wait till the honeymoon."

"But wait," I said, trying to get all this straight in my head. "It can't be the bed." What was it Nick had said? *Georgie always claimed it gave her nightmares.* Which suggested she'd slept in it rather a lot, resulting in nothing more injurious to her health than a few bad dreams.

And then I read on.

. . .though, according to the circumstances of the curse, he specifically made exception of the constant women who truly loved their husbands, as good wives are wont to do.

Women who loved their husbands.
Women who loved their husbands.
Oh God, oh God.
Was this it?
This had to be it. Now it was all making sense. Sort of.
So long as Georgina had loved Nick, she'd been safe. But the instant she'd stopped loving him, probably around the time she'd found out about him and Ginny, her days were numbered.
And Alice . . .
Alice didn't love her husband.
Alice loved *me*.
I leapt to my feet, sending my chair flying, and tried not to yell, "What time is sunset tomorrow?"

Janie took my strange behaviour in her stride. "Oh, I don't know, around five o'clock. Look it up on the internet . . ."

"Five o'clock," I repeated. "Five o'clock in the afternoon?"

"Well it's not going to set in the morning, is it," Janie said sensibly.

I righted the chair I'd knocked over, trying to suppress the mounting panic. Less than twenty-four hours. The fuse had been lit, but what I could I do? Alice and Nick would be halfway to Venice by now. Maybe they were already there.

But she'd have her mobile with her, wouldn't she. I could contact her with that.

Unless, of course, she maintained radio silence, the way she'd been doing this past few days.

On the other hand . . .

With a superhuman effort, I jerked myself out of my lassitude and headed towards the door. "I have to go."

Janie looked at me in amazement and, if I wasn't mistaken, no little disappointment. "So soon?"

"I have to get to Venice."

Janie's face was a mask of wide-eyed astonishment. Then she let out a little squeal of pleasure and clapped her hands together delightedly.

"We all knew you were stuck on her, but I never thought you'd go this far!"

"I'm not stuck on her," I sighed, knowing she wouldn't believe me for a second, "but I do need to speak to her urgently, Janie. A matter of life and death."

"Really," Janie said doubtfully.

"Yes, really," I said, and there must have been something convincing in my manner, or maybe she just fancied me, because I had no trouble at all persuading her to set off for London without delay, not even stopping long enough to track down her boyfriend, and drop me off at Stansted on her way down the M11.

ON THE motorway she talked about Nick with a vehemence that surprised me. I wondered, finally, if maybe there hadn't once been something between them, something that had turned sour and left her feeling vindictive. I wondered why I hadn't spotted it earlier. But then, there were an awful lot of things I hadn't been spotting lately.

"And how long has he been shagging Ginny?" I asked.

Janie took her eyes off the road for so long that I grew nervous.

"He's shagging Ginny?"

"I thought it was common knowledge," I said, mentally adding, *In other words, everybody was in on it except me. And you, apparently.*

Janie still seemed to be having trouble concentrating on the road.

"Where did you hear that? I can't believe it's true. And if it was true, it would be sick. You do know they're cousins?"

Now it was my turn to forget the road.

"They are?"

"Maybe not first cousins. Distant ones. But they're pretty much related. I thought you knew."

She shot me a keen sideways glance. "I mean, I thought the two of you were involved."

"Not any more."

And with those three little words, I felt liberated.

Or maybe it was just relief at putting distance between myself and Framptons.

A FEW HOURS later, I was trapped on one of Bud-Jet's crummy old 727s, utterly unable to sleep and groaning in pain as the pressure in my blocked-up ears reached critical point. My head felt ready to explode. A flight attendant gave me painkillers, which helped, but not much. By the time we landed, I'd started bleeding from one of my ears, like someone who'd strayed too close to Chernobyl.

I stumbled off the plane and through what looked more like a World War Two airfield than a commercial airport, then on to a waiting coach, where an alarmingly drowsy-looking driver was waiting to transport me and my fellow night-fliers the rest of the way to La Serenissima..

TWENTY THREE

ALICE AND Nick would have flown first-class directly to Marco Polo and thence been whisked by *motoscafo* straight to the private dock of their luxury hotel.

I, on the other hand, had to endure the eighty minute coach ride from hell.

I couldn't sleep, not for a second. As the coach bumped over corrugations in the road and my skeleton rattled around my body like loose change in an empty tobacco tin, I stared fixedly at the back of the driver's head, ready to lunge forward and grab the wheel if he nodded off.

But in a way it was good that I had something to occupy my brain, since it limited my fretting about what I would do when I arrived. Was I really hurtling across Italy at this ridiculous hour in the morning in the faint hope that a new bride would leave her husband of only a few hours, at my behest? If I hadn't been able to convince her in London or Norfolk, what chance would I stand in Venice?

What if the only way to persuade her was to pretend that I really did love her?

And what if she *did* leave Nick for me? What then? How could I possibly tell her it had all been a charade, that I was no more in love with her than she had been with Nick, or Nick with her?

Would I have to *marry* her? Would I find myself saddled with Alice for the rest of my life?

But I wasn't sure I had any choice now. The facts were simple. If I couldn't somehow prise Alice out of Nick's grasp, something terrible was going to happen to her, and it would be my fault, because it had taken me all this time to work out that Fitch women who failed to love their husbands were doomed.

There was still a faint hope we could sort it out without melodrama, that we could discuss it like adults. Maybe Nick would see reason. Maybe once he knew the jig was up he would yield with a good grace. Maybe if I just stuck close to Alice nothing would happen.

Or maybe if I stuck close to Alice, whatever was going to happen to her would reach out and get me too, the way it had got to Tubby Clegg. I didn't want to end up with half my head missing. But I tried not to think about that. In any case, I would have to arrange for Alice and Nick to get the marriage annulled, and pronto, but how on earth would I do that? Was there a British consul in Venice? What if Nick were simply to repudiate her, like a Muslim? Would that be official enough?

The coach finally dumped me, red-eyed and mouth fixed open in a more or less permanent yawn, on the greasy Piazzale Roma with dawn still only a hint on the horizon and the *vaporetti* not yet in service.

As I struck out on foot towards the city centre, I rehearsed desperate dialogue in my head. *Alice, you've got to ditch that bastard right now.* I was going to have to make her think it was a crazy romantic gesture, that I was so desperately in love with her that I would stop at nothing, including trying to ruin her honeymoon. How could any woman not be susceptible to such a passionate appeal?

Or maybe I would have to be direct, like Michael Biehn in *The Terminator*.

Come with me if you want to live.

The problem was, this wasn't a sci-fi movie; this was real. And Alice was stubborn, I already knew that. She'd devised her life's plan and now she finally seemed to be getting everything she'd always wanted she had no intention of abandoning it. I wished now I'd brought *Old Egbert's* to thrust under her nose, but the book was so cumbersome I'd left it in Janie's care, together with strict instructions that she was not to eat while reading it.

As I headed south I glimpsed a skinny grey cat creeping across a deserted piazza. I stepped forward with my hand out, to greet it, but it flattened its ears against its head and backed away, and I felt a yearning for Boris so acute that I nearly passed out.

On the other hand, it was more than likely I was simply feeling faint from the hunger that a few scraps of leftover wedding cake had failed to assuage, so I stopped off at a small cafe for a couple of slices of toast and a large cup of steaming cappuccino so hot that it stripped the surface off my tongue. As I drank, I propped myself up at the bar alongside broad-shouldered men in overalls who kept using the word *puttana*.

The breakfast did me good and I set off again with renewed vigour. In any other circumstances I might have enjoyed a stroll through the traffic-free streets with their hump-backed bridges and alluring shop windows full of leather-bound notebooks and saucy lingerie, but the clock was ticking and I didn't dare loiter, particularly since the laughably inadequate map I'd plucked off a stand at the airport kept sending me down the wrong route, through dank labyrinths terminating in even danker stretches of canal, forcing me to backtrack repeatedly. It was impossible not to be reminded of *Don't Look Now*, but I tried not to think about the way that film had ended.

Finally I broke through a cordon of closed shops and restaurants into the unmistakable expanse of St Mark's Square, where early-rising tourists were already posing for photos with the pigeons. Not far now. After another ten minutes toiling through narrow alleyways, I glimpsed the top of a massive pink brick building with DI LUSSO spelt out in large gold letters against a crenellated roof. It looked like the sort of chateau Barbie might have lived in had she been European instead of American.

Finding the place was one thing, but getting to it required a PhD in orienteering, and possibly one in quantum physics as well. It seemed to have been constructed on an inaccessible parcel of land, forever on the far side of a canal with no bridges in sight. And if I could see bridges, I couldn't work out how to reach those either.

But I persevered, scurrying back and forth like a rat in a maze, and at last found myself propelled through revolving doors that spat me out, dishevelled and footsore, on to the thick red carpet of the hotel lobby.

The morning hum of the real world was instantly replaced by a churchlike hush. The porter looked me up and down with an expression of ill-concealed contempt. I couldn't have done much about the purple eye that was still so puffed out I could barely see out of it, but I was beginning to wish I'd taken the time to shower and shave and change my clothes.

"Mr and Mrs Fitch . . ."

"Scusi, Signor?"

I spoke slowly and clearly. "I must. See. Mr and Mrs Fitch. Nicholas Fitch."

The porter's expression said, So what?

I looked him straight in the eye. "It's very important. *Molto importante.*"

He replied in virtually accent-free English. "Room number, please?"

I hesitated, then decided that Nick was the kind of guy who would have done things properly.

"The honeymoon suite."

He looked mildly surprised, consulted his computer screen in frigid silence and at length said, "And you are Mr . . .?"

"Croydon," I said, relieved that for once the name was unlikely to be greeted by the usual snigger. Unless of course *Croydon* turned out to be Italian for tosser.

"Take a seat, please," said the porter, picking up the phone and directing me towards a sofa beneath a small glade of potted palms. I perched on the edge of the seat and tried not to tear at my fingernails with my teeth, sensing I was there on sufferance and that the merest hint of autocannibalism on my part would result in swift ejection.

But it was impossible to stay in one place for long; I was soon back on my feet, wearing a hole in the carpet as I paced back and forth, glancing imploringly at the porter who was no longer on the phone but diligently refused to catch my eye. Each time I drew near to the desk, he warded me off with an impatient shake of his hand, as though trying to dislodge something slimy that was clinging to his fingers.

At last, just as I was beginning to despair, he ceased shaking and started beckoning instead.

"Mister Croydon? I am informed that Mr and Mrs Fitch have specifically requested not to be disturbed."

It had taken him ten minutes to come up with *that?* I felt my one good eyeball rolling back in my head, but the porter was smiling as he inclined forwards, as though about confide a secret. The corners of his eyes went all sentimental and crinkly.

"They are on their honeymoon."

He winked at me, like Janie Carruthers. But this was a man-to-man sort of wink, the sort that said, *Yes, and we know what they're probably doing right this moment, don't we?*

He probably thought I was winking back at him.

"*Molto importante,*" I pleaded again. "A matter of life and death." And added, "*Sola, perduta, abbandonata,*" for good measure.

At this, his expression changed. He eyed me warily, as though he thought I might whip out a razor and slit my wrists right in front of him; anyone could see I'd already had a go at my face.

Then, cautiously, he slid a notepad across the desk and suggested I leave a message.

He'd given me an idea. Maybe Alice would be more receptive if she thought it was my life hanging in the balance.

So I scribbled, *Am here in Venice. MUST SEE YOU. Otherwise, not responsible for what I might do . . .*

That seemed sufficiently dramatic to get her worried enough to agree to a meeting. I added the number of my mobile, just in case she didn't have it with her, and tore off the sheet and folded it and printed *Alice Fitch* on the outside.

Alice Fitch. *Fitch.* It seemed like such a done deal. And now I was here to bugger it up.

The porter said, "I'll make sure she gets it," and winked again, and for a second there, I was able to fool myself into thinking he was on my side.

Then I thought I heard him mutter something like, *Canny probity,* but before I could ask him to repeat it, he'd turned his back on me to greet a newly-descended guest who wanted directions to the Accademia.

Since I was afraid that if I lost sight of the hotel I might never be able to find it again, I thought it best not to wander too far. I installed myself in the window of a small cafe on the far side of the canal and drank one cappuccino after another, repeatedly glancing from the hotel to my mobile to my watch and back to the hotel again.

I saw many people coming and going through the revolving doors, but no sign of Alice or Nick. Were they still asleep? Or making love? I tried not to imagine what their lovemaking might be like and began to smoke my way through a softpack of Marlboro, feeling increasingly like a soul stranded in limbo, earthly ties growing feebler by the minute as the café grew ever more crowded and the smoke swirled around me in lazy coils.

By mid-morning there was still no sign of the happy couple, the café was standing room only, and I was so twitchy from caffeine and lack of sleep that I switched to Vecchia Romagna in an effort to stop myself bouncing off the walls.

It was a bad decision. The glasses were small but the measures enormous, and after my second or third, or possibly even fourth, things started to slip.

I WAS JERKED back into consciousness by a spasm of shivering so violent it made my teeth knock together.

I'd been waking up in some rum places lately, but this was the rummest to date: I was curled up on a windswept bench, surrounded by tall, unfriendly-looking buildings and not a landmark in sight.

I sat up for a better look. It was some sort of godforsaken piazza, definitely off the beaten track. To my right, half a dozen stray tourists were huddled together, despondently licking green and red *gelati* on the leeward side of a shabby kiosk. To my left, a couple of skinny cats were tearing at a pile of reddish ordure that looked suspiciously like the remains of one of their relatives. As I stood up they instantly stopped what they were doing and scattered, slipping away as fast as their legs could carry them.

There was a watery lemon yellow light in the sky and the shadows were lengthening. Surely it couldn't be evening already? In a panic, I checked my watch.

Mid afternoon. Alice would be safe until sunset, at least. But what time did the sun go down around here? It was impossible to tell simply by looking, since it was hidden somewhere behind a wash of greenish-yellow cloud. I didn't even know where I was—I assumed it was somewhere in Italy; I just hoped it was still Venice. I felt around in my pockets, but passport and credit card and what remained of my euros were still present and correct, so I obviously hadn't been mugged. More like drugged—it seemed I was still in thrall to whatever the doctor had shot me full of the day before, and the sleepless night followed by a stomachful of Vecchia Romagna and lack of solid food had done the rest.

At least I now felt vaguely rested, though so dehydrated my tongue kept sticking to the roof of my mouth; I bought a can of eye-wateringly sweet orangeade from the kiosk and took great gulps from it as I studied my map and scrutinised my surroundings. It seemed I was about as far from the Di Lusso as I could possibly get. How the hell had I ended up here? And how would I get back? I decided it would be simplest to return by the quays rather than risk getting hopelessly lost in the labyrinthine streets.

As I set off the sky was so overcast I could no longer tell if it was due to approaching twilight or a gathering storm. There was no logic to the shadows; they flitted across my sightline, across the surface of buildings, over balustrades and cobbles as though the light were constantly shifting, though as far as I could see the sky overhead was the same old glowering grey.

By the time I reached the Canale di San Marco a wind had sprung up and was tossing damp sheets of newspaper back and forth. The water in the canal was choppy, the waves flecked with angry foam, and I felt large spots of rain splashing down on my head. I took the map out of my pocket to check my bearings but the wind tried to snatch it from my grasp; soon it was in tatters, so I gave up and shoved it back into my pocket and simply kept going in what I hoped was the right direction.

It wasn't until I found myself back in St Mark's Square that I thought to check my phone. While I'd been out for the count, my mobile had kept busy. I'd slept through several missed calls and text messages.

The first was from Alice.

LOBBY 17H30 LUV U2

LUV U2?

Something told me she wasn't referring to the band of that name.

What the hell? She was on her *honeymoon*. Of course I was relieved she'd responded to my note, but reflected it was just my luck; the one woman so passionately in love with me that she was prepared to send me digital billet-doux only a few hours after getting married to someone else was someone who wasn't my type, someone I didn't fancy at all, someone I wasn't ever likely to fancy. Why couldn't it have been Kate? Why not Ginny, damn her?

On the other hand, the thought of Ginny was no longer warming my cockles the way it had done.

The second text message was unambiguous.

KEEP AWAY FROM ALICE

I had no idea who'd sent that one, and I didn't care.

Fuck you, asshole, I thought. I'd crossed Europe to reach this woman; nothing could keep me away from her now. But five thirty . . . Wasn't that around sunset? I would need to catch up with her earlier than that. I checked my watch again. Jesus, it was already coming up to four. Had it really taken me an hour to get from the Castello to my current position?

I broke into a sprint. Actually it was more of a cautious canter, but the stones were slippery and the last thing I needed now to was to slip and break my neck. But where was that bloody hotel? After being suckered into the usual false trails leading to the usual dead ends I finally spotted a sliver of pink brick, and soon the Di Lusso was once again in view, with only a narrow strip of canal separating us.

Sixteen minutes past four. I paused to catch my breath. I could see a bridge, but in order to cross it I would have to retrace my steps, which would mean losing sight of the hotel again. The rain was still coming down in the same big isolated splotches, making circular ripples in the surface of the canal.

The sun was still nowhere to be seen. Oddly enough, that gave me heart, for if the sun wasn't visible in the first place, then how could it possibly matter what time it set?

Or maybe, just maybe, it didn't matter, none of this mattered. Maybe the curse was a load of old cobblers and this whole thing, the flight to Venice, the hike through the drizzle, the desperate race to stop whatever unspeakable thing was going to happen at sunset from happening, maybe all this was nothing but a fool's errand.

Christ, how I hoped it was.

But there was either something wrong with the light, or something wrong with my wacky one-eyed vision. The shadows were back in force, but now they seemed to have more to do with my own eyesight than with anything external. The world seemed increasingly leeched of bright colour, like the drab countryside around Little Yawning. A woman with a red umbrella passed by; I knew it had to be red, but it was my brain telling me this rather than my one good eye. Was it an incipient cataract, or just another consequence of the phlegm filling my head? Oh Lord, maybe Nick's fist really had done permanent damage.

Or then again, maybe it was just how things were in Venice—the cold, the damp, the watery chill . . .

"John! What the hell are you doing here?"

The voice at my ear wasn't loud, but I'd been so lost in contemplation of my faulty vision that it made me jump. I turned and found myself face to face with Nick.

I felt a selfish twinge of satisfaction when I spotted the bandage on his left hand, but he was grinning, as though pleased to see me. Though there had to be some mistake—after what had happened over the past couple of days, why would Nick be pleased to see *me*?

I looked around; no sign of Alice, and it was already twenty-five past four. When was it that damned sun was supposed to go down? Five? Five thirty? There was no time to waste. I grabbed Nick by the lapels of his jacket and yelled, "*Where is she?*"

Gently he extricated himself and stepped back, smiling amiably, as though having his collar grabbed by a semi-hysterical rival was the most natural thing in the world. His jacket was a stout green, I noted, and yet it wasn't—it didn't seem to be any colour at all.

"Steady on, old man. I know you're enamoured, but wouldn't you say this was taking things too far?"

All the fight went out of me. "You don't understand. I have to reach her by sunset, or . . ."

He narrowed his eyes. "Or what? You'll turn into a pumpkin?"

I sneezed several times in quick succession and Nick said, "Hey, keep it to yourself, we don't want to catch your cold."

I blew my nose noisily. "The curse . . ."

Nick burst out laughing. "You mean the Fitch curse? Oh, you've got to be kidding. Hey, calm down. You look done in, old man. What on earth are you doing here? Last time we saw you, you were flat out on the bed. No, no need to apologise. You were a real pain in the arse, but hey, the best man won."

"I need to talk to Alice," I said. "I need to talk to her, I need to talk to her *right now.*"

"OK, OK, don't freak out on me. She's over there."

He indicated a spot directly across the canal. I followed his pointing finger and saw her. She was bundled up in a stout jacket, just like Nick's, and a plaid skirt and the usual ridiculously impractical shoes: criss-cross straps that might have been lime-green, shiny heels that could possibly have been gold, though with my eye problem I was finding it difficult to tell for sure. She had her back to us; she was gazing into a brightly lit shop window full of fancy notebooks, clutching a small carrier bag as though it contained the doge's treasure.

The bag might have been orange.

"She bought you a present," Nick said proudly, as though buying a gift for a man who wasn't your husband was a philanthropic deed that merited a pat on the back.

The scene in front of me turned suddenly crepuscular, as though someone had hit a dimmer switch. Somewhere, a clock struck the half hour and a dog began to bark.

Yap yap yap

I'd heard that yapping before.

I looked frantically around, but there was no dog to be seen. Vast mountain ranges of goose pimples suddenly erupted on every last centimetre of my skin as a horrible suspicion gnawed at the back of my brain, trying to tear its way in and capture my attention. But it was too late.

Nick shouted Alice's name, and the sound carried through the twilight, and she whirled round, and though it was too dark to see her face, I thought I saw her raise the small carrier bag and wave it frantically. Or at least she waved her arms, though my eyes must have really been playing tricks because I thought I saw lengths of cotton hanging from her sleeves, like vapour trails.

And then I realised I'd made a mistake and, this time, I hadn't been looking at Alice at all. Alice was further along, she was already moving away from us, towards the nearest bridge. I'd been looking at . . .

What, exactly? Because there was no-one there now. Behind me, Nick started whistling absent-mindedly.

Don't talk to strangers . . .

No, I corrected myself, it wasn't Ronnie James Dio; it was that folk song about the Devil. That was OK, because I didn't believe in the Devil, but this didn't stop me from clutching myopically at Nick's arm. "That tune . . ."

"Tune?" he said, which was when I realised it hadn't been him whistling at all. I looked around but couldn't see anyone else. But by now, I couldn't see anything much.

An awful thought struck me. "What time is it?"

"Five thirty," said Nick.

I felt as though I'd been hit by an anvil. "Five thirty?"

"What? Oh, I see, you forgot to set your watch. You're still on English time, old man."

"English time," I mumbled to myself. "Venice is an hour ahead of Norfolk. Which means the sun has already gone down."

"Of course it has," Nick said cheerfully. "Which means it's time for aperitifs. Perhaps you'd join us? Hey, look at that dog, haring across the bridge like a mad thing."

He sounded so reasonable. So . . . civilised. An Englishman

abroad. I wanted so much for everything to be normal. I wanted so much to be joining them for drinks . . .

And then the rest of what he'd just said finally sank in.

Dog?

"What dog?" I said, and then I said, "You've got to stop it."

But Nick had already turned his back to me and stepped up to the edge of the canal to watch Alice approach the bridge. Things were falling into place like the elements in an elaborate set-piece. Something terrible was about to happen, and I was the only one who could see it.

I stepped right up to where Nick was standing, right to the very edge of the canal, and bellowed at the top of my voice, "Alice! Watch out!"

For an instant I couldn't breathe at all. It was though I was caught in a freezing tornado that snatched the air out of my lungs and rinsed all the snot out of my head—and then my flu was gone, my mind was free of the cobwebs that had been clogging it up, and the fog was stripped from my eye. I understood everything—but too late. And now that my one-eyed vision was once again sharp, pin-sharp, I no longer wanted to see. But I couldn't look away.

Alice heard me. She must have heard me, because she glanced back over her shoulder. And she saw something, because even from where I was standing, I could see her expression change. In the space of a split second, her whole body language changed. She went stiff. And then she turned and started to run.

I'VE BEEN going over the sequence in my head, replaying it again and again, but I have yet to get the order of events and all the elements straight. It happened in the blink of an eye, and yet it seemed to be unfolding in slow motion in front of me, as though I might have been able to step in and stop it, if only I hadn't been trapped in the slo-mo as well.

Did she begin to run because she was impatient to reach us? Or because she saw something behind her? Something that frightened her?

I saw the figure emerge from the shadows as Alice went past, or maybe it was simply a part of the shadow that splintered off and took on a life of its own. I saw Georgina racing after Alice with her peculiar loping barefoot stride, sleeves trailing uneven lengths of cotton like thin dark streams of vapour, arms outstretched, trying to touch her, trying to grab her, trying to pull her back and stop what it knew was going to happen next.

Afterwards, no-one else thought to mention this figure, and even though I saw it clearly I didn't mention it either, but I'm prepared to swear that Alice saw it too, and it wasn't a pretty sight, which was why she'd started to run.

Because now I knew—and it was too late.

Georgina was not the problem.

If only I hadn't shouted, Alice would never have looked back. If she hadn't looked back she might never have seen Georgina. If she had never seen Georgina she might never have tried to run. And if she had never tried to run, what happened next might never have happened.

They said afterwards it was because of those shoes she'd been wearing. Running like that, in those strappy shoes with high heels, was just asking for trouble.

According to witnesses, it was a small dog that tripped her up. Most likely a Jack Russell, or something closely related to the breed, but it had to have been a stray, because it wasn't on a leash, nor was it muzzled, the way dogs in Venice were supposed to be. Everyone saw the flurry of brown and white that launched itself playfully at Alice's ankles, but before anyone had really taken it in, it had somehow got tangled in her feet and she'd lost her balance and pitched sideways and I must have imagined rather than actually heard the hollow thud, like the sound made by a cricket ball hitting a coconut, as the side of her head connected hard with one of the stanchions planted at intervals along the bank of the canal.

The dog scampered on towards an archway, and I could have sworn that just before it was swallowed by the darkness there, it turned back to look at me, and I saw its eyes gleam yellow.

For a stunned moment Alice was left half-kneeling, half-crouching, one hand against that same stanchion that had so nearly brained her, the other poised in the air, as though she'd remembered a question she wanted to ask but couldn't work out how to put it into words.

Nick and I held our breaths.

An elderly couple who'd just crossed the bridge briskly changed direction to go and help, but while they were still a dozen yards away, she pulled herself together and hauled herself to her feet, and waved as if to say it's OK, I'm fine, and Nick and I relaxed and the couple, convinced she really was all right, returned to their rambling pace. I waited for her to start off again towards the bridge, now only a few paces away, but she didn't.

The stumble had turned her around, and now she was facing me and Nick, swaying lightly, one hand still touching the stanchion, as though using it to get her bearings. The other hand she raised slowly to the side of her head, as if to smooth down her hair, but all she did was pat it. She seemed about to repeat the action, but this time something caught her attention and she paused. She was gazing at her hand with a puzzled expression, and as she gazed, I saw a fine line, horribly red against the waxy pallor of her face, run in one swift fluid movement down from her hairline, like a dark crack opening up in her forehead. Still with the same puzzled expression, she swayed again and this time toppled sideways into the canal and sank quite gracefully beneath the surface, and the water closed over her head and she was gone, just like that, leaving nothing but a few bubbles to indicate she'd ever been there.

There was a moment of total silence as time stood still, and then all hell broke loose.

The elderly couple were the first to start yelling. There was a great deal of scurrying and shouting in half a dozen different languages, not just Italian, and people leaning over the parapet of the bridge and pointing, others kneeling by the canal and plunging their arms uselessly into the water, like washerwomen. I remember Nick's face—he'd turned grey and his mouth was hanging open, as though someone had punched him in the solar plexus.

And I remember jumping into the canal and making frantic efforts to swim over to where I'd seen her go under. But all I did was flounder, and as I splashed uselessly around with my jacket ballooning around me, I felt something attach itself to my trouser-leg and before I knew it I too was being pulled beneath the surface and I couldn't see anything and the water, once I was submerged in it, was blacker than ink and tasted like sewage and I really thought it was the end of everything until I felt strong hands grabbing me by the armpits and whatever had been dragging me down me decided I wasn't worth it and relinquished its grip and I was lifted out of the water with an ease that was almost insulting.

I learned afterwards that Nick had also jumped into the canal, but whereas I'd been rescued by a lone waiter from a nearby restaurant, it had taken three men in a gondola to pull him out of the water. All I remembered after that was a flotilla of boats and a team of divers and a small crowd of onlookers being held back by police, and someone giving the kiss of life to a shrunken bundle of wet rags, and a small orange bag bobbing on the surface of the water.

NICK AND I were taken to hospital for massive shots of anti-biotics to ward off whatever viruses we might have picked up in the canal, though ironically my head now felt clearer than it had all week. My flu had vanished, just like that, but I wasn't in the mood for celebrating.

Nick and I sat side by side in the waiting-room. He stared fixedly at the ground, apparently as miserable as I was, as though what had happened to Alice had had absolutely nothing to do with him or his blasted family or his wretched house. I felt like killing him, but a curious lethargy weighed me down.

More than anything else I wanted to go to sleep and wake up to find it had all been a nightmare. Alice would come barrelling through the door at any second, laughing and saying, *Had you there, guys!*

She could have done what she wanted with me—hell, she could have had me as her toyboy, I didn't care, just so long as she was alive and well and talking out of the corner of her mouth in that droll way she had.

OK, so she'd never been my type, and I'd only known her a

week, but that didn't mean I wasn't going to feel bad about what had happened for a long, long time.

AFTERWARDS, DRESSED in someone's sweatshirt and tracksuit bottoms so large they had to be gathered in around my waist with a horrible plastic belt, I went with Nick to the police station, then on to the *obitorio* and thence back to the police station, and then finally back to the Di Lusso.

I got the impression that Nick wanted to be alone, and I had no real desire to spend any more time with him than I had to, but the brutal fact was that I couldn't afford a hotel room of my own, so I was forced to invite myself up to the honeymoon suite so I could sleep on the sofa. Though, in the end, neither of us did much sleeping. We drank the mini-bar dry and had to call down for refills.

"Why do you do it, Nick?" I asked wearily. "Why do you go on marrying them?"

"I like getting married," he muttered into his cognac. "I guess I'm a romantic."

"Yeah, and you're not just after their money."

"Alice didn't have any."

"I knew that."

"And I'm grateful you shared that information with me." He looked up at me. His eyes were horribly bloodshot. "We took out life insurance on Friday."

That stopped me in my tracks.

"OK," I said after a while, still fighting down the urge to punch him. "Let's forget the money. Let's leave that to one side. Why keep the bed?"

"Bed?"

"The one with the Hammer horror bedhead."

"It's the family bed."

"Yes?"

"I don't understand. Why would I want to throw out an antique?"

He seemed genuinely not to know. I reflected that maybe I was the only one who worried about these details. Everybody else just got on with their lives and did what they had to do, whether that involved curses, or tattoos, or human sacrifices, and they didn't stop to think too hard about what they were doing or whether it was unnatural or immoral. Maybe I was the only one who saw the skull beneath the skin.

"Do me a favour," I said, "and burn that piece of pernicious crap. Burn the house down while you're at it."

He looked shocked.

"Can't do that, old man. It's been in my family for generations."

All of a sudden he seemed pathetic, an empty shell, a shadow of his usual self. He didn't even seem particularly charming, just shallow and ingratiating. I wondered if maybe I'd been looking at him through Alice's eyes, as the incarnation of all the things she'd ever wanted from life, and now she was gone he was exposed as the vacuum he'd always been.

"That photo of Georgina," I said.

"What are you talking about?"

"The one in your flat. Hair's blowing across her face. Not a very good likeness."

"I took it the day before she died," he said with something that sounded oddly like nostalgia. "I know it's not a great picture, but it's the last I ever took of her."

"Didn't you see the dog?"

"What dog?"

"There's a dog in the background."

"Is there? I never noticed."

When we, or rather I, had run out of things to say, we sat and chain-smoked and stared vacantly at movie after movie on the hotel cable; Hollywood thrillers, Italian romantic comedies, kiddy cartoons, hardcore porn—they went in one eye and out the other, or in my case in and out via the same eye, and I couldn't tell you a single thing about them.

Alice's belongings were all around us—not strewn, as they'd been in her room at Frampton's, but in tidy piles. Nick eventually moulded her clothes into a sort of nest and curled up in the middle of it and fell into a restless sleep in which he mumbled, and once or twice cried out for his mother, while I sat by the window, gazing out at the small boats chugging across the lagoon, and wondering why I'd failed, completely failed, to recognise that Georgina hadn't been the problem.

Georgina had never been the problem.

Georgina had been trying to warn Alice, keep her safe, stop what had happened to her from happening to her friend.

She'd meant well. It wasn't her fault she was scary. She couldn't help it. She was dead.

Because Georgina hadn't been the Fetch.

The barman had been right all along.

It was the dog. Black Shuck, the Hell Hound or whatever it was called. Except that it hadn't been black, and it hadn't been very big.

In the end, though, it didn't make much difference what size or colour or breed it had been. It could have been a Chihuahua, and it wouldn't have made any difference.

Alice would still be dead.

THE NEXT thing I knew there was hammering on the door, and Nick was sitting up and groaning and clutching his head. Strangely enough, I didn't feel hungover, though maybe that was only because I was still drunk.

I opened the door and there stood Jeremy, who pushed past me without a word and took one look at his old school chum and picked up the phone and ordered a long list of items that included orange juice, toast and bananas.

It hadn't just been Alice propping up Nick's personality, I realised. Jeremy had done his fair share of propping as well, and I had no doubt that Ginny had also done her bit.

Nick was like the Wizard of Oz, I decided, and it had been the Evil Twins behind the curtain, pulling the strings. They'd had incentive enough to keep him dancing; Fitch money had paid for Ginny's flat, and I was prepared to bet it had paid for Jeremy's shop as well. No wonder they were so keen to supply him with sacrificial virgins when his funds ran low.

I wondered how many of his other friends had been in on it.

I drank some of the juice and endured several hours of Jeremy's withering sarcasm before it became obvious, even to someone as obtuse as me, that my presence was no longer required, so I took the water-bus to the airport and caught the next available flight home, and sat on the plane with people giving me funny looks, and the smell of sewage seeping out from the plastic bag containing my damp clothes.

TWENTY FOUR

NICK CALLED, more than once, but though he left messages I never replied. Alice had been the tie binding us, and now she was gone we had nothing in common. Heavy metal song lyrics, games of squash, artistic litter trays—they were all so much dust in the wind, and I was left feeling nothing but indifference.

I didn't care what he did, just so long as he didn't get married again. Not that he would need to, once the insurance policy coughed up. Naturally there would be an investigation—to paraphrase Oscar Wilde, losing one wife was unfortunate, but losing a second in equally tragic circumstances was beginning to look like carelessness—but since there would be dozens of witnesses prepared to swear that Nick had been on the other side of the canal when Alice had fallen in, he would once again be let off the hook.

Dozens of witnesses who had seen the dog.

I, on the other hand, couldn't let myself off so lightly. Shortly after I'd got back to the barge, my phone started burbling again and this time I answered it. No point in putting it off any longer.

"Johnny? Is that you, Johnny?"

"Of course it's me, mum. Who else would it be?"

And she was off.

"I'm surprised you dare show your face after what you did to that poor girl, you really are the worst child a mother could ever have, you should have kept away from her but no, you insisted on playing the big hero and you killed her, dashing around like a madman, hopping on planes at all hours of the night, lammy dammer rung skin you as good as hit her on the head and pushed her into the canal yourself, you're just like your father, you murdered her . . ."

She continued in this vein for another ten minutes, and this time I listened, even though it was depressing as hell, because I knew what she was saying was fundamentally the truth. When, finally, her voice died away I called up my archived messages and reread that last one from Alice.

LOBBY 17H30 LUV U2

I stared at it for a long time, feeling a tempest of mixed emotions. I decided not to erase it.

Then I reread the message that came after it.

KEEP AWAY FROM ALICE

Without any expectations whatsoever, I did what for several days now I hadn't bothered to do, since there were never any results. I hit callback.

And this time saw the number come up. Only it didn't make any sense.

Because it was my own.

I didn't waste time wondering how a mobile phone could call itself. It hadn't been a threat, I realised now. It had been a warning, though whether from my mother or my own sub-conscious or some other agency, such as Georgina, I couldn't tell. I lay on my back on the sofa and stared at the ceiling as the missing pieces fell into place.

The Big Picture was complete at last.

I'd done my job as lightning conductor too well.

Canny probity. *Cani proibiti.* Dogs prohibited.

The dog hadn't been hanging around Ginny; it had been hanging around me. I'd drawn it away from Alice. She'd been safe for a while. She might have stayed safe, if only I'd kept my distance.

But then I'd gone and led it straight back to her.

A FEW MONTHS later I ran into Nick at Gnashers. He looked right through me as though I were invisible, but I don't think he intended it as a snub. He was so drunk he could barely place one foot in front of the other, let alone place a face that would inevitably remind him of something he preferred to forget.

By this time, anyway, most of my bitterness had melted away. I'd heard Ginny had dumped him and I was pleased about that, though I had no desire to see her again, let alone resume almost-but-not-quite-having-sex with her. Besides, by this time, my friendship with Janie had taken an interesting and unexpected turn that made Ginny redundant. But this didn't stop me from wondering what had finally prompted her to ditch Nick after all these years. Might it have been due to a new rumour that was circulating—a rumour suggesting that even extra-marital sex with Nicholas Fitch might be fraught with peril? That the family curse was moving with the times and was now extending its reach beyond wedlock, bedhead and Little Yawning?

Actually, it hadn't been so very hard to spread that rumour. I'd dropped hints to Janie, who had never been able to resist an opportunity to do Nick a disservice. And sure enough, she'd smiled, and winked, and duly passed it on. Those hens, they were a superstitious lot. Like mediaeval peasants, really.

I thought that was the end of it, but it wasn't.

Not quite.

AFTER VENICE I tried to get back to normal, but there was no such thing as normal, not for me. I tried not to think too much about Alice, and actually managed to stop drinking for a while, but there were a lot of dark nights of the soul all the same. I hung out with Sol, and helped Eddie with his accounts, and the Barnum brothers fixed me up with a brand new laptop and broadband connection in return for putting them in touch with someone who could hack into the files of their local electricity board for reasons I considered it best not to inquire about.

Life went on much as it had before, but with one or two changes. Janie and I were getting along just fine. Better than fine in fact, and though she gave no sign of wanting to dump Willy, when I thought about it—which wasn't very often—I found I didn't really care. It was better this way.

Janie seemed to sense there was something eating away inside me, but preferred not to ask about it, even after accidentally overhearing one of my mother's infamous phone calls. I wasn't sure I would have wanted to explain it to her anyway. Alice had died because of me. How was I supposed to explain that to one of her friends?

I didn't tell anyone about what I'd done, of course, apart from Sol, who was always understanding about my mistakes.

"It's not your fault, John," he said. "You did your best."

I couldn't help beating myself up about it, all the same. Feeling bad was my way of trying to deal with the guilt. If only I'd known more about Fetches and Curses and Waffs, I might have realised what was happening from the very beginning, and Alice would have done whatever I'd asked, maybe even cancelled the wedding, because I would have had the authority of someone who'd known what he was talking about. I would have been an *expert*. You never know, I might have been able to make a difference. I might have been able to do something.

So my bedside reading had changed. I'd put Proust on hold, and was now working my way through *Old Egbert's Almanac* in the hope that next time someone like Alice came to me asking for help, I would know what to do. I wasn't going to make the same mistakes twice.

Old Egbert's wasn't any easier to read than Proust, of course. After several months, I was still bogged down in the Bs. One night, propped up against pillows, I was struggling through BANSHEES and BAOBHAN SITHS and BARGUESTS, and my eyelids were starting to droop when I was jerked back into wakefulness by a soft scrabbling from the porthole behind my head.

By now I'd heard this sort of thing so often it had ceased to worry me, because I knew what would happen next: I would pull the curtain back and outside there would be nothing but the still black waters of the canal, maybe the faint shadow of someone loitering over on the towpath, but nothing more, and certainly nothing worth losing any sleep over.

So as usual, in a swift movement and without thinking too much about it, I flicked the curtain aside.

Alice was outside.

I couldn't move or react, not even to let the curtain fall back down, so there was nothing for it but to stare back into the face that was pressed up against the porthole.

Although she was right up against the glass her breath, if breath there was, left no trace of condensation. One of her hands was clawing at the window, but the perfect manicure was a thing of the past; now her fingernails were yellow and discoloured. The expensive tan was gone as well; her skin was now white, almost luminous, paler than any skin I'd seen on a living person, the colour of something that had been a long time in the water.

I looked into her eyes, but I'm not sure if she saw me. I'm not sure she saw anything, but her lips were moving, forming words, and she seemed to be trying to say something.

Suddenly I was overcome with a sorrow more piercing than any I'd ever known and I knew I had to stop staring at her or my heart would burst. I decided I didn't want to know what she was trying to say, not right now, maybe not ever, because it would undoubtedly have something to do with my abject uselessness and how terrible it was being dead, and asking me if I still loved her and what was I going to do about it.

And, of course, there wasn't an awful lot I *could* do. Because one thing I was sure of. And, in the end, it didn't make much difference whether she was alive or dead.

She just wasn't my type.

Anne Billson is a film critic, novelist, and photographer. She has lived in London, Tokyo, Paris and Croydon, and now lives in Brussels.

Also from The Brooligan Press
THE SEBASTIAN BECKER NOVELS
Stephen Gallagher

Chancery lunatics were people of wealth or property whose fortunes were at risk from their madness. Those deemed unfit to manage their affairs had them taken over by lawyers of the Crown, known as the Masters of Lunacy. It was Sebastian's employer, the Lord Chancellor's Visitor, who would decide their fate. Though the office was intended to be a benevolent one, many saw him as an enemy to be outwitted or deceived, even to the extent of concealing criminal insanity.

It was for such cases that the Visitor had engaged Sebastian. His job was to seek out the cunning dissembler, the dangerous madman whose resources might otherwise make him untouchable. Rank and the social order gave such people protection. A former British police detective and one-time Pinkerton man, Sebastian had been engaged to work 'off the books' in exposing their misdeeds. His modest salary was paid out of the department's budget. He remained a shadowy figure, an investigator with no public profile.

THE KINGDOM OF BONES
After prizefighter-turned-stage manager Tom Sayers is wrongly accused in the slayings of pauper children, he disappears into a twilight world of music halls and temporary boxing booths. While Sayers pursues the elusive actress Louise Porter, the tireless Detective Inspector Sebastian Becker pursues him. This brilliantly macabre mystery begins in the lively parks of Philadelphia in 1903, then winds its way from England's provincial playhouses and London's mighty Lyceum Theatre to the high society of a transforming American South—and the alleyways, back stages, and houses of ill repute in between.

"Vividly set in England and America during the booming industrial era of the late 19th and early 20th centuries, this stylish thriller conjures a perfect demon to symbolize the age and its appetites"
—New York Times

THE BEDLAM DETECTIVE

...finds Becker serving as Special Investigator to the Masters of Lunacy in the case of a man whose travellers' tales of dinosaurs and monsters are matched by a series of slaughters on his private estate. An inventor and industrialist made rich by his weapons patents, Sir Owain Lancaster is haunted by the tragic outcome of an ill-judged Amazon expedition in which his entire party was killed. When local women are found slain on his land, he claims that the same dark Lost-World forces have followed him home.

"A rare literary masterpiece for the lovers of historical crime fiction."
—MysteryTribune

THE AUTHENTIC WILLIAM JAMES

As the Special Investigator to the Lord Chancellor's Visitor in Lunacy, Sebastian Becker delivers justice to those dangerous madmen whose fortunes might otherwise place them above the law. But in William James he faces a different challenge; to prove a man sane, so that he may hang. Did the reluctant showman really burn down a crowded pavilion with the audience inside? And if not, why is this British sideshow cowboy so determined to shoulder the blame?

"It's a blinding novel... the acerbic wit, the brilliant dialogue—the sheer spot-on elegance of the writing: the plot turns, the pin sharp beats. Always authoritative and convincing, never showy. Magnificently realized characters in a living breathing world . . . Absolutely stunning"
—Stephen Volk
(Ghostwatch, Gothic, Afterlife)

"Gallagher gives Sebastian Becker another puzzle worthy of his quirky sleuth's acumen in this outstanding third pre-WW1 mystery"
—Publishers Weekly starred review

Printed in Great Britain
by Amazon